Bonny Kate's
Honeymoon

Blessings! Mark Strength

Victory at King's Mountain

A Novel by Mark Strength

Based on a true story of the American Revolution

To order additional copies of this book, contact:
Bonny Kate Publishing Company
1-888-822-7585
www.bonnykate.com

Contents

Acknowledgements

Since the publication of *Bonny Kate: Pioneer Lady*, I have had the honor and privilege of meeting and corresponding with many members of the Sevier and Sherrill families. I cannot adequately convey to them my deep appreciation for their many expressions of encouragement and enthusiasm about my work.

I wish to thank Tom Windle, a descendant of Bonny Kate and John, for his many communications and references to rare documents known only to family members and direct descendants of John Sevier and his wives, Sarah and Bonny Kate. Tom is also descended from Sarah's sister Mary Hawkins Windle, connecting him to the families of both of John Sevier's wives. I treasure every conversation, e-mail, and especially our meeting at Sycamore Shoals for the Gathering of the Over-mountain Victory Trail Association. Tom's knowledge comes from a lifetime of interest, travel to historic sites, and maintaining connections to every branch of the Sevier family.

I thank Stephen Little, also descended from Bonny Kate and John. Stephen discovered my first book right after its publication and helped to alert hundreds of family members to its existence. I thank Stephen's wife Lois, the artist who generously provided the portrait of Bonny Kate that graces the cover of this volume. A picture is truly worth a thousand words.

I thank Lynne Coen who bought a book from me the first time I ever set up at a craft fair at the Governor John Sevier Historic Farmstead, Marble Springs, near Knoxville. She turned out to be a direct descendant of Valentine, John's brother. Her information led me to an appreciation for Sherriff Val and his remarkable wife Amy, characters I came to adore.

Thanks go out to talented actress and fashion model Kimberly Coen-Frank, the daughter of Lynne Coen. I met her by an act of Divine Providence while searching for a model to appear in Bonny Kate posters and magazine ads. She was working at the modeling agency office and had heard about the book from her mother. When the lovely Bonny Kate look-alike told me of her relationship to the Sevier family, I knew I had found the right lady for the photo work.

I also extend thanks to Margarette Stout and D. Jack Smith, descendants of Bonny Kate's brother John Sherrill, for their information about the Sherrills, and to Donna Sherrell for granting me access to the Sherrill/Sherrell family website.

Thanks also go to Chuck Sherrill, descendant of Bonny Kate's brother George for his extensive research and published works on Revolutionary War pension applications, all generously shared with me.

Wayne Hamilton, another direct descendant of John and Bonny Kate, honored me by writing a long and enthusiastic review of my first book. Wayne's own published books are remarkable contributions to geological science, so his praise for *Bonny Kate* was especially appreciated.

I thank Marinella Charles for her help in clearing up who was who concerning the case of the two Joseph Seviers and who and when they married. Her expertise in Sevier genealogy was a recent discovery for me, but a valuable one for the last several chapters of this work.

I thank David Daily of the Governor John Sevier Home at Marble Springs for his hospitality and the informative conversations. I appreciate the many other historical site curators in Tennessee, who have added Bonny Kate to their bookstores and gift shops.

I thank the historians who did the research, found the sources, and wrote marvelous books: Pat Alderman, Lyman C. Draper, James R. Gilmore, John Haywood, Hank Messick, J.G.M. Ramsey, Francis Marion Turner, Samuel Cole Williams, and especially Cora Bales Sevier and Nancy Sevier Madden. Their masterpieces became the golden threads used to weave the fabric of this story.

Thanks go also to my production partners. Jeanmarie Martin of *A Way With Words* provided the proofreading and editorial services. Brenda McClearen, Terri Morris, and Amanda Purcell at McClearen Design Studios provided the book design services.

I thank the members of my own family for their forbearance and support through the creative process, especially my wife Lynn, who exemplifies all that is good in American womanhood. She has always been my first love and best friend, and the truest model for how Bonny Kate has been portrayed. I have yet to prove any kin relationship to any of the characters in my books, but the spirit of the pioneer is the bind that ties us together. I thank my mother Ellen for a lifetime of love, encouragement, and enthusiasm for sharing my books with others.

I thank all the people of the states of Tennessee, North Carolina, Virginia, Kentucky, Georgia, Alabama, and South Carolina for preserving the nature and the character of the over-mountain pioneer in their present-day family relationships. I have only to look among my friends and neighbors of the region to see why victory at King's Mountain was inevitable. It remains my purpose to bring to remembrance the importance of our illustrious and heroic forbears, and to honor with gratitude all the participants of the King's Mountain campaign, who sacrificed so much to win American independence, and went on to build modern commonwealths in the states of Middle America.

M. S.
Smyrna, Tennessee
April, 2009

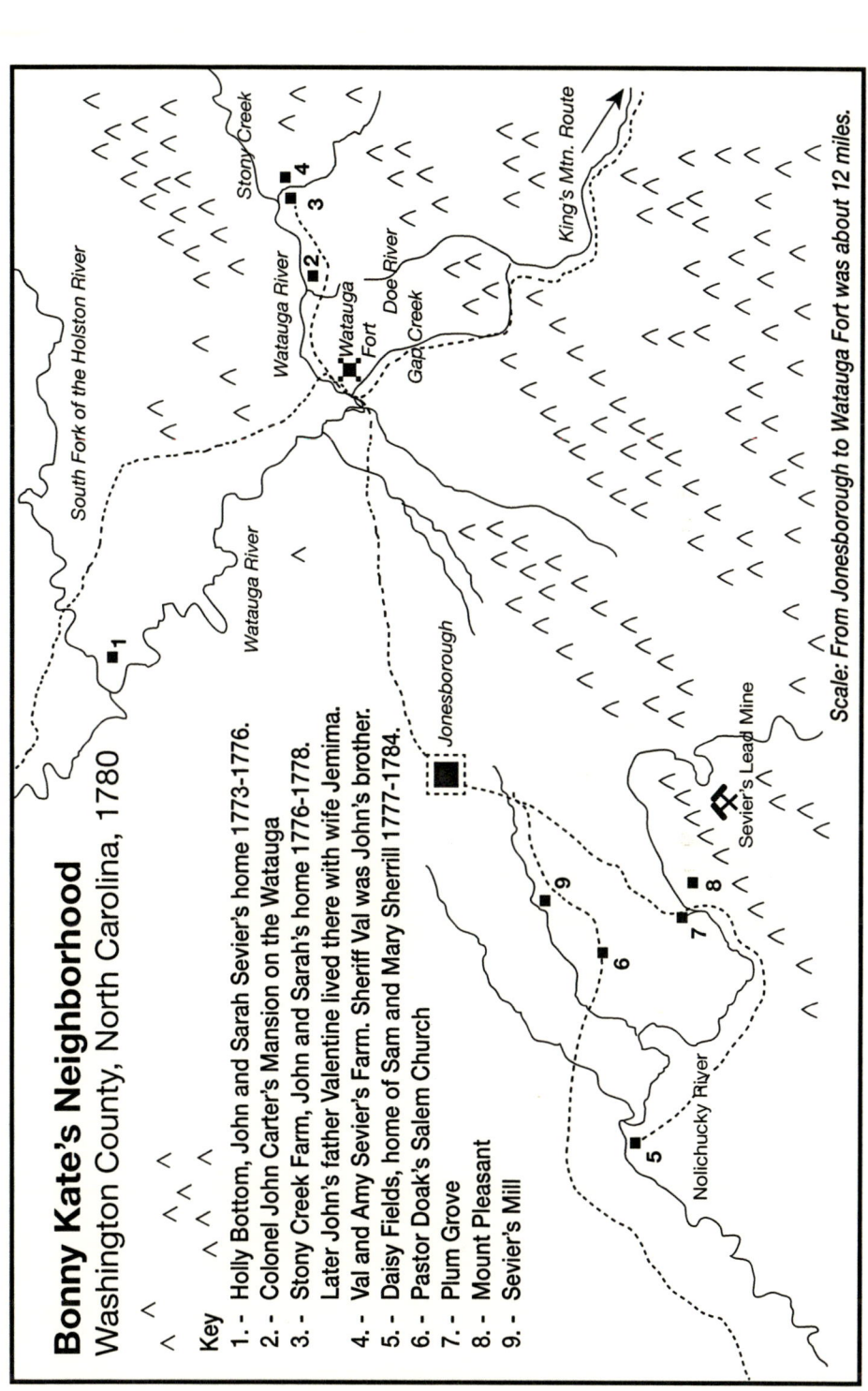

Bonny Kate's Neighborhood
Washington County, North Carolina, 1780

Key

1. - Holly Bottom, John and Sarah Sevier's home 1773-1776.
2. - Colonel John Carter's Mansion on the Watauga
3. - Stony Creek Farm, John and Sarah's home 1776-1778.
     Later John's father Valentine lived there with wife Jemima.
4. - Val and Amy Sevier's Farm. Sheriff Val was John's brother.
5. - Daisy Fields, home of Sam and Mary Sherrill 1777-1784.
6. - Pastor Doak's Salem Church
7. - Plum Grove
8. - Mount Pleasant
9. - Sevier's Mill

South Fork of the Holston River

Stony Creek

Watauga River

Doe River

King's Mtn. Route

Gap Creek

Watauga Fort

Watauga River

Jonesborough

Sevier's Lead Mine

Nolichucky River

Scale: From Jonesborough to Watauga Fort was about 12 miles.

The Route of the King's Mountain Expedition
September 26 - October 7, 1780

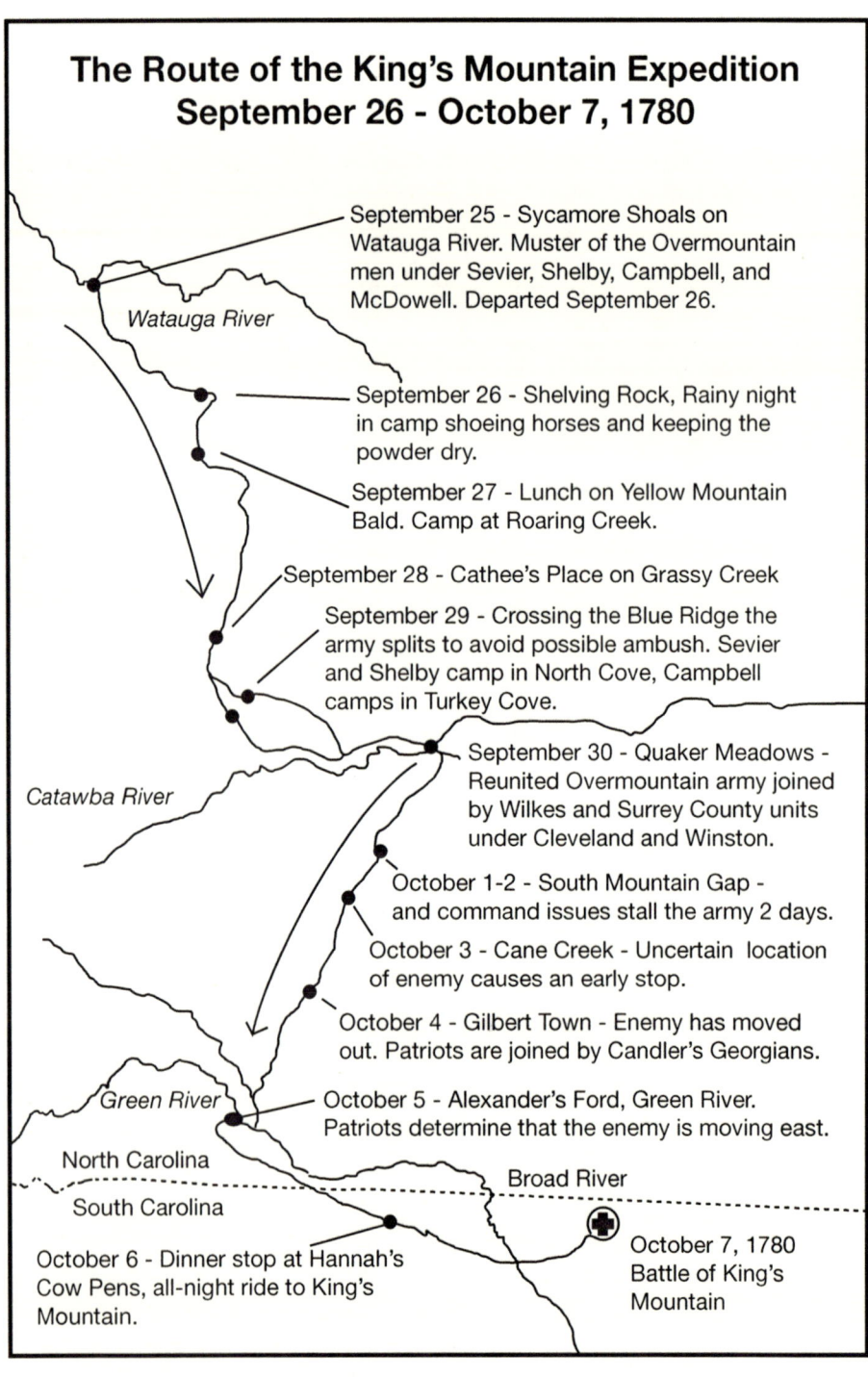

Preface

Welcome to Washington County, North Carolina, in the year 1780. You are about to embark on a fantastic journey in time through the magic of your own imagination. The book you hold in your hands is the doorway to a community of people, most of whom actually lived in a mountainous part of present-day east Tennessee that was first settled along the rivers Holston, Watauga, and Nolichucky. Imagine, then, that every farmstead and cabin is new. Your friends and neighbors all came from somewhere else; most are from Virginia, North Carolina, Maryland, Pennsylvania, and South Carolina. The community leaders set up a system of self-government, county courts, and organized militia units completely independent of the British Crown's colonial administration. When you explore the forested mountains and cane-blanketed river bottoms of the unclaimed virgin wilderness, you are very likely to run into hunting parties of the Shawnees or the Cherokees. There is an uneasy peace with the red men of the forest, hard won in the Cherokee War of 1776 and secured in the treaty talks that took months in 1777. Even now you had better have your rifle at the ready for the Chickamaugas, a breakaway faction of the Cherokees sworn to ignore all treaties and always looking for trouble. However, the greatest concern in the neighborhood is making good the claims of ownership to the land on which the white people live; especially after all the hard work put in to clear it, plant crops, and build cabins.

I'm sure you know the rest of the world has gone completely mad. The British attacked and took Savannah last fall, they captured Charleston in May of this year, and now there's serious fighting in South Carolina that threatens to engulf the state of North Carolina. We westerners turned out pretty solidly for the Liberty boys in 1776. And at this very moment one hundred of our Washington County volunteers are serving in the eastern part of the state, trying to prevent the British invasion.

It's now August 14, 1780, and you are invited to a wedding at the home of Sam and Mary Sherrill. Sam is pretty well off with his horse breeding business, but seven sons and three daughters all work hard at it. It's not Sam's eldest daughter Susan who's getting hitched; she married Leroy Taylor some years ago. It's not the prettiest of the three, either. Mary Jane is only twenty, but she drives the young fellows to distraction with her natural beauty and mysterious air. No, it's the middle girl Catharine, the one they call Bonny Kate, who nearly became an old maid for being so particular. She just turned twenty-six on the third of this month, and she's never been married.

You might be wondering about this Bonny Kate, because she's earned a reputation as someone to watch out for. She can outrun, outjump, outshoot, and ride more gracefully than any female on the continent. Some have said she can outtalk any female too, but that's a little harder to prove. There is a book called *Bonny Kate: Pioneer Lady* that tells the story of her early life and romantic involvement with the man she's about to marry. If you have read it, you'll understand about Bonny Kate; but if not, just pay close attention and you'll pick up on the story.

I guess I should tell you what sort of fellow would marry a girl like Bonny Kate. Well, he's the handsomest man in the West, the darling of every widow in Jonesborough, the bravest, most enterprising, natural leader of men, officer of the county court, lieutenant colonel of the militia, and father of ten children, John Sevier. Yes, I said father of ten. Our friend John has been married before, but he married his childhood sweetheart at the age of sixteen, tragically lost her last winter, and today he's only thirty-four years old. The poor fellow still has a few good years left, and Bonny Kate is crazily in love with him. That's why we are going to the clearing on the south bank of the Nolichucky River at Sam Sherrill's horse farm today to watch the ceremony, enjoy the games, eat the food, sample the drink, and dance late into the night. I hope you are ready for some fun!

Chapter 1

Domestic Tranquility

On the warm moonlit night of August 14th in the year 1780, John Sevier, the handsome, blond, blue-eyed, fit and trim lieutenant colonel of the Washington County militia, walked his new bride Bonny Kate, a tall, slender, raven-haired, blue-eyed beauty, up the footpath to the door of the guest cabin on Daisy Fields Plantation. They lingered at the threshold, and she looked back toward the main house of the Sherrill family farm where the music of the wedding dance continued.

"Do you think anyone noticed that we slipped away?" Bonny Kate asked.

John looked into her eyes and concentrated very hard to remember every detail of her appearance at that moment in her beautiful wedding gown. "All eyes have been focused on your beauty the entire evening. I think everyone watched as you walked out of the dance circle into the dark with me."

She blushed. "There's no escaping notice, I suppose. I've always lived in the center of attention, but tonight I want some privacy." They kissed tenderly in the dark. Then John reached into the candle box on the wall beside the door and took out a candle. He lit it and gave it to Bonny Kate, and opened the cabin door.

"Bonny Kate, my cherished bride, light of my life, may our love always shine as brightly as it does this night."

"Dear husband, may the Lord make the light of his love shine upon us and bless us, all the days of our lives!"

John lifted her in his arms and carried her into the cabin. He closed the door behind them and kissed her again before crossing the room and laying her gently on the bed.

"This bed seems a bit rickety," John observed.

"It was my Granny Sherrill's. It means a great deal to me."

John took off his uniform quickly as she watched in the soft glow of the candlelight. When he had dressed down to his night shirt, she rolled off the bed and stood beside him.

"Make yourself comfortable while I lay aside my finery," she said. He got upon the bed carefully as it creaked ominously. Bonny Kate was out of her wedding dress and into her nightgown quickly. "John dear, do you remember the first thing you said to me at the wall of Watauga Fort the day you rescued me from the Indians?"

"Yes, my love. I said, jump for me, Kate!"

"Catch me then," she warned and sailed across the room into his arms. With a sudden crash, the bed collapsed beneath them and they found themselves on the floor amidst the wreckage. After a stunned silence she began to laugh. "I think I broke the bed! I'm going to be in so much trouble with Papa!"

"No, you won't. Papa Sherrill gave you away today. You are now a Sevier, and as my dear wife, you are free to make all the trouble you want. Forget the bed and let me show you the mysteries of marriage!"

The next morning sunlight found the cracks in the shutters on the windows and streamed into the little guest cabin. John lay on a blanket on the floor, holding his new wife and surveyed the damage they had done to the bed of Granny Sherrill. The ancient cording that suspended the bedding had dry rotted and broken in several places. It would be an easy repair to restore the treasured family heirloom, if anyone had time to do it. He knew a militia colonel in a country at war certainly had no time for such things. He had resisted tremendous pressures to go on the summer campaign east to fight the British invasion. Then he had refused to help a force from Virginia on an Indian campaign. He had risked his entire military career to stay home for his ten children and grieve for the loss of his first wife, Sarah.

It had been only seven months since Sarah died from complications she suffered after giving birth to little Nancy. Sarah, on her deathbed, had extracted a promise from her best friend Bonny Kate to care for the children until John could remarry. John searched far and wide for a love as deep as he had with Sarah, but none of the widows he considered dared to get involved in a family with ten children. Then he noticed Bonny Kate, already involved with his children as a sort of volunteer governess, and his feelings for her began to deepen. He found he preferred her company to the many women that well-meaning matchmakers had paraded past the lonely colonel. Scarcely a week had passed, since he, ready to declare his love for her, discovered that Bonny Kate loved him too. It seemed almost pre-ordained by Divine Providence that the girl he rescued four years earlier from certain death at the wall of Watauga Fort, would eventually become his second wife.

John could hear the distant activity of breakfast cooking, and outside he heard a rooster crow. He watched Bonny Kate's eyelids flutter open and was amused by the surprised look on her face as she became aware of who she was with. "Good morning, Mrs. Sevier."

"Good morning, Mr. Sevier," she responded cheerfully, rising enough to lean over and deliver a good morning kiss.

"A great way to start the day," he approved.

"Then this is how we will start every day." She kissed him again more slowly. "Did you sleep well, my love?"

"It was too hot for sleep, but I enjoyed a great peace of mind and soul this morning as I lay here beside you."

"We were not very comfortable on the hard floor," she said. "I'm sorry I destroyed the bed."

"It appears to me like the cording had dry-rotted. It will be easy to fix."

"Easier to fix than our reputations, once word of this gets out," she said. "I can already imagine what the wagging tongues of Jonesborough society will say; Colonel Sevier broke the bed with his passionate love-making!"

John laughed. "I'm not the least bit concerned with my reputation among the gossips of Jonesborough, are you?"

"Yesterday it would have ruined me, but today I'm free to love you for all I'm worth! I don't care what anyone may think."

"Don't you think they'll pity the poor virgin who received such passionate play?"

"Pity me not, when they learn it was me that broke the bed! Married love governed the passion, and that justifies all in God's good plan. Under the circumstances, I would highly recommend the play we performed last night!"

"Well spoken, my dear! Let us dress for breakfast. It will be a busy day as we move the celebration to Plum Grove."

When they had dressed, she opened the shutters and sunlight flooded the room. She knelt at the open window and breathed deeply the summer air. She prayed the Lord's Prayer out loud as was her custom to always do, and finished with a psalm of thanksgiving. She was now living a new life that promised to fulfill her destiny.

"So now we have three grandmas?" wondered five-year-old Dicky Sevier.

"That's right," his sister Betsy told him. "You can now call Mrs. Sherrill, Grandma Sherrill. And we still have Grandma Sevier and Grandma Hawkins, but they live farther away than the Sherrills do."

"Three grandmas," Dicky marveled.

"That's right," Betsy answered. "And Mr. Sherrill is our new grandpa."

Sam and Mary Sherrill worked at cooking a big breakfast with their two other daughters, Mary Jane Sherrill, who was twenty and Susan Sherrill Taylor, who was twenty-eight and married to Leroy Taylor. Outside the cookhouse the Sherrills had set up a table in the shade of the sycamores. Nine of the Sevier children sat around the big table, enjoying animated conversation in anticipation of the morning feast. Joseph Sevier was the eldest at eighteen, and he enjoyed flirting with Mary Jane Sherrill as she set the table, trading admiring glances and smiling at each other's attentions. They had been dance partners the night before. John Sevier Jr. was fourteen and as handsome as his famous father. Betsy was twelve; Sarah, who was named for her mother but nicknamed Dolly was ten; Mary Ann was nine; Little Val was seven; Dicky was five; Rebecca was nearly three; and Nancy was just seven months. The only member of John's family who was missing was James, a sixteen-year old who rebelled at the idea that his father would marry again so soon, and to a much younger woman. Indeed, Bonny Kate was twenty-six, to John's more experienced age of thirty-four. James Sevier had hurt his father's feelings and disappointed his young stepmother by staying away from the wedding and sulking at the Sevier plantation they called Plum Grove. There were family issues to resolve, but on the morning of August 15, 1780 with the sweet bliss of marriage fresh on his mind, John Sevier found a scene of domestic tranquility beneath the shady sycamores at Daisy Fields as he and Bonny Kate joined the family for breakfast.

"Good morning, bride and groom," Mary Sherrill called from the doorway.

"Good morning, Mother." Bonny Kate left her husband and entered the cookhouse.

"I trust the night passed pleasantly," Mary said with a knowing smile.

"Most pleasantly, thank you." Bonny Kate stood at the hearth with only her mother and sisters close enough to hear her report. "Nothing you told me, Mother, prepared me adequately for what I experienced last night."

"What happened?" Mary Jane asked with great interest.

Bonny Kate looked at her younger sister. "I'll say nothing of the mysteries except that I was very pleased."

"Oh please, Bonny Kate, you can't leave it like this. Tell me all of it!" Mary Jane pleaded.

"No, I'll say nothing else."

"Tell me later, then."

"Never, dear sister. You must discover the mysteries of marriage for yourself."

"Hold on there," Father Sam interrupted the sister play as he entered the cookhouse. "Mary Jane will do nothing of the kind until her own wedding night. Let me serve the eggs and bacon before the breakfast gets too cold and the conversation gets too hot."

The women carried the prepared food out to the table, and after Sam blessed the breakfast Bonny Kate served the children and sat down beside her husband. The discussion then turned to the wedding, the dance of the previous evening, and the plans for more celebrations in the days to come. Many well-wishers from the Watauga and Nolichucky Valleys would assemble in the pastures around Plum Grove Plantation to pay their respects to the happy couple and enjoy the feasting, the games, the handiwork, the trading, and the gossiping that always accompanied such celebrations. No man was more popular and universally admired than John Sevier, and no woman was better known for her beauty, domestic skills, athletic abilities, farm management, and strength of character than Bonny Kate.

After breakfast the Sevier family made preparations for the ride to Plum Grove. The children needed to settle back into the routines that were so important to their growth and development. Bonny Kate knew that the week of wedding preparations and community celebrations had greatly disrupted their young lives. She wanted to reestablish the life disciplines of work and instruction that would someday make them helpful and useful citizens. There were unmet affectionate needs as well among the youngest of the brood. She and John must address those individually with each child as soon and as often as they could.

Bonny Kate took much time and invested much feeling in departing from her family home. Although her life had been very busy with daily trips to Plum Grove since early February as the caregiver to the younger Sevier children, today was different. She knew she would not return that night, and it saddened her. She deeply loved her mother and father and her nine siblings. She was the second daughter of three to get married, and her seven brothers were mostly grown men except Aquila, the littlest boy who was only a year old. The leave-taking required some time, some tears, and warm embraces all around before Bonny Kate could mount her horse at the head of the column beside her husband.

John felt the sadness expressed in his wife's formal separation from her parents and siblings and tried to comfort her. "We will see them all again tomorrow, when they come over for the pig roast. I doubt you'll ever go a week without a visit with your folks as long as they remain my nearest neighbors."

"I know, John," Bonny Kate laughed through her tears. "I'm acting as though I'm setting off on some great journey around the world or something. I know it's foolish of me to carry on so, but this is a day I have long dreamed of, and I realize it has finally arrived. This is still a big step for me."

"I know, my dear," John empathized. "It is a big step for me too."

The family troop, when mounted, made an impressive show with fine-looking children on finely bred horses. The stepmother was justifiably proud of her new family as they took the river road up the Nolichucky to Plum Grove Plantation.

The Nolichucky River was a west-flowing river of the over-mountain country remotely situated from the home state of North Carolina. John Sevier and the other great men of the west had worked tirelessly to gain recognition and inclusion in the affairs of the state of North Carolina and were now finding greater acceptance as the eastern parts of the state reeled under the effects of a British offensive to take back the southern states in a war that had dragged on for five years. The two western counties, Washington and Sullivan, had provided a total of two hundred of their best fighting men, sent east to protect the state from invasion. The problem for Colonel John Sevier was keeping peace on the frontier in the face of hostile Indians and troublesome British loyalists called Tories.

By the time the Seviers arrived at Plum Grove, unburdened the horses, and set the children at their various chores, the morning was well spent. Bonny Kate went looking for James Sevier, who had opted to stay home rather than attend the wedding. She found him brooding at the edge of the river.

"I want to talk to you, young sir!"

"About what?"

"You didn't come to my wedding, and I very much wanted you there."

"Why? What difference would my presence have made in the outcome?"

"It would have pleased and honored your father."

"I don't believe your wedding pleased and honored my mother," he answered sharply.

"James, I am so sorry you feel that way. Your mother was my dearest friend, and she required of me a promise to care for her children until your father could remarry. That was not an easy promise to keep, but I tried my very best."

"Nobody gave you the right to take her place."

"No, I have no right to take her place in the affections of your heart, or in the hearts of any of your brothers or sisters. And I have no right to take her place in the affections of your father's heart."

"Then what are you doing here?"

"I'm making my own place in the affections of your father's heart and in the hearts of his children. You see, the human heart has an unlimited capacity to love, so there is room for all of us in your father's heart, including a full measure of love for your mother's treasured memory."

"I will never call *you* mother."

"Just call me Bonny Kate, and let me love you as a mother would."

"No, I'll have nothing to do with you. You married for property and position, and to plunder my inheritance. I resent you for that."

"That is absolutely not true! Who gave you that idea about me?"

"Everybody knows it, but Aunt Kesiah had the guts to say it."

"She did, did she? Then I have accounts to balance with Aunt Kesiah," Bonny Kate said with a coolness that concealed a rage that began to rise in her hot blood. James walked away without another word, and the young stepmother was left more hurt and disturbed than when she began her talk with him. Aunt Kesiah Sevier was about the same age as Bonny Kate and married to John's favorite brother Robert. She was also the daughter of Major Charles Robertson, John Sevier's next-in-command over the Washington County militia. Captain Robert Sevier and Major Robertson were at that time in the eastern part of North Carolina, leading a force of one hundred men against a British invasion of the southern states. Bonny Kate wondered how she might set the record straight with young James and discount Kesiah Sevier's influence in the John Sevier family. Kesiah had never been friendly to Bonny Kate, but now as a sister-in-law, Bonny Kate would have to learn how to deal with Kesiah's trouble-making behavior without upsetting the delicate workings of Sevier family relations and Washington County politics. It would prove to be challenging.

The next day, John's friends, neighbors, and business associates arrived for the gathering by the wagonload and there was more work to do than ever. Bonny Kate went to it with characteristic enthusiasm and cheerfulness, fulfilling her public role as the colonel's new wife. The days of hard work and gracious hospitality would reveal to her whom she could depend upon and who in the community could not be trusted. In years past, when helping Sarah at such gatherings, she had observed and learned much, so she felt equal to the task.

Among the first to arrive were Sam and Mary Sherrill, with Bonny Kate's sisters Mary Jane and Susan Taylor and her brothers Sam Sherrill Jr., Adam, John, Will, George, and baby Aquila. Bonny Kate's own family was always very supportive and patriotic. Some of her brothers rode with Colonel Sevier's light horse companies patrolling the western frontier. George Sherrill at age seventeen had even joined the Lincoln County militia on a visit east and seen action at Monck's Corner before the fall of Charleston. The governor of North Carolina ordered his army home after the disaster in South Carolina and reorganized the militia for home defense. George had come home in late June and provided Colonel Sevier a first-hand description of the situation in South Carolina and of preparations being made in the eastern counties of North Carolina. Sam Sherrill was just glad to have his boy back home and had scolded George for being just a little too adventurous.

Valentine Sevier, John's father, was the patriarch of the Sevier family. He and his second wife, Jemima Young Douglass Sevier, arrived with the Sherrills, having attended the wedding on the fourteenth and staying at Daisy Fields an extra day visiting. He helped Sam Sherrill repair Granny Sherrill's bed and together they speculated about the forces that had produced such wreckage. Bonny Kate was well liked and admired by her father-in-law because of the money he had always won betting on her in foot races and shooting matches. Jemima was a good stepgrandmother to John's children, and she too was fond of Bonny Kate.

Naomi Douglass Sevier and her children traveled with Big Val and Jemima. She was married to John's brother Valentine, the sheriff of Washington County who had gone east with the militia as captain of a company of horse rangers. Naomi, whom everyone called Amy, was warm, kind, trustworthy, and funny. She had grown up a Douglass and was the daughter of her husband's stepmother, Jemima. Amy was a solid woman who could make cattle ranching pay and ran one of the best dairies in the west.

Colonel, sometimes Judge, John Carter and his wife Elizabeth arrived about mid-morning. They were among the richest leaders of the community. Bonny Kate had assisted Elizabeth Carter through a nasty encounter with camp fever during the three-week siege of Watauga Fort. Ever since then, Mrs. Carter had held the highest regard for Bonny Kate as her "dear girl." Landon Carter, their son, was a close friend of John Sevier and always accompanied him on military campaigns and hunting trips. Sarah, John's first wife, had complained privately to her husband about Colonel Carter's practice of holding on to his official rank of colonel, even after his appointment to Judge of Washington County. By doing so, Judge Carter had withheld from John a long-deserved promotion. That's why John was still a lieutenant colonel, even though he was in fact, the actual and acknowledged commander of the county militia.

Susanna Cunningham Robertson, wife of Major Charles Robertson, arrived with her daughter Kesiah Sevier just in time for the midday meal. Their men-folk were away defending the country, and great respect was paid them in polite conversation. Kesiah had a month-old baby her husband Robert had never seen. The infant was named Val in honor of the Sevier family patriarch. Kesiah also struggled to manage a very active two-year-old son Charlie, named for Kesiah's father. Bonny Kate greeted them as the gracious hostess, but wanted to find the opportunity to talk things out with Kesiah.

After lunch, the children went down for an afternoon nap and Bonny Kate drew Kesiah aside for a talk.

"Kesiah, thank you for coming to the gathering," Bonny Kate began as they walked through the plum orchard.

"Mother advised it. We must keep up appearances for the family, you know."

"I had hoped we could enjoy warmer relations now that we are sisters-in-law. But you do not speak kindly about me and have even said things that are not true."

"What things?"

"Young James, for example, reports that you said I married for wealth and position."

"When the kettle is black, I call it black," Kesiah replied.

"I married for true love! And I will not tolerate anyone saying otherwise, neither inside nor outside the family."

"You have been used, Bonny Kate, and you are too stupid to see it." Kesiah laughed wickedly. "Yours is a marriage of convenience. He needed somebody to take care of his children so he can run off to play soldier."

"That's a lie! John Sevier loves me deeply and passionately, the way I love him!"

"Then I suppose you two got this thing going before Sarah died."

"I never betrayed Sarah. She was my best friend! I did everything in the proper order and according to the leading of Divine Providence."

"When did you seduce him?"

Bonny Kate was losing her temper. "Kesiah, you don't know what you are talking about, so I'll thank you to keep your mouth shut and not give expression to evil thoughts."

"You are not the boss of me, Bonny Kate Sherrill. I may not be popular and pretty like you, but people respect my ability to uncover and report a scandal."

"The wedding was yesterday, Kesiah. Now I'm Bonny Kate Sevier. It is well known that I have boldly faced mountain lions, and I have backed down Tories and horse thieves, and I raced against Indians and beat them at foot racing and target shooting. Who between the two of us is better at cat fighting?"

"I suppose you are," Kesiah answered.

"Then before you say anything that might annoy me, remember these two words, *cat fight*. You could save yourself a lot of pain and me a lot of embarrassment if you can remember those two little words. Do you understand?"

"Yes, but I want to warn you about something."

"Warn me about what?"

"I suppose you think your fondest dreams have come true marrying into this family. But I can tell you all about being married to a Sevier, and you'll discover soon enough it is no sweet bed of roses. He's always gone when I need him most, and it is all for the cause, the great cause of liberty."

"I'm sorry you feel that way, Kesiah, but your own father is Robert's commander on the eastern campaign, so in a sense he is in service out of loyalty to *your* family right now, not the Seviers."

"But I labor from early dawn to the middle of the night tending to guests at the tavern, and it was never *my* dream to live like this. Now I have two boys who cry all the time. They are not perfect little angels like Sarah's children. I feel like I'm drowning with two, and you don't seem to be having any trouble with ten. Where's the difference in you and me?"

Bonny Kate sighed and reached for Kesiah. The bitter girl recoiled at the prospect of a cat fight, but Bonny Kate caught her and quickly pulled her into a sisterly hug. "The difference lies in how you and I look at the world. Kesiah, I don't know if you'll ever have the patience to learn my point of view, but I'd like to show you, just the same."

"Show me what?"

"A book that I have lived by all my life; it's a book of wisdom, a book of history, a book of destiny, and a book about how to live your life so it makes sense in a very crazy, mixed-up world."

"Who could write such a book?"

"God Almighty caused this book to be written; it's called the Holy Bible. And I'm going to give you a copy and show you where to find the answers to your questions."

Kesiah broke free of her embrace and pushed her away. "You can't seduce me with psalms and proverbs. You're no better than me or anyone else. Keep your old book."

"It's yours, I promise, and if you don't take it we will have that cat fight!"

Kesiah ran away to the main house and found her mother seated amongst a group of women sewing, engaging in pleasant conversation. She joined the group and found a quilt square to work on.

"Kesiah, did you have a nice visit with your new sister-in-law out there in the plum orchard?" Mrs. Robertson asked her daughter.

"Mama, she's bad tempered and crazy mean when she's been drinking!" Kesiah declared.

Mary Sherrill raised an eyebrow and exchanged surprised glances with Mary Jane Sherrill. "Kesiah, it's good for you to know that about her, right from the start!" The Sherrill women laughed, and soon all the women enjoyed the joke. The backwater community would enjoy many days of raucous celebrations, but the storm clouds of war were building over distant lands to the east, storm clouds that would threaten the domestic tranquility prevailing in the homes of the hardy frontier folk.

Chapter 2

Men at War

In the spring of 1780, Governor Richard Caswell of North Carolina called all militia units into the field for a campaign to defend the mother state from a British invasion that had overrun Georgia and South Carolina. The British policy in the occupied territories forced fathers, husbands, and sons to serve in militias loyal to the English crown or suffer cruel reprisals on their own families. That was creating a bloody civil war throughout the south. North Carolina would be the next to suffer as the British army moved north out of Charleston.

Major Charles Robertson from Washington County, the westernmost county of the state, led one hundred citizen soldiers on a march to the eastern part of the state. Robertson was a powerful man and wealthy. He was an original member of the Watauga Association, the group of men from Virginia and North Carolina who first settled over the mountains and negotiated land leases directly with the Cherokees. For eight years he had been active in building a community in the west, and gaining recognition as a county in the state of North Carolina. Civil government, negotiation, and compromise were his particular strengths. Military enterprise was not his best game, yet that responsibility fell to him when his commander Lieutenant Colonel John Sevier lost Sarah, his wife, and chose to stay home from the war for the sake of his ten children.

The Washington County committee discussed several options about what to do to make Colonel Sevier answer the call to arms. Some members even engaged matchmakers to bring suitable widows to Colonel Sevier's attention, to lure him into a marriage of convenience that would quickly solve everyone's problems so the state could get on with the war. It seemed an easy fix since Sevier was rumored to be rich and considered the handsomest man in the west. They might have found hundreds of willing candidates for the position of wife, if only the heartbroken Colonel had been more cooperative, but he clung to the silly romantic notion of finding a love as deep as he had with Sarah. It had become a frustrating business for the county, so Major

Charles Robertson rose to the occasion and provided the leadership for the militia company. Robertson planned to combine forces with Sullivan County to the north whose commander was the talented Colonel Isaac Shelby, a younger, impetuous, and enterprising officer.

When Colonel Shelby and Major Robertson arrived in the theater of operations, they were placed under the command of Colonel Charles McDowell of Burke County. Others serving under McDowell were Colonel Elijah Clarke from Georgia, Colonel Andrew Hampton from North Carolina, and Colonel James Williams from South Carolina. These units made up a force of nearly a thousand men, eager for action. Colonel McDowell was the strategic planner, sending his officers on missions rather than leading them.

The frontiersmen, natural hunters, men of the long-rifle, and hungry for action, went to work immediately. McDowell sent them south probing for the advancing enemy. Colonel Shelby found a group of Tories in a stoutly defended fort on Thickety Creek and surrounded it. He sent up Captain William Cocke, who under a flag of parley demanded the surrender of the fort and all the weapons. After an initial refusal, Shelby arrayed his riflemen in an impressive show of force and sent a second request, convincing the loyalist militia officer that the mountain men could take his fort quickly and easily. The men in the fort surrendered rather than fight such rough-looking characters as the mountaineers.

On their next mission they got into a pretty hot fight with a detachment of British regulars near Wofford's Iron Works, and it proved to be more difficult than fighting Tory partisans. The fight lasted several hours, and Charles Robertson received saber wounds from the British cavalry charging through their lines. The courage of the western riflemen and their uncanny marksmanship saved the day, and the British were forced to withdraw. The liberty boys returned to McDowell's camp more experienced and more determined to continue the fight.

While Charles Robertson recovered from his wounds, Isaac Shelby spread the rumor that John Sevier had suddenly arrived from the west and was taking part in the operational planning. Such news had the effect of boosting the confidence of the westerners. They would do anything for Colonel John Sevier. Shelby even went so far as to ride through camp on an inspection tour with Sheriff Val Sevier, John's brother, dressed like the colonel to keep the rumor fresh. So effective was Shelby's pretense that Colonel McDowell eventually came looking for Colonel Sevier, thinking it strange that the popular officer had arrived in his camp and not observed the courtesy to call upon the camp commandant.

"Where is Sevier?" Colonel McDowell demanded of Isaac Shelby.

"Which Sevier?" Isaac asked. "We have Captain Robert and Captain Valentine."

"Colonel John Sevier; I heard he arrived in camp yesterday, and I believe he should have had the courtesy to report to me."

"The last time I saw Colonel John Sevier he was making time with the widows of Jonesborough," Isaac said. "He's campaigning to find a new little wife to take care of those ten children of his!"

"Then why did I hear about his arrival in my camp?"

"I started the rumor to boost morale. The mere mention of his name, and the belief in his presence among us, makes these mountain men fight like there were a hundred more of us!"

"Well, it's a shame he's not in camp to help you plan your next mission tonight." McDowell grinned as he produced a map from his pocket and spread it out on Shelby's camp table.

Shelby was intensely interested. "What's the news?"

"I've decided to follow up on your recent successes with a deeper strike into enemy-controlled territory." McDowell pointed to the map. "These are the last reported positions of the various elements of the British army. The main army under Cornwallis is marching on Camden. General Gates is marching his Continental regulars to oppose Cornwallis before the British can bring up their supply trains and artillery out of Charleston. Opposing us, out here in the west, is a British major named Patrick Ferguson recruiting an army of loyalist militias in the South Carolina uplands. His raw recruits are untrained and under-equipped at the present time. I believe a rapid strike at the recruiting camps could discourage the loyalists from organizing and make them more reluctant to answer the recruiting calls of the British. What do you think?"

"The timing is good," Isaac answered. "The British will concentrate on Camden when they detect the approach of the army under Gates. We can slip into their barnyard and raid the chicken coup, so to speak."

"The place I want you to target is here on the Enoree River," Colonel McDowell continued, pointing out the place on the map. "There's a mill there owned by a man named Musgrove. You will have two hundred men with Colonels Clarke and Williams going with you. Is Major Robertson feeling better today?"

"Some, but not well enough to go with us," Isaac told him.

"Then leave him in camp, and we will see that he is properly cared for until you return," McDowell said. "You will take the back roads tonight, skirting around that group of regulars you tangled with the other day. Surprise the recruiting camp at dawn, disperse the recruits, destroy their supplies, and return by the same route."

The two hundred men rode all night on quiet country lanes and covered a distance of nearly forty miles before the sun lightened the eastern sky. Scouts traveled out in front about a half mile, with outriders on either flank of the main column for protection against ambush. Isaac Shelby, Elijah Clarke of Georgia, and James Williams of South Carolina rode together at the head of the column. Distant shooting sounded a warning, and the officers stopped the column to listen.

"It sounds like our scouts have found something," Isaac said. The men waited and listened. Presently the scouting party appeared from the woods galloping toward them. Isaac recognized the leader of the detachment. "There's Robert Sevier."

"A half dozen Tories spotted us," Robert reported, breathless from the excitement. "We dropped two, but the others made good their escape down to the river."

"There goes our chance of surprise," Isaac noted with disappointment. "We rode all night to get around Ferguson's army for nothing!"

"Maybe we can still do some good," Clarke said.

Captain Val Sevier rode up from the left of the column with a prisoner. "Colonel Shelby, sir," Val reported. "We captured this Tory farmer. He says he has information."

Isaac looked at the countryman, an older fellow he was, with a smile on his face, possessing information he was only too eager to share.

"Good morning, sir," Isaac greeted him politely. "What information do you have?"

"I think you may be rebels," probed the farmer.

"Patriots," Isaac corrected him.

"Then you'll soon be up to your necks in trouble, trying to make good your escape."

"How far is Musgrove's Mill?" Isaac asked.

"Half a mile, but you would be a damn fool to go there, if you be rebels." The farmer appeared very pleased. "Last night six hundred of His Majesty's troops joined the two hundred militia men that were already camped there."

"Who commands the force?" Isaac demanded.

"Colonel Alexander Innes, and I understand the army of Major Ferguson is coming, too. I suggest you ride away and not cause our district any trouble."

Isaac sat straighter in the saddle. "I appreciate your concern, but as long as the British invade American soil they will find nothing but trouble. Good day, sir."

"Good day to you, rebel, but don't say you wasn't warned," the man gloated.

"Val, escort this gentleman to a place of safety. There will be a fight presently." Captain Val Sevier directed the farmer away from the officers.

Colonel Williams was clearly distressed by this new information. "The British are reinforced, and the element of surprise lost. What's left to be done here?"

"If we run, they'll be hot on our trail with fresh horses," Isaac reasoned. "Our men and horses are exhausted and hungry. I say we stand and fight!"

"I'm for it!" spoke up Colonel Clarke. The Georgian was a daring officer and like Isaac Shelby, willing to take risks advancing his objectives. "We'll pile up some brush and old logs along this ridge. I'll take the left, Colonel Williams will cover the center, and Colonel Shelby, take the right."

They could hear distant drums and bugles alarming the enemy camp to action. "They are forming up to fight us," Isaac observed. "Let's get to it and defend ourselves the best we can. Maybe a bold stand will fool them into thinking we outnumber them."

The men were ordered to dismount and secure the horses. Then they ran to the ridge collecting brush and fallen timbers, making them into defensive breastworks. The officers continued to confer when Captain Shadrach Inman, one of Colonel Clarke's Georgia troopers, rode forward with an idea.

"Colonel Clarke?"

"Yes, Captain Inman?"

"I have an idea how we can regain the element of surprise."

"Let's hear it," Clarke replied.

"They don't know our numbers, and they don't know we have Colonel Shelby's riflemen. I want to take my company and attack them as they cross the river. Then we quickly retreat. The British will pursue, thinking they can catch my small force. As they charge up this hill, Shelby's riflemen can fire at least two volleys before the enemy ever sees them."

"Sounds like a good plan," Clarke approved. "What do you think, Colonel Shelby?"

"I agree. I think it will work to our advantage. Are you with us, Colonel Williams?"

"I am," replied the proud South Carolinian.

"Captain Inman, carry out your plan," ordered Colonel Clarke. "We'll have a hot reception ready for the enemy when you come back. God be with you!"

"Thank you, sir!" Captain Inman saluted smartly and turned to signal his mounted Georgia troopers. They rode forward and followed their brave captain down the hill toward the river at a gallop.

"All right, men, let's throw up some cover," shouted Elijah Clarke. "We've no time to lose!" The men worked quickly to gather logs, branches, and brush.

Isaac Shelby turned in his saddle looking for one of his officers. He spotted Captain Samuel Moore and called out, "Captain Moore!"

Samuel Moore rode up to the head of the column. "Yes, Colonel?"

"Sam, the enemy is approaching from the river. Take your men and circle around to the right. Cross the river and get behind them. When you hear the shooting start, make as much racket as you can. Distract their reserves and destroy their camp if possible."

"Yes, sir!" Captain Moore obeyed enthusiastically. He and his men rode quickly away toward the right wing.

Isaac looked at Colonel Williams and Colonel Clarke. "Well, gentlemen, let's get the men situated and pray we have a successful venture!" He dismounted and walked toward his appointed place in the line.

"Isaac!" called Elijah Clarke. "I'll have about forty men in reserve. Call if you need them!"

Isaac saluted an acknowledgement and walked on.

Colonel Williams dismounted. "Elijah, I don't like putting our two hundred against eight hundred of the enemy. If I weren't so saddle sore from the all-night ride, I would have urged that we withdraw to seek an easier target."

"Courage, my friend," Elijah responded. "One unconfirmed report by a Tory farmer should not interfere with our grand designs."

Williams smiled at him and replied dryly, "Courage we have in full measure. It is good sense that is lacking in your backwater compatriot."

"Don't worry, Colonel Williams; my reserves are available to back you up, too."

"My men won't flinch at the bayonet charge," Williams assured him. "You better worry about Shelby's boys. They are green to this kind of warfare. Their home-forged hunting rifles don't even fit the bayonet."

"I'll keep an eye on them," Clarke promised.

In thirty minutes the hastily thrown together breastworks provided ample protection and screened the Americans from view as they lay on the ground, grasped their weapons, and breathed their prayers. They watched a distant line of trees, down the slope, and across an old Indian field, for any signs of movement. They listened as the sounds of firing came closer and closer.

Isaac Shelby walked along the lines speaking words of encouragement. "Men, hold your fire until you can see the buttons on their coats. Then fire only on my signal. I don't want anybody shooting our friends from Georgia." The sounds of shooting and shouting came closer until Inman's troopers appeared on the other side of the clearing. The horsemen charged across the open ground and sped past the men concealed on the ground. Enemy foot soldiers emerged from the woods in hot pursuit, followed by their mounted officers.

Captain Inman found Colonel Clarke as his men dismounted behind the breastworks. "Here they come, Colonel!"

"Steady men; aim carefully and wait for them all to get clear of the woods," Colonel Clarke told his men.

At the other end of the line, Isaac Shelby crouched behind his men. "Hold your fire, men. Hold on!" Shelby let the enemy troops come within seventy yards, hoping the first volley could give them a good effect while leaving enough space for an effective second round.

"Fire!" Isaac shouted. The guns blazed all along the line, catching the advancing enemy completely unaware of the presence of the hidden ambush. Colonel Williams' men in the center opened up next, and Clarke's men an instant later. Many of the king's friends fell to the first volley. Those remaining looked franticly for signs of an enemy. They fired their muskets wildly over the heads of the unseen patriots and turned to run. Shelby's men worked quickly to reload.

The British troops and officers riding behind the vanguard stopped the retreat at the edge of the clearing and turned the soldiers around. They ordered a full bayonet charge. The second volley of the patriot force caught them again in the open and ripped holes in their ranks. Shelby's riflemen aimed at the officers on horseback and took down every one. Colonel Alexander Innes, the highest-ranking British officer, was severely wounded at that moment. The British vanguard reached Shelby's concealed men, and the fighting turned hand to hand, bayonet against tomahawk. Isaac's men fell back, darting behind trees for cover from the bayonet thrusts. Suddenly Clarke's Georgia reserve joined the mountaineers, and the British were stopped. The backwater men shouted the Indian war whoop, and the British retreated. Shelby's men had time to reload their deadly rifles and fired again as the battle became a rout. Captain Inman and his troopers were back in the saddle, gallantly charging the dispirited British and Tories who ran headlong downhill back toward the river. Horsemen brought horses forward for Isaac Shelby and Elijah Clarke who quickly mounted for the pursuit.

"I think they'll try to regroup beyond the river," Elijah shouted. The officers rode out across the battlefield, and Colonel Williams joined them. The Watauga men could reload on the run and kept up a destructive fire throughout the pursuit. The officers followed in their wake until they encountered a group of Georgians dismounted and kneeling around a fallen officer.

"Who is it?" Isaac called out.

One of the Georgia troopers answered, "Captain Inman, shot dead!"

"It can't be!" lamented Elijah Clarke. "He is my finest officer and hero of the day! Oh, what a cruel loss is this!" He dismounted and knelt beside his friend.

Isaac turned to Colonel Williams. "Come, Colonel Williams, let us honor the fallen by securing our victory." Shelby and Williams left the sad scene and rode on to the river, where they found a scene of confusion. American forces had already crossed the river, driving the British before them. Captain Val Sevier splashed back across the river and saluted Isaac.

"Captain Moore reports a successful action on the enemy rear," Val reported. "The enemy broke and ran down the road toward Fort Ninety Six. We captured their camp and are burning everything we can't carry."

"Very well," Isaac approved. "Tell Captain Moore to finish his work and rejoin us on this side of the river."

"Yes, sir," Captain Sevier saluted and wheeled about to splash again across the river. As Isaac and Colonel Williams looked across the battle scene, Colonel Clarke rejoined them.

"What happened over there at the mill?" Elijah asked.

"We routed them completely," Isaac replied. "They are retreating to Fort Ninety Six."

"Well, let's be after them," Clarke urged. "It's only thirty miles. We could be accepting the surrender of that fort by nightfall!"

"I'm for that," Colonel Williams chimed in. "We could free all of upland South Carolina in one great sweep!"

"And then free Georgia!" Colonel Clarke suggested. "Let's go on to Augusta!"

"Let's take one objective at a time," Isaac cautioned. "What's the casualty report?"

Elijah Clarke had the information. "My men reported four dead and nine wounded on the field. They counted sixty enemy dead, and we have taken scores of prisoners."

Isaac was surprised. "Only four dead?"

"That is correct," Elijah confirmed.

"Well, if that isn't a sign from heaven, I don't know what is! Let's get the men in the saddle. We are going to Fort Ninety Six!"

At that moment the officers spotted a courier, approaching from the west riding hard. "Colonel Shelby? Colonel Clarke?" the courier called.

"Over here! I'm Shelby!" Isaac hollered.

The youthful courier arrived and saluted. "Good morning sir, my name is Francis Jones, and I have an urgent dispatch from Colonel McDowell. I also have your orders and other documents, Colonel Shelby."

"All right son, let's have it," Isaac answered. The courier handed over the packet. Isaac read the first letter quickly and passed it to Clarke.

"What happened here?" Francis asked.

Isaac glanced up from his reading momentarily. "We just won a great victory over British and Tory forces twice our size, but it looks like we will have to change our plans." Clarke finished reading the orders and passed them to Williams. Captains Val Sevier and Robert Sevier joined the other officers.

Robert Sevier could tell they had just received important dispatches with serious implications. "What's wrong, is it bad news?"

"The worst," Isaac replied. "The whole American army under General Gates was destroyed at Camden two days ago."

"Surely there's some mistake," Val Sevier ventured.

"No," Shelby said sadly. "Colonel McDowell included a letter from Governor Caswell describing the whole fiasco. I recognize his handwriting. McDowell says to get the hell out of the way, because the British will certainly cut up the remaining corps of the American armies within their reach."

Francis Jones, a precocious youngster, felt great comfort among the straight-talking frontier leaders and volunteered more information than he had been sent to deliver. "General Gates was among the first to run off the field, and he's still running for all I know!"

Isaac was shocked and disgusted. "Are you sure about your facts, young fellow?"

"Yes, sir," Francis answered confidently. "I heard it straight from the rider out of

Charlotte that delivered the news to Colonel McDowell."

Elijah Clarke was livid. "Congress sends us a great hero, an experienced general they promised us. He leads the army to destruction and runs like a yellow-bellied coward! I swear, how can we beat the British with such poor leadership? Gentlemen, we have only our own resources to rely upon, and that's the way it has always been!"

"Ferguson's whole force stands between us and McDowell," Isaac reminded his companions. "I'm sure he knows about the defeat at Camden and will most certainly come after us immediately."

"You will have to ride hard to rejoin McDowell," Francis Jones informed them. "He broke camp and was marching north this morning."

"There goes our support and our provisions," Isaac responded angrily. "We will have to go far west to get around Ferguson and move fast before he figures out the game."

"What about these hundred prisoners?" Colonel Williams asked.

"They'll have to go too," Isaac answered. "I don't want Ferguson receiving any reports about our strength or our movements from prisoners left behind."

"I'll deliver the prisoners to the governor at Hillsborough, and give him a report of our victory," Williams volunteered. The other officers had no objections.

Isaac looked at his subordinates, Captains Val and Robert Sevier. "Gentlemen, we have done all we can do. We are going home, to the safety of the mountains."

"I'm going back to Georgia," Elijah Clarke declared. "I still think Augusta can be retaken."

"I'll tell you one thing, gentlemen," Isaac said in all seriousness, "I'm not coming east again without John Sevier."

"The fellow you keep bragging about?" Elijah Clarke grinned. "The one you call the peacekeeper of Washington County?"

"That's right!" Isaac exclaimed. "Washington County is a safe haven for the patriot cause, and John Sevier is the reason, but we need his talents here, now, to stop the British invasion."

The officers rode up the hill as their men prepared to march. The pursuit of the defeated enemy was recalled, horses were retrieved, the dead were buried, the prisoners organized, and the captured weapons loaded for travel.

The patriot army moved west within the half hour. The tired horses moved too slowly to satisfy the officers. Concern for the safety of the small army marked every step. The rear guard waited impatiently while the column filed by. They worked quickly to erase the signs of the passage of the army through the woods.

Lunchtime came and went for the men without stopping for rest. The officers were unrelenting in their drive to reach the safety of the mountains and escape the reach of Major Ferguson's dragoons. The American rear guard created diversions and false trails for the pursuers, and none of the officers on either side realized how close an escape it really was. Shelby drove the men and horses through the night, and the only food they had was what they could reach from the saddle as they trailed through a corn field or peach orchard.

Late the next day, the detachment rejoined Colonel McDowell at his new camp in the temporary safety of North Carolina. The exhausted men and horses rested while the officers conferred. Colonel McDowell agreed that it would take more men than they had in the field to stop the invasion, and he welcomed Isaac Shelby's offer to go home and organize a larger over-mountain army with Colonel John Sevier at its head. Elijah Clarke received approval to attempt his plan to retake Georgia, and Colonel Williams conveyed the prisoners from Musgrove's Mill to Hillsborough, the emergency capital of North Carolina. Williams would report their success to Governors John Rutledge of South Carolina and Abner Nash of North Carolina, both of whom were governing their states from the same little town in the northern part of the Tar Heel State.

After the officers' meeting, Isaac Shelby found Major Charles Robertson still recovering from his saber wounds, and described for him the battle at the mill and the situation caused by the defeat at Camden. Major Charles Robertson had a story to tell Isaac Shelby as well, concerning the mood in the camp.

"While you were gone, McDowell and Hampton had a set-to and nearly came to blows," Charles told Isaac.

"Why?"

"Colonel Hampton blamed McDowell for not posting pickets out far enough the night the British rode into our camp at Cedar Creek. It resulted in the death of Hampton's son, Noah. Then Hampton brought up all kinds of examples where McDowell showed ineptitude, indecision, and unfitness for command. I tell you, Isaac, it was ugly to see two powerful and proud men go at it like that in front of their junior officers. McDowell took it like a man until Hampton charged him with cowardice. Then McDowell dismissed him from camp. Hampton left with all his men, even before the news from Camden reached us. Losing Hampton's company was one of the factors that made McDowell move his camp so quickly."

"I was damn mad at McDowell for deserting us like that," Isaac said. "We nearly died in the saddle for want of provisions."

"Isaac, we don't need to answer to such officers as these when we have better men commanding our over-mountain boys," Charles confided.

"I appreciate your confidence in me," Isaac said proudly. "Elijah Clarke is another good man we can depend upon."

"With all due respect, Isaac, I was thinking about John Sevier." Charles grinned.

Isaac laughed. "How are you going to convince old lover boy to join the fight?"

"John Sevier's love life very nearly cost me my own life," Charles declared. "When he hears how we suffered for the cause without the benefit of his leadership, I think his manly pride will get the better of him and he will leave off the widows of Jonesborough long enough to win the war for us."

"I suppose if we both go to work on him, we might be able to bring him around," Isaac said thoughtfully. "The quickest way I know would be to get him married off so he could feel right about leaving those ten children."

"I wonder if those matchmakers have made any progress since we've been gone," Charles wondered.

"I doubt it," Isaac said gloomily. "I even tried to talk Bonny Kate Sherrill into marrying him when I visited Plum Grove. She's already taking care of his children."

"Was she agreeable to the idea?"

"She threw me off the place, insulted me, and threatened me! That girl has a hell of a temper!"

"Yeah, that sounds like Bonny Kate," Charles laughed. "You're lucky she didn't shoot you! Imagine if Jack Sevier ever did marry that little shrew."

"He would become the greatest general in the whole country!" Isaac roared with laughter. "He would *always* be ready for campaigning, just to avoid going home to her!"

Chapter 3

The Horse Race

The golden days of September arrived before John and Bonny Kate knew it. They had enjoyed two weeks of wedding celebrations with feasting, games, races, and dancing for the entire Nolichucky community. The farming folks came and went steadily, spending some days at home tending animals and harvesting crops and returning to the "Sevier frolic," as it was called, for more fun and games. Finally the festivities were set to conclude with one final horse race and one last dance before everyone went home to their farms and regular routines of hard work and continuous agricultural production.

On the day of the race, John and his father-in-law, Sam Sherrill, stood beside the horse track watching Bonny Kate warming up her horse. She walked the horse past the men and smiled. "Wish me luck, Mr. Sevier!"

John grinned at her. "I wish you all the luck in the world, my darling Bonny Kate!" She turned her horse and trotted to the starting line.

"Of my three daughters, Bonny Kate has always been the most naturally cheerful," Sam told John. "But I've never seen her as happy as she's been these last few weeks."

"Sam, your daughter has made me the happiest man in the world! I sure wish it would last." John's gaze looked far beyond his friend as he noticed a distant rider approaching at a rapid pace.

"And why shouldn't it?"

"Yonder approaches the very reason I've been dreading."

Sam looked in the direction of John's attention and recognized the rider. "Isaac Shelby!"

"Yes, the personal emissary of Mars, god of war."

"Let's hope he brings good news."

"Does he look like he's got good news?" John asked.

"No, I'm afraid not."

Isaac Shelby arrived and wearily dismounted his exhausted horse.

"Welcome to our celebration, Isaac" John greeted him. "You're just in time for the horse race!"

"I've already had my horse race today, a full forty miles from Sapling Grove. I've no time to spare, John. We need to talk."

"Very well, Colonel Shelby, come on up to the house. I want you to drink a toast to the bride and groom."

"Whose wedding are we celebrating?"

"Mine!" John exclaimed.

"I can't believe my ears!" Isaac seemed genuinely delighted. "How in the world... I mean, who's the lucky lady?"

"Bonny Kate Sherrill," John announced.

"Well, if it isn't Lady Luck personified! She's a remarkable woman! Congratulations, John."

"Thank you, Isaac, and of course, you know the father of the bride, my good friend, Sam Sherrill."

"Yes sir, we are well acquainted," Isaac shook hands with Sam warmly. "Mr. Sherrill, I expect you warned your daughter about what she was getting into by hitching up to this old horse soldier."

"She knows, and I believe she's equal to the challenges," Sam spoke confidently.

"Let's hope so. Now, John, I have an urgent matter. Can we talk?"

"Come along, then." John started for the house. "Sam, tell Bonny Kate I'll be back at the house."

"I will," Sam nodded. John and Isaac walked toward the house just as the horse race began.

"Riders, are you ready?" the race master shouted. "Get set!"

Crack! The starting rifle sounded and the horses took off! Bonny Kate captured an early lead as the horses thundered across the meadow and into the forest. Her horse maintained the lead on the forest trail, splashing through brooks, jumping fallen trees, and running through the hills and valleys of the pristine country. Finally she emerged from the forest trail at the far end of the meadow leading the field and crossed the finish line first. The crowd cheered madly and passed around the winnings of many serious wagers. A jubilant Bonny Kate, flushed with excitement, rode over to her father to celebrate.

"Did you see how she ran?" Bonny Kate spoke excitedly. "It was magnificent. We have another champion!"

"Yes, she won easily," Sam agreed. "That was a good ride."

"Where's John?"

Sam's smile faded quickly. "He's gone back to the house with Isaac Shelby."

"Isaac Shelby?"

"Yes, he rode up just before the race started. I reckon he had news of the war."

"Only a serious war would make John Sevier miss a horse race! What did Colonel Shelby say?"

"Not much, except that it was urgent."

"I'll find out what's going on."

"Bonny Kate, you may not like what you hear."

"Papa, I knew this was coming when I married him. I just didn't expect it so soon."

"You are a colonel's lady now, in a country at war. You know what that means."

"I know...I'll be brave." She started her horse toward the house with a determination to be strong.

When Bonny Kate entered the parlor at Plum Grove manor house, the men stood up from their chairs and regarded her solemnly.

"Good evening, Mrs. Sevier," Isaac Shelby greeted her.

Bonny Kate smiled. "Good evening, Colonel Shelby. I'm not yet accustomed to being called Mrs. Sevier. It takes some adjustment, you know. Welcome to our wedding celebration."

"Thank you, ma'am, and congratulations to you both," Isaac said as he bowed courteously.

"The boys pit-roasted a pig today," she said. "I expect you'll stay for supper and a night's lodging."

"Yes, ma'am," Isaac accepted. "That would be a great pleasure were it not for the terrible nature of the news I bring. You may feel justified in withholding your hospitality once you hear my report."

"Your news must concern the end of the world to make John Sevier leave his guests and miss a horse race; especially a race I won."

"Well done, Sweetheart. That's wonderful!" John stepped over to take her hand and pulled her into a warm embrace. They lingered that way several moments, embarrassing Isaac with such a display of affection. They kissed and Isaac turned and walked to the doorway, gazing out to the yard where some Sevier kinfolks were making preparations for the dance.

Isaac spoke again without looking at the happy couple. "I must say, John, you are a fortunate man when it comes to marriage." A few moments later he turned to see that they had not ceased their affectionate demonstrations. He sighed and walked over to the table, producing a piece of paper from his pocket. "I hate to spoil the moment, but read this when you come up for air." Isaac laid a letter on the table and sat down.

Bonny Kate pulled away, looking John in the eye. Then she turned and looked at the letter. John followed her gaze to the letter but didn't move. She picked up the letter and gave it to John. He looked at her, then at the letter, and slowly opened it and began reading. John's alertness and intensity returned as he looked over at Isaac. "This comes from a British Army officer named Ferguson."

"The same Major Patrick Ferguson that's been stirring up the Carolinas and recruiting all the Tories to the king's standard. Go ahead and read it out loud."

"To the rebel officers west of the mountains," John read. "Gentlemen, if you do not lay down your opposition to the British arms, I will march my army over the mountains, hang your leaders, and lay waste your country with fire and sword."

Bonny Kate gasped. John looked up at her and then turned to Isaac. "Where did you get this?"

"My cousin, Sam Phillips, was captured. Ferguson paroled him to deliver this message to me."

"You are the leaders he's talking about hanging," Bonny Kate realized. "He's threatening our lives, our families, and our homes. How could he know who we are, let alone find us here in the safety of our mountain homes?"

"The same Tories we ran out of our country these last several years would be only too happy to lead the wolves right to your door," Isaac answered with a chilling edge in his voice.

"And he would destroy our country with fire and sword," Bonny Kate repeated with a shiver in her voice.

"It's already happening in the Carolinas," Isaac pointed out. "Every day it gets worse."

"I have many Carolina relatives," Bonny Kate said. "They are all in danger." A silence fell over the room as her words had their effect. John was deep in thought as they pondered the gravity of the threats.

"We must never stop fighting for our freedoms," John began slowly. "We declared our independence clearly, according to the laws of reason, and with faith in Divine Providence. No foreign king has the right to force his will on us. This Ferguson must be defeated!"

"What will we do?" Bonny Kate searched her husband's face for an answer she knew was coming.

"My dear wife," John looked into her eyes. "Where would you kill a skunk?"

Bonny Kate smiled at his reference to folk wisdom she had often heard from her Granny Sherrill and replied, "As far downwind from the house as possible."

Isaac and John laughed.

"Are you thinking what I'm thinking?" Isaac asked John.

"Suppose we don't wait for Ferguson to make good his threats. We go after him quickly, without warning, and hit him so hard that King George feels the blow all the way over in London!"

"It's brilliant!" Isaac declared.

"It's dangerous," Bonny Kate cautioned.

"But I'm afraid it's the only way," John concluded seriously. He sat at the table and became very quiet, obviously deep in thought.

"Something troubles you, my love." The lady stood behind him and massaged his shoulders as though to relieve him of a burden that he would soon shoulder because of his office.

"The Chickamaugas intend to attack our homes and families at the first opportunity," John reminded them. "An expedition to rescue the Carolinas might mean the extinction of all families on the frontier."

"Don't you think that Charles Robertson staying here with a strong, well-organized home guard could effectively counter that threat?" Isaac asked.

"If we limit the number of men we take on the expedition, and our families go into the forts, they might withstand a general Indian uprising until we could return and run them off," John answered.

"We can't fort up with the crops in the field, ripe for harvest," Bonny Kate objected. "We would starve next year."

"There's also the risk that Ferguson can't be taken by surprise," John added. "What would we do if so many Tories joined him that he became too powerful to stop? The Carolinas would fall anyway, and Ferguson would be free to carry out his threats against our families."

"John, my aunts and uncles and cousins all live over in the Carolina country," Bonny Kate said. "This fellow, Ferguson, invades the land of my birth. Can't you stop him?"

"I can. You know I can! But we have to understand the risks we face with this adventure and plan the project down to the last detail, allowing for every contingency. Besides, my dear, it is a horrible way for us to spend our honeymoon!"

"I know, my love," Bonny Kate agreed. "Mr. Ferguson should have had better sense than to interfere with our happiness, but I know what must be done."

"Then I shall do it! I resent him and his king all the more, because the business takes me away from my dear Bonny Kate!"

"Oh, how I will miss you," she cried. They rushed together again, hugging and kissing, obviously forgetting that Isaac was present.

"Surely, this is the most difficult part of the whole campaign for me to watch," Isaac protested.

"Then, don't watch," Bonny Kate said.

"I'll just leave you lovebirds alone for awhile," he offered.

"No, we will get started planning immediately." John released his wife and stepped over to his desk where he took out pen and paper.

"And I'll get your supper," she volunteered. She realized she had just been involved in an important military decision, and had even been supportive of her husband's involvement. She chose not to speculate on the "what ifs," because she knew such thinking would drive her insane. She knew that now was the time for action.

"We'll plan the whole thing out to the last detail," Isaac said. "But remember, the entire project must be cloaked in secrecy. Bonny Kate, you'll have to keep the secret too."

She smiled at John. "I can keep secrets, especially when the lives of my beloved family are at stake. John, what about the dance tonight? Won't our guests suspect something is wrong when they miss their exuberant host?"

"No, you can make up some excuse," Isaac replied.

"No excuse would work for John Sevier to miss a dance or a horse race!"

"She's right, Isaac. No excuse would make any sense. My people know me too well. Besides, I'm not missing a chance to dance with my lovely wife!"

"I can see I'm outnumbered here," Isaac grumbled. "But we'll work double hard tomorrow to make up for the lost time."

"It wouldn't hurt you, either, Colonel Shelby, to spend a little time dancing with some of our pretty Washington County belles," Bonny Kate prescribed.

"That's right, Isaac. I could introduce you to Bonny Kate's sister."

"You have a sister?"

"Two sisters; but Mary Jane is the one not yet married."

"Yes, and she's one to watch out for," John recommended.

"I can believe that!" Isaac laughed.

As the colonel's lady, and hostess of the dance, Bonny Kate spent a lot of time socializing and making sure everyone had a dance partner. She introduced Colonel Shelby to Mary Jane, but both seemed reluctant partners. Isaac thought visiting among the men would speed up the progress of organizing and equipping a military expedition, while Mary Jane seemed to have romantic interests elsewhere. Bonny Kate was also occupied by the needs of her stepchildren during the evening. She found a partner for twelve-year-old Betsy Sevier, John's oldest daughter, who was developing into a popular young lady, and ten-year-old Dolly needed a partner too. Mary Ann, the precocious nine-year-old, also wanted a partner. Bonny Kate could already see John's girls would break many hearts. Bonny Kate never got back to her sister Mary Jane and didn't observe who she danced with the rest of the night.

Bonny Kate and John won the dancing contest as John had so many times in the past when Sarah was his partner. Many of the women remarked that the colonel was once again his old charming self, and that the marriage to Bonny Kate had completely restored his playful nature and his family fortune. Many of the men wondered if the colonel could ever pull himself away from such a wife to restore his reputation as their militia commander.

Isaac Shelby met with Charles Robertson during the course of the evening. Charles had recovered from his saber wounds, but the experience had shaken him and made him realize he was getting too old and too slow for hand-to-hand combat against professional British soldiers. He was eager to return John Sevier to his rightful position of active leadership.

"Did you talk to Jack about leading the next expedition to the east?" Charles asked Isaac.

"It was the very first thing we discussed upon my arrival," Isaac answered.

"You don't waste any time, do you Isaac? How did it go?"

"Much easier than I thought."

"Do you think Bonny Kate is going to try to stop him?"

"No," Isaac replied. "She was there and encouraged him to go."

"That's a surprise," Charles marveled. "I thought she would raise a ruckus to keep him home!"

"She didn't. It kind of surprised me too."

"They are already acting like old married people," Charles observed. "Maybe she's ready to get some relief from ol' Jack. Did you hear about the wedding night?"

"No."

"They got so rough, they broke the bed!" Charles laughed.

"You don't say!" Isaac responded. "Who is spreading such wicked gossip?"

"It's true, old man Val Sevier told me," Charles testified. "He saw the wreckage and helped old man Sherrill make the repairs."

"It looks like we missed a hell of a wedding!" Isaac laughed.

"I'll say," Charles agreed.

Late that night as the dancing turned into visiting and the fiddlers retired for the night, the hostess and the gallant colonel excused themselves from the few remaining guests sitting around the bonfire and retired to the main house.

"John dear," Bonny Kate said. "I just want to check on the children, and then we can ride up to our special place."

"Not tonight, my love," John said gently. "I have some correspondence to take care of and some orders to issue at first light. There's going to be a lot to do in the next couple of days. Why don't you sleep in the loft with the children? I'll be at my desk in the parlor, but every other thought shall be of you."

"Come to me softly when you are done," she whispered. "Just let me hold you every night."

He kissed her long and passionately. "Run along now."

John entered the parlor, and she went into the great room where she found Mary Jane waiting up for her. The rooms of Plum Grove were filled with guests and family members sleeping on every surface where a bedroll could be spread. That's why she and John had pitched a tent in their special place, a hilltop that commanded a sweeping view of the Nolichucky Valley and Plum Grove Plantation. It was a mile distant so that she and John would not embarrass anyone with their passion.

"Bonny Kate, I must talk to you!"

"Oh, Mary Jane," Bonny Kate sighed. "It's very late. Can we talk in the morning while we cook breakfast?"

"It can't wait. I need to discuss this tonight!"

"Very well then," Bonny Kate agreed. Mary Jane took her by the hand and led her back out into the yard.

"I am going to elope," the twenty-year-old Mary Jane Sherrill declared.

"Not tonight, you won't! Papa would tan your hide, and Mama would be heartbroken!"

"No, I'm not talking about tonight, but some night soon. And Papa will thank me for it!"

"What are you talking about?"

"It's not easy being your sister. You put on such a big show, with your wedding and everything, and now here you are the leading lady in the community. Papa spent a fortune on your wedding, and now I very much doubt there will be much of a dowry for me."

"Papa loves you very much! He would want the same kind of wedding for you. I know he would. Give him a year or two, and he will have the resources built up again."

"But I'm in love now! That's why I think it best that we elope."

"Who are you in love with?" Bonny Kate asked, amazed that she had missed the signals.

"Isaac," Mary Jane drawled his name dreamily.

"Isaac Shelby?" Bonny Kate asked in shock.

"No, it's Isaac Taylor, the surveyor. You know, the Taylors of Gap Creek!"

"Yes, I know him. I'm sorry for the confusion. I just have Isaac Shelby on my mind tonight."

"Why?" Mary Jane looked at her sister with concern.

"Oh, he's John's best friend, and he arrived today almost too late for the celebration. I was just trying to make a favorable impression, that's all."

"So you tried to set him up with me?"

"I'm sorry, Mary Jane. I didn't know you were engaged."

"I'm not engaged, but I wanted to know what you thought about me eloping."

"Please don't, Mary Jane. Mama and Papa would not be happy with that. Take your time and get to know his family. You'll be glad you did. Has Mr. Taylor proposed?"

"Not yet, but he has hinted a time or two, since the day you and John got married."

"Promise me you won't elope. There's really no need for that."

"I promise," Mary Jane said solemnly.

"Papa would like your Mr. Taylor very much for a son-in-law. Mr. and Mrs. Taylor, isn't that funny?"

"What?"

"That you and Sister Susan would both marry a man named Taylor. And Isaac and Leroy are not even related."

"Not that we know of," Mary Jane laughed.

"Thank you for confiding in me, Mary Jane." Bonny Kate yawned as they returned to the house. "Maybe we should get some sleep now."

"Sweet dreams," Mary Jane teased as she kissed her sister good night in the hallway. When she was gone, Bonny Kate saw that the candles still burned in the parlor and she heard the voice of Isaac Shelby droning on with John about the details of the campaign.

"Sweet dreams indeed," Bonny Kate sighed. She thought that after the traditional farewell breakfast in the morning, and after the fond farewells to all their important guests, friends, and family members, she ought to ride up alone to their special place on the hilltop and take down the tent where she and John had enjoyed so many intimate moments of pleasure.

Chapter 4

John's Jubilee

The morning was half spent before Bonny Kate could get away to the special hilltop place where she and John had spent their nights of the wedding celebration. It was less than a mile southeast from Plum Grove house, across the Nolichucky and partway up Cherokee Mountain. There the hill flattened like a tabletop, with room enough for a home site and garden, and two springs of sweet water were not very far from the crest. It commanded a spectacular view of the valley, and behind it rose Cherokee Mountain another seven hundred feet. A storm in recent history had blown down some trees and created a natural clearing.

Bonny Kate felt safe there and happy; and although she had not yet discussed it with John, she had decided that someday she would like a house built there. She would call the home Mount Pleasant, because of the beautiful memories that she and John had made there. She tied her horse, walked over to the tent, and removed all the camp bedding they left behind the previous morning. She shook out the quilts and packed them on her horse. She hadn't slept well and doubted that John had slept at all. He never came to bed in the loft at Plum Grove last night and was wearing the same clothes when she served him and Colonel Shelby breakfast in the parlor that morning. He had barely acknowledged her, so focused was he on the secret discussions.

Bonny Kate pulled up the stakes and let the tent topple to the ground. She was folding it when she noticed Kesiah Sevier approaching on horseback. The appearance of Kesiah, strangely out of place, in John and Bonny Kate's special place, Cupid's Garden, as he called it, was unsettling to her. It was like discovering a hog in the turnips.

"The mystery is solved," Kesiah exalted. "Everyone has been wondering where the two of you go every night!"

"Well, now you know," Bonny Kate said without her usual cheerfulness.

"So what have you been doing up here every night?"

"Use your imagination, Kesiah. You likely will, anyway."

"It looks like you and John have knocked down all the vegetation like bears in heat. You made a nice little clearing up here."

"A storm did that. Why don't you climb down and help me pack?"

"You seem to have everything under control, Bonny Kate."

"Then go find your husband to play your catty games with."

Kesiah dismounted her horse and stepped over to where Bonny Kate worked. "Your husband sent my husband on a patrol to the French Broad this morning. He won't likely return until tomorrow, so you are not the only one who has a right to be out of sorts today."

"I'm not out of sorts," Bonny Kate replied unconvincingly.

"I warned you what it would be like, married to a Sevier. You can't control what happens from now on. A report of Indians or Tories on the prowl sets them into action, and they are gone before you know it!"

"You are right, Kesiah. We can't control what happens. That's why I always trust in Providence to control events."

"Oh, there you go preaching the gospel again."

"Yes, Kesiah, I'm trying to explain the source of my happiness. Jesus Christ is Lord of my life, and while he controls all things, I am happy. When I try to take control of things, something almost always goes wrong!"

"Does John believe these same things?"

"He will understand it all, in time. I believe that his talents for leadership and his ability to make loyal friends are the gifts of Divine Providence. His entire life is an instrument in the hands of God to bring about God's will on earth. The purpose of my humble life is to be his helpmate."

Kesiah laughed. "Your life is anything but humble, you big show-off!"

Bonny Kate laughed at her reaction as she lifted the tent and other equipment onto the back of her horse and tied it to stay.

"Bonny Kate, Bonny Kate!" shouted Betsy Sevier as she rode up the hill on her father's horse.

"How did *she* know where I was?" Bonny Kate wondered.

"The children watch you closer than I do," Kesiah said.

"Bonny Kate, Papa wants you," Betsy announced. "What are you doing up here?"

"I came up here to enjoy the view. Wouldn't this be a pleasant place for a picnic?"

"A picnic indeed," snorted Kesiah. A glance from Bonny Kate silenced her.

"Pleasant enough, but Papa needs you right away."

"Did he mention why?"

"I hope you can put him in a better humor," Betsy answered. "Colonel Shelby has him upset about something. I don't think they got any sleep last night!"

"Isaac Shelby is always trouble," Kesiah complained. "What are they up to, Bonny

Kate?"

"I can't tell. You never know whether it's horse racing, target shooting, cock fighting, or wagering who can spit the farthest." She untied her horse, mounted, and galloped down the hill toward Plum Grove.

Bonny Kate found the parlor at Plum Grove dark and smoky as she breezed in like a breath of fresh air and closed the door behind her. "Good morning, gentlemen," she lilted. "Colonel Sevier, I have come to collect my wages, sir."

John looked up drowsily and noticeably brightened at the sight of her. "Wages?"

She held her arms open for an embrace, and he rose to comply with a hug and a lingering kiss.

"Oh, for goodness sake," Isaac groused. "Doesn't Miss Sunshine have some other dark corner of the world to illuminate?"

"I sent for her, Isaac. I want her to shed some light on the quality of the horses we possess in these Washington County muster rolls. Besides that, she provides excellent companionship."

"She talks too much. She'll compromise our security."

"No, she won't."

"Yes, she will," Isaac insisted.

John turned to Bonny Kate. "You won't talk too much will you, my darling?"

"I'm not saying a word."

"See Isaac, she's going to be a big help to get us back on schedule."

"As usual, you have me out-numbered." Isaac returned to a letter he was writing.

"We need to move the planning operation to a more secure location," Bonny Kate suggested. "I know a place where we can open the shutters and let in the daylight, have plenty of fresh air while we work, and no one can hear what we say."

John thought a moment and came up with the same idea. "The old blockhouse over the horse barn; it is perfect! And I can post some sentries to keep the children and our other relatives from learning too much about the operation before we have the plans complete."

Isaac stood up and stretched. "I could use a breath of fresh air. What time is it getting to be?"

"Almost lunch time," she informed the officers. "Let's get moved to our new quarters, and I'll have Betsy and Kesiah prepare us something to eat."

Plum Grove was built on the site of old Fort Williams, a hastily constructed duty station for the North Carolina troops who had been sent out to protect the settlers from the Indians during the summer of 1777. The only blockhouse the soldiers built during the one season of occupation had been converted into John Sevier's horse barn when he settled the property as his family home. The upper level was roomy, and the shutters could be opened for fresh air, southern daylight and a beautiful view of the Nolichucky River Valley with the mountains rising majestically beyond. The greatest advantage was the privacy that kept the secret work of the campaign planning from being discovered by the friends and family constantly coming and going at the main house.

That afternoon found Bonny Kate quietly conversing with John about the quality of the horses owned by every member of the Washington County militia. She knew the families and horses of the community through her work in her father's horse-breeding business. They used a muster roll and a local map to guide the discussion.

"Now tell me about these Smiths over here on Big Limestone Creek," John directed.

"You don't want to involve those people in this," she reacted. "I'm surprised Mr. Smith is even enrolled in the Washington County militia."

"Why is that?"

"Their daughter married a Tory."

"Bonny Kate, these militia companies were set up for defense against the Indians, not to divide the community along political lines. Did you hear that, Isaac?"

"What's that?" Isaac looked up from a letter he was reading.

"Bonny Kate brings up a good point. Many of our citizens out here on the Nolichucky, who have been useful to us against the Indians, have loyalist political leanings. That ought to disqualify them from service in the coming campaign."

"That is a good point," Isaac agreed. "We must only draft men who have good horses *and* the correct politics."

"Horse quality I can easily judge, but a man's political thoughts are not so easy to fathom," John said. Isaac went back to his reading, while John stood and walked to the open window and breathed deeply.

"How many qualified men do you need?" Bonny Kate asked.

"I'm halfway through the muster rolls for Washington County," John calculated. "I'm taking eight companies, and that's two hundred forty men, all equipped and mounted. The real challenge is deciding who to leave behind to fill the rosters of the home guard. I'm pretty sure I'll have more than enough volunteers when I announce that I'm leading the Washington County contingent."

Isaac looked up and laughed. "Pretty sure of yourself, aren't you?"

"I've never had any trouble before. When I lead men on campaigns, it's just like a big hunting trip. My men will go for the fun of it."

"Wait until you have to hang the deserters; you'll see how much fun it is."

"I've never had deserters or cowards among my men."

"They haven't faced the bayonet charge, or advanced across open fields against British artillery. Even the best men will turn yellow before such terrors."

"Isaac, there is no reason to maneuver our men into such horrific situations. I intend to choose a more advantageous battlefield where cannon and bayonets cannot be employed against us. With our men mounted and the superior range of our hunting rifles, we should never have to face the bayonet."

"The British have mounted dragoons that can move just as fast as we can."

"But no dragoons can outshoot our riflemen."

"John, you are not running an independent command here. You are going to have to follow orders from whoever gets put in charge. I just hope it's not Charles McDowell. I've had my fill of him."

The conversation distressed Bonny Kate, and she sought to change the subject. "Mr. Sevier, you know you can count on the Sherrill family. Every one of my brothers will volunteer, and so will Papa."

"I can't take them all, my dear. Mr. Sherrill and at least two of your brothers are needed for the home guard. I have decided to take Sam Jr., Adam, and George."

"Papa told me whatever you are cooking up, he wants to go. Please don't hurt his pride."

"In battle we have to move fast. I can't be encumbered with worrying about your father."

"Oh, that would be a hurtful thing to say to Papa."

"I don't want to hurt his feelings. Our friendship runs too deep for that."

"Then let him go with you."

"I need him here to safeguard you and your mother."

"We will manage," Bonny Kate spoke confidently, but she understood as clearly as John did the incredible risks that they had resolved to take for the cause of liberty. "Where will you likely encounter Mr. Ferguson?"

"In the valley of the Catawba," Isaac replied.

"Who knows the valley of the Catawba better than any man under your command, Mr. Sevier?" Bonny Kate gazed into her husband's eyes with determination.

"Your father has often made that claim. Are you intent on confirming that?"

"You need his experience and knowledge of that country. You know you do."

"Very well, Mrs. Sevier, I have warned you of the dangers, and I will give your father one more chance to back out."

"He'll not back out. Take my word for it."

"You cannot hold me responsible for what happens, but I will do everything in my power to keep him safe from harm."

"Treat him no different than any of your other warriors."

"Done, madam," John said tenderly. She moved into his embrace and he held her close.

"Oh, for Pete's sake," Isaac exclaimed. "Are we going to suffer this woman's interference in every decision we have to make?"

"No, Colonel Shelby," she answered with a smile, "only the important ones."

"Send her back to her pots and pans," Isaac ordered.

"I kind of like having her around," John said.

"Are you thinking about taking her on the campaign?"

"I can ride and I can shoot, and everybody loves my cooking," she offered.

"But when would old lover boy ever get around to fighting?"

"Isaac has a point, my dear," John said. "We could never make it work; and what would we do about the children?"

"What indeed?" Bonny Kate sighed, and John noticed a little frown of disappointment.

"We have guests coming tonight, my dear. The Reverend Samuel Doak and Mr. Waightstill Avery will dine with us. Afterwards we are having a little business meeting I want you to attend, my Bonny Kate. Cook something that will put us all in a fine humor, my love."

"Yes, something to celebrate our last night at Plum Grove," Isaac added.

Bonny Kate gasped and looked to her husband.

"I'm afraid it's true," John confirmed. "We are going up to Watauga Fort tomorrow and talk things over with Charles McDowell, but I'll be back in a few days. It could be that our North Carolina and Virginia friends might reject our idea of a campaign as too risky. There may be no campaign at all."

Soothing words to the worried wife did little to allay her concerns. It would be their first separation since the wedding, and she knew she would miss his loving arms wrapped around her against the chilly nights of September in the mountains.

Despite John's request for good humor with their dinner, a somber mood prevailed. Isaac Shelby had never been a free-spirited talker, and Pastor Samuel Doak's mood was reflective and deeply thoughtful. Perhaps he was preoccupied with some great sermon he was planning. Waightstill Avery, the lawyer, was a great talker when arguing a case but of no particular help on this occasion. So it was up to the wives, Esther Doak and Bonny Kate, to take up the slack, but women speak of things that are of interest to women, and rightly so. John smiled politely as though he was listening intently to the female chatter, but it was his own internal conversation about religion, economics, politics, and war that occupied his consciousness that evening.

After the dinner was cleared away, John's guests repaired to the parlor. The fireplace gave off a cheerful glow, and Pastor Doak lit three candles on the table. Waightstill Avery brought out some papers, and all was in readiness for their meeting.

John had seen Bonny Kate and Esther Doak taking the dishes out to the wash pot in the yard, and he followed them. "Bonny Kate, it's time for our business meeting, and we want you and Esther to attend."

"We were about to do the dishes," she answered.

"Leave them to soak. I want to get this done now." She looked at his face in the firelight, and he was as serious as she had ever seen him. She and Esther looked at each other and moved toward the door of the house and entered. When everyone was seated, John closed the door and nodded the order for Mr. Avery to begin.

"Colonel Sevier has caused me to draw up two documents that will be signed here tonight in the presence of these witnesses and subsequently recorded in the record books of Washington County. The first document is the Last Will and Testament of Lieutenant Colonel John Sevier, Esquire, of Washington County, North Carolina. In it, Colonel Sevier has listed all of his property, his businesses, his personal effects, his assets, as well as his debts and obligations. His children are the beneficiaries of his personal effects, and everything else goes to his wife, Catharine Sherrill Sevier, to hold and manage in trust for the benefit and sustenance of said children of Colonel John Sevier, until each child reaches the age of majority, at which time they will each inherit one twelfth of Colonel Sevier's present land holdings and those lands that may be due him for services rendered to the State of North Carolina and Washington County."

Bonny Kate wept openly. Esther Doak gave her a handkerchief to manage the tears. She was unable to lift her tear-streamed face to look at her husband as he stepped over to stand beside her chair. "Excuse me, Mr. Sevier. Might I be given leave from the rest of this?"

"I'm sorry, my dear, but the most important arrangements are still to come," he answered. "Please proceed, Mr. Avery."

"Nothing in this Last Will and Testament and the responsibilities laid out for the care of Colonel Sevier's children shall bind or prohibit the said Catharine Sherrill Sevier, widow of Colonel John Sevier, from pursuing a speedy and happy remarriage, after an appropriate period of mourning."

"Oh, John, losing you would mean the death of me!" Bonny Kate could not control her feelings. She stood and embraced her husband tightly. Everyone in the room was affected with sympathy for her. "Why are you doing this to me?"

"I'm going away to war, my dear, and we both understand the risks. I need to put my affairs in order and simplify things as much as possible for you. I'm sorry this has upset you." She continued crying, struggling to catch her breath between sobs. John sighed. "That's enough, Mr. Avery. I'll sign it now, and Pastor Doak and Colonel Shelby can witness."

"I'm sorry, John, but because of my priestly office, I cannot serve as signatory on any kind of covenant." Pastor Doak rose as he spoke. "I am under exclusive and eternal covenant as priest of the God Most High, so I make it a practice never to enter into any other kind of inferior covenant, don't you see?"

John looked at the Reverend Doak and nodded. "I'll get Sam Sherrill to be the other witness. The Sherrills are staying with us down at the guest house. I'll send for Mr. Sherrill immediately." It wasn't long before Bonny Kate's parents had joined the group and observed their daughter's distress.

"Are you all right, darling?" Mary Sherrill asked with great concern.

"This whole war business is already breaking my heart!" Bonny Kate tried hard to hold back another round of tearful demonstrations but was not successful.

"What is it?" Mary asked.

"John is signing his Last Will and Testament and wants me to be a witness," Sam Sherrill explained from the table where he watched his neighbor sign the document.

"Oh," Mary nodded, understanding completely the scene they had been invited to observe as she held her daughter close. "Maybe Mr. Sherrill should be doing likewise with his own estate, but he'll get no tears from me until he earns them. When you get to be as old as me and have as many children as I have, you'll understand."

"I already have as many children as you have," Bonny Kate said.

"So you do!" Mary laughed, and the mood in the room brightened a bit.

After the will was signed, witnessed, folded, and sealed, Mr. Avery reminded the group of another document still to process. For this he yielded the floor to Pastor Doak.

"Colonel Sevier asked me to prepare this next document, and I have searched the scriptures and engaged in much prayer to fully understand his request, but here goes. In the book of Leviticus, Chapter 25, and again in Deuteronomy, Chapter 15, God gave Moses the laws and ordinances concerning the Sabbath, where rest is granted from all our labors on the seventh day of the week. There was also a Sabbath year, when fields were granted a year of rest every seventh year. Then every seven Sabbath years there was a year of Jubilee, held forty-nine years apart from the last Jubilee. All debts were cancelled, all slaves were freed, and all obligations forgiven." Pastor Doak picked up the document from the table before continuing. "After the year of Jubilee, God always performed great and wonderful miracles in the land of Israel. Colonel Sevier believes that in the present times, we need God's presence amongst us. He has declared his own personal year of Jubilee. He has cancelled all debts owed to him and erased all obligations that any other people of this community might owe him. This will become effective on John's thirty-fifth birthday, Saturday, September 23, 1780. Have I explained it clearly enough, John?"

"Yes, Pastor," John nodded. "Better than I ever could. Even in the Lord's Prayer it says *forgive us our debts as we forgive our debtors*. So I have decided to simplify my affairs and forgive all my debtors."

Mr. Avery looked at the list of debtors John had supplied him with and at the amounts each owed. "Yep, there's my name up there with the Allisons, the Algoods, and the Andersons. This debt cancellation represents quite a fortune you are giving up.

Are you sure you want to go through with it?"

John looked at Bonny Kate and discerned a great many questions and concerns in her expression. "I need to explain a few things to my wife, if you will excuse us for a few moments," John said. "And don't be reading out the names, Mr. Avery. I want all the letters you send out to be personal and confidential; do you understand?"

"Yes, of course, Colonel Sevier. You can always trust your attorney to be confidential."

John and Bonny Kate walked out on the porch and stepped down into the yard. She took his arm as though they were out for a stroll. "John, he said you were giving up a fortune. Is this true?"

"The only fortune I might collect would be if I foreclosed and took away the homes of my neighbors. I'll never see that money again, anyway. You know how hard Sarah worked to collect on those loans, and I know you have no joy in that kind of work."

"How much money is it?"

"This simplifies my business dealings a great deal, and just think about how it will stimulate the Washington County economy."

"What about the money *you* owe to other people?" she asked.

"I still have to pay that. If only everybody would observe the year of Jubilee, like I do, what a splendidly blessed land this would be."

"It sounds good for everybody but us," she admitted. "What about the slaves in this year of Jubilee?"

"All the slaves go free. They may choose to stay another seven years or go anywhere they wish at the time of Jubilee."

"I don't think you will ever get this idea universally accepted. How do you know it will work?"

"I did the same thing seven years ago when I left Virginia, and look at all the blessings I have received since then. I even see the hand of God in the circumstances I was forced to face this year. You, my dear, are living proof of God's good Providence."

Bonny Kate's heart overflowed with love and admiration for her most exemplary man. His unique and profound private convictions had finally surfaced and found voice, more deeply rooted in Holy Scripture than she could have ever imagined. She marveled at his depth of understanding, and his wisdom, which almost always lay hidden beneath his flamboyance, and what appeared at most times to be a certain vanity in his dress and manners. She knew she had been granted a rare privilege to glimpse the inner man, and her estimation of his worth to the world at that instant soared. Her response was simple and inadequate to encompass all she felt. She embraced him tightly and said, "I have always placed my trust in Providence."

"So are you with me in this decision?"

"We can only go forward in faith," she affirmed.

The quarter moon had returned in its glory, shining as it did the week before their wedding. There had only been a scant three weeks of happiness before the weight of the cares of the world came crashing in on their lives. She pulled away from the embrace an arm's length so she could cock her pretty head and gaze into his eyes with a smile. The moonlight bathed her face and twinkled in her eyes.

"What are you thinking, my love?" he said.

"Let's finish what we need to finish, and go to Mount Pleasant," she whispered.

"I'm with you in that." He slipped his arm around her slender waist.

"Confound it!" she said.

"What's wrong, my dear?"

"I took down the tent this morning and packed it away."

"That's all right. All we need is blankets under the stars and that glorious moon. We'll be back before the dew falls. I have to get an early start."

Chapter 5

Financing the Expedition

After three days of intense discussions and planning, the men were ready for action. In the orange-pink glow of pre-dawn, John Sevier and Isaac Shelby packed their horses for a journey after Bonny Kate had prepared them a full breakfast. John was dressed in his military uniform and pulled on the blue officer's coat Sarah had made for him years before. It was the only coat Bonny Kate had ever seen him wear when he was on active duty. He had worn it at their wedding and looked dashingly handsome.

"You are out of style there, John," Isaac observed. "That's an old Virginia officer's coat."

"Sarah made it for me. I've taken very good care of it."

"General Washington sent down an order that all North Carolina militia officers need to be wearing his new design."

Bonny Kate wrapped her shawl a little tighter against the September morning chill and spoke her mind. "It seems that General Washington ought to fill his time with more important matters than to be designing fashions for his backwater militiamen."

John laughed. "What could be more important than out-dressing the enemy?"

"Hold on, you two," Isaac replied. "Before you go off on another silly escapade, let me show you the order." Isaac went through his portmanteau and quickly found the document. "Read this, so you will know I'm telling the truth."

John received the order and read aloud. "By order of General Washington, October 2, 1779, the dress uniform of the North Carolina Regiments should be blue, faced with blue, and the buttonholes bound with white tape or lace." John folded the paper and passed it to Bonny Kate. "This order is nearly a year old."

"It went out to all the county colonels in the state, John. Why didn't you receive it?"

"Because I'm not the colonel," John answered. "Judge Carter is still the official colonel of Washington County, and he doesn't pass along important communications."

"It's going to get pretty messy when you are only a lieutenant colonel and have to start taking orders from me."

"That will be the day," John grinned. "You and I have too much history to let a little thing like rank spoil a friendship."

"The fact remains, John, old man Carter has rendered you powerless in the rough and tumble politics of the North Carolina military establishment."

"Isaac, never mind about that. We can discuss that on the ride to Watauga. Well my Bonny Kate, summon my dear little minions. I wish to give the children my charge and my benediction."

"John, if you need a new uniform coat I can make it for you this week. Just leave me your old coat to use as a pattern."

"No, my dear, don't trouble your pretty little head about that. My uniform will be fine just as it is."

"Come now, sir, we must not suffer those eastern county colonels to poke fun at our backwater officers over a simple matter of dress. I can cut and sew and embroider as well as any woman on the continent. No one shall find any fault in the way my husband turns out for assembly."

John looked at her sternly. "The matter is closed to further discussion. Now, madam, fetch me my children."

"Yes, sir," Bonny Kate obeyed. She entered the house to gather the children for the customary tearful good-byes. But she grinned as she took General Washington's order concerning uniform design and slipped it into her pocket. She was resolved from that moment forward to make her husband a new uniform.

The officers rapidly rode the twenty-five miles to the valley of the Watauga where they had several stops to make. First they visited Matthew Talbot, the gristmill owner and operator on Gap Creek. He was one of the earliest settlers who came out in 1772 with James Robertson. They found the miller hard at work in the mill and greeted him.

"Ah, Colonel Sevier," Mr. Talbot said. "Take a look around at all this work. Your little mill at Little Limestone Creek hasn't hurt my business at all!"

"I told you it wouldn't, Matthew," John replied. "The way this county is growing, there should be enough business for a dozen gristmills."

"What can I do for you gentlemen today?"

"We want to place an order with you," John said.

"That's a strange request from a man who has his own gristmill."

John grinned. "I know, but I'm going to be a might too busy to attend to my milling business for quite awhile."

"Busy with that new little wife, are you?" The men laughed.

"I can only wish my life was as simple as that, Mr. Talbot," John said. "No sir, we need to provision a thousand men for a thirty-day enlistment."

"Militia business then," Talbot guessed.

"Yes, sir, but we are forced to keep the details of this a closely guarded secret."

"I understand. When and where do you want the delivery of the parched corn?"

"On the morning of September twenty-sixth we are marching right past your door. We will have our men draw their rations as they pass."

"You sure know how to make it easy for me," Mr. Talbot laughed. "Where are you are going to get a thousand men for this little adventure?"

Isaac laughed. "We have been trying to figure that out for two or three days."

"We Talbots are up for just about anything that Colonel Sevier wants to do, whether it be hunting, fighting, bear wrestling, or moccasin dancing. What do you say, Colonel?"

"I appreciate your kind offer, Mr. Talbot, but you are too valuable to the local economy to spare for such a long, hard campaign as this. You see, I am not going to be in command this time. We might even be forced to take orders from fellows like him." John grinned as he nodded in Isaac's direction.

"Hey, I'm not the one you have to watch out for," Isaac protested. "McDowell and Hampton are already fighting over who is going to command."

"Colonel Sevier, what about Matthew Jr.? He's always asking me when he can join up, and it sounds like you could use him on this trip. If you won't take me, at least take my son. He's a good lad, strong and obedient. I know he'll serve you well, and come home a better man for riding with you."

"Can he handle a horse?"

"With ease, and it's a good horse too, raised and trained by the Sherrills."

"There is no better recommendation for a horse," John declared.

"I knew you would approve." Mr. Talbot was sure he had made the sale, so he silently waited for the colonel's decision.

"Have him report to Captain Valentine Sevier at Watauga Fort on the morning of the twenty-fifth. I'll tell Val to be expecting him."

"Thank you, Colonel Sevier, you won't be sorry," the proud father said.

"Don't forget that everything has to be kept a secret," John warned. "Please bill me personally for the provisions so this doesn't come before the county commission before we are ready to present our plans."

"Yes sir, Colonel," Mr. Talbot nodded. John and Isaac left Talbot's Mill and headed for Mary Patton's Powder Mill, the next stop on their morning tour.

"Jackie, Jackie, Jackie! You are a great disappointment to me!" The widow Mary Patton shook her head and clicked her tongue. She was an active outspoken woman who had learned to mill powder from her father and continued to make a good living at it after she married. An unfortunate accident took her husband a few years back.

but her prosperity and her valuable service to her country had only expanded as the war dragged on. Grinding charcoal and mixing in sulfur with saltpeter for her special gunpowder recipe always gave her a somewhat grimy appearance, but underneath was a firm, fit, formidable female who passed for pretty when properly cleaned up.

"How have I disappointed you, Mary?" John replied.

"You went off and married an old maid when an experienced widow woman would have served you better. You never even called on me to let me know you were shopping."

John grinned. "It all happened kind of fast, Mary. I didn't even realize I was shopping until I'd already agreed to buy."

"That Bonny Kate Sherrill is a shrewd horse trader. I've seen her in action a time or two. What makes you think you got a fair deal?"

"I've always heard it said that there is no one better at spinning, weaving, sewing, cooking, cleaning, child caring, foot racing, hunting, riding, dog washing, and horse breeding."

"Is that all you wanted in a marriage?"

"I was looking for love, and I found it in far greater measure than I ever dared to hope for!"

"Then I suppose you two will be happy, but that's little comfort to me," the widow sighed.

"Colonel Shelby is still available," John said with a grin.

Isaac reacted with surprised awkwardness. "What?"

"Yes. He's younger, has more land, no mob of noisy children, and he carries a higher rank in the state militia."

"I'm sorry, Mrs. Patton, but all my interests lie in Kentucky just now. Colonel Sevier has misrepresented my availability, and I am much annoyed with him."

"No," Mary said. "Colonel Shelby would not be a good match for me. Our tempers are too much alike; hot enough to set off the powder that surrounds me here."

"Well, if we can't accomplish any matchmaking, we ought to at least purchase some of your best black powder," John said.

"How much do you need?"

"Five hundred pounds for Washington County and another hundred for me personally," John answered.

"That's a mighty big order, Colonel. You can make a lot of trouble with that much powder."

"We intend to, but please keep secret the details of this transaction," John requested. "We risk great peril if we allow such information to go abroad."

"You can trust Mary Patton," the lady replied. "I won't say a word about it. Shall I pack it in hundred-pound barrels?"

"No, we need it in twenty-five pound kegs," Isaac said. "We will be traveling great distances on horseback where no wagons can go."

"When do you need this order?"

"September twenty-fifth, at Sycamore Shoals for the first five hundred pounds," John answered. "Then, send the last hundred pounds to my wife at Plum Grove."

"Are you giving her this as a wedding gift, Colonel?" Widow Patton grinned.

"Not exactly, but it will be a surprise for Bonny Kate just the same."

"Shall I also surprise her with the bill for it?"

"No ma'am, I'm paying for everything in advance," John promised. "Can you deliver?"

"I can deliver," Mary replied sweetly. She winked at Isaac and he blushed.

"Good day to you, Mrs. Patton." John tipped his hat and Isaac followed his example.

When the men had regained the trail to Sycamore Shoals, Isaac questioned his confident companion. "John, you're flat broke. How are you going to pay for all that powder and corn?"

"I'm working on it, Isaac. We have one more stop to make before we call on our friends McDowell and Hampton at Watauga Fort."

The land office was a small cabin beside the home of John Adair, the entry taker for state land grants. John and Isaac tied their horses to the hitching post and entered the building. John Adair, a recent settler from Ireland who spoke with the accent of his ancestors, looked up from his correspondence.

"Well, what a surprise," exclaimed Mr. Adair. "Always look for something big to happen when John Sevier and Isaac Shelby travel about together!"

"You guessed correctly, Mr. Adair," John greeted him. "A big deal is cooking."

"Come on in and take a seat," Adair welcomed. "Jack, may I offer my congratulations on your marriage. It was some shindig. Most folks here have never seen the likes of that! And to think you married Bonny Kate Sherrill. What's it like being married to the *sweetheart of the mountains* who can outrun, outride, and outshoot anyone in the country?"

"She is the love of my life, and everything I could have hoped for."

At that moment the door to the office opened and Mrs. Adair walked in. The three men rose politely as Mrs. Adair pretended to be surprised at their presence.

"Oh my, it's Colonel Shelby and Colonel Sevier! I didn't know we had such distinguished visitors. I have Mr. Adair's dinner ready. Shall I set two more places at the table?"

"No, ma'am," Isaac declined. "We plan to dine with Colonel McDowell at Watauga Fort, but we appreciate your kind offer just the same."

"My dear, I have some business with these gentlemen but I'll be up to the house shortly."

"The dinner will keep," she said. "Colonel Sevier, you must bring Mrs. Sevier down here for a visit. We enjoyed the wedding celebration so much, and many of us want to know her better."

"Thank you, Mrs. Adair. We are planning a visit here sometime this month; I'll convey your regards to Mrs. Sevier." The colonel smiled and bowed politely.

Mrs. Adair curtsied, "Well, good day, gentlemen."

"Good day, ma'am," John and Isaac spoke almost in unison. She left as quickly as she had appeared.

"Forgive the interruption," Mr. Adair continued. "What can I do for you, gentlemen?"

"Isaac has just returned from the war, and the fair state of North Carolina is being invaded and overrun," John informed him.

Isaac supplied the details. "The disastrous defeat at Camden last month reduced the American army, under General Gates, to a tattered remnant nursing their wounds at Hillsborough. North Carolina is open to invasion by Cornwallis, and then even Virginia will fall. The British Major Ferguson has swept over western North Carolina and pushed McDowell's forces with their poor families over here to Watauga."

"As the ultimate insult, Ferguson claims he will cross the mountains, hang our leaders, and lay waste our lands with fire and sword," John reported. "I ask you, Mr. Adair, by what right and authority does this cocky little dog, owned by a foreign king, make such threats to free self-governed men?"

"I'd say no right at all," Adair proclaimed.

"I'll tell you," Sevier continued boldly. "A threat like that, made in these mountains, does not go unanswered!"

"You're right, Colonel," Mr. Adair agreed. "You ought to go over and answer that blustering, bragging bastard in person!"

"That's exactly what we had in mind," Isaac said. "A large army of mountain men, well equipped and moving swiftly, could take Ferguson by surprise and lay the whipping on him!"

"Good plan!" Adair encouraged.

"There's just one problem," Sevier cautioned. "I know the men will all serve out of duty and love of country, without any pay. But we still need money for food and equipment, and that requires cash, perhaps public cash—State of North Carolina cash."

"I see what you are getting at. You suppose that the public funds in my possession raised from state land sales ought to be channeled into your military adventure."

John and Isaac looked at each other a moment; then John turned to Mr. Adair and said, "Yes!"

Public servant, state appointee, John Adair walked to the door of the land office and gazed at his beautiful view of the Watauga Valley. John and Isaac stood up to await his response. Adair produced a key from his pocket and walked to a trunk behind the desk. He slowly opened the trunk and turned to speak.

"Colonel Sevier, I have no authority by law to make that disposition of this money; it belongs to the impoverished treasury of North Carolina, and I dare not appropriate a cent of it to any other purpose; but if the state is overrun by the British our liberty is gone. Let the money go too! Take it. If the enemy, by its use, is driven from the country, I can trust that country to justify and vindicate my conduct. So take it!" Mr. Adair lifted several sacks of silver coins onto his desk.

"Well said, Mr. Adair! You are a true patriot," John exclaimed.

"Yes, thank you, Mr. Adair," Isaac agreed. "We will personally pledge our own property to repay the money if the State demands it."

"Then may the saints preserve us, until all accounts are settled," Adair said most seriously. "I do have just one small request, Colonel Sevier."

"What is that, Mr. Adair?"

"That you allow my son and I to enlist and serve with you on the expedition."

"You would be most welcome," John shook his hand warmly. "But I beg you to keep the details of the expedition secret so we won't be ambushed on the way over the mountains. We will muster here at Sycamore Shoals on the twenty-fifth of September."

"Splendid! Your secret is safe with me," promised the Irishman. "Good day, Colonel Sevier. Good day, Colonel Shelby."

John and Isaac carried the bags of money to their horses and secured them to their saddles for the short trip over to Watauga Fort.

John Sevier had many fond memories of Watauga Fort, from the days he supervised its construction to the many nights he spent guarding its walls during the three-week siege of 1776. He met Bonny Kate Sherrill there the first morning of the Indian attacks and pulled her up over the high wall to save her life. He held her safely in his arms for only a short time as she clung ferociously to his coat. He never realized the deep impression he had made on her young untried heart as they innocently flirted during the siege. Flirting had been merely a pastime for the handsomest man in the West, because at that time his heart belonged completely and securely to his lovely wife, Sarah. Those were simpler days, when youthful idealism promised all the best things in life, until he suffered the crushing blow of losing his beloved wife. Months of grieving and brooding followed the heartbreaking loss. Fortunately Divine Providence intervened, and there came again Miss Bonny Kate as volunteer caregiver to his children, and new love blossomed in the summer.

John and Isaac rode into Watauga Fort, saluting as they passed the sentries. They dismounted and tied their horses. Colonel Charles McDowell came out to greet them.

"Colonel Shelby, welcome! And you must be Colonel John Sevier?"

John nodded respectfully. "Your servant, sir. And you are Colonel McDowell?"

"Yes, and already deeply indebted to you, sir," McDowell replied.

"I hope all your needs have been supplied here at Watauga Fort," John said.

"Your men have provided for us most generously, sir. Thank you for your hospitality."

"It's my pleasure," John said sincerely.

Isaac spoke. "Colonel McDowell, we bring good news. We raised the funds to finance the expedition to drive the British from the state of North Carolina!"

"Good news indeed! How did you manage that?"

"We applied for state funding and received a grant," John replied.

John and Isaac unloaded the sacks of money and carried them into one of the cabins. McDowell watched as John and Isaac placed the money sacks in some empty gunpowder kegs and nailed on the lids.

"Well, I'll be!" marveled Colonel McDowell. "This seems to be a land of plenty!"

"Nothing will be lacking in our support for the cause of liberty!" John declared.

"Thank you, Colonel Sevier. Your support is most encouraging."

"Colonel McDowell, we place these State provisions in your care," John proclaimed as though he were conducting a ceremony. "Guard them well, sir."

"I certainly will," he promised.

"I wish we had twice the number of men," John continued less formally. "Isaac, we really need the Virginians in this enterprise. When will we hear from Colonel Campbell?"

"I sent my brother Moses, and I told him not to return without an answer," Isaac replied.

"Listen, if Campbell refuses to join the campaign, you write him again," John instructed. "Remind him of his last visit to Plum Grove when he enjoyed Bonny Kate's cooking so much. Tell him I insist that he join us, and I'll even have Bonny Kate cook for him again. Don't take *no* for an answer."

"I won't, John."

The three officers strolled across the commons of the fort, and John noticed an energetic young woman who reminded him a bit of Bonny Kate working at an outdoor cook fire. Charles McDowell guided them over to the woman for introductions.

Grace Bowman, a spirited, patriotic widow looked up and smiled, wiping her hands on her cooking apron. "Colonel McDowell, can I interest your guests in a bit of dinner? Roasted chickens make a fine meal, gentlemen!"

"We would be delighted, ma'am," John answered politely.

"Grace, my dear, allow me to introduce Colonel John Sevier. And of course, you remember Colonel Shelby from our summer camp?"

"Yes indeed, Colonel Shelby. It's good to see you again," she smiled. "And Colonel Sevier, I've already heard so much about you and your lovely new wife from the people in the community. It will be a pleasure getting to know you."

"Likewise," John bowed. "But I did not catch the lady's name."

"I'm Grace Bowman. My husband was Captain John Bowman, late of McDowell's militia. He fell valiantly at Ramseur's Mill."

John removed his hat and respectfully placed it over his heart to honor the fallen officer. "I offer you my deepest condolences, ma'am."

Grace was moved by his manner of address and recognized his qualities as a gentleman. "Thank you, sir," she replied softly.

The McDowell party had erected a shade tent on the commons and that was where they served the midday dinner. McDowell's soldiers arrived to serve the meal, allowing Mrs. Bowman to sit at table and charm the officers with her conversation. Charles McDowell led them in prayer. "Gracious heavenly father, we thank you for this safe haven where we have found refuge. We thank you for these new friends, who from their own means have shared in abundance the things we need to support us. Bless this food to our use and us to thy service. Amen."

Grace looked up. "Now, Colonel Sevier, tell us about your recent marriage."

"Well, I married the daughter of a good friend and neighbor, and her name is Bonny Kate."

"I love that name!" Grace approved.

"I do too, because in a moment of lighthearted humor I named her that."

"Ah, we must hear more of this."

"Yes ma'am," John continued. "The wedding was the fourteenth of August; not even a month has passed."

"Oh, that's sweet," Grace said. "How did you attract her attention, and what did you do to win her?"

"Well actually, it happened right here at Watauga Fort about four years ago. I saved her life from about three hundred howling savages. I think that got her attention. I don't remember doing anything to win her. I guess you could say she won me, when she saved me from a whole flock of widow women who were chasing after me."

"I marvel at your modesty in telling me this, Colonel Sevier," Grace remarked, not sure exactly how to understand such a story.

"You should ask Bonny Kate her version of the story," John said. "She tends to take longer with the details and would tell it more completely and clearly than I can."

"So if we are to believe you, Colonel Sevier, we might conclude that you are some sort of a great hero," she scoffed.

"Believe it, Mrs. Bowman," Isaac advised. "John Sevier is the most honest and modest man on the continent. Everything he just said is true, even if he did not say it as well as he should have."

"So Mrs. Sevier won you in some kind of a chase by a flock of widows?"

"You could say that," John replied with a smile. "But I've been a very poor prize for my dear Bonny Kate, now that the war has come to the western waters."

"Oh, how cruel a war this is, to take you away campaigning and leave the poor young bride alone!" Grace lamented.

"She won't be alone," John corrected her. "She'll have nine of my children to keep her company."

"What?" Grace was shocked at the revelation.

"This is his second marriage," Isaac explained. "His first wife died last winter."

"You're such a young man, to have so many children! Oh my, the new Mrs. Sevier has so many responsibilities. How does she manage?"

"Very well, thank you," John replied. "Mrs. Sevier possesses many unique talents with a gift for organization. In fact, I consulted with her frequently when planning the details of this campaign."

"Amazing," Grace said.

Charles McDowell was ready for a change of subject. "Colonel Sevier, I am delighted with how quickly everything has come together, but I still have one concern. Mrs. Bowman and her little girl will be without safe haven when we leave on the campaign."

"I'm going with you," Grace declared.

"Absolutely not, my dear, I forbid it. Great danger looms before us."

"I will not be left behind. I know what needs to be done on the battlefield. You might need me!"

"No," Charles said flatly.

Grace broke into tears and rose from the table. "Excuse me, gentlemen..." She rushed to the cabin and closed the door. "You must forgive Mrs. Bowman," Charles explained. "She is a spirited and courageous woman, but the loss of her husband on the field of honor was only in June. Captain Bowman was one of my most able officers and a cousin of mine. She rode forty miles that day to be with him at the last. He died in her arms. Her grief overcomes her at times."

"Not a day goes by that I do not grieve for my Sarah," John empathized. "But Bonny Kate knows and accommodates my moods, and I love her for that."

John and Charles fell silent with their thoughts and concerns over women's business.

"Enough melancholy," Isaac renewed the conversation. "Let's get on with the war. The support of Virginia is crucial to the success of our project..."

John held up his hand and silenced the red-haired, impetuous Shelby. "Just a moment, Isaac. Colonel McDowell, I want Mrs. Bowman to be our guest at Plum Grove. My Bonny Kate brings great comfort to anyone who is grieving."

"I hate to further burden your wife, who seems to have more than her share of responsibilities," Charles expressed his concern. "Don't you think you should talk it over with her before you extend such an invitation?"

"I know my wife, Colonel McDowell. She would never turn away the refugee. It is best for Mrs. Bowman and her daughter to stay at Plum Grove."

Charles thought for a moment and lacking any better offer decided to accept. "Thank you, Colonel Sevier. You and I are going to get along famously. I see great things in your future. I do have some influence with Governor Nash."

Isaac laughed looking at John. "He may need the governor's influence after that deal he pulled at the land office today!"

.

Chapter 6

The Rescue of Colonel Sevier

Bonny Kate worked at the loom while Betsy worked at the spinning wheel. At nearly thirteen, Betsy Sevier was cute as a button, lively and quick to perceive the dynamics of human relations. Betsy was very much her mother Sarah made over in personality, and loveliness. She had always been Bonny Kate's closest ally in the struggle to keep the family together in the hard times that followed Sarah's death, and supported Bonny Kate's candidacy as John's second wife. She even cooperated with the matchmakers to bring about the happy conclusion of that business. Bonny Kate sang a love song as she worked.

"I haven't heard you sing that song before," Betsy noted when Bonny Kate had completed the last refrain. "You must be thinking about Father."

"Yes! I can hardly wait to see him tonight."

"Will Father be home to stay?"

"A few days maybe, but then he'll be gone again."

"Then why are you singing so happily?"

"Because every moment we have together is a gift to be cherished!"

The sound of a horse out in the lane broke the peacefulness of the morning. "I hear a horse coming," Betsy announced. "Do you think he could be home this early?"

"See who it is!"

Betsy rushed to the window to look. "It's a lady, but I don't know her." There were footsteps on the porch, and a young woman of twenty-five entered the open door of the cabin. She was dirty, bruised, and battered. Bonny Kate rose from the bench of the loom.

"Why, Mary Dyckes," Bonny Kate greeted. "Hello, dear girl! I haven't seen you in months. I missed you at my wedding."

"I know. I so wanted to see it, but...well, my own marriage has taken its toll."

"To what do we owe this unexpected pleasure?" Bonny Kate asked politely as she assessed the deplorable condition of a formerly close friend.

"I wanted to see how it was with you."

Bonny Kate noted the bruises were defensive, and not typical of those caused by the hazards of farm work and homemaking. She pulled out a chair at the table for her guest. "Please, sit down. Mary, this is my stepdaughter, Betsy Sevier."

Betsy curtsied, "Pleased to meet you, ma'am."

Mary looked at her coldly, "Hello."

"Betsy, this is my friend, Mary Smith," Bonny Kate explained. "But two years ago she became Mrs. Jacob Dyckes. That was a fine wedding!"

"I reckon it was, but I've had trouble. I just need someone to talk to." Mary glanced up at Betsy and then looked at Bonny Kate.

"Betsy dear, would you get Mrs. Dyckes some cool cider?" Bonny Kate requested. "I think she needs some refreshment."

"Yes, ma'am." Betsy complied and left the room.

"I heard you married into a big family," Mary observed.

"Yes, Colonel Sevier had ten children when his sweet wife Sarah died last winter. She was such a dear friend of mine, the shock was terrible."

"It must have been a shock to be suddenly taking care of ten children."

"It's not so different than what I've always known. I was raised in a family of ten children. I helped Mama raise my younger brothers and my sister."

"What about your husband?" Mary asked. "Does he give you much trouble?"

"Well, we have only been married for a little over a month, but he's no trouble. John is the love of my dreams!"

"But when he beats you, is he excessive?"

Bonny Kate became indignant. "John Sevier has never beaten me! I don't think he has ever raised a violent hand against any woman!"

"What about when he's drunk?"

"I've never seen him drunk. He's a man of balance and moderation."

Mary began to sob quietly. Betsy entered with the cider and put the cup on the table in front of their guest. Betsy looked at Mary curiously and then at Bonny Kate.

"Thank you, Betsy, honey. I think it's time to start the lunch we planned. Would you go out to the cookhouse and see to that?"

"Yes, ma'am." Betsy obeyed, but she really wanted to stay and learn why their guest was so distraught.

Bonny Kate walked over to the washstand and poured a basin of water and took a clean washcloth and towel down from a shelf on the wall. She returned to the table and began washing Mary's hands, arms, neck and face, taking great care where she encountered cuts and bruises. "You'll feel better when we get the road dust off you."

"Oh Bonny Kate, I'm so confused. Forgive me for coming here like this."

"There's nothing to forgive," she comforted her friend. With the dirt cleaned away she could see the effects of abuse, and it angered her.

"We haven't any food at the house, and Jacob finally comes home with his friends, expecting me to cook something for the lot of them. When I don't have what he wants he gets so angry."

"Well, why didn't you say so earlier? Come on out to the smokehouse. I'll give you the fixings for a dinner that will make your man prefer to stay home!"

Bonny Kate helped her up out of the chair and led her by the hand out into the yard. They stopped in at the cookhouse where Betsy worked, and Bonny Kate produced a sack of corn meal and gave it to Mary Dyckes. Then she led the way to the smokehouse.

"Bonny Kate, what about your husband; what will he do to you when he learns you gave me food?"

Bonny Kate stopped and turned to her friend. "He will take me in his arms and lovingly praise me!"

"He will?"

"John Sevier is the very soul of generosity!"

"What if he knew my husband's friends were...were Tories?"

"John always says that Tories may make worthy people and good citizens, if they are not kept continually ashamed and mortified by being reminded of their bad conduct." Bonny Kate opened the door of the smokehouse and lifted down a ham. She brought it out and offered it to her friend.

In the next instant, Mrs. Dyckes fell to her knees weeping loudly and clutching Bonny Kate's skirt. Bonny Kate was surprised and confused by so sudden an outburst. "Madam, get hold of yourself! What is wrong with you?"

"Oh, Bonny Kate," she wailed. "I know your John is a good man, and I see how you love him. You don't deserve to die!"

"Mary Dyckes, get up and stop this foolishness! What are you saying?"

The hysterical woman turned her tear-streamed face upward, and Bonny Kate saw the terror that tormented the wretched woman. "They are going to murder you all in your beds tonight and cut you up to make it look like Indians did it!"

"Who?" Bonny Kate demanded.

"The Tories from the east; they planned the whole thing last night at my house. And I'm ashamed to say Jacob is in on it."

"This cannot be!" Bonny Kate felt sickened by such inhumanity intended for her dear family. "They wouldn't murder me and the children."

"They will, and do horrible things to you to make it look like Indians!"

Bonny Kate dropped the ham in front of the kneeling Mrs. Dyckes and started back toward the house. She was dazed by the news of this threat, and her mind raced as she made it as far as the cookhouse. She leaned against the door frame and looked in on sweet Betsy, a fellow intended victim of planned Tory cruelty. "Never," she uttered.

"Ma'am?" Betsy replied sweetly.

"Never!" Bonny Kate repeated with more force. "They'll never do that to us!"

"Bonny Kate, what's wrong?" Betsy cried, feeling the intensity of Bonny Kate's reaction to the impending danger.

"I've got to send word to John!" Bonny Kate decided.

Mary Dyckes caught up with Bonny Kate, bringing with her the gifted ham. "It's too late for him, Bonny Kate! Save yourselves. Take the children and run!"

Bonny Kate whirled to face her with frightening ferocity. "What else do you know?"

"The Tories will kill him from ambush today as he leaves Watauga Fort. Jacob bragged about it as he beat me last night. But you can still save the children."

"Betsy! Johnny! Come quickly!"

Betsy stepped out from the cookhouse, and Johnny came running from the horse barn. They knew Bonny Kate well enough to see she was greatly agitated and would have done anything to provide her relief.

"What is it?" Betsy cried.

"Your father's life is in danger! Get all the children ready to travel. Johnny, go find Joseph and James, saddle all the horses, and bring every rifle!"

Bonny Kate entered the main house, with Mary at her heels. Like a mad woman she flew about the great room, gathering her shot pouch, powder horn, and rifle. Then she packed things the children would need for a journey—food, clothing, water in canteens, and bedding for overnight. She debated in her mind where to leave the children in safety, with Betsy in charge, while she would take the elder Sevier boys up the road to Watauga.

"What are you doing?" Mary asked. Bonny Kate turned and looked at her and an inspiration hit her that brought the whole plan into focus.

"I'm taking you to Pastor Doak's church for safety. Then, the boys and I are riding for Watauga to save John's life!"

"Can you do that?"

"With God's good Providence I can! Mary, I promise you this: If I live through this night, anyone who tries to beat you again, will answer to me!"

"Oh dear!" Mary reacted.

"Come on!" Bonny Kate ordered, and they rushed to move all their baggage out to the porch for Johnny, Joseph, and James to load on the horses.

A peaceful September afternoon prevailed at the New Salem Church. Mrs. Esther Doak rocked her baby on the sunny front porch of Pastor Doak's cabin. Bonny Kate, her family, and Mary Dyckes galloped into the yard and up to the porch. Bonny Kate and the boys remained in their saddles while the rest of them dismounted in the yard. Esther rose and laid her baby in a cradle. She stepped down into the yard to where Bonny Kate's big racer stood.

"Bonny Kate, what's wrong?"

The colonel's lady could not hold back her tears. "The Tories are out to ambush John on the Watauga road. They mean to kill him! Is Pastor Doak here?"

"No, he's up at Jonesborough for the day," Esther answered with deep concern.

"I need a place of safety for the children while I go for help."

"I'll keep them for you."

"Thank you, Esther! I also have a friend here who needs your protection and prayers. This is Mary Dyckes. She told me about the Tory plot. Can she stay here too?"

"Yes, of course! So you are riding to Watauga?"

"That's where John's been working all week."

"Bonny Kate, ride straight to the courthouse in Jonesborough. Court is in session today, and you'll find plenty of good men to help you."

"Great idea, thank you Esther," Bonny Kate and the three eldest Sevier boys urged their horses onto the Jonesborough trace and were gone.

Mary Dyckes and Betsy Sevier shepherded the younger Sevier children from the yard up to the porch. Esther reached out and took Mary by the hand and saw her bruises.

"Poor dear, you've had a hard time."

"I worry about Bonny Kate," Mary said. "I hope she gets there in time."

"I know she'll move heaven and earth to save her man," Esther said softly. "I pray she does."

Jonesborough, at that time, was the only town in the over-mountain settlements. The courthouse was at the center of a scattered collection of new houses arranged on orderly little streets where many lots were still vacant. Bonny Kate and the three Sevier boys arrived at the courthouse yard to find men crowded around the doors and windows of the one-room courthouse listening to the proceedings.

Bonny Kate's voice, desperate and pleading, invaded the courtroom and disturbed the peace of Jonesborough. "Robert Sevier! Val Sevier! Are you in there? Robert, Val, come out! John needs you!"

Robert and Val Sevier appeared at the door, while Judge Carter stuck his head out the window. Bonny Kate was comforted to see her father Sam and brother Adam Sherrill among the spectators.

"What's all the ruckus, Bonny Kate?" Judge Carter demanded. "Don't you know Court's in session?"

"I'm sorry, Judge, but the Tories are out to kill my John, and I'm going to stop them! I need Robert and Val and anyone else who can ride fast and shoot straight!"

Judge Carter recognized the need and decided quickly. "By all means, Court adjourned!" The men ran out to the shade trees, where their horses were tied, and they mounted quickly. Sam Sherrill, Adam, Val, and Robert rode over to surround the colonel's lady, and she immediately felt comforted to be among loving kinsmen.

"Which way?" Captain Robert Sevier called out.

"He's on his way home from Watauga!"

"We're ready; give the order!" Sheriff Val Sevier said to Bonny Kate.

"Let's go, my brave boys!" she shouted, and spurred her horse ahead. The men responded with their familiar war whoop, and she led the forces into the Watauga road.

John was tired from ten days of too much work, communication, and negotiation that accompanies organizing a military campaign. Much of the work that he would ordinarily have delegated to subordinate officers he had to do himself because of the tight secrecy that had to be maintained. A surprise attack on a more powerful enemy was always a risky proposition. He was glad to be heading home for a couple of days rest before the muster planned for the twenty-fifth of September. On the twenty-third he would get to celebrate his thirty-fifth birthday with his family and Bonny Kate. As John rode alone on the familiar route that sunny afternoon, his thoughts turned from military matters and focused on her—the smiling face, the open arms, the ready lips, and the gentle laugh. She waited for him, just hours away, he thought.

John was in a hurry to get home to Plum Grove and left Watauga Fort without an escort and without the companions who often enjoyed his jokes and stories when he traveled on business. Isaac Shelby had gone home to Sapling Grove to organize the affairs of Sullivan County for the campaign. Isaac was anxious to hear the answer they expected from Colonel Campbell about the Virginia participation in the expedition. Fearless John had not expected any trouble, so he had not taken the usual precautions to prevent it.

A covey of quail was startled into flight from their nests beside the road ahead, and that alerted John to the proximity of possible danger. He drew his horse to a stop and listened. Sounds on the road behind him confirmed that mounted men were back there, but when he turned to look he saw nothing. Normally he would have welcomed the company, but these riders acted suspiciously. He drew a pistol from the saddle holster and primed the pan. As he looked up he saw a rider confronting him in the road ahead. The rider held a pistol in one hand and a noose in the other. John did not recognize the man.

"John Sevier?" the stranger addressed him.

"Who wants to know?"

"The king's men have come to hang a traitor!"

Suddenly four men came on the gallop around a bend in the road behind him. A glance over his shoulder confirmed that the company was not friendly to the cause of liberty. John spurred his horse straight ahead at the Tory in front of him and fired his pistol at the same instant, but missed. The Tory fired his pistol as John flashed by, but his horse bucked and the shot missed John. A deadly race developed with five Tories in pursuit. John knew he had one of the fastest horses in Washington County, but the Tories seemed to be gaining. He struggled to reload his pistol as the horse galloped along, but such a trick was never easy. His pursuers fired their pistols, but luckily all shots missed.

A mile away Bonny Kate and her war party charged up the road at a gallop. She could hear distant gunfire.

"Pistol fire," Sam Sherrill called to her as their horses raced at full stride.

"Please Lord, protect him!" Bonny Kate prayed. The men of the rescue party drew their rifles as they turned a curve in the road and entered a clearing where a small creek crossed the road. John's horse trotted riderless in the clearing. She spied him lying in the creek bed, hunkered down by the stream bank, sheltered from Tory pistol fire. The Tories had drawn up some distance away, having heard the approach of the larger party. They turned and raced away as the patriots arrived at the creek.

"Let's get 'em boys!" Robert Sevier shouted. He and his company of militia charged after them. John waved to his brother's men as they passed. Then he got up slowly and brushed off his clothes. Bonny Kate dismounted and rushed into his arms.

"Oh sweetheart, did they hurt you?" she asked breathlessly.

"No, I came through well enough, but another mile and they would have caught me for sure. Those horses were as fast as Sherrill horses!"

Sam Sherrill spoke up. "Those *were* Sherrill horses, stolen from my place a week ago!"

"Well, Robert and the boys will have a hard time running them down," John predicted.

"So, Mr. Sevier, aren't you going to kiss me?" John embraced his lady and complied passionately as the men cheered the good fortune of a timely rescue.

The evening of John's birthday, the colonel and his lady retreated to the parlor at Plum Grove to complete the last minute details of the campaign. Bonny Kate sewed the buttons onto another uniform coat. Her long slender fingers worked rapidly and skillfully with needle and thread even in the dim candlelight.

"Thank you for surprising me with my new uniform," he said. "I could have made do with the old one."

"No, John, this is very important to me to have you properly dressed for the campaign. Your appearance is a reflection on me; and you know enough about the Sherrills to understand we never do anything half way."

"I understand that," he replied tenderly as he watched her work. "I thought you had finished the work on the uniforms for Joseph and me."

"Oh yes, days ago," she replied. "I made uniforms for my brothers too. This coat is an extra in case one of your men has need of it. It will likely snow in North Carolina before you return from the campaign."

"Bonny Kate, I hope you are not conspiring with a certain young James Sevier to defy my wish that he stay home."

"Mr. James Sevier is not on speaking terms with me. He has never forgiven me for marrying the man I love. You said you would speak to James, and arrange our reconciliation but I have seen no change in his attitude."

John sighed, "It is obvious I haven't had the time."

"I know you want him to stay home and protect me, but that would just give him one more reason to resent me."

"Then you want him to go?"

"It's not my decision," she answered. "I'm just suggesting that he would be of greater use to you in the field than he would be to me on the farm."

"Thank you for your opinion," John said, returning to his paperwork.

Bonny Kate doubted her opinion counted for much. The Sevier men were proud and stubborn. They didn't waste a lot of time revisiting their decisions.

Bonny Kate sewed on her last button and held up the coat to admire the look of it. Betsy had cut and sewn the large panels and had done remarkably well. She listened for the children in the loft, and the silence indicated they were sleeping. She looked at John and appreciated that moment as a gift from Providence. She fully realized how close she had come to losing him the other day. She also knew this was their last night together at home, but she couldn't think of a way to propose a trip to Mount Pleasant. Then another campaign detail flashed up from her memory and she addressed the colonel again. "John dear, Moses Embree made the delivery yesterday of all the lead shot you ordered. I stored it in the horse barn until Papa brings the big wagon over tomorrow. He will carry it to Watauga for you."

"There's an important detail! We must have ammunition to fight the war, and for the first time ever, we don't have to order shot from the Virginia mines!"

"I knew you would be pleased to hear about that, my dearest."

He placed his papers in his small travel trunk and closed the lid. Standing and stretching, he looked at his lovely wife. "Do you know what would please me even more, dear wife?"

"Is it the same thing that would please me, dear husband?" She grinned.

"Is it the sort of thing that happens on a hilltop?"

"Can the gentleman saddle a pair of horses, while I collect the blankets?"

"Can somebody stop asking silly questions and just say yes?"

"Yes!" She laughed.

"Then I'll meet you out front with the fastest horses in Washington County!"

Chapter 7

The Gathering at Sycamore Shoals

On the afternoon of September 24, 1780, the families of the western waters began to gather in the meadows beside the Sycamore Shoals of the Watauga River. They set up camps and began the routines of cooking, visiting, playing, and working in preparation for an expedition. Most of the men didn't know where they would be going or how long they would be gone, but of course, the rumors flew. Some guessed an Indian campaign, while others thought there might be trouble in Kentucky again. The most popular idea, however, was another eastern campaign like the one some of the men had endured in the summer. The presence of Colonel Charles McDowell and Colonel Andrew Hampton gave great weight to that theory. These eastern leaders and their men were anxious to get back to the unfinished business they had left behind at home.

For the women, the gathering was another chance to assemble and visit, deepening friendships and exchanging necessary information vital to their survival in the absence of their husbands and sons. Bonny Kate took on her leadership role as the colonel's wife in collecting and dispensing useful information. She was constantly being sought by the women of Washington County for advice and emotional support, and gained great popularity by the quality of her information and the care with which she delivered it. The women of Sullivan County likewise turned to her for the same needs, because their own Colonel Shelby was a bachelor and failed to understand the first thing about women's business.

Bonny Kate's responsibilities also extended to the refugee families of the eastern counties who were living in exile in Watauga Fort. Bonny Kate met Grace Bowman and immediately liked her. She admired Mrs. Bowman's courage and commitment to a cause that had taken the life of her gallant husband. She felt compassion for the little Bowman girl, whose future had been seriously compromised by the loss of her father. The Bowman family tragedy gave Bonny Kate reason to contemplate her own situation if anything were to happen to John. An economic and political empire so beneficial to the prosperity and progress of the people of the West would immediately come crashing down without its unique and chief personality.

Among the men, campaign leadership immediately became a point of contention. The top officers seemed united in purpose, but intense rivalries and resentments festered beneath their friendly relations while their subordinate officers acted out their struggle for control. The most useful and talented Lieutenant Colonel John Sevier was immediately discounted and placed at a disadvantage because of his inferior rank. In Washington County, Judge Carter had never relinquished the official title of colonel of the militia, even though Sevier ran the whole organization. John had allowed this out of respect for his senior mentoring friend, who was then too old and infirm for active duty. This injustice had always enraged Sarah, and now Bonny Kate observed how it threatened John's ability to lead when he shared his concerns with her after a meeting of the officers.

"My fellow officers are a contentious lot, Bonny Kate. All they want to do is argue about strategy."

"Why don't they listen to you, John? You have more good sense, talent for leadership, and concern for the troops than the whole lot of them put together."

"They say I have no experience in regular warfare. I am an Indian fighter. And of course, the fact remains—I'm only a lieutenant colonel."

"Good old Washington County politics has always held you back. Why, even your old sidekick Isaac Shelby outranks you. If they were to put you in charge, I know you would find the enemy, win the battle, and come home quickly without losing a man! That ability makes you popular with the men, but more importantly it makes you very popular with the women!"

John laughed. "There's only one woman I wish to be popular with, my dear."

She hugged him tightly, communicating her regard for him. "It isn't fair!"

He gently lifted her face and her lips found his, ending the conversation.

John finally had to pull back and straighten his uniform. "I must return to my duties. Good day, Madam Sevier." He bowed politely.

"Good day, Mr. Sevier, my handsome prince!" She smiled and curtsied.

In midafternoon great excitement attended the arrival of two hundred Virginia militiamen on the north bank of the Watauga River. About half were horsemen who rode across the river to the old fields where they dismounted. The others were foot soldiers who waded across the wide shoals in water just above the knee. They crossed in companies, and each company paused in midstream to fire a volley to salute their North Carolina comrades. It made an impressive show. They set up camp and prepared their cook fires after their day of marching. John Sevier was the first officer to greet Colonel William Campbell. "Bill, you will never know how relieved I am to see

Virginia committed to our campaign."

"I'm not convinced it is in the best interests of the Commonwealth; but the fact that you are involved in this, Jack, helped make my decision."

"How many men did you bring?"

"Two hundred, but tomorrow morning Cousin Arthur is bringing two hundred more."

"Praise the Lord," John said. "With four hundred Virginians we can whip the whole British Army!"

Campbell grinned. "I appreciate your enthusiasm, Jack. Now, show me where you are camping, so I can collect that dinner you promised me in the last letter. What is Bonny Kate cooking tonight?"

"It's a surprise, even to me, but I promise it will be good!"

On the hill near the walls of the fort, Bonny Kate watched the troops assemble in the fields and practice their drills. Small groups of friends and family members stood about visiting while the men worked together to prepare themselves. Young James Sevier found Bonny Kate and greeted her with surprising warmth. His purposes were soon evident.

"I want to go fight for my country," James declared. "But nothing I can say will persuade Father to change his mind."

"So you have discussed it with him?"

"Yes, many times, but it does no good. Apparently I have no influence with the colonel."

"I'm sorry you are disappointed," she said looking him in the eye.

"And I'm sorry I missed your wedding," James said. "I wasn't feeling well that day."

"I know how badly you miss your mother. I miss her too, as the best friend I ever had."

"I was hoping you might help me the way she would have done."

Bonny Kate knew where James was going with this rare interview and wondered about his sincerity. Despite his obvious attempts to manipulate his father, and now his attempt to manipulate her, she did love Sarah's boy. "What would you have me do?"

"Ask Father if I can go on the campaign."

"It's not my place to question one of the colonel's staffing decisions."

"Please, Bonny Kate, he'll listen to you!"

"James, your father made it abundantly clear that you are to stay at home with me. We may have our own war to fight before he gets back."

"The home guard can take care of the Cherokees just fine without me. Bonny Kate, I'm sixteen; I can ride and shoot as well as any man here! Why should I miss the most important campaign of the war? Even your brother George gets to go, and he is only a few months older than me."

She understood his desire and his great need to prove his budding manhood to his father. James Sevier's problem was not only the loss of his mother at a critical time in his social development, but his changing relationship to his famous father. James was trying to relate to John as one of the fiercely loyal men under his command, and to Bonny Kate that seemed an honorable aspiration.

"James, if this means so much to you, I'll ask your father about it when I have the opportunity. All I can do is tender the request. I'm not going to argue the case for you and anger him."

"Oh, thank you, Bonny Kate!" James seized her and hugged her awkwardly, a first time for the surprised stepmother.

"I made an extra outfit just like Joseph's. Be ready to go in the morning in case your father says yes."

"I'll be ready!" He ran away toward the family camp, rejoicing as he went.

"I wonder what Sarah would have done," Bonny Kate said to herself as she turned and walked through a flood of memories within the walls of Watauga Fort. It was there where she first met John four years ago. The siege lasted three weeks for the starving, under-supplied garrison while death stalked them at every moment day and night. Forty men protecting two hundred hysterical women and helpless children was not a formula for survival, but somehow they lived to tell about it. And many of the funniest stories became legends, the retelling of which always delighted her.

Bonny Kate encountered a group of children playing in the bed of a wagon, pretending it was a stoutly defended fort. She watched as some girls lined up beside the wagon while an older boy in the wagon leaned over the edge and shouted, "Jump for me, Kate!" The first girl ran and leaped for the boy's outstretched hands. He caught her and pulled her up into the wagon. "A bonny lass for a footrace you are, my Bonny Kate!" the boy pronounced. The children laughed with delight each time the act was repeated for each girl in line.

"Look, there's the real Bonny Kate!" shouted nine-year-old Mary Ann Sevier, the next girl in line.

"Nuh-uh," answered the nay-sayers. "That's a grown-up lady. Bonny Kate was just a girl!"

"It is too Bonny Kate! She's my new mother!" Mary Ann insisted.

Bonny Kate grinned. "She's right, boys and girls. I am the Bonny Kate of Watauga Fort." The little audience was surprised and delighted.

The boy in the wagon looked at her with admiration. "Who was the man that pulled you over the wall?"

"Why, it was Lieutenant John Sevier."

"Chucky Jack?"

"Yes, the now-famous Colonel John Sevier," she confirmed.

"I'm Chucky Jack," the boy said, completely satisfied with his pretend role as the hero of Watauga Fort.

Bonny Kate retold the story of her rescue and many other stories of those days of desperation for the benefit of the children. She was amazed at how incomplete their understanding was of the game they played. She remembered something she heard Pastor Doak say with much sadness about proclaiming the Gospel. The truth of his observation was impressed upon her by this chance encounter with children at play. He said, "All the truth that's ever been revealed to the world can be lost in one generation if we don't keep telling the stories to our children!" Yes, she decided, there is much value in a thorough education for the young!

Late in the afternoon Bonny Kate witnessed the outbreak of a fight in camp. She ran to the crowd of men who are betting and cheering the contestants, a mountain man and an eastern man. John arrived at the scene quickly, and she followed him as he charged through the crowd to restore order.

"Stop this! Stop it now!"

Several of the men took up his call. "It's the colonel! Hold up! Stop the fight!" Some of the men stepped up to restrain the combatants, and the crowd quieted down.

"I'm going to have to break this up," John said. "There is a lady present." The men noticed Bonny Kate and immediately straightened up out of respect for her gender. "Now, what's this all about?"

"This here Catawba man claims that his Colonel McDowell will command the army. I said the commander should be you, Colonel Sevier," the mountain man stated his case. The crowd rumbled with men expressing their own opinions. John held up his hands for silence and the noise died down again.

"Men, please, Colonel McDowell and I, in council with the other officers, will decide these details. It does no good for you to fight about it!"

"But he started it," the mountaineer grumbled.

"A British major named Ferguson started it!" John shouted angrily. "Remember that, and save your fighting for the right time and the right place! Now, you men know the penalty for fighting in camp..."

"Please, Colonel Sevier," a feminine voice spoke soothingly behind him, and he recognized it as a voice that he adored. "I appeal for mercy on behalf of these men. I understand well the differences of opinion that often occur between men of the East and men of the West. I was born and raised on the Catawba, but I have embraced the West as my own. I can assure you, we are all the same people, like a blue hen's chickens!"

John turned to face her, and thought he might express his displeasure at her interference, but her words struck him as quaint and delightful. "A blue hen's chickens, Madam?"

"Yes sir, Granny Sherrill used to say we are all going to be who we were born to be, like a blue hen's chickens," she explained. "There's not very much we can do about it without the intervention of Divine Providence."

"That sounds reasonable," the mountain man said thoughtfully. "We are who we were born to be, like a blue hen's chickens."

"There's no sense fighting about that," the Catawba man said. "We should save the fighting for Ferguson. We are all, every one of us, a blue hen's chicken." He offered his hand to his recent opponent, and the two men shook hands.

Broad smiles appeared all around as John shrugged his shoulders and said, "Well, I guess there's no sense arguing with that. The case is dismissed!" The men returned peacefully to their camp activities.

Colonel Sevier escorted his lady back toward their campsite. "Shouldn't I come with you to help keep order in camp?"

"I desire nothing more than your sweet company, my dear, but who would keep order at Plum Grove?"

"I know my place," she assured him. "Our welfare lies in your hands, and you, sir, are an instrument in the hand of Providence. I have faith in that, and faith that the Lord will lead you through safely."

John stopped and responded with precious words from his own brave and pure heart, "Bless you, my love."

Her only answer to that was another loving embrace, so sincere, so lingering, so demonstrative of feeling, and so public, that many men would later ask John about the occasion. "How do you get a woman to love you like that, especially one so ornery and mean as Bonny Kate used to be?"

John laughed as he explained, "On my father's side, I'm French!"

The next morning the Sevier family walked down to the assembly together with all their children, from Joseph and James down to the smallest, Nancy, cradled in the arms of the once ornery and mean Bonny Kate, the only mother the baby had ever known. John and Joseph led their horses and wore all their traveling gear. They stopped on a small rise overlooking the gathering grounds where the 1,040 volunteers had assembled intermingled with a myriad of family members.

"Mr. Sevier, I have a gift for you," Bonny Kate said. "Betsy, make the presentation." Betsy stepped forward smiling and from a rolled-up piece of parchment she drew forth a magnificent white ostrich plume for his hat.

John was surprised. "Where did you get that?"

"I have a cousin in the millinery trade back at Lincolnton," Bonny Kate replied.

"I remembered hearing you tell the story of Jean Xavier, your illustrious ancestor, who always wore one of these on his hat when he went into battle. I had my brother Uriah purchase it and send it out."

John attached the plume to his hat and placed the hat on his head. "Yes, Jean Xavier was a knight of King Henry of Navarre. His battle cry was 'Follow the White Plume!' That is where the fighting was always the thickest!"

The children seemed most impressed. "Papa looks like a pirate!" Dolly Sevier exclaimed.

"No chief of the Cherokee has a bigger feather than that," Little Val declared.

Bonny Kate grinned, "The other colonels may outrank you, sir, but none can out-dress you! Do you like it, my dear?"

"I love it," he answered. "Thank you, my sweet Bonny Kate. No gift could be more appropriate!" Nobody present could have understood the full impact on subsequent events of that simple gift of a feather.

"I found a Bible verse that's perfect for this occasion," Bonny Kate announced. "Deuteronomy 24, verse five says: *When a man hath taken a new wife, he shall not go out to war, neither shall he be charged with any business: but he shall be free at home one year, and shall cheer up his wife which he hath taken.*"

John nodded his approval. "That would suit me just fine. I'd love to stay with you for a year to cheer you up. But I'm sure this war won't wait, and many a wife suffers the absence of her husband every day, until this business is decided."

"I know, but I can't help dreading the separation from you."

"I'm sorry, my love. I wish it were not so," John comforted her. Bonny Kate stretched out her free hand to James and pulled him gently forward, presenting him before his father.

"Here, Mr. Sevier is another of your boys who wants to go with his father and brother to the war–but we have no horse for him, and poor fellow, it is a great distance to walk!" She pouted and turned her sad eyes appealingly to the natural parent.

"Bonny Kate, you know how reluctant I am to leave you unprotected."

"James, get your things," she ordered confidently with her eyes locked on John's.

"Father?" James respectfully awaited his father's approval.

"Do as the lady says," the colonel directed.

"Thank you, Father! Thank you, Bonny Kate! I'll make you proud!" He hugged her and kissed her on the cheek.

"We know you will," she replied.

"Go find Uncle Val and tell him we need another horse for a new private in the Washington County militia."

"Yes, sir! Thank you, sir!" James saluted and ran off to carry out his first order.

"So many good men volunteered, we had to draft men for the home guard," John said.

"Yes, Colonel, but did you see the look on his face? You won't find a more willing soldier on either side of the mountains!"

"You already had him outfitted, knowing he wanted to go."

She nodded. "Had all your ten children been sons, and large enough to serve on the expedition, I could have fitted them out!"

"You did what his mother would have done."

She looked into her husband's eyes. "Did I?"

"Yes, I have always felt that Sarah would have chosen you as the stepmother to her orphans," John said seriously.

"I'm feeling more like a mother to them every day." Bonny Kate looked down into baby Nancy's smiling blue eyes.

John was ready to move on and started forward, but Bonny Kate handed Nancy off to Betsy and walked a few steps to catch him. She looked up to him with tears in her eyes. "I know what must be done in the name of country, liberty, and self-defense, but John, please, take every care. Come home to me and the children!" Softly sobbing she pressed her face against his neck. He took her in his arms and held her close.

"We'll be home, my darling, in God's good providence!" John kissed her, and released her. "Now, you be a brave wife while I'm gone."

"The wife of John Sevier knows no fear!"

"That's my lady! I sure wish Mrs. Bowman had your courage." It suddenly occurred to him he had not spoken to his wife about his commitment to Colonel McDowell.

"What's wrong with Mrs. Bowman?"

"Well, Colonel McDowell refuses to take her and her little girl back to Burke County while the fighting goes on. She and the child will have to stay here in the fort or move to the tavern in Jonesborough."

Bonny Kate reacted strongly. "I won't hear of it! Mrs. Bowman deserves better than that! She will stay with me at Plum Grove!"

"Oh, my dear, you have your hands full already."

"No, John, I insist. I'll go find her at once and extend the invitation. Poor woman, she was driven from her home without a friend west of the mountains, and with that sweet little girl to care for. I'll show her some Sevier hospitality." Bonny Kate walked away looking for Grace Bowman, and John smiled with pride at his good wife's sense of hospitality.

It was midmorning on September 26, 1780, when the soldiers and their families knelt or sat in groups surrounding a stately sycamore tree for a simple prayer service. Colonel William Campbell of Virginia had arrived the day before with two hundred soldiers, and then his cousin Arthur Campbell brought two hundred more, making Virginia the largest contributor of manpower for the expedition. Bonny Kate, in surveying the crowd, counted her own family's contributions to the force. Her husband, John, commanded the Washington County troops with her stepsons Joseph and James. Her husband's brothers, Valentine, Robert, Joseph, and Abraham were there. Her father, Sam Sherrill, and her brothers, Sam Jr., Adam, and George were assembled and ready for duty. Her uncle, Captain William Sherrill, would bring his company, including her brother Uriah from Sherrill's Ford, to join forces with the westerners once the army had crossed the mountains. Her sister Susan's husband, Leroy Taylor, was going, and so was Mary Jane's boyfriend, Isaac Taylor, the land surveyor. Bonny Kate watched Mary Jane flirting with Mr. Taylor, and she could tell by the way they acted, they both intended more than friendship. Bonny Kate considered the risks her family was taking, but they were united in their determination to be free of British tyranny, and all prepared for the ordeal confident in Colonel Sevier's leadership.

Reverend Samuel Doak had been invited by Colonel Sevier to say a few words of inspiration. He stood beneath the sycamore tree and preached with his magnificent voice.

"My countrymen, you are about to set out on an expedition which is full of hardships and dangers, but one in which the Almighty will attend you. The mother country has her hands upon you, these American colonies, and takes that for which our fathers planted their homes in the wilderness–our liberty. Taxation without representation and the quartering of soldiers in the homes of our people without their consent are evidence that the Crown of England would take from its American subjects the last vestige of freedom. Your brethren across the mountains are crying like Macedonia unto your help. God forbid that you shall refuse to hear their call–but the call of your brethren is not all. The enemy is marching hither to destroy your homes. Brave men, you are not unacquainted with battle. Your hands have already been taught to war and your fingers to fight. You have wrested these beautiful valleys of the Holston and Watauga from the savage hand. Will you tarry now until the other enemy carries fire and sword to your very doors? No, it shall not be! Go forth, then, in the strength of your manhood to the aid of your brethren, the defense of your liberty, and the protection of your home. And may the God of justice be with you and give you victory! Let us pray."

The men and their families bowed their heads as the Reverend Doak continued. "Almighty and Gracious God! Thou hast been the refuge and strength of Thy people in all ages. In time of sorest need we have learned to come to Thee—our Rock and our Fortress. Thou knowest the dangers and snares that surround us on march and in battle. Thou knowest the dangers that constantly threaten the humble but well-beloved homes which Thy servants have left behind. O, in Thine infinite mercy, save us from the cruel hand of the savage, and of tyrant. Save the unprotected homes while fathers and husbands and sons are far away fighting for freedom and helping the oppressed. Thou who promised to protect the sparrow in its flight, keep ceaseless watch, by day and by night, over our loved ones. The helpless woman and the little children, we commit to Thy care. Thou wilt not leave them or forsake them in times of loneliness and anxiety and terror. O God of battle, arise in Thy might. Avenge the slaughter of Thy people. Confound those who plot for our destruction. Crown this mighty effort with victory and smite those who exalt themselves against liberty and justice and truth. Help us as good soldiers to wield the sword of the Lord and Gideon! Amen."

A silent moment passed as Colonel Sevier walked over to Reverend Doak and shook his hand. Then the colonel turned to his men, placing his magnificently plumed hat on his head. He dramatically drew his sword and held it high, shouting the battle cry, "The sword of the Lord and Gideon!"

The men took up the cry and repeated it three times with increasing intensity, "The sword of the Lord and Gideon!" Then they broke out in cheers that filled the valley and resounded from the hillsides as they prepared to march.

The Colonels John Sevier, Isaac Shelby, William Campbell, Andrew Hampton, and Charles McDowell mounted their horses and watched as the majors, captains, and lieutenants organized their ranks and began their companies marching toward the Gap Creek road. Major Charles Robertson, commanding the Washington County home guard, walked over to Colonel John Sevier and reached up to shake his hand.

"Think you have enough men to do the job?" Major Robertson asked.

"I do," John replied confidently. "My two hundred and forty from Washington County and Isaac's two hundred and forty from Sullivan County can whip anybody. We have Campbell's four hundred Virginians for good measure, and McDowell's force of one hundred and eighty will triple in size when we cross the mountains. The question is Charles, do you have enough men to protect our homes and families?"

"We may have to gather in the forts," Charles replied. "I'm as worried about Tory activity as I am about the Indians. After that attempt on your life the other day, the dangers are all too clear. It's a good thing your wife uncovered their plot."

"Don't let anything happen to those prisoners until we get back. In the case of Jacob Dyckes, there are circumstances that warrant consideration because of what his wife did for us."

"I've got them locked up under guard, Jack," Charles replied. "They will keep."

"Look Charles, since I've become a walking target for Tory and Chickamauga alike, I wonder if you could post some men close to Plum Grove, to give Mrs. Sevier a warning if trouble comes her way."

"I'll see to it, and let me do the worrying. You just concentrate on getting Ferguson."

"I'll see to that!" John grinned. The men saluted each other, and John turned his horse for Gap Creek. He scanned the crowds of women and children, locating his beloved family grouped together. He waved his magnificent hat to them as his horse carried him to the head of the column. Bonny Kate and the children could recognize him by his plumed hat for a long time as the army moved into the distance down the Watauga Valley and up the Gap Creek road.

Mary Sherrill walked over to her daughter to discuss their uncertain future. "Well Mrs. Sevier, what are you going to do now?"

"I don't know, Mother," Bonny Kate replied. "The last three weeks have been all about planning for today. I guess I'll call on the Carters, and Jemima Sevier and Amy Sevier while I'm up here at Watauga, then I'll go to Jonesborough for a day or two, and then I need to buckle down to the work of running the grist mill, the lead mine, and Plum Grove Plantation."

"Why not spend some time with me at Daisy Fields?"

"I can't, Mama. I have responsibilities for the welfare of the community. Any family that needs help is supposed to come to Plum Grove. I need to be at my post faithfully until John returns."

"I think that's her polite way of saying she's stuck with entertaining me and my daughter," Grace Bowman said.

"Oh Mother, I want you to meet Grace Bowman, from Burke County. Colonel McDowell placed her here for protection. She is a very important lady, and I enthusiastically offered the Sevier hospitality to her and her little girl."

Grace laughed. "Important, my eye! Charles McDowell left me stranded out here in the wilderness when I could have served the cause better tending the dying and wounded of the army."

"The only dying and wounded will be the men of the enemy," Bonny Kate declared confidently. "When John Sevier is in charge, he very rarely suffers any casualties. Out here we will arm you to fight the savage, and you will find better service on the frontier than going with the army."

Grace laughed at the outrageous claims of her hostess, but Bonny Kate seemed sincere. She stopped laughing and eyed her hostess curiously.

Grace received a warm hug from the mother of the colonel's lady. "Welcome, Mrs. Bowman. If you can't shoot now, Bonny Kate will soon teach you to fire four rounds a minute and accurately hit moving targets. I think we will all benefit from having you here with us!"

Chapter 8

The Summit Meeting

Colonel Sevier's men were mounted, as were Colonel Shelby's. More than half the Virginians had horses, but the fact that many of them had to walk slowed down the army as they made their way through the backwater river valleys toward the steep mountain passes. A herd of cattle donated by the people of Washington County had been brought along to feed the army its first week out, so the foot soldiers were further slowed by the responsibility for cattle driving. Colonel Sevier was already friends with Isaac Shelby and William Campbell, so he spent his time in entertaining conversation trying to get to know Colonel McDowell better. Colonel Hampton, the other eastern colonel, would not associate with McDowell, so he rode further back and conversed quietly with William Campbell.

"I posted my men at every mountain pass to keep a watch out for the enemy," McDowell announced.

"I know, Colonel," John answered. "My scouts report what a fine job they are doing too."

"Your scouts?" McDowell showed surprise.

"Yes sir, my scouts have been moving all over these mountains for the last two weeks. I took the liberty of providing your men with fresh provisions, whiskey, and blankets to make their duty more tolerable."

"Well, thank you, Colonel Sevier, but why wasn't I advised?"

"Your men didn't tell you? My scouts report everything, every little detail. They even told me about the dropping temperatures in the high country. I insist on that degree of intelligence."

"I get the feeling you don't trust my intelligence gathering."

"I trust your friendship, your patriotism, and your sincerity, Colonel McDowell. But you may trust I will always send out my own scouts. They know what I look for when I, myself, go scouting. I will never ride into an ambush, or let an enemy force catch us sleeping."

McDowell frowned. "So Colonel Shelby told you what happened to us at Cedar Springs?"

"I heard about it and learned a lesson from your unfortunate experience." Far ahead a scout appeared at a bend in the road. Sevier urged his horse ahead of the column to meet with him. "Excuse me, Colonel McDowell, while I ride forward and get another scouting report."

McDowell turned to Shelby. "Perhaps Colonel Sevier is too cautious. I'll have to employ him carefully in this campaign. A cautious man makes a poor commander, in the heat of battle."

Isaac laughed. "Yes, Colonel, you keep a sharp eye on Colonel Sevier. You could learn a thing or two about commanding in the heat of battle!"

Isaac spurred his horse ahead to where John talked with his scout. McDowell next turned to Colonel Campbell.

"Colonel Campbell, you'll have to help me maintain my authority over those two backwoods officers. I know I can count on you."

"Colonel McDowell, as far as I'm concerned, you have no authority over any of us *backwoods* officers. I told Isaac Shelby no when he asked me to join this campaign. I had better things to do in the defense of the Commonwealth of Virginia. But when he told me John Sevier was committed to this project, I changed my mind. I'm here because of Sevier. I want you to understand that." They rode on in silence after that.

On the Little Doe River, the vanguard of the army arrived before the humble cabin of John Miller, best blacksmith in the over-mountain country. Colonel Sevier stepped down to renew an old acquaintance, and Sam Sherrill joined in the visit. Almost four years ago Sarah Sevier, Mary Sherrill, and Bonny Kate had attended Mrs. Miller at the birth of her first child. It was a miraculous birth, and the baby was named in honor of Sarah Sevier. Sam Sherrill and John Sevier had joined their wives and became snowbound with the Millers for a week. Mr. Miller was a large, strong, good-natured man, with a love for the writings of Shakespeare. Mrs. Eliza Miller was a healthy pioneer woman; witty, cheerful, and talkative. Her eldest daughter, Sarah was three and a half and already very helpful around the cabin. Her second daughter was just over a year old.

"Mr. Sherrill, we named our new baby Mary after your wife," Eliza introduced the happy little girl. "And there's little Sarah, named for Colonel Sevier's wife. Your wives were truly a godsend when they came here to help me!"

"Colonel, we were so sorry to hear about your Sarah," Mr. Miller said. "That happened back in the winter, didn't it?"

"Yes," John said sadly. "It seems ages ago, but you never completely recover from the loss of a wife."

After a moment of reverent silence, Mr. Miller sought to change the subject. "Say Mr. Sherrill, whatever happened to that Bonny Kate of yours? Ah, she was a girl with spirit, a take charge kind of a girl!"

"She finally married last month," Sam answered with a grin.

"Well, that was a long time coming. She was in full bloom and ripe for the picking when we first met her."

"She got to be right choosy about picking a husband," Sam explained. "She had to find a handsome one who was handy with the ladies, rich, and powerful, like a fairy tale prince."

"My goodness!" Eliza exclaimed. "Who did she end up with?"

"Me," John volunteered. "She ended up with me."

The Millers laughed and congratulated the colonel, and praised his choice of a worthy woman for his new wife. "Well done, sir," Mr. Miller clapped John on the shoulder. "You sure got a good one in Bonny Kate!"

"Yes, Mr. Miller, I love her dearly."

Mr. Miller had a busy afternoon and evening reshoeing horses at the forge. The army filed past his house and camped just up river at the Resting Place at the Shelving Rock as it was known to travelers of the time. Mrs. Miller hosted the officer's mess that evening, and Colonels Sevier, Shelby, Campbell, and McDowell enjoyed a good meal and friendly camaraderie after the first day of the journey. Colonel Hampton chose to have his dinner later to avoid any contact with Colonel McDowell.

After dinner John Sevier invited Charles McDowell to take a stroll in the darkening valley of the Little Doe River. In John Miller's neatly farmed bottom land Colonel Sevier wanted to sort out a few misunderstandings. "Charles, what is it between you and Andrew Hampton that causes him to regard you so icily?"

"The incident at Cedar Springs where his son Noah was killed," Charles answered. "He blamed me for the placement of the pickets. We were attacked by fast riding dragoons. They were in the camp before anyone knew it."

"I see," John said. "That could have happened no matter where you placed your pickets."

"But I was in charge that night. I take full responsibility for what happened, and Hampton will never forgive me. He has probably poisoned the minds of Shelby and the others against me."

"I think the command of a force this size warrants the talents of a general," John suggested. "Is General Rutherford available?"

"No, he was wounded at Camden and captured by the British."

"I'm sorry to hear that. What about General Davidson?"

"I'm the commander of this force," McDowell insisted. "As long as the fight with

Ferguson is in my district, I have the natural right to command! Governor Nash is a personal friend of mine, and he will back me up in this."

John could see that McDowell was proud and stubborn and would not yield easily to suggestions from the other colonels that someone else should command. "There are too many kernels in this sack of corn," John declared. "Only an officer with abilities that command the respect of all will be able to make this expedition work."

McDowell glanced up at the big feather in John's hat. "So you think by being friendly to me, you can grab the glory of command for yourself? You are no better than the others!"

"I don't covet your command, Colonel McDowell. I only want to secure the success of our mission. Besides, the others would never consider me a likely candidate. I'm only a lieutenant colonel with no regular military experience."

John's grin and charming tone disarmed Charles McDowell's anger and opened the way for further conversation about the expedition. McDowell possessed a wealth of information about the British commanders, the Tory militia leaders, and the physical landscape of the eastern foothills of the Appalachian Mountains where the battles would likely be fought. John learned as much as he could and spent the next hour gaining the trust of Charles McDowell.

Rain began falling, and John suddenly took leave of Colonel McDowell. He raced across the meadow where the men tried to find refuge from the rain. He found the wagon he was looking for and then ran to the Shelving Rock where men huddled together for shelter. One of the men greeted him good-naturedly, "Is it wet enough for you, Colonel?"

"It's too wet for that gunpowder!" John shouted. "Help me move those powder kegs in here!"

The men quickly followed John to the powder wagon, and soon they had all the kegs of powder under the shelter of the overhanging rock. John made sure the men covered the powder kegs with canvas, and issued orders to a company of Burke County men to post guards and prevent the men from smoking and lighting cook fires inside the natural shelter.

Isaac Shelby showed up and breathed a sigh of relief to see that the powder had been saved. He walked over to John. "I might have known you would be the first to get up here and see about that powder."

"Who was in charge of the ammunition?" John demanded.

"Colonel Hampton," Isaac answered.

"I'll have words with Colonel Hampton. Where is he?"

"He was just down at Miller's cabin having a late dinner."

John ran down the road in the heaviest rain toward the home of the blacksmith. He removed his hat as he entered the cabin, bowed politely to Mrs. Miller, and greeted

Colonel Hampton. "Forgive the intrusion, Mrs. Miller, but Colonel Hampton is in charge of the gunpowder, and it is raining cats and dogs out here." Andrew Hampton jumped up, charged out the door, and ran up the road. John smiled at Eliza Miller. "He will be right back, Mrs. Miller, after we handle a small matter of great importance." John bowed again and ran after Colonel Hampton to the campground.

Andrew Hampton was an older man with grown sons very useful to the cause of liberty, so John easily caught up with him by the time he reached the powder wagon. Finding the wagon empty, Colonel Hampton looked around in panic until John motioned him toward the Shelving Rock where the treasured gunpowder was deposited. Hampton was relieved to find everything in order. Isaac Shelby stood nearby watching as Lieutenant Colonel Sevier worked his political magic.

"Who did this?" Hampton demanded.

"I had these men take care of it," John answered. "But they tell me they are under the command of Colonel McDowell."

"Where are my men?"

"Somewhere dry, I hope." John grinned.

"I'll post guards from my command and relieve these men of duty."

"Wait, Colonel. Don't you think you ought to thank these Burke County boys for saving the whole campaign tonight?"

Hampton looked around the circle of men and realized the value of Sevier's suggestion. "Colonel Sevier is right. You men have rendered a great service to the state of North Carolina tonight. On behalf of a grateful and generous people, I thank you." He turned and went in search of his officers to take over the guard duty. John followed him out into the rain, and Isaac followed to see what would happen next.

"Colonel Hampton, could I have a word with you, sir?"

Hampton wheeled about to face the lieutenant colonel. "I suppose you want me to thank *you* too?"

"That won't be necessary. I just want the campaign to run smoothly."

"McDowell is just looking for a reason to drum me out in disgrace, and tonight you gave it to him."

"I paid for that powder with money I borrowed against my own credit, and the lady that milled it took great personal risks to deliver it into my hand," John replied. "I have some interest in keeping it dry."

"Why did you have to use McDowell's men?"

"They were the first men I found. I didn't care whose men they were. Besides, you and Charles need to come to an understanding, for the good of the country."

"What do you know about any of this?"

"Isaac told me everything, and I feel the greatest measure of sympathy for you, Colonel Hampton, in the loss of your son, but the present emergency requires reconciliation and unity."

"Reconciliation, my ass!" Hampton then turned on Isaac. "What are you grinning at, you Judas? You have delivered me up to this Pharisee."

Isaac became defensive. "Jack is on our side in this, Colonel Hampton. He will not betray us, but you have to be reasonable and keep a cool head."

"Stay out of my way, both of you." Hampton then looked at John directly and disdainfully. "That's an order." He left John and Isaac standing in the rain.

"Damned if he didn't just pull rank on you, John," Isaac remarked.

"These things never turn out the way I expect." John looked to the sky, spread his arms and said, "Lord God, send me guidance." Lightning flashed and thunder rumbled.

Isaac reached out and pulled John toward the shelter of the rock ledge. "Let's get out of this infernal rain."

The men in the shelter of the rock ledge of the Resting Place proved good company for John and Isaac, and all were impressed with John Sevier's jovial nature and skill at frontier story-telling. Gathered was a mixture of Burke County boys under McDowell, Isaac's Sullivan County men, and some of John's Washington County lads, but none of John's kinsmen were present. When the late September storm finally subsided, a chill set in with the brisk north wind blowing up the valley.

John decided to stroll down to Mr. Miller's forge, where he was sure to find a warm fire. At the forge he found Mr. Miller, pounding away at the anvil, assisted by Sam Sherrill and his sons Sam Jr., Adam, and George. The boys worked the bellows while Sam the father was shoeing the horses.

"Ah, Romeo arrives," Mr. Miller announced. "Perhaps Mr. Sevier will play the role if we can get him to oblige."

John grinned and answered. "A glooming peace this morning with it brings; the sun, for sorrow, will not show his head. Go hence, to have more talk of these sad things; some shall be pardoned, and some punished. For never was a story of more woe than this of Juliet and her Romeo."

"Well said, good sir!" Mr. Miller said. "Rare is the backwater man that knows his Shakespeare."

"I've known more tragedy this year than comedy, and find some comfort in reading from Pastor Doak's library. Forgive me for not performing an encore, but I'm weary of the drama we have played tonight among certain officers of this command."

"Having trouble with McDowell?" Sam asked.

"And Hampton," John answered.

"Boys will be boys," Sam said as he hammered on another horseshoe. "They'll fight like roosters until they find out who has the biggest...uh...feather in his hat." John removed his hat and smoothed out his plume with thoughts of his lady fair.

"I've had some fine help this evening, Colonel Sevier," Mr. Miller said. "But they don't share my love for Shakespeare."

"But nobody knows horse care better than the Sherrills," John replied.

"Funny how people just let something like horseshoes go until it's almost too late," Miller mused. "Some of these mounts would not have lasted the trip if we hadn't done something about them tonight. The Virginia horses were the worst off."

John warmed himself at the fire. "Mr. Miller, the state of North Carolina will compensate you for your services if you present me a written bill. Include the Virginia horses in that as well. How late are you working tonight?"

"We are working on the last horse now. I have to get packed for the journey myself."

"Taking a trip, Mr. Miller?"

"I'm going with you, Colonel Sevier. I just have to find a place of safety for Eliza and our girls."

"Plum Grove is the safest place I know," John said. "One of my scouts can escort them to Watauga Fort, and Eliza can send word to Bonny Kate from there."

"Then it's all arranged," Miller decided. "And tonight you and Mr. Sherrill will be guests in my home. You'll have warm, dry beds in my loft. Are you ready to turn in now?"

John looked at Sam. "I'll be along later. I want to have a private conversation with Colonel Campbell." He put on his hat and left the forge.

In the Virginia camp John discovered that William Campbell had already retired for the night, so he spent some quality time with Campbell's men getting to know some of the junior officers. John's Virginia roots and his encouraging manner made him very popular among Campbell's officers and men. Half an hour later John checked in at his own camp, where his brothers Robert and Val had things very much under control, but there were concerns.

"That storm made the cattle very restless tonight," Val told him. "Some of the boys are out there now trying to settle them."

"Do what you can, but don't lose too much sleep over it," John advised. "I saw today how the cattle slowed our progress. If you need me for anything, I'll be spending the night in Mr. Miller's cabin. He's an old friend."

Val laughed, "John, it seems like you have friends in every corner of the world!"

John grinned. "Yes, but a brother is the best friend a fellow can have."

"After his rifle, his hunting dog, and his wife," Robert called out from his seat near the campfire.

John looked at Robert. "Keep an eye on him, Val. If he gets to missing Kesiah too much, he'll likely desert."

"Keep an eye on me, for I'm missing my Amy," Val said. "And I know you are missing your Bonny Kate."

"It's that hunting dog I'm a-missing," Robert joked.

John laughed. "Good night, men."

When John finally lay down in the warm dry loft in Miller's cabin, Sam Sherrill was still awake. "First day out and you are already carrying more than your fair share of the load, John. You can't patch up these old resentments and cause these colonels to behave civil toward each other overnight."

"We have to cooperate or the cause is lost, even before we begin."

"What did Campbell have to say about it?"

"He was already asleep when I got over there."

"He's a sensible man. He's not worried; why should you be?"

"If he knew what I know, he would not sleep so soundly."

"It's all in the hands of Divine Providence," Sam reminded him.

"That's exactly what Bonny Kate would say."

"There now, think of her and have sweet dreams." Sam fell silent after that. Soon John could tell he was asleep, but not even thoughts of Bonny Kate could drive away his concerns about the campaign.

The next morning the cattle problem had to be solved. They had stampeded in the night and caused many soldiers to lose sleep getting the herd under control. Colonel Sevier considered the options, since the cattle had come from his home county, and he talked it over with Sam Sherrill and Isaac Shelby.

"John, we might as well send these cattle back home," Sam reasoned. "The trail to the top of the mountain is steep and narrow, and we are not going to be able to keep these cows in line."

"We will have to subsist on eastern beef once we get over the mountains," Isaac said. "Let's slaughter as much meat as the men can carry and send the rest of the cattle home."

"I agree, gentlemen," John said. He gave orders to his men to carry out that plan.

John's scouts came down from the high country and reported that it had snowed in the mountains overnight. "Colonel, it's the prettiest blanket of soft white powder I ever did see," declared the young scout Joseph Greer, who stood seven feet tall.

"How deep is it?" John was immediately concerned about the foot soldiers.

"Ankle deep, but the trail is passable all the way."

"Good. We will march as soon as the commissary detail finishes packing the meat."

Half the morning was gone when Sevier's men led the army up the steep, narrow trail that wound through the gap between Yellow Mountain on the north and Roan Mountain on the south. Near the summit there was an open meadow called the Bald of the Yellow where the men stopped for lunch. The hundred-acre table land was covered in about four inches of snow.

"It's cold up here," Isaac Shelby remarked. "That snow is ankle deep!"

"Isaac, let's march the men out before lunch and take roll of who we have with us," John suggested. "That will give them something to do while the meal is being prepared."

"Sounds like a good idea," Isaac agreed.

The company captains soon had the men moving about in orderly drilling and then lined them up in companies to take roll of the men present and accounted for. Captain Robert Sevier came running to report a situation that angered him greatly. "Two men from my company are absent from roll call."

"Who are they?" John asked.

"Sam Chambers and James Crawford," Robert replied.

"John, what do you know about these men?" Isaac demanded.

"Chambers is a simple lad, easily led astray," John told the other officers. "But Crawford might be mercenary enough to sell information to the enemy."

"Then we have to assume we've been betrayed," Isaac concluded. "I thought you said your men never desert. There are two for the hangman."

"I'm sorry I brought them," John expressed his dismay. "That'll be a sad story to tell their womenfolk."

"And we have lost the element of surprise, the only part of the whole enterprise that gave us any advantage!" Isaac's anger was evident. He knew how difficult it had been for Colonel Sevier to make judgments about the political leanings of his neighbors.

Charles McDowell was equally disturbed. "Well, it won't be long before Ferguson will know our plans and lay traps for us as we come out of the mountains!"

Colonel Campbell was more optimistic. "There's plenty of ways we could go. We could even split up and meet again on the other side."

"I'd feel better if the Burke County scouts had already located Ferguson and were watching his movements," Isaac shot a barb at McDowell. He thought Charles McDowell's district where Ferguson supposedly waited should have been well enough organized to report British movements all along.

John Sevier, painfully aware of his own responsibility for the breach of security, did not want the meeting to disintegrate into a squabble over command issues, so he advanced a suggestion. "Colonel McDowell, couldn't your men, who know the country so well, ride ahead and determine the whereabouts of the British?"

"To be sure," McDowell answered quickly. "I'll lead the advance party myself. I'll assemble my detail and leave my brother Joseph in charge of my Burke County men. Gentlemen, I'll see you in a few days." Colonel McDowell walked away toward his group.

John turned to his brother Robert, "Captain Sevier?"

"Yes, Colonel Sevier?"

"I suggest we end the drill with the firing of a volley and let the men get their lunch."

"Yes, sir!" Robert saluted smartly and returned to his company. The command was passed to load and fire a volley into the rare mountain air. Almost a thousand rifles discharged, but the thinness of the air at the mile high altitude made the volley sound noticeably weak. The men dispersed to various cook fires for lunch.

John turned to Isaac. "That was weak sounding. Were they using a full charge?"

"It must be the thin air at this altitude that made it sound that way," Isaac reasoned.

Charles McDowell, leading one company from his Burke County force, rode by heading east. As they passed, Colonel McDowell saluted and the officers saluted back. The other four colonels sat down to enjoy their lunch around a cook fire where Sam Sherrill and his sons cooked steaks and boiled potatoes and carrots.

"Gentlemen, I'll speak plain," Isaac Shelby began.

"You generally do," John said with a grin.

"I'm worried about what we're going to do when we get down to Carolina and end up with McDowell in command."

"What's the problem with McDowell?" John asked to stimulate the conversation.

Isaac took a bite of his steak and continued. "When we served with him in the summer campaign, he was all strategy, sending us here and there but never leading. His brother Joe fights like a wildcat, but Charles is a planner—a paper soldier! Don't get me wrong. Colonel McDowell is a fine man and a great patriot, but he's so determined not to get beat that he's forgot how to win."

"Some would level the same criticism at General Washington," John pointed out.

Isaac stood up and paced around the fire speaking forcefully. "Our mountain boys need a leader who can think fast, move like lightning, strike like thunder, and get us home to our families. And that ain't Charles McDowell!"

"I believe he is the most senior officer on this expedition, and we will be operating in his home district," John observed. "How do you think we are going to work around this little problem?"

"Hell, John, you're the politician," Isaac replied. "You'll think of something."

John stood up and strolled thoughtfully away from the warmth of the fire, gazing far away to the east. "Politics, now there is a dangerous game!"

"Yes," Isaac said. "And speaking of dangerous games, the British Indian agents won't waste any time stirring up the Chickamaugas when they learn of our absence from home."

Sevier abruptly turned his gaze west. "I have thought about that constantly since we left the Watauga."

"We can't go dancing down to the Catawba and play camp soldiers the way McDowell wants to do it," Isaac said. "Our men expect us to lead them down there, fight, win, and get them back home!"

"We have a bigger fight waiting for us back home with Dragging Canoe," Sam Sherrill interjected from his place at the cook fire. The officers grinned at each other to hear one of Sevier's privates speaking up in a council of officers, but none took issue with his sober assessment.

"Aye," Colonel Campbell agreed. "Mr. Sherrill has a valid point."

"It's our way or no way with McDowell; am I right?" Isaac polled the others.

"Damn right," Colonel Andrew Hampton said bitterly.

"Whatever it takes," Colonel William Campbell said in agreement, still unsure what way Isaac was talking about.

Colonel John Sevier continued to gaze west, silently pondering the alternatives. Isaac noticed John's apparent lack of attention. He walked closer to John and spoke in a softer tone. "We have to think of our families first. John, you have to think of Bonny Kate!"

John didn't need an invitation from Isaac Shelby as he still stared at the western horizon. "I have thought of little else since we left Watauga; I do miss my Bonny Kate!"

After the meal, the army marched downhill beyond the snowline into Elk Hollow and camped for the night beside a beautiful spring that supplied Roaring Creek. It was a departure from the regular route that travelers would have taken. The officers were improvising a route that would prevent detection and ambush if the two deserters were to find Major Patrick Ferguson of the British army and warn him of the gathering storm.

Chapter 9

Washington County Queen

Bonny Kate Sevier had gathered around her a fair flock of frontier female friends. They were attracted to her strength of personality, her optimistic encouraging nature, and her position as the colonel's lady. She held court at Watauga Fort, where she moved into one of the cabins vacated by McDowell's officers. She used the fort as a base from which she made day visits, riding the length of the Watauga Valley to spend time with friends and relatives from Jemima Sevier, John's stepmother who now lived at Stony Creek farm, to Elizabeth Carter, old Colonel Carter's wife, and many other women of note. In her entourage were Mrs. Grace Bowman, Mrs. Mary Sherrill, Mrs. Susan Sherrill Taylor, Miss Mary Jane Sherrill, and Miss Betsy Sevier. The other Sevier children stayed at the fort and played hard each day supervised by some of the older women.

Bonny Kate especially enjoyed the company of Grace Bowman, and one day when they were riding back from a visit with Mrs. Talbot on Gap Creek, Bonny Kate remarked on what a pretty name she thought Grace was.

Mrs. Bowman laughed. "Grace is not my given name!"

"What is it?" Bonny Kate wondered.

"Oh no, Bonny Kate, I'm not telling you that. You would laugh your head off!"

"No, I wouldn't."

Grace smiled. "There's much mystery about you, Bonny Kate Sevier, much more I want to know. Let's make a game of it. I'll tell you the secret of my name if you tell me some of your secrets."

Bonny Kate laughed, "A lady has to be careful with a game like this! What do you wish to know?"

"What are you willing to tell?"

"John Sevier named me Bonny Kate the day he rescued me at Watauga Fort. I didn't know it at the time, but he got that name from his favorite tavern song, *The Bonny Lass of Fisher Row.* Isn't that flattering, to be named for a naughty tavern song?"

Grace laughed. "Tell me about that rescue."

"Not so fast, Grace; it's your turn to tell me something."

"All right, here's one. My father arranged the perfect marriage for me, to an elderly gentleman with a large plantation and a hundred slaves. On the day of the wedding, when the pastor asked me, 'Grace, do you take this man?' I said, '*No, I do not!*' Then I ran to my father's horse, and I rode home as fast as the horse could go."

"You were a runaway bride?"

"Yes, I was. He was a sweet old man and very rich, but I never loved him, and I realized that day I never would."

"So you held out for a man you could love, just as I did," Bonny Kate said.

"And I'm so glad I did! Captain John Bowman came into my life the same year, and he was the love of my heart's desire. He ardently courted me, with his natural charm and gallant courtesy. He stirred my hot blood like no one else ever did. I would tell you more were it not for the virgins who travel with us." Bonny Kate and Grace turned in their saddles and caught Betsy Sevier and Mary Jane Sherrill listening eagerly to the romantic conversation.

"Don't stop on our account," Mary Jane encouraged. "We have much to learn about passionate love, and you ladies are the best teachers available."

Bonny Kate laughed. "Grace, do you see how they watch me hoping to catch a glimpse of the mysteries of marriage? It is so difficult to give free reign to my passion when I have to be concerned about being observed. John and I have gone to great lengths to prevent embarrassment to those around us."

Betsy Sevier laughed, "Bonny Kate, you haven't gone far enough! We know all about the place you call Mount Pleasant!"

Bonny Kate blushed. "Betsy, don't tell that!"

Mary Sherrill couldn't resist adding her observation, "They broke the bed on their wedding night!"

"Mother!" Bonny Kate exclaimed, but she could not keep from smiling at the memory.

"Wait, hold up there," Grace said. "That's not how we play the game! It doesn't count to have second-hand information. It only counts when we hear it straight from the source! If Bonny Kate chooses not to share those intimate details, then we cannot admit them as evidence of a colorful character!"

"Thank you, Grace, my character is colored enough. Let us get back to learning your given name."

"I just finished relating the story of my courtship and marriage to Captain Bowman," Grace reminded her. "It's your turn, Bonny Kate. Tell us about the rescue."

"I think I'm getting the worst of this game, thanks to my dear kinswomen, but I can't stop now. The rescue happened like this: I was among the women sent out to milk the cows that morning. My family's cow, Flowerbelle, had strayed to the far end of the Old Fields surrounding Watauga Fort. When I reached out to untangle her lead rope from the dense shrubbery, an Indian warrior grabbed my wrist. I struggled and contended with him for my liberty while his companions, twenty or so in number, appeared from their hiding places, armed and painted for battle. The milk bucket in my other hand became the instrument of my release, for the big Indian could not continue restraining me as he received the bucket in his face. Fear is a stranger to me, but on this occasion I admit I did run, and run my best I did. My screams alerted the other women to seek the safety of the fort. The men at Watauga Fort discovered more than three hundred Indians had surrounded us and meant very seriously to do us harm. By the time I reached the fort, they had already closed the gates and I could see that another party of Indians had cut me off from approaching the front gate. I turned and ran around to the back wall, and there I found a brave man who reached down for me and called for me by name. I did not know the man before that morning, but it was no time for formal introductions. The bullets and arrows came like hail. It was now leap or die, for I would not live a captive! I jumped for his outstretched hands, and he pulled me over the wall. That was my first introduction to Mr. John Sevier. He said I was a bonny lass for a foot race, and after that he always called me Bonny Kate."

"Amazing story," Grace sighed.

"It is your turn, Mrs. Bowman," Bonny Kate said. "Have I yet earned the right to know your given name?"

"We are getting closer," Grace replied. "Last June, the Tories of North Carolina received payments of money to enter the service of the king. Two hundred of them gathered at a place called Ramseur's Mill. Major Joseph McDowell and my husband, Captain John Bowman, rode to break up the Tory gathering. They added some men from Rowan County and boldly attacked with a force half the size of that belonging to the king. At the moment of victory, Captain Bowman fell on the field of honor. The news reached me the same day from Colonel Charles McDowell himself, and he escorted me the forty miles to the battlefield, with me carrying my two-year-old daughter with me. I found my lover in great distress, mortally wounded, his life ebbing away, and I cared for him the best I could, providing every comfort. I hoped against hope that he could somehow recover enough for me to take him home, but the angels took him first. He died in my arms as I tenderly caressed him and bitterly wept. My ministry did not end there. I arranged a warrior's funeral, and had him buried with honor in a nearby churchyard. Colonel McDowell, a cousin of my husband, has since been my protector and healer. His kindness has been a great comfort to me, even to the removal to Watauga to protect me from the cruelty of the invaders."

"That is so sad!" Bonny Kate sympathized. "My dear Mrs. Bowman, you have suffered more than any wife I know in the cause of Liberty!"

"I curse the king who paid for the destruction of my family, and I curse the hirelings who carried out the crime!" Grace declared. A moment of silence fell over the ladies as they rode on. In the distance Watauga Fort could be seen. "We have time for one more story before we arrive back at the fort. It's your turn Bonny Kate, and then I shall tell you my name."

Bonny Kate drew a deep breath, clearly affected by Mrs. Bowman's bravery and the sadness of her story. "The siege of Watauga Fort lasted twenty days, as the specter of sudden and violent death hung over us constantly. Mr. Sevier worried unceasingly about his wife, Sarah, and their children who had taken refuge at John Shelby's fort some twenty-five miles distant. We had no news of their fate the entire time. We all did our best to keep spirits up at Watauga Fort, and there was much jesting and practical joking between Mr. Sevier and Captain James Robertson. I developed a dangerous fascination for Mr. Sevier as the model of the perfect man for an old maid's dreams. I enjoyed flirting with him and behaved very recklessly, but you have to understand the feelings and the imaginings that my rescue had aroused, compounded by the daily perils we suffered. It made me look at my wasted life where I never could find a man who was my equal in nerve and ability, until suddenly there he was! I confess that during the siege I did in my heart covet that which belonged to another. Mr. Sevier, to his great credit, never took me seriously and playfully indulged my attentions without any feelings of his own. Betsy knows that her father always loved Sarah and only Sarah, as long as the good lady lived. Anyway, I confessed it all to Sarah Sevier when we became neighbors at Stony Creek Farm, and she in her kindness and understanding forgave my transgressions. Sarah was superior to me in all that respects housewifery, midwifery, hospitality, matchmaking, and Christian kindness. She welcomed me daily under her roof and took me under her wing. She became my mentor and confidant. I became to her somewhat of an apprentice, or sidekick if you will, in many grand adventures and misadventures. Sarah did her best to find the perfect match for me from among the best bachelors in the west, and I know I caused her a great deal of frustration."

"We were all frustrated!" Mary Sherrill added.

"You can say that again, Mother!" Mary Jane laughed.

"Here's the point," Bonny Kate continued. "As Sarah lay dying at Nolichucky Fort last winter, she called me to her side and expressed to me how much our friendship had meant to her. I in like manner declared my devotion to her as my well-beloved friend. Then she made me promise to care for her ten children until John remarried. I made that promise and did my best to fulfill it."

"Oh Bonny Kate, you always leave out the best parts!" Mary Jane complained.

"When did he first notice his feelings for you, and how did he tell you? When did you realize you truly loved him as a woman loves a man? How did it all happen?"

"It was all in God's good providence," she replied mysteriously.

"Beautiful," declared Grace. "That is the most beautiful story I have ever heard!"

"And now my fair lady, a name," Bonny Kate insisted. "We shall have a name!"

"My maiden name was Grizelle Greenlee," she laughed. "And by the grace of God I changed it!" The other women could not hold back from joining her in the amusement and laughed with her.

"Amazing Grace," Bonny Kate said. "You are truly amazing!"

When Bonny Kate's party arrived at Watauga Fort, they found it surrounded by a small herd of cattle that had been returned to the settlement from Mr. Miller's mountain forge. Eliza Miller and her two daughters came out to greet them as they dismounted their horses.

"Eliza Miller! What a wonderful surprise!"

"Hello, Bonny Kate. My husband decided to go campaigning with your husband, so they sent me here for safekeeping."

"You are always welcome to stay at my home. And here are your darling daughters!"

"Yes, ma'am. You were there when my Sarah was born, and now we have Mary, named after Mrs. Sherrill."

Mary Sherrill climbed down from her horse and took the Miller baby in her arms as the other women gathered around to view her too. "Ah, she's absolutely adorable, Eliza!"

"You were right about second babies, Mrs. Sherrill. This one was so much easier."

Bonny Kate and her mother looked at each other with the memory of a snowy night when the blacksmith's wife miraculously survived a childbirth gone wrong. Sarah Sevier, Mary Sherrill, and Bonny Kate had prayed long and hard for that miracle. Bonny Kate looked into the angelic face of the three-and-a-half-year-old Sarah Miller. The blue-eyed blond with a head full of soft curls smiled proudly at her baby sister.

"I bet you are the best big sister a little baby could have," Bonny Kate acknowledged her. "Are you Mother's big helper?"

"Yes, ma'am."

"Sarah, do you know who this is?" Eliza asked her daughter. "This is Mrs. Bonny Kate Sevier, the colonel's wife. She and her mother were there to help me the night you were born."

"Are you married to the handsome colonel with the big feather in his hat?" the child wanted to know.

"Yes, I am."

"I want to marry a colonel like that," little Sarah declared. The women all laughed as Bonny Kate knelt and hugged the child.

"Then always do your best to be useful and helpful to everyone, beginning with your own family," Bonny Kate instructed.

"Yes, ma'am."

Bonny Kate stood up smiling at Eliza. "I see they sent back some of the cattle."

"Yes, we need to know where to settle them," Eliza replied.

"They should go to Val Sevier's farm, where Amy will take good care of them. I'll see to that in the morning."

"Bonny Kate, did you know that out of all those men who camped at our farm, only one rose early enough with the idea of writing a letter to his wife and sending it down with me?"

"Let me guess who that was," Mary Sherrill said. "Was it Colonel Sevier?"

"Yes," Eliza replied with a smile. "And here's the letter."

Bonny Kate took her prize and found a quiet corner of the fort where she could read her letter over and over. There was very little news, and only a few concerns. Most of the letter was heartfelt expressions of a man very much in love, and it was read eagerly by a lady very much in love.

Early the next morning Bonny Kate was back in the saddle, driving the cattle up the Watauga to Val Sevier's farm at Stony Creek. Her sisters helped, as did two of her brothers, John Sherrill and Billy Sherrill, members of the home guard. It was only four miles to the farm, but they had to pass Colonel Carter's mansion, and they worked hard to keep the cattle out of Colonel Carter's corn fields.

"Mary Jane, there's one astray on your side."

"I see her," Mary Jane called back. She spurred her horse to a gallop, intercepted the cow, and expertly directed the animal back into the lane. Bonny Kate appreciated Mary Jane Sherrill's many skills and reflected on her sister's near elopement with Isaac Taylor. How like the stray cow's behavior would have been Mary Jane's elopement.

"I'm glad she *didn't* elope," Bonny Kate said aloud.

"What's that you say?" Susan Sherrill Taylor called from the saddle of her nearby horse.

"I was thinking about Mary Jane," Bonny Kate explained. "I'm glad she didn't elope."

"That was a ruse, Bonny Kate," the elder sister said.

"A ruse?"

"Yes, a trick, a deception, a stratagem!"

"I know what a ruse is. Why did Mary Jane set forth a ruse?"

"To see what you would say, and what Father would do. But when it became clear that Colonel Sevier was acting on the news that accompanied the men returning from the summer campaign, Mary Jane had to drop the whole idea."

"Then I suppose I can put my mind at ease about that."

"One less thing for you to worry about, Bonny Kate," Susan said. "And you sure have more than your fair share of worries these days, dear sister."

"Don't I know it?"

Mary Jane galloped back toward them with her dark brown hair flying loose in the gentle morning breeze. Her fair skin, laughing blue eyes, and slender agile form created a natural beauty rarely seen in those or any other days. Bonny Kate knew it was just a matter of time before the third daughter of Sam Sherrill would also find the man of her dreams.

Amy Sevier was cooking a late breakfast for her eight youngsters when the herd of cattle arrived at Stony Creek Farm. While Johnny and Billy Sherrill turned out the cattle to graze in the meadows beside the Watauga, Bonny Kate and her sisters entered the cabin for a visit. Amy had her children seated around a long table, with the older ones helping the younger ones. Peace, order, and politeness prevailed among the children of Sheriff Val Sevier under the authority of Amy Sevier, who possessed a sweetness of spirit and kindness of hospitality that Bonny Kate greatly admired. Their eldest child was twelve-year-old Elizabeth. She was the same age and bore the same first name as John's Betsy, and their personalities were similar as well. Amy's next child was John, named for his uncle; he was eleven. Ann was nine. Little Valentine, named for his father and grandfather, was seven. Seated together at the end of the table were the five-year-old twins, Robert and William. James was three, and Jemima was a few months short of being two.

"Good morning, sisters," Amy called out cheerfully.

"Good day, Amy dear," Bonny Kate answered. The sisters-in-law hugged each other in greeting.

"Would you care for some breakfast?" Amy offered.

"No, ma'am," Bonny Kate said. "We had a good breakfast at Watauga Fort. We brought back some of the cattle from the campaign. I was told the men didn't want to have to drive them over the steep mountain trails."

Amy smiled. "I don't blame them. Watauga Valley cows are very unruly, as a rule. What do you want *me* to do with them?"

"I thought you could return them to their rightful owners."

"But the cattle are yours, Bonny Kate. Colonel Sevier paid hard silver in advance for every head."

"Where did the money come from?"

Amy shrugged. "Maybe it was county money. Why don't you ask Judge Carter if he knows anything about it?"

"I'll stop by his place on my way back to the fort. May I leave the cattle with you until I figure this thing out?"

"Certainly, dear sister," Amy replied. "I'll help you any way I can. I understand the challenges you face with the eight children entrusted to your care. You and I find ourselves in almost identical circumstances. I was delighted and relieved when John decided to marry again, and I'm glad it was you."

"Thank you, Amy. Others in the family did not extend so warm a welcome."

"Let's talk about that," Amy invited. She removed her apron, hung it on a wall peg, and walked over to the door. "Susan, you and Mary Jane make yourselves at home, and do not spare the rod if that's what is necessary to maintain order at this table." Amy led Bonny Kate out into the yard, while Susan and Mary Jane were amused at the suggestion of how to maintain order at Amy's table. No greater scene of domestic tranquility could be imagined than at that neat and orderly table where Amy's little angels received their nourishment.

Amy began the conversation. "Kesiah has never been kindly disposed toward you, and has never been able to articulate to me any reasons why."

"I assure you, I have always tried to be civil and accommodating," Bonny Kate said.

"Kesiah practically worshipped Sarah Sevier from the first time they ever met. Sarah had great respect for the Robertson family, which was perhaps the reason she first suggested Kesiah as a match for our brother Robert. It was the only time I ever saw Sarah make a misjudgment. The girl proved to be jealous and overly possessive, but Robert loves her deeply despite her faults. I can only imagine how it must have hurt Kesiah when Sarah preferred your friendship and companionship to hers."

"Sarah was the best friend I ever had."

"With your marriage to John, the whole family situation has changed. Now it is Kesiah's responsibility to be civil and accommodating."

"I will always hope that we can reach a common ground where we can at least get along."

"Understanding her nature is the first step toward toleration."

"I'll do my best."

"I know you will." Amy took Bonny Kate's hand in hers and patted it gently. "Now, we have more important concerns to worry about than women's business."

"Like the cattle?"

"More important than that," Amy said seriously. "Val told me how Isaac Shelby won the battle at Musgrove's Mill."

"It was a great victory, two hundred of our best men against eight hundred of the king's men."

"Val was disgusted by it. Do you know what Shelby ordered the men to do?"

"No."

"Shoot down the officers first. Empty every saddle and the foot soldiers will run like rabbits; that's what Shelby told his men."

"Isn't that what war is supposed to be about, killing the enemy?"

"No, Bonny Kate, it's about courage, honor, leadership, and stratagem to persuade an enemy force to lose their resolve and quit the field with minimum loss of human life."

"Oh."

"If we start killing officers, the enemy will order their soldiers to do the same until both armies become leaderless rabble whose passions for violence will naturally turn to rape and plunder. That is not what war is supposed to be about."

"What can we do about it?"

"Pray for a miracle, because our husbands are officers. Isaac Shelby might hide behind his men and order them to shoot officers, but do you think that is the way of the Sevier? I think not! John and Robert and Val will be at the front of the charge leading their men boldly. They lead like officers, they act like officers, and they look like officers in dress, in conduct, and in example! Bonny Kate, I am sure you have heard that story Big Val tells the boys about their ancestor, Don Juan de Xavier, who led the forces of King Henry of Navarre. *'Follow the white plume; for there you will find me in the thickest part of the fighting, and there you will find the glory!'* That is the example our men will follow."

"Yes, I've heard it." Bonny Kate began thinking about the big feather she bought to give to her husband at Sycamore Shoals. She realized then that she had unknowingly made him a marked man for enemy riflemen ordered to shoot down officers first. She became greatly agitated. "Why are you telling me this?"

Amy wept. "It was too great a burden for me to bear alone, and there was nothing I could do to stop it."

"Oh, Amy, I've done a terrible thing. I gave John a white plume to wear in his hat, like the gallant cavalier!"

"I know, and I would have stopped you if I could have."

"But John seemed so pleased with it, and his children were so proud of him."

Both women were overcome with dread for the safety of their husbands, and embraced as the tears flowed freely.

"I'm too young to be a widow, Bonny Kate, and too much in love to marry any other. What man would accept a widow with eight children?"

"Whatever would I do if I lost my John? It took forever to find him, and it took an act of Divine Providence to discover the love we had for each other. Please, Holy Spirit, suffer no harm to ever come near him!"

"Yes, Bonny Kate! We should call upon God to save them, and God will save all of us. Miracles do happen, don't they?"

"Yes, of course they do, Amy. We will pray for our husbands to be delivered safely out of the midst of the tumult."

"Naomi! Naomi!" A voice sounded from far away.

Amy pulled away. "That's my mother, Bonny Kate. Pull yourself together. We must not let her see our distress. We must show the brave face at all times. We are the wives of officers. Set the good example."

Bonny Kate laughed at Amy's sudden change in demeanor as they hastened to dry their tears. Jemima Sevier was Amy's mother, and because of her marriage to Amy's husband's father, was also her mother-in-law. Jemima came hurrying down from her cabin, which was on a hill not too far away.

"Naomi, I saw Bonny Kate out here with you, and I wanted to hear the news. Have you seen my husband, Bonny Kate?"

"Not since the gathering."

"Big Val said he was going fox hunting, but he went without taking his hounds," Jemima explained.

"Mama, he's probably down at Robert's Tavern with Charles Robertson and the rest of the home guard."

"I should have watched him like a hawk," Jemima said. "All the signs were there, but I didn't read them like I should have. It was too much for the old man. He couldn't resist the temptation."

"Mother thinks he went on the campaign with all his sons," Amy explained to Bonny Kate.

"He asked me if he ought to go, and I told him absolutely not, and that's when the conversation stopped," Jemima said. "The man is seventy-seven years old and acting like he's forty."

"I helped John with the muster rolls, and Mr. Valentine Sevier was reserved for the home guard." Bonny Kate said. "I'll ask Charles Robertson to find him for you. I'm leaving today to return home through Jonesborough, where Major Robertson has set up his headquarters. Don't worry, Mrs. Sevier, I'll locate him."

"Thank you, Bonny Kate," Jemima said. "You are such a blessing to our family!"

"Thank you, ma'am," Bonny Kate curtsied. "I am likewise blessed to be a part of this family."

After a rushed visit at Amy Sevier's, the five Sherrills and Bounder, the cow-herding dog, made their way back down the beautiful Watauga. Bonny Kate had decided to stop in and visit Colonel Carter and get some information that might ease her concerns. She had little reason to suspect that Colonel Carter would have a full measure of his own concerns to unload on her.

Bonny Kate sent her companions on ahead as she stepped down in the yard at Judge Carter's mansion. The judge met her at the door and ushered her into his parlor, where he sat back down at his writing desk.

"Bonny Kate, those men who attempted to take your husband's life last week were part of a wider conspiracy. What was the name of that woman who warned you about it?"

"Mary Dyckes."

"And what became of her?"

"I left her with Pastor Doak's wife, but she went home after we rescued my husband. What do you mean by a wider conspiracy?"

"We believe the Tories are planning more mischief directed against the county commissioners. Where does this Mary Dyckes live?"

"On Third Creek north of the Big Limestone," she answered. "What do you think these Tories will do?" Judge Carter wrote down the information she had given him, then he looked up at her.

"First they will communicate with that British commander, Major Ferguson, and alarm him about the approach of the over-mountain men under Lieutenant Colonel Sevier. Our side shall likely lose the element of surprise."

"Oh, dear!"

"Then they will try to hang other members of the county commission the way they tried to hang Lieutenant Colonel Sevier."

"Well, what are you doing about it, Judge Carter?"

"Major Charles Robertson tells me he is restructuring the home guard to respond to the threat. So I think you have nothing to worry about since your husband has gone into the mountains surrounded by two hundred and forty of our best fighting men."

"Have you considered recalling the expedition in the light of these developments?"

"That's beyond my authority," Colonel Carter explained. "The various colonels involved in the expedition are seeking the approval of Governor Nash to embody their forces in defense of North Carolina and its neighbors. When that happens, they are under the Governor's authority. Now I want to caution you, Bonny Kate, that whatever we discuss this morning must be kept in the strictest confidence. That means you can't talk about it to anyone."

"I understand strict confidence, but I have some questions for you."

"Ask away, but be quick. I am a busy man."

"Who owns the cattle that were sent back from the campaign yesterday?"

"So Lieutenant Colonel Sevier sent back those cattle you drove past here this morning?"

"Yes, sir."

"How did Lieutenant Colonel Sevier happen to possess said cattle?"

"Amy Sevier said he paid for them in hard silver."

"I recall that Lieutenant Colonel Sevier borrowed a large sum of money in hard silver from the State of North Carolina to finance the expedition," the judge said.

"So the cattle belong to the state?"

"No, the cattle belong to him. You cannot use the cattle to repay his debt to the State Treasury. He owes hard silver for the hard silver he borrowed. Mrs. Sevier, your lack of understanding of the workings of state and county affairs is deeply disturbing to me. Sarah Sevier was never as confused as you seem to be."

Bonny Kate was offended by Judge Carter's unfair comparison of her to Sarah Sevier. Telling her she seemed to be confused was the same to her as saying she was stupid. Bonny Kate might have been inexperienced, and perhaps unsophisticated, but she was certainly *not* stupid. She held back her temper because she had one more question to ask Judge Carter.

"Judge Carter, could you tell me where I might find the elder Val Sevier? His wife is worried about him."

"She has good reason to worry about the old man. The day the men left I wrote out a commission to Major Valentine Sevier, Sr."

"Why did you do that?"

"Lieutenant Colonel John Sevier requested that I make that appointment," the judge said.

"Why did you make him a Major?"

"Major is an appropriate rank for a quartermaster. A quartermaster is the officer in charge of all the provisions of an army."

"I *know* what a quartermaster is! Where is Val Sevier now?"

"How would I know? Perhaps he's gone fox hunting."

She rose to leave. "But he didn't take his dogs!"

"Good day, Mrs. Sevier. Be careful going down my front steps. I must have Landon repair that loose board before it lands me in litigation."

Bonny Kate left Judge Carter's home with more concerns than she had arrived with. She suddenly felt a great urgency to get home to Plum Grove and throw herself into the management of family, home, and John's businesses. She thought she might find answers to the enigmas she had uncovered that morning in that stack of papers in John's great secretary, the finest piece of furniture in the house.

Chapter 10

A Dangerous Night at Home

Jonesborough was the seat of Washington County. It was the first real town on the over-mountain frontier and consisted of several cabins on neat little town lots surrounding a courthouse and a tavern. Bonny Kate's transportation resources consisted of six horses and the Sherrill family's ox-drawn Conestoga wagon. When Bonny Kate's party arrived in town, John Sherrill and William Sherrill relaxed in the shade of the trees on the courthouse square and watched the Sevier children play and entertain their new friends. The ladies were welcomed at Kesiah Sevier's tavern, where they had the large taproom to themselves with all the men away on the campaign. Hardly a customer came in while Bonny Kate, her mother, her sisters, Eliza Miller, and Grace Bowman visited.

Kesiah served the ladies refreshments and sat at the table with them. "I'm going to close this place and move home until the men come back from the campaign. This town is really dead when court is not in session, and with the men gone until God knows when, I'd be much happier at Mother's."

Bonny Kate was of the opinion that the women had to carry on as if the men were still among them. To do otherwise might give the Tories the idea that they could ride in and take over the institutions of the county. And Sevier's Tavern in Jonesborough was an important institution in Washington County. She knew also it was no use trying to persuade Kesiah to change her mind, so she let it pass. "Kesiah, anytime you want some company and some good fun, you come on over to Plum Grove," Bonny Kate invited. "Mrs. Bowman is my guest and I assure you, she can tell an entertaining story!"

Major Charles Robertson arrived at the tavern, tied his horse in the yard, and came into his daughter's establishment to get a drink. "I'll enjoy a drink of rum and company so fair to go with it." Kesiah got up and poured her father a tankard, which he raised in toast. "I drink to the leading ladies of Washington County!"

"Thank you, Major Robertson," Bonny Kate acknowledged his gallant gesture. "We are here for a brief visit in town before returning to our farms."

"Good, the tavern here is as safe a place as any from Tories on the loose." The fact that he didn't go into detail, and the fact that there were always Tories on the loose, did nothing to alarm Bonny Kate to any extraordinary danger. She let the remark pass and shouldn't have.

"How's the restructuring of the home guard proceeding?" Bonny Kate asked.

"Well enough."

"Did you find a job for the newly promoted Major Valentine Sevier?"

Robertson laughed. "The old boy showed me his commission and told me he was going on the campaign. I can't understand why John would let an old man endure the rigors of such a trip."

"I can't understand it, either," she said. "It was nearly impossible to persuade John to take *my* father along. So you actually saw old Val march away?"

"Yes," Charles replied. "But it was strange to see him amongst the Virginians, instead of riding with his own kin."

"I find that very strange too," Bonny Kate agreed.

"Listen, Bonny Kate, the home guard is still short of horses. Whose horses are those outside the tavern?"

"Three belong to me, and three belong to my father. But my brothers John and Billy will be riding two of them in the home guard, and mother should have one for her use at Daisy Fields."

"I sure could use any extras you might have."

"I need my good broodmare, but I could spare the other two," Bonny Kate volunteered. "Write me a receipt and a certificate of indemnification, and I can deliver them into the service immediately."

"Mrs. Sevier, what sort of requirement is that?" Major Robertson asked.

"I want Washington County to agree to indemnify me if any harm comes to my horses while in the service of the county."

"Your husband doesn't require that, and I've never heard of your father doing that, either."

"These are *my* horses, and that's what *I* require."

"I have the authority to just take the horses in a military emergency."

"Exercise that authority and see what happens. I'll wager the outcome will be much more onerous to you than writing me a certificate of indemnification."

"Very well, I'll write you that certificate." He walked over to a table, removed his riding cloak and hat, and sat down. "Kesiah, bring me a writing kit so I can transact some county business with this shrewd commercial contractor."

"Yes, Father," Kesiah answered, moving quickly to deliver the requested paper, inkwell, quill, and blotter.

"So Major Robertson is Kesiah Sevier's father?" Grace Bowman asked.

"Yes," Bonny Kate replied. "And her husband is my John's beloved brother."

"I didn't realize the connection," Grace said.

"Kesiah has two adorable boys, Charlie, named after this grandfather, and Valentine, named after the other grandfather," Bonny Kate explained.

Kesiah delivered the writing equipment and joined the conversation. "My Robert ought to serve a tour of duty in the home guard for a change, so his boys will have a chance to know him. I don't know why the major, here, couldn't exercise his authority and influence to grant my request to leave Robert out of this latest campaign."

"Boys will be boys," Charles Robertson said without looking up from the certificate he was engaged in composing. "And those Sevier boys are so competitive, if one goes they all want to go."

"Not so with John," Kesiah said. "He got out of the summer campaign by sending you in his place, Father."

"Colonel Sevier had a very good reason for staying home," Bonny Kate spoke up in her husband's defense.

"Yes, he was hotly courting Miss Bonny Kate Sherrill," Major Robertson said.

"That version of the story is about as far from the truth as man can imagine," Bonny Kate answered. "He was heartbroken from losing Sarah, and grieving long and deep. I had nothing to do with his reasons for staying home with his dear little children."

"Didn't you?" The major grinned at the colonel's lady.

"He cared nothing for me until it was almost too late."

"Tell it all, Bonny Kate," Mary Jane cheered on her sister.

"Hush, Mary Jane. Colonel Sevier was happily hunting widows on the very day he first took notice of me, and that's the truth. It was Divine Providence that caused the man to take a second look and direct his attentions toward me."

"Well, we can't argue with Divine Providence now, can we?"

"No, sir, that would not be wise, especially since *you* were hundreds of miles away all summer long and completely ignorant of what was going on here."

Major Robertson stood up from the table, having truly enjoyed the entertainment provided by riling up the colonel's lady. "Madam, here is your certificate of indemnification, in case any harm comes to your horses."

Bonny Kate read the words and reacted sharply. "Major Robertson, you are the shrewd one between us. You have written this certificate so the expense of any claim is to be charged to the county clerk, personally!"

Robertson laughed. "Yes, ma'am, Colonel Sevier is in charge of the military department, and he pays for all military expenses out of his own pocket."

"How is that fair?"

Robertson shrugged and grinned. "That's just the way we have always done it. So there's little chance you would file a claim like that."

"Oh, rest assured, Major Robertson, if I am entitled to indemnification, I'll file my claim, and I *will* be satisfied, one way or another." She winked at him as she folded the certificate and slipped it into her pocket.

Major Robertson picked up his hat and cloak. "Ladies, I have enjoyed this chance encounter." He bowed respectfully, and the ladies curtsied. "Mrs. Sevier, I will take very good care of your horses, and feed them of the best the county can provide."

"And of course, send the feed bill to the clerk of the county, the way it's always been done," she added.

"Of course," he agreed as he left the tavern.

Kesiah moved to put away the writing kit, but Bonny Kate stopped her. "I have a letter to write, Kesiah, and it is not going to be easy. I have to tell Jemima Sevier that her missing husband was last seen marching away with a band of Virginians."

Mary Jane Sherrill laughed at her sister's expression. "There's some consolation that it was a band of Virginians and not a band of virgins."

"Mary Jane, this is no laughing matter."

Kesiah understood the gravity of the situation. "You mean our father-in-law failed to tell his wife he was marching away to war?"

"That's what it looks like to me. And he also failed to tell his colonel. John never would have allowed it."

"Poor Jemima," Kesiah empathized. "I warned you, Bonny Kate. Now you can see for yourself what a burden it is to be married to a Sevier. They are always so ready to abandon us to run off and play soldier. They leave us with businesses to run, babies to care for, and nothing but lives of drudgery."

"Hush, Kesiah," Bonny Kate ordered. She extended her hand toward Eliza Miller and Grace Bowman. "These are my new friends from other parts of the state. They are very eager to formulate an opinion about the character of Colonel Sevier, in whom their husbands have placed their trust and hope of salvation from the cruel invader. The things you want to discuss would be better handled in a private conversation, and I don't have the time for that now."

Bonny Kate picked up the quill and began to write her letter. Kesiah began cleaning up the tavern, straightening the chairs and tables.

"It's getting late, dear," Mary Sherrill addressed her middle daughter. "Susan, Mary Jane, and I wanted to stop and visit with Mrs. Doak this evening. We will likely spend the night there and go on to Daisy Fields in the morning."

"Mother, could you let Brother John ride up to Stony Creek and deliver my letter to Jemima Sevier? It would greatly ease my mind to have that task accomplished."

"Of course, my dear," Mary replied. "I still have Billy, who can escort us safely to Pastor Doak's church."

"You are welcome to stay the night here, Mrs. Sherrill," Kesiah offered.

"Thank you, dear Kesiah, but I need to make some progress toward home." Mary Sherrill politely declined with a laugh. "If I should die before I wake, it would be a great comfort to Mr. Sherrill to know they found me in the church and not in the tavern."

At Plum Grove Plantation that dark night, an eerie quiet prevailed as Johnny Sevier, a trusted lad of nearly fifteen, drove the big oxen-drawn wagon into the yard and stopped the team at the edge of the porch. Bonny Kate climbed down from her horse and helped the sleepy children out of the high wagon. She also helped Grace Bowman and her daughter down and unloaded their belongings onto the porch. Next Eliza Miller and her two daughters received the same care.

"We shouldn't have stayed so long at Jonesborough," Bonny Kate said, looking around warily. "I don't like keeping the children out so late."

"The ladies of Jonesborough were very gracious hostesses," Grace Bowman said. "I should have liked staying longer, but I had no idea your farm was so far from town."

"It's a big country," Bonny Kate answered. "I can't wait to show you the farm!"

"Can it wait until tomorrow? I'm exhausted."

Bonny Kate laughed. "Of course, Grace. These children should go straight to bed."

Johnny lit the porch lantern and opened the door. The children filed into the dark cabin as Bonny Kate crossed to the mantle above the fireplace where she had some candlesticks. As Johnny crossed the threshold with his lantern, strange men emerged from the dark corners of the room.

"Nobody move and nobody gets hurt!" growled a gruff voice. Bonny Kate whirled around and saw three desperate men armed with pistols. She suddenly noticed the unmistakable offensive odor of unbathed men. Johnny charged the closest man, but the bully knocked him down with one blow to the head.

"Don't be a fool, boy! You'll just get yourself shot for nothing!"

Bonny Kate moved quickly to Johnny's side and helped the dazed lad to his feet.

"Everybody into the corner!" the intruder ordered. Bonny Kate gathered her family over to the bed in the corner of the room, where the children huddled together behind their stepmother, her new friend Grace Bowman, and her old friend Eliza Miller.

"Nobody moves until we figure out who you are," the man continued. Several more candles were lit, revealing three men and six pistols trained upon Bonny Kate's family. She was greatly angered and prepared to defend her own with every ounce of fight she could muster. She figured the men were Tories and even thought she recognized two of them. The door opened and another man entered the room.

"That's all," reported the fourth man. "Nobody else rode in with this bunch."

"Where is Sevier?" demanded the man with the gruff voice.

"Which one are you looking for?" Bonny Kate stalled.

"I'm looking for John Sevier, but tonight any of them would suit my purpose."

"What is your purpose?"

"I mean to hang the lot of them from the highest tree in the yard. Now, who are you?"

"I am Bonny Kate Sevier, and you have no right to invade my home and frighten my children."

"How are you related?"

"I am the wife of John Sevier."

"I thought his wife died."

"I'm his new wife."

"Well then, Mrs. Sevier, tell us where to find your husband and we'll do no harm to the children."

"I'll tell you nothing. Get out of my house and leave us alone!"

"That's no way to talk to the official agents of His Majesty, your king."

"My only king is the Prince of Peace; your king is the lapdog of the devil!"

"Why, you treasonous little witch!" The angry bully slapped her across the face, and she fell back onto the bed where the children broke her fall. She sat up and collected her senses, stunned and angered at the cruel treatment. Johnny charged to her defense, but the other men quickly subdued him.

"Tie up that troublesome boy," the leader ordered. "We can hang him with the others once we round them up. What's your name, boy?"

"Tell them nothing!" Bonny Kate called to her brave stepson.

"If the boy is old enough to hang, he's old enough to speak up for himself."

"Leave him alone," Bonny Kate demanded. "It's me you have to deal with!"

Another Tory stepped forward and waved his pistol menacingly. "She's just a stepmother. She doesn't care what happens to Sevier's children. But she'll sing to save her own skin." He cocked his pistol and pushed the weapon into her face. "Now, tell us where to find John Sevier or I'll blow out your brains!"

Bonny Kate took a deep breath, straightened up defiantly, and answered with fire in her eyes. "Shoot! Shoot! I am not afraid to die. But while a Sevier yet lives on this earth, my blood will not be unavenged!" She stared beyond the gun barrel into the eyes of her adversary as tense moments passed. The Tories all understood that the stubborn stepmother had spoken her last words and nothing more could be gained by threatening her with sudden violent death. The Tory leader also considered the weight of her counter threat and knew something of the avenging nature of the Sevier brothers.

"Put away your gun, Bart," the leader ordered. "Such a woman is too brave to die."

The gunman stepped back slowly and lowered his weapon. He gently released the hammer of the pistol and tucked it into his belt. He turned away from her intensely defiant gaze and strolled over to the door. "I'll take another look around," he said and stepped out. Everyone exhaled a sigh of relief.

"We'll just sit down here for the night and wait for Mr. Sevier," the leader said, settling into a chair at the table. "We have plenty of time. Who's this?" He pointed his pistol in the direction of Grace Bowman.

"She's my cousin Grace," Bonny Kate replied. "She's just visiting."

He removed his hat, tossed it on the table, and looked at Grace. "It's a pity you can't pick your relatives. Please excuse the inconveniences of war, ma'am."

"I am well acquainted with the inconveniences of war," Grace said with a steely haughtiness that matched Bonny Kate's. "Your cruel king has ever been my natural enemy, and has already aggrieved me more than you will ever know!"

"Boys, keep an eye on Cousin Grace. I think she's more dangerous than the other one. What about you there, what's your name?"

"Eliza Miller. I'm a friend of Bonny Kate's."

Bonny Kate, encouraged by Grace's boldness and Eliza's calm, had recovered enough to renew the war of words. "Colonel Sevier will be here soon with a hundred of his best fighting men. You have no chance against them!"

"I have my own hundred men posted along the trail out there ready to shoot them down like dogs! What do you think about that?"

"I think you are lying."

"So it doesn't concern you that my men have prepared an ambush for your husband?"

"Why should I be concerned about the men of your imagination?"

The Tory studied her face to read her reactions, but she gave nothing away in useful information. "You are a cool one," he decided. "But you will change your tune when I hang those rebels for what they did to Jacob Dyckes."

"Jacob Dyckes will get a fair trial," she said confidently.

"Dyckes is dead. He was hanged by the Seviers, just this morning."

"That's not possible. He's in custody."

"We broke him out. Then they ran us down at Big Limestone Creek and hanged Jacob. They hanged Holley too, but the rest of us got away."

"Oh, poor Mary Dyckes! This is horrible news, but I know the Seviers had nothing to do with it!"

"They were Sevier's men, acting upon his orders!"

"No," she denied the accusation. "John wouldn't have ordered that. He couldn't have even known about it!"

"Why not?"

"I won't tell you!" She resolved to say nothing else until dawn. The children drifted off to sleep on the crowded bed. Bonny Kate watched the Tories as they watched her. The Tories took turns sleeping. Grace and Eliza managed to sleep some, too. Bonny Kate dared not sleep in the presence of her enemies, for the concern that the violent vile men might try to molest her loved ones and friends.

At dawn she heard the sound of a single horse in the lane. She prayed it wasn't anyone of her acquaintance that the Tories might rob or kill. She listened intently for a clue to the identity of the rider. She heard boot steps on the porch that aroused all the Tories in the room. Unfamiliar voices spoke as the lookout greeted the newcomer. The door opened to reveal a man the other Tories apparently knew. "Get your horses. It's time to travel. Sevier and two hundred and forty men slipped over the mountains four days ago to join other forces against Major Ferguson."

"Four days! We have to warn Ferguson. Let's go!"

The Tory who had threatened Bonny Kate looked at the family in the corner of the room. "What do we do with these rebels, shoot 'em or hang 'em?"

"Leave them be," the leader ordered. "We have a real war to fight now. I should have known their army was on the move when we couldn't find a single horse to confiscate in the entire Nolichucky Valley. These rebels never make a move without taking their horses." The Tories rode off without even plundering the smokehouse, which greatly surprised Bonny Kate. Peace returned to Plum Grove Plantation with the departure of the villains.

Bonny Kate ventured out on the porch as the king's men disappeared up the Jonesborough road. She guessed they would not keep to the road as they sought to elude the light horse companies of Major Robertson's home guard. Grace and Eliza joined Bonny Kate out in front of the house. "I thought we would be safe here," Grace said.

"It seems we are not safe anywhere until our men settle their differences with Mister Ferguson. That's what I think about the condition of this country. I know the names of some of those Tories, and I promise you, they will be brought to justice. I'm sorry they frightened your daughters." She looked into the faces of her friends and saw concern but not fear.

"Do you think those men will warn Ferguson?" Grace asked.

"The light horse companies can stop them," Bonny Kate replied confidently. "We need to get the children some breakfast and put them to work on some useful chores. Then I'll send Johnny to Jonesborough to find Major Robertson and report this outrage." The ladies turned and entered the house, but Bonny Kate rushed out to the horse barn. There she found her good broodmare, still saddled, standing at the feed trough as though expecting a breakfast. The horse had gone straight to the barn last night and escaped the notice of the Tory partisans. Bonny Kate breathed a sigh of relief to still have the horse. She prepared its feed and offered prayers of thanksgiving for the escape of her family and friends from some desperate men.

Later in the morning Bonny Kate brushed and groomed her only remaining horse as Major Charles Robertson visited with her at the horse barn. A company of citizen soldiers milled about in the yard, having been called to assemble at the Sevier home for action against the Tories.

"They said that Jacob Dyckes was hanged," Bonny Kate said. "Is that true?"

Major Robertson eyed the colonel's lady and determined that she was one woman worthy of his complete confidence. "Yes, he escaped from my farm with three others, but by the time we found them, two of them were hanged."

"John will not be pleased with this report. Who did it?"

"We are investigating. Some say it was the Regulators."

"Regulators! There haven't been any Regulators out in these parts for years."

"Bonny Kate, it's time to move the people into the forts."

"No, Major Robertson, I won't go. I'll stand by my post until my husband comes home!"

"I had no idea you ladies were planning to leave Jonesborough last night."

"We wanted to get home. There's work to do now with my menfolk gone. It's time for the pumpkin harvest."

"Those Tories might have killed you last night. This proves what I've been saying all along. The families have to go into the forts."

"I won't do it! The wife of John Sevier knows no fear!"

"Spare me the bravado, Mrs. Sevier."

"How would it look for the colonel's wife to hightail it to the fort the first week he's gone? Who would stay out if his family forted? What kind of example would I be setting? Panic would cause folks to desert their well-stocked farms, right at harvest time. Tory plunderers and savages would take all our goods and stocks for the winter. The ruination and starvation of our home country would surpass any defeat our brave men might encounter in the east. Don't you see, Major Robertson? I can't allow it."

"Jack Sevier would never forgive me if anything happened to you, Bonny Kate. Won't you consider your personal safety and the safety of the children?"

"I've considered all things, and I'll take my chances here," she said decisively. "Besides, whenever you crowd people into the forts, the fever breaks out and runs rampant."

Charles noted the determination in her eyes and saw the strength of her character shining through. "Very well, have it your own way. I'll post a company here at Plum Grove."

"Major Robertson, I know you can't spare a whole company of men, and then I'd just have so many more to cook for."

"All right then, I'll send just a pair of sentries."

"That will be fine. Just don't ask me to go to the fort."

"I understand," said the major, placing his hat upon his head. "I'm sending half the men on the trail of those Tories. With the rest, I'm riding down to Daisy Fields this morning to check on your mother. We are going to be using your Papa's place as a watch station against Indian trouble."

"Major Robertson, could you do me a great favor there? Pack up mother and my sisters and escort them here. It would be a great help to me to have them staying at Plum Grove."

"On that point, we can certainly agree. I'll deliver them here today."

"Thank you, sir."

Major Robertson gave the orders that divided his command, and they pursued their different missions, one to stop the Tories and one to defend against Indian trouble. Charles Robertson mounted his horse and tipped his hat to Bonny Kate, Eliza Miller, and Grace Bowman, and then he led his men down the lane.

Chapter 11

A Town Named Sevier

At the crest of the Blue Ridge, the patriot army paused to take in the magnificent view. John Sevier, Isaac Shelby, William Campbell, and Andrew Hampton dismounted, and the order went down from Colonel Sevier for all the men to dismount and rest their horses. Sam Sherrill walked over to Colonel Sevier and offered him a telescope to scan the terrain ahead.

"Where did you get this, Sam?" John asked.

"I got it from Jacob Brown a few years back. Give it a try."

John scanned the valleys and ridges in the distance and marveled at the detail the telescope afforded. He turned to his father-in-law and confided in a low voice, "I wish I knew this country better, Sam. It puts me at a disadvantage around these other officers to be so ignorant of the geography."

"Nobody knows this land better than me," Sam said. "I hunted these coves and valleys for years after the French and Indian war. I'll tell you what lies ahead each morning at breakfast, if you like."

"Yes, I would appreciate that. How do we get to the Catawba and Quaker Meadows from here?"

"All of these coves drain down to the Catawba, but they are narrow. A large army like this could get mighty strung out and open to ambush."

"It sounds like we need to split up our forces," John said. "I'll recommend that since we don't know where Ferguson is waiting."

"If I were you, I'd take about half the men south, down Turkey Cove," Sam instructed. "Do you see that notch down there in the ridge to our right? That's Turkey Cove, the home of Colonel Wofford. Then I'd take the other half east through North Cove. Look over here on the left and you'll see North Cove. This way the horses will have plenty of forage and the men won't get too spread out. We can rejoin the parties on the Catawba tomorrow and just follow it on down to Quaker Meadows."

"Thanks, Sam, and thanks for the look through your telescope." John tried to return it.

"No, sir. You keep it until we get back home. The officer in charge needs it to see what's ahead."

John smiled and walked over to confer with the other senior officers. "We have received no word from Colonel McDowell, and my scouts haven't seen any sign of Ferguson."

"So far, so good," Isaac said.

"Where do we go from here?" Colonel Campbell asked.

"Still south, then east," John answered confidently. "All of these coves drain down to the Catawba, but they are narrow. A large army like this could get mighty strung out and open to ambush. Since we don't know where Ferguson is hiding, I think it would be best if we split up and approached the Catawba by two principal routes. Colonel Campbell, you will take your men down through Turkey Cove to Colonel Wofford's place." John pointed the cove out on the horizon. "The Carolina men will accompany me through North Cove. We will meet on the Catawba tomorrow and proceed to Quaker Meadows."

"That's agreeable to me," Colonel Campbell approved. "I wouldn't want the whole army lost to ambush in a narrow valley."

"This way the horses will have plenty of forage and the men won't get too spread out. If either branch of the army is attacked, the other can march to its assistance along the Catawba and catch the enemy in the rear."

The officers were pleased with the plan and called over their junior officers to put the plan into action. Colonel Campbell knew of Sam Sherrill's experience in the area and wanted a guide to help him get to Turkey Cove. "Colonel Sevier, I would like to have Mr. Sherrill guide my company."

"I'm sorry, Colonel Campbell, but a great deal of domestic trouble awaits me if any harm comes to my wife's father. Bonny Kate made me promise to look out for him, so I can't let him go."

"She made me promise to look out for you, John!" Sam laughed. All the officers laughed who understood the family influence that Bonny Kate Sevier was capable of exerting over great distances.

"I'm sure Colonel Hampton can provide you an experienced guide," John suggested.

Andrew nodded and said, "I'll get you a good man, Colonel Campbell."

"Well gentlemen, let's ride," Isaac Shelby urged the others. The officers shook hands and parted company.

The afternoon was uneventful, and the Carolina men easily found their way into North Cove and pitched their camp in the forest beside a fast tumbling stream of sweet water. There was a small settlement there, and the residents provided a cabin for the officers to use. The patriotic citizens also offered a herd of swine for the soldiers to cook for dinner, and then they requested an interview with the commander of the troops. Isaac looked at John, "You take care of the locals, John. You are the one with the big feather in your hat. I'm tired." Isaac laid down to rest on one of the beds in the cabin.

John performed the duty of commander and met with the local citizens committee. "I'm Colonel John Sevier, from Washington County in the over-mountain settlements."

"Are you by any chance the man who rescued Bonny Kate Sherrill?" a woman asked.

"Why yes, I am; and last month Bonny Kate did me the honor of becoming my wife." The people of North Cove seemed very pleased with his answer.

The woman became excited. "Oh! That's one of our favorite stories! We even have a song about it that our children sing."

"Thank you very much," John said as he bowed politely.

"We wanted to thank you and your men for coming to our rescue and saving us from the Tories," the leader of the village said. "We had resolved to name our little town after the officer in charge, but lo and behold, we find out he's the savior of Bonny Kate Sherrill, a real hero of the frontier!"

"It's an amazing coincidence, isn't it?" John smiled with satisfaction.

"May we have the honor of naming our little town Sevier, North Carolina?"

"The honor would be mine. I can't wait to tell Bonny Kate about this. She will be so pleased as well."

"Tonight we will have a feast and a dance in your honor, and we will present you with a key to our city," the leader of the town promised.

John surveyed the ramshackle huts, the pig pens, the tobacco patches, and the dirty children playing happily in the mud of the little vegetable gardens. He would have the key to all this? *Well, it is the thought that counts,* he told himself. Nobody had ever named anything after him, and it almost moved him to tears.

Back inside the guest cabin, John awakened Isaac when the hinges on the door squeaked loudly. "What great grievance did the local yokels try to charge you with today?"

"They wanted to name their town after me."

"Oh, come on, John, tell me the truth! Civilians are constantly complaining about armies moving through their lands and creating a swath of destruction. The ungrateful wretches even gripe about the armies that fight to win them their own liberties."

"I'm telling you the truth," John insisted. "They are naming the town for me and presenting me with the key to the city!"

"Bullshit!" Isaac said and rolled over in his bed. "And the next thing you know they'll be asking you to autograph a tree in the center of their stinking little hamlet!"

"It could happen," John said.

After Isaac's short nap, he and John had some time to discuss the command issue while Major Joseph McDowell and Colonel Andrew Hampton posted the pickets further down the valley and all around the perimeter.

"John, you were impressive today up on the ridge. The other colonels went right along with everything you said. The men in every unit have the greatest respect for you, and they all acknowledge the leadership of the man with the biggest feather. I reckon you are getting yourself ready for the role of commander of the army."

John removed his hat and admired the plume, the sign of his lady's favor. "I've been working on the command problem, Isaac."

"You spent the whole first night chatting with Charles McDowell. Hampton suspected you of getting too cozy with McDowell, and defending McDowell's claim to command when the moment of decision comes."

"No, you can tell Andy Hampton that his fears are unfounded. I agree with you about Charles McDowell, but I did learn that he's a proud stubborn man and will not yield his right to command easily."

"Aw, hell, John, just take over and send McDowell home. The men will support it, and the circumstances will justify it."

"No, Isaac, there is a better way. I want to come out of this thing without losing the friendship of Charles and Joseph McDowell."

"I don't see how you can do that, or even why you would want to bother."

"Charles McDowell and Burke County are critical ingredients to any military operation in the mountain region of North Carolina. Burke County offers a host of patriotic men and generous supplies because of the excellent stewardship and skillful management of Charles McDowell. He is very popular with his people and extremely well liked at the General Assembly, not to mention his deep friendship with Governor Nash. We can't just sweep him aside like he doesn't matter. Besides, my wife and his fiancée are probably dearest friends by now."

"Oh, for Pete's sake! I knew there would be a petticoat somewhere in your reasoning. There always is!"

John grinned. "You can never deny the power of the petticoat, my friend!"

The door of the cabin opened, and Joseph McDowell stuck his head in. "Colonel Sevier, one of your scouts has come up from the Catawba, sir. He's the real tall one."

"Thank you, Major McDowell," John replied. He and Isaac walked out to the yard of the cabin where John put on his plumed hat, thinking of the lady that he loved.

A young scout by the name of Joseph Greer stood an impressive seven feet tall beside his horse and saluted as soon as Colonel Sevier arrived for the report.

"Good evening, Joseph," John greeted him. "What did you find out today?"

"Colonel, I rode all the way down to the Catawba River and went downstream several miles talking to settlers on both sides of the river, and no one has seen any signs of British or Tory patrol activity."

John shook the lad's hand. "Excellent! Do you have anything else?"

"We found Colonel McDowell and his North Carolina militia. I left Adam Sherrill to guide them into camp."

"Well done, Joseph. Does Colonel McDowell bring us any news?"

"None that he will share with the likes of me, but I'd say by his attitude he brings good news for the expedition."

"Thank you, Joseph. Get some food and rest tonight. I won't need you again until morning."

"Thank you, Colonel." Joseph saluted and led his tired horse away.

"He thinks McDowell has good news," John said. "I pray it is good news."

Isaac Shelby turned to Major Joseph McDowell. "Why don't you ride out and welcome your brother. I'm sure he'll have news of your home and family."

"I was just about to," the younger McDowell said with a grin. "Won't you gentlemen join the welcome party?"

"Colonel Sevier and I have a disciplinary matter to discuss," Isaac replied.

"Very well, Colonel Shelby." Major McDowell turned to his horse and rode out of camp.

"John, what have you decided to do about Charles McDowell?" Isaac asked with new urgency.

"I said I was working on it."

"He will arrive in a few minutes and insist on his right to command," Isaac warned.

"Let me handle him. There's no point in doing anything until Colonel Campbell rejoins us."

"I suppose not, but you had better be ready with a plan. I'm not serving under Charles McDowell again; not for a single day!"

When Charles McDowell arrived with his thirty men, John and Isaac were there to greet him. "Good evening, Colonel McDowell!" John said cheerfully.

"Good evening, Colonel Sevier," Charles responded. "Hello, Shelby. I'm glad you found your way over the Blue Ridge." McDowell dismounted and shook the hands of the officers present.

"Where is the enemy?" John asked. "We expected a much warmer reception on this side of the mountains."

"My scouts report that Ferguson occupies Gilbert Town," McDowell answered. "He has not moved, and not changed his patrol activity, so I think he is unaware of our approach. Our friends, Colonel Cleveland from Wilkes County and Major Winston of Surrey County, intend to join our force with three hundred and fifty more men. I have also learned of a force of South Carolinians under Thomas Sumter. They have stationed themselves between Charlotte and Hillsborough, close enough to join us if they can be persuaded to share in the glory."

"How close are Tarleton and Cornwallis?" John asked.

"Cornwallis has taken Charlotte. Now he is waiting for his supply wagons to catch up. I don't know the whereabouts of Tarleton."

"That information is critical," John said. "Tarleton is the only one who can move as fast as we can."

"Tarleton, that butcher," Isaac Shelby condemned the enemy officer. "He ignored a flag of surrender and cut down Colonel Buford's Virginians. That's Tarleton's idea of quarter." A moment of silence followed his outburst.

"Tarleton's quarter," John labeled the massacre. "We can't let that happen again."

Charles McDowell looked around at the size of the encampment and discovered half the force was missing. "Where is Colonel Campbell? The Virginians didn't turn back, did they?"

"No," John replied. "We split up at the crest of the Blue Ridge. Colonel Campbell went down Turkey Cove to Wofford's place. He will rejoin us tomorrow on the Catawba."

"As soon as he arrives, we will hold an officer's council to plan the next move," Colonel McDowell said.

"Until then, let us have feasting, dancing, and a good night's rest!" John invited.

After the dinner of roast pork, the citizens gathered in the center of their community around a stately beech tree and officially named their town Sevier, North Carolina. Colonel Sevier was given a beautifully crafted hunting knife. They referred to the ceremonial gift as the key to their city. Colonel Sevier was deeply moved and made an impressive but short speech.

"Colonel Sevier would you autograph this beech tree as a memento of our evening celebration together?" requested the community leader.

John glanced at Isaac to see the surprise on his face. "Why certainly, and may I make a small request that these other gentlemen of my company also be allowed to autograph your tree. Some of them may someday become famous as well."

So it was that the officers of the army of liberation carved their names on the stately beech with the ceremonial hunting knife, and for generations the monument to their passage could be viewed. As Colonel Shelby and Colonel Sevier made their way to the dance, Isaac laughed, "You set that up very cleverly, John. McDowell and Hampton couldn't have been more surprised."

"I set what up?" John asked.

"Oh, don't pretend that you didn't!"

"I thought you set it up. The tree autographing was certainly your idea."

"And thanks for your magnanimous gesture of letting us put our names up there with the great John Sevier. Some of us may someday become famous as well?"

"Tell me the truth, Isaac, did you or did you not set up that ceremony?" John asked.

"Hell no," Isaac flatly denied it. "Don't you think I have better things to do with my time than to go around playing practical jokes on my fellow officers?"

"Well if I didn't set it up and you didn't, who did?"

"How would I know? Ask your family. It could have been one of your brothers or even old Sam Sherrill."

The dance was a good time for all, but not as exciting as the romantic affairs of the community gatherings back home. The small community of Sevier, North Carolina, had little to offer in the way of charming female companionship to the five hundred man army of the west. Many of the men made an early night of it, choosing instead the warmth of their campfires, a cup of rum, and their reflections on home and family.

John Sevier made his rounds from group to group as was his custom, to visit with and listen to the thoughts and ideas of his men. "Good evening, men," John greeted one of the groups.

"Good evening, Colonel," the men answered in chorus.

"Everyone get enough to eat?" John asked.

"Yes, sir," answered Robert Young, a respected man of the Watauga community. "We are doing well, like a blue hen's chickens!" The men laughed at the quaint expression introduced to them some days ago by Bonny Kate Sevier.

"That's good," John approved. "Well, look who we have here, Robert Young Jr., newly married and answering the call to arms. Robert, I'm proud to have a patriot like you along!"

"Well Colonel, you're newly married too, and I'm mighty proud to have you along!" young Robert answered as the other men laughed.

"It is a sorry way to spend your honeymoon, isn't it, Robert? This fellow Ferguson prevents me from spending my nights with my lovely bride, Bonny Kate. That's the reason I want to give him a whipping he'll never forget!" The camp erupted again in laughter.

"Hey, Colonel," the elder Young said. "I named my rifle 'Sweet Lips' in honor of my wife, Mary. I remember how you did the same thing to honor your wife, Sarah."

"Something about that rifle looks mighty familiar. May I see it?"

"Sure thing, Colonel."

John examined the rifle and discovered that it *was* the original Sweet Lips that had once been his. Bonny Kate had presented it to the Cherokee War Chief Oconostota as a gift without his permission. "How did you come to possess this fine rifle?"

"I took it in trade for a shipment of cast iron cooking utensils I delivered down to Chota," he replied.

"Well, I hope Sweet Lips speaks well for you, Robert," John said, handing the rifle back to its new owner. "Take good care of her!"

"The wife or the rifle?" Mr. Young joked.

John smiled broadly. "Both! Good night, men. Rest well." He left the cheerful campfire circle and walked toward the next group.

Somewhere in the darkness men were singing a song that reminded him of Bonny Kate. "Amazing Grace" was a song he first heard Bonny Kate sing in Pastor Doak's little log church many months ago when he was deeply grieving the loss of Sarah. It was the moment he remembered as the first time he really noticed how beautiful Bonny Kate was. It was the turning point in his recovery, as he wondered why such a gorgeous, talented woman wasn't already married. His investigation into that question had led him through the process of heart healing to a most remarkable conclusion. John listened to the men singing and longed to be with his lovely bride at Mount Pleasant. He wondered how she was passing her evening, what she was thinking about surrounded, as she was, by eight of his ten sweet children. He missed home as never before!

Chapter 12

Quaker Meadows

The reunited patriot armies of Virginia and North Carolina arrived at the stately home of Charles McDowell, at a place on the Catawba River known as Quaker Meadows. The five colonels, McDowell, Sevier, Shelby, Hampton, and Campbell, dismounted at the broad porch, and McDowell's soldiers led the horses away for rest and feed.

Charles McDowell turned to John and said, "Colonel Sevier, I hope McDowell hospitality may repay, in some small measure, the hospitality you have shown me and Mrs. Bowman."

"That's very kind of you, Colonel McDowell," John answered. "I wonder how our ladies are getting along."

Isaac Shelby interrupted. "I wish we had time to enjoy the hospitality, but Major Ferguson is eager, I'm sure, to make our acquaintance. We should move on as soon as the men have rested."

Colonel McDowell ignored Isaac Shelby and continued addressing Colonel Sevier. "I have fresh beef for the men, and they can build their fires with my fence rails."

John smiled at his friend Isaac. "Major Ferguson can wait at least one more day for his undoing."

A messenger arrived from the northeast and rode up to the officers. He saluted Colonel Sevier, the man with the biggest feather in his hat. "Colonel McDowell, I am pleased to report that Colonel Benjamin Cleveland of Wilkes County sends his compliments, sir. He has joined forces with Major Joseph Winston of Surrey County, and they are marching here to join you tonight."

"I'm Colonel McDowell," Charles corrected the messenger.

"Sorry, sir," the messenger saluted again. "I thought the officer with the biggest feather would be the chief commander."

"I'm Lieutenant Colonel John Sevier. The feather was a gift from my lady."

"Very well," Colonel McDowell answered. "Tell Colonel Cleveland to come straight away. We will feed his men their supper when they arrive."

"Very good, sir!" saluted the messenger, and he rode away in the same direction from which he had come.

"There you are, gentlemen. With Cleveland and Winston, the army has increased in size to more than fourteen hundred!" Colonel McDowell smiled with satisfaction.

"That is cause enough for celebration," John said. "Colonel McDowell, you have done a fine job of assembling the finest company of riflemen in the world and enlisting them in the cause of freedom. It is a fitting tribute to your devotion to the cause that so many men have answered your call with their service and their resources."

"In the case of these easterners, I believe it is less a love for McDowell and more a fear of Ferguson that has stirred up the answer to the call," Isaac Shelby remarked to Colonel Campbell. McDowell regarded Shelby sourly but showed remarkable restraint by ignoring his biting comments. In a command where Hampton was openly hostile towards McDowell, where Shelby spoke his mind without regard for feelings, and where Campbell was trying to remain above the Carolina squabbling, only the consummate political skill of John Sevier held the little army together. John sought to understand all sides of the command problem, and his impeccable manners, and effusive compliments delivered sincerely were the only reasons the army had reached the size it had. John wondered how the dynamics would change with the arrival of Colonel Cleveland and Major Winston.

The officers were pleased to meet the indomitable Mrs. McDowell, the mother of Charles and Joseph. It was a rare privilege to meet a woman of so much character and courage, and John Sevier was as charmed by her as she was by him. John was seated beside her at dinner that night, and they enjoyed much pleasant conversation.

After the soup was served, a soldier stepped in to announce the arrival of Colonel Benjamin Cleveland, a tall, 250-pounder, and his companion Major Joseph Winston, a handsome, slender, but serious-looking man. They immediately entered the dining room, and the officers rose to greet them.

"Welcome, gentlemen!" Colonel McDowell greeted them. "You are just in time for dinner."

Benjamin Cleveland's good humor was not to be obscured by either fatigue or hunger. "It should be obvious, Colonel McDowell, that I never miss a meal!" the big man boomed. The officers laughed heartily along with the giant from Wilkes County.

"Gentlemen, allow me to introduce our hostess, my mother, Mrs. McDowell."

"A pleasure, Mrs. McDowell," Cleveland bowed politely. Joseph Winston did likewise.

"I should also like to introduce these officers," Colonel McDowell indicated those standing at their places around the table. "I present my brother, Major Joseph

McDowell, Colonel Isaac Shelby of Sullivan County, Colonel William Campbell of Virginia, and Lieutenant Colonel John Sevier of Washington County." All the men shook hands politely.

"I know all these men from my trips to the west. I was placed in command of Fort Caswell briefly back in the summer of '77," Cleveland said.

"The first time I ever met you, Colonel Cleveland, you were on your way to the Indian towns looking for some horses," John recalled.

"Yes, a group of Indians took everything we had, including our shoes, and we had to walk all the way back to Robertson's store to get refitted. Then we went to the Indian towns. Those chiefs treated me with great courtesy. I told them I was staying and eating with them until I got my horses back. They produced the missing horses in less than a day, and gave me an escort home. It was either that or starvation for those poor red devils." The officers enjoyed a good laugh.

"Gentlemen, let's eat," invited Charles McDowell. The men took their seats, with Mrs. McDowell at one end of the table and her son Charles at the other.

"Mrs. McDowell, I admire your courage to stay here when the British invaded," John said. "My Bonny Kate would have welcomed you at Plum Grove where Mrs. Bowman is staying."

"I thought I could make myself useful and pass along information about the enemy's plans when they used my home as their headquarters," Mrs. McDowell explained. "But they locked me up overnight with the servants and took everything we had to eat. The Tories have been dreadful in their rude treatment of our women and families. Major Ferguson himself sat at this table and boasted about what he would do to any rebels they caught."

"It's the same thing we do to Tories we catch!" Cleveland laughed. "We just have to work faster than the other side, and we will come out all right!"

"We drove our cattle into the hills as a precaution," Charles McDowell said. "Some of my men who stayed behind have been supplying Major Ferguson with beef taken from Tory farms. Apparently His Majesty's troops can't taste the difference!" The officers laughed.

"I have been eager to discuss the matter of a commander for the expedition," Isaac Shelby began. "Now that all these officers are gathered, it might be time..."

"Excuse me, Colonel Shelby," John interrupted and stood up quickly. "But I believe my scouts were to have returned by now, and I need to dispatch additional patrols."

"But John, we were just about to settle some things," Isaac protested.

"I'm afraid you will have to wait until later, Isaac," John spoke quickly and elegantly. "Mrs. McDowell, please excuse me. I shan't be away but a few minutes. We wouldn't want old Mr. Ferguson sneaking up on us tonight."

"Certainly, Colonel Sevier," Mrs. McDowell replied. "Do what you must do."

"Isaac, why don't you attend me while I see to my errand," John invited his friend. "We can make sure your men are not brawling again." John walked to the door and picked up his hat from the table where the men had left their hats. Isaac stood up, bowing to the host and hostess, and followed John out.

In the yard, Isaac found Colonel Sevier gazing out toward the setting sun beyond the western mountains. "Why did you stop me? I was about to get our problem settled."

"Not now, not here, at the man's own dinner table, in front of his mother; that would be poor form, Isaac. Have you no sense of timing?"

"But everyone's here, now. If Ferguson camps at Gilbert Town, that's just a two-day march from here. We need a commander immediately, and McDowell thinks he's going to be it!"

"No, he doesn't. I have been working on Charles all day, but I need more time. You have to back off, Isaac. Besides, we have to consult with Cleveland and persuade him to our point of view. Everyone has to agree that we need a general to lead us into battle."

"A general, you say? Just where are we going to find a general on the eve of battle?"

"Let me and Charles McDowell worry about that," John said confidently. "We'll march in the morning to get away from Quaker Meadows to a place where we can all see things a little clearer. Then we will wrestle out the problem of who will command."

"Wrestle it out?" Isaac wondered what his complicated but creative friend had in mind. "Well all right, we'll do it your way, but why can't you tell me what you are planning to do?"

"Because if I did, it might not work," John said with a grin. "Now, let's get back to that roast beef. I'm hungrier than ever!"

On the porch of the McDowell home, John noticed a wounded man on a stretcher attended by a Wilkes County private. The wounded man shivered and obviously suffered much pain.

"Who is this?" John asked.

"Lieutenant Larkin Cleveland," the private replied. "He was wounded today by Tory bushwhackers as we crossed the Catawba at Lovelady's Ford. We brought him the rest of the way by canoe."

"Lieutenant Cleveland, are you any kin to Colonel Cleveland?"

"His brother," the wounded man responded.

"He's taken a chill on the river. We brought him up here to get him out of the wind."

"This man is in shock," John said. "Take him inside the parlor and let him rest by the fire. Isaac, go fetch Dr. Cozby from my camp. Lieutenant Cleveland has a serious wound in the thigh." Isaac left on his errand as John continued directing the care of wounded man. "Let's get a few more men over here and take him inside the house. He looks a lot like his brother."

"We think the Tories were gunning for Colonel Cleveland and thought Larkin was him," the private said.

"Easy now, boys," John directed as he joined the other stretcher bearers for the lift. "Rest easy, Larkin, I'll take care of you. We lieutenants have to stick together."

The dinner of the officers was interrupted by the arrival of the wounded lieutenant, and Mrs. McDowell pitched right in to make him comfortable. Doctor Cozby cleaned and dressed the wound and prescribed food and rest in the warmth of Mrs. McDowell's parlor.

Later that evening, as Colonel Benjamin Cleveland sat with his brother and reflected on the day's march, Larkin questioned his brother about the lieutenant who had helped him upon his arrival. "Who was that lieutenant who gave all the orders for my care and comfort? He is a fellow who can take charge when he recognizes a need."

"You mean the fellow with the big feather in his hat?"

"Yes, that's the one."

"He's Lieutenant Colonel John Sevier of Washington County."

"He told me he was just a lieutenant," Larkin said with a smile.

"He strikes me as being a very modest man," Benjamin said.

"He gives orders like he's making suggestions, and everybody goes along, even the men of higher rank."

"He's talented but has no experience in regular warfare."

"He has a great heart for his fellow man," Larkin assessed.

"They say he's very handy with the ladies too," Benjamin laughed.

"Benjamin," Larkin became serious. "I know I'm done campaigning for this season, but when you need somebody you can trust like a brother, Sevier would be your man."

Benjamin looked at his brother and knew Larkin's suffering had been intended for him. He became serious too. "I'll remember your wise counsel."

After dinner, John walked back to the Virginia camp with Colonel Campbell. They discussed the operational strategies and the condition of the men and horses. When they got around to the issue of supplies, Colonel Campbell had no complaints. "John, you have to meet my new quartermaster. He has completely reorganized my commissary and made the supply of my troops run smoother than I have ever seen. The man says he's from Watauga, and I bet you know him."

"What's his name?"

"Major Reives," Campbell replied with a grin. Then he spelled the name for John; "R-E-I-V-E-S." When they reached the camp, Campbell spoke to his sentry. "Go get Major Reives and tell him I need to see him."

"Charlotte Robertson was a Reeves, but they don't spell it the same way," John said.

The sentry returned a few minutes later with a big, tall, powerful man, and the officers watched as the man entered the campfire light.

"Papa, what are you doing here?"

"Hello, Sonny, surprised to see me?" Big Val Sevier grinned.

Campbell was quite amused at the father and son reunion. "Major Reives is Sevier spelled backwards. Pretty clever, isn't it John?"

"I'll admit the man is clever, but reckless, irresponsible, insubordinate, and a deserter."

"Now hold on, Johnny, I'm no deserter. I told my commanding officer I was going on the campaign, and he raised no objection."

"Charles Robertson knows about this?"

"Yes, sir, I told him exactly what I was going to do."

"Then I'll court martial him, too. You are under arrest until I figure out what to do with you."

"Hold on, Lieutenant Colonel Sevier," Campbell protested. "You can't just walk into my camp and arrest the best quartermaster I ever had. He is an officer of Virginia, sir, and should be treated as such."

"This man is an imposter, and a deserter from the Washington County home guard. His commission is an honorary one without any validity outside the county."

Colonel Campbell held up his hand and spoke formally. "I hereby reinstate Valentine Sevier Sr. to his original Virginia rank of captain of the militia of Augusta County, by the authority of the Emergency Powers Act. Orderly, bring us some rum; we will drink a toast to Old Dominion!"

"You can't do that," John objected.

"I can drink to old Virginny anytime I damn well please," roared big Bill Campbell.

"I mean you can't reinstate him as a Virginia officer. He's not even a citizen."

"I say once a Virginian, always a Virginian," Campbell declared.

"Papa, how did you persuade Jemima to let you go? I was counting on you to take care of her and Amy's family. You left the ladies of Stony Creek unprotected."

The rum arrived, and Campbell poured out three mugs. "To the ladies of Stony Creek," he said, holding his mug high. Val joined him, and John felt obligated to toast his defenseless stepmother and brother's wife.

"I feel bad about that, Johnny. I told her I was going fox hunting."

"Here's a toast to fox hunting, the greatest sport in Virginia!" Campbell held up his mug and waited for the others. "Don't fall behind here, Johnny. There's plenty of rum, thanks to the best quartermaster Virginia ever saw!" John raised his mug and took another sip.

"That's unforgivable, Papa. Jemima will be worried sick, but I can't spare any men to carry you home."

"Home, we haven't toasted home yet, lads," Campbell shouted. "To Virginia, the sweetest home this side of heaven. Come now, Johnny, drink deep this time. You may have married a North Carolina girl, but your first love was always Virginia!"

"To Virginia," John said as he raised his mug and drank. "Papa, we have to talk about this. You have put me in a very awkward position with regards to the family."

"To family!" Colonel Campbell refilled his mug and raised it high.

"My family is here on this campaign," Val said. "Five sons and two grandsons are my family, and I want to be there when God's glory is revealed to the victorious army of Liberty."

"To Liberty!" Colonel Campbell shouted. "And bring more rum."

"I'll drink to that," Val agreed.

"Major Reives, when you have finished your service to Virginia, you can surrender yourself to the sheriff of Washington County. I expect to see you tomorrow morning in his custody, in my camp." John turned to leave.

"Aren't you going to stay for another round?" Campbell invited.

"I've had enough. Good night, gentlemen."

The next morning was Sunday, the first of October. John rose early and while they ate breakfast, Sam Sherrill drew maps and described the landscape they would see that day on the march. John absorbed it all quickly and asked insightful questions. He questioned Sam about the layout of Gilbert Town as well, where Ferguson was thought to be headquartered. When John fell silent, Sam looked up from the map and saw a faraway look in the eyes of his commander.

"Colonel?" Sam tried to regain his attention.

"God, how I love that woman," John sighed.

"Keep your mind on your work, son. Fourteen hundred men's lives are depending on your intelligence and judgment. Don't allow thoughts of Bonny Kate to cloud that judgment. Isaac Shelby and your brothers are already saying you will take over the command in the next day or two. How are you going to manage that when all five of the other colonels outrank you?"

"I accomplish all my purposes with congeniality."

"Congeniality, what's that?"

"Being polite and friendly to everybody else; it builds trust and once you are trusted, you can pull the strings that need to be pulled. I don't need superior rank to lead the army. I just pull the right strings."

"I hope you know what you are doing."

"I have always been successful at creating alternative realities to the ones that exist in the minds of my adversaries. When sufficient confusion is generated, I simply suggest the best course of action and that's the one they usually accept."

"You have lost me." Sam shook his head. "But I do enjoy watching you work."

"Thank you, Sam. Having you and your sons along provide a great comfort to me, and your knowledge of the land is extremely valuable!"

Sheriff Valentine Sevier steadied his father, Big Val, as they approached the colonel's campfire.

"Look who showed up this morning at my tent," the younger Valentine Sevier announced. "He said he was making a name for himself in the Virginia militia."

"Yes, Val, he was making an assumed name for himself. He was serving as their quartermaster calling himself Major Reives, R-E-I-V-E-S."

"That's Sevier spelled backwards," Big Val explained.

"I understand, Papa," Val said kindly. "What are we going to do with him, John?"

"Sober him up and give him a useful job."

"Aren't we going to send him back home? He was supposed to look after my family at Stony Creek."

"I know, Val. He's let us both down. Amy and Jemima will have to bear the greatest burden of his absence."

"They are resourceful women, and if they need anything they can go to Bonny Kate," the elder Valentine said.

"I wanted to prevent such worries from descending on my Bonny Kate while I was gone. I don't yet know how much of a burden my new wife can bear in these family responsibilities."

"Don't worry, John. Bonny Kate will bear up under any circumstances. After all she is a Sherrill," Sam declared proudly.

"Don't ever get old and useless like me, Mr. Sherrill," Major Val warned his friend. "They will take all your experience, wisdom, and advice and toss it all out with the wash water."

"Papa, don't talk that way," John responded.

"I'm only seventy-seven, strong, clear-minded, steady of nerve, and ready for action. But they say I'm too old."

"Nobody said you were too old," John replied.

"Jemima did when she laughed at my desire to go and forbade me to consider it. Judge Carter did when he wrote out an honorary commission to humor his lieutenant colonel's old man. Then he ordered me to stay out of Major Robertson's way. Major Robertson laughed at me as I showed him my commission and told him I was joining the campaign. The Virginia boys all said I was too old when they ignored my rank and made up nicknames for me like Old-timer, Gramps, and Pops."

John stood up and paced thoughtfully before speaking. "Stand at attention, Major Sevier." His father straightened up to his full stature. "Not one of my officers or men holds his position because of patronage or family connections, and neither shall you. They all are courageous, tenacious fighters who hold rank based on merit. It is just a coincidence that three of the finest officers on my staff just happen to be my two brothers and my beloved father. But when I have to discipline my officers, as I am required to do by military convention, it is especially difficult for me because of the impact that has on my life at home. You are alleged to have deserted your post in the home guard, and that is a serious charge. But since you left with the knowledge and consent, as you say, of Major Robertson, I cannot bring these charges against you without witnesses and formal written complaints. Therefore, I appoint you my quartermaster in chief to coordinate supply efforts with all the other branches of the army. Your position in battle is to defend the supply train. Is that clear?"

"So I will miss all the action?"

"Unless the enemy attacks our supply train, and I will do all in my power to prevent that from happening. Is that clear?"

"Yes, sir. For the next thirty days, you are not my son, you are my colonel," Big Val answered.

"That's correct, Major Sevier. As for the nicknames, you will just have to grin and get used to it. Applying nicknames to their officers is one of the favorite sports in the life of the common soldier."

Isaac Shelby joined John after breakfast and presented a South Carolina scout, dressed in the style of the longhunter, with a reputation for usefulness. "John, this is Anthony Twitty, a man who was a great help to us in finding the enemy at Musgrove's Mill. He is willing to go find Ferguson for us."

"How do you do, Mr. Twitty?" John greeted him with a warm handshake.

"Right pleased to meet you, Colonel Sevier," Twitty replied with a grin. "Colonel Shelby says you are in charge of intelligence in this here camp."

"I have a high regard for intelligence, and my scouts are highly skilled trackers who are well compensated for their trouble. But today I need a local scout who knows upland South Carolina like a native son."

"Colonel Shelby says you need to know the whereabouts of Ferguson."

"Not just his whereabouts, but I need to know everything about his troop strength, artillery, horses, baggage train, his officers, the organization of his army, how he selects a campsite, where he places his pickets, how his scouting service operates, who his camp followers are, who cooks his meals, who does his laundry, and where and with whom he usually sleeps. I especially want to know which way he is headed on a daily basis."

"Whew!" The scout removed his hat respectfully. "You are that rare officer who wants to know it all. And I bet you will use it all in the formulation of your strategy, and the development of your tactics."

"You come highly recommended as one who can gather that kind of information with one stroll through Ferguson's camp."

Twitty grinned. "Getting in is easy; it's the getting out that always presents the challenge."

"Are you up to the challenge, Mr. Twitty?"

"Always, Colonel Sevier," the scout replied.

"What do you need for your journey?"

"Won't take nothing for my journey now. You'll pay for my performance."

"And handsomely," John promised.

The trustworthy scout left the camp with a written pass provided by Colonel Sevier that allowed him to ride by the sentries and pickets.

Chapter 13

South Mountain Gap

The patriot army assembled and made ready to leave Quaker Meadows in fine spirits. John was pleased that no sickness had developed among his men. The health of his regiment was always important to him. He believed in camp cleanliness and moving the camp daily to always provide clean water to his men and horses. The men had been well fed from the start, and that was always a boost to morale. The morning started bright and sunny, but as the soldiers marched to the east, clouds began to overtake them from the west.

John put aside his thoughts of the command problem and began to work on the battle strategy. He had already decided that any actual battle would have to be identical to an Indian fight. His men had the best chance of winning if they were firing their long rifles from behind trees in a wooded area, catching the enemy by surprise in the open. The patriots would have to find the right place for the battle with Ferguson. If the British had field artillery, or were allowed to mass their musketry, or mounted a bayonet charge, the day would be theirs almost certainly. John began an important conversation with Charles McDowell addressing his concerns.

"Colonel McDowell, how many field cannons does Ferguson have?"

"I'm not sure they have any," Colonel McDowell answered.

"How many men do they have at the present time?"

"Fifteen hundred was the last report."

"How old is your last report?"

"It came in the day I rode west to rejoin you."

"That's two days old. How can we rely on information two days old, Charles? Where is Cornwallis this morning?"

"Still at Charlotte, I suppose."

"And what do we know about Tarleton?"

"I told you before I don't know."

"How many men did you send into Ferguson's Camp?"

"Colonel Sevier, my most trusted scouts are well known to their Tory neighbors. I can't risk losing them sending them into Ferguson's camp. Why don't you send your own scouts?"

"I already have, but no reports have come back," John replied. "What about the selection of a battlefield?"

"We will fight them wherever we find them."

"That's not acceptable, Colonel McDowell. My men fight best in the forest, firing from behind trees. It would be good, however, if the enemy were out in the open."

"I hope Mr. Ferguson will oblige you then," Charles said sarcastically.

"Major Ferguson makes mistakes; all military commanders do. We have to catch him making a mistake and time the attack to take full advantage of it. Colonel McDowell, are you up to this?"

"Of course I am. I just recognize the fact that we will win this campaign by pinprick after pinprick, hit and run, hit and run."

"No, sir," John objected. "That is not the deal! Ferguson threatened us and he will be destroyed in one colossal stroke, completely, utterly and decisively, the way we destroy a rabid skunk!"

"It doesn't work that way, Lieutenant Colonel Sevier," Charles said, reminding John of his inferior rank. "I understand your zeal for the cause far exceeds your experience in regular warfare. Still, I think you and your men can provide some useful service in the months to come."

"Not months, Colonel McDowell," John said seriously, "days, and this thing will be over. We came to get Ferguson, and when we are done with him, we have an Indian war waiting for us. The entire frontier is about to explode in bloodshed, and my wife and children are in danger—and so is Mrs. Bowman!"

Charles McDowell was suddenly vulnerable, realizing the danger John described would indeed engulf his dear Mrs. Bowman. "Why didn't you warn me of this earlier?"

"Your invasion of redcoats became a more urgent problem than our troubles with the redskins, but the Indian war is coming whether we are ready for it or not. My men are committed to a thirty-day enlistment, and when that is up they are going home. If this thing is not settled with Ferguson by then, you will be about a thousand men short."

"So Shelby and Campbell would pull out too?"

"The Indian problem is theirs too. We guard a thousand-mile frontier against determined and savage enemies who kill women and children as easily as they kill the armed soldier. I'm sorry, Charles, but that is why you have to trust me to get the Ferguson job done on my schedule, not yours."

"That's impossible!"

"Is it? Campbell doesn't think so; neither does Shelby. And most importantly, the men of the West don't think getting Ferguson is impossible. So I ask you again, Colonel McDowell, are you up to this?"

Charles McDowell took a deep breath and exhaled slowly. "The first night of the march you suggested getting a general officer to bring all these colonels into a unified command. Maybe it's time to propose that to the others."

"Colonel McDowell, I wouldn't know where to find a general officer with the required capabilities in the whole South."

"Leave that to me," McDowell said. "I have the connections to get it done."

"Colonel McDowell, I knew you wouldn't let us down. I'm going to sleep a lot better tonight after you convince the other colonels we need a general to lead us into battle."

A heavy rain commenced that afternoon and lasted all night. The army reached South Mountain Gap and pitched their camp the best they could in the pouring rain. Cook fires could not be started, so the men ate cold whatever they had of parched corn and jerky. Colonel Sevier made certain that each man had a cup of rum dispensed from the common stock, and that raised spirits somewhat. The officers chose not to meet that night, but Sevier and Shelby played cards with Major Winston and Colonel Cleveland in Cleveland's tent. They had an opportunity to describe the command problem to the new members of the expedition, and knowing Colonel McDowell very well, they agreed to cooperate.

Benjamin Cleveland dealt the next hand of cards. "If McDowell steps aside as Colonel Sevier has predicted, then who will command? We could do a lot worse than Charles McDowell as commander."

"John Sevier is the most talented Indian fighter in camp, and the men of the West love him like a father!" Isaac Shelby said.

"This is not going to be anything like fighting Indians," Cleveland replied. "Ferguson has a combined force of British regulars and Tory militias who have been training for the invasion of the southern states since the British came back to Savannah. They love their Patrick Ferguson like a father!"

John Sevier shared an idea. "I thought it would be best if the colonels ran the army like a committee, working together on strategy each evening and then appointing an officer of the day to carry out the execution of the strategy. One day it could be Colonel Campbell, another day we might have Colonel Cleveland, the next, Colonel Shelby, and so on until everybody has had a turn."

"He's joking!" Cleveland bellowed. "Shelby, please tell me he's joking!"

"I never can tell anymore. His arguments have nearly convinced me."

"Good God, man," Cleveland said with a laugh. "Nobody on earth can run an army like that, especially an army made up of all these pop-in-jay colonels. None of you boys have any experience in dealing with someone like Major Ferguson. He's regular army through and through. He's tough, tenacious, stubborn, and he expects the same of his officers! Someone asked earlier if he has any artillery. Damn right he does, and he's got hard-riding, saber-swinging dragoons and infantry skilled in the bayonet charge, too. Have your Indian-fighting citizen soldiers ever faced artillery, sabers, and bayonets, Colonel Sevier?"

"No, but Major Ferguson has never faced the finest riflemen in the world in an Indian-style ambush. He won't know how to deal with something he hasn't seen before."

"The first time we fight him you might get away with that, but he will adapt quickly and soon be beating you at your own game!" Cleveland threw down the ace of spades and took a trick.

"You wasted that ace," Winston pointed out. "Your partner had it with the king."

"Damn it, Sevier's talking is distracting me."

"There's only going to be one battle," John said. "We will annihilate Ferguson the first time we engage and fight to the finish!"

Cleveland breathed deeply, and as he studied Colonel Sevier their eyes met. The big man saw determination, resolve, intelligence, sincerity, and confidence. "He's *not* joking, Colonel Shelby. He actually believes what he is saying!"

"And I believe my men are more than a match for anything Ferguson has in an Indian fight," John affirmed.

"Then all you have to do is maneuver Major Ferguson into an Indian-style fight," Colonel Cleveland said. "I doubt very much he would cooperate with you, Sevier."

Major Joseph Winston had been listening intently to the discussion up to that point. "Colonel Sevier, you are going to need an act of Divine Providence to catch Ferguson in an ambush like you have described."

John smiled. "I always trust in Providence. Are you Presbyterian, Major Winston?"

"I am," he answered.

"So is my wife," John said.

"Don't let him start talking about his wife," Isaac warned.

"She's at home with my eight youngest children. My two eldest sons came with me on the campaign."

Isaac Shelby played his last card of the hand. "Sevier's got ten children, and if we don't keep him away from Bonny Kate, he'll have ten more!" Winston took the final trick.

"You ought to do it like Winston here," Cleveland spoke up. "His wife had three at once just the other day!"

"Triplets?" John asked with surprise.

"Yes," Winston declared proudly, "and all boys!"

"Congratulations, Joe." John poured a portion of rum for each of the officers. "I propose we drink a toast to Mr. and Mrs. Joseph Winston." The officers raised their cups and drank a solemn toast.

Benjamin Cleveland had not done well at cards. All the luck seemed to be running with the family men Sevier and Winston. He stood up and stretched. "It's getting late. We have talked about the situation and all the obstacles we face. If you believe in what you are saying, Colonel Sevier, your first obstacle is Charles McDowell. Handle that one, and we will consider whatever else you have to propose."

"Fair enough," John agreed. He and Isaac left Cleveland's tent and walked through the rain to their own quarters.

"Cleveland is not completely sold on your ideas, John," Isaac observed. "What do we do now?"

"You get some sleep, Isaac," John advised. "We have a lot of politicking to do tomorrow. I'm going to spend some time with my boys before I turn in."

"That's what I like about you, John. You always have time for the common soldier, no matter how lowly his position. I'll see you in the morning."

Captain Jacob Brown approached John as he walked through camp. "Hey, Jack, why don't you come over and give my men a speech. They are pretty discouraged after a pointless march through this miserable rain."

Jacob Brown was an old friend and hunting buddy of John Sevier. He was among the first settlers and had become wealthy in land speculation and betting on the outcomes of frontier games, especially those contests where Bonny Kate Sherrill had been a player.

"We have to keep up their spirits, Captain Brown, and let them know they have nothing to fear. Jacob, you are a betting man and a natural optimist. What is your opinion on our chances at beating Ferguson?"

"I wouldn't take that bet, even if every man in the outfit could shoot like Bonny Kate."

John stopped and looked at his old friend in the flickering light of surrounding campfires. "Care to explain?"

"Nobody commands, nobody respects, nobody trusts; it's as simple as that."

"I'll speak with your men."

"Shall I sound assembly?"

"No, if some of the men are already asleep, let them sleep. I'll talk to the men around the campfire, informally. I want to listen to what they have to say rather than me doing all the talking."

About a dozen men sat huddled around the campfire with blankets pulled up to their necks and the light rain dripping off their broad-brimmed hats. They all knew John Sevier from years of frontier gatherings, hunting trips, and Indian patrols. They knew about his leadership, his family, his recent personal tragedy, and his very recent marriage.

"Good evening, men. It's a little damp out here tonight, so I'll make my remarks brief. When I mustered the Washington County militia, I had no authority to do so. Colonel Carter and I thought it was necessary to defend our country from a certain Major Patrick Ferguson, who had rattled the saber and threatened our homes and families. I believe you all heard Reverend Samuel Doak explain our reasons for making this expedition. I assure you that nothing has changed in our purpose. We came out here to find this fellow Ferguson and defeat him so severely that he will never again entertain a thought to come west and disturb our homes and families."

The men listened attentively, and other men who could hear the voice of their colonel came out of their tents and listened too.

"You will no doubt hear from other divisions of this army about certain differences of opinion among the colonels as to strategy, tactics, and methods. Do not be discouraged by any of this kind of talk. If it is the will of Divine Providence that we accomplish our purpose, we *will* accomplish it. If not, I will give you leave to go home when your enlistments are up."

"Colonel, we keep hearing about the British having cannons, cavalry, and the bayonet charge," one of the men spoke up. "How do we stand and fight against such things without losing all our men?"

"We have horses, long rifles, and tomahawks," John answered. "And we all know how to use them. As a strategy we have to make the enemy fight our kind of fight, where our weapons work better than theirs."

"Those Wilkes County and Burke County boys can march around in neat little squares and form lines and ranks in the field. We can't do any of that."

"They do that to enforce discipline and keep order in camp," John explained. "It also comes in handy for fighting out in the open on foot. Well, I'm not interested in that kind of fight, and I will do everything I can to give every man a tree for his shield and an open target for his rifle. Those are the proper tactics for Indian play."

The men thought about his tactics and nodded with satisfaction.

One of the younger men rehearsed his moves out loud. "Colonel, if I'm hiding behind a tree and the enemy comes at me with the bayonet, he has to make a choice which side of the tree to attack me from. I'll just go around the other side and hit him with the tomahawk."

"That's how it works," John replied. "And if we do get caught out in the open, lay down, for Pete's sake. You can reload and keep up a very destructive fire from the prone position, and the enemy will have a much harder time targeting you."

There was a large group gathered by the time John finished, and all of them were more confident in their expectations and in John's proposed tactics. The colonel smiled and wished the men a good night. He turned and saluted Captain Brown and left the company.

John went back to his own campfire and found the men who gave him the most comfort, Captain Robert Sevier, Captain Val Sevier, Major Val Sevier, and Privates Joseph Sevier, James Sevier, Sam Sherrill Sr., Sam Sherrill Jr., George Sherrill, and Adam Sherrill.

"You boys get anything to eat tonight?" John asked.

Sam grinned. "Sherrills and Seviers won't ever go hungry, Colonel. We had some leftovers from the big dinner last night that we packed up. We also passed some apple trees along the way."

"You made out better than I did, then," John said.

"Do you have the details worked out yet?" Robert Sevier asked.

"No, McDowell still thinks that we can go against Ferguson like a regular army, out in the open," he replied in disgust. "The others doubt that we can catch Ferguson in the right terrain for Indian play, so they don't pay any attention to my proposals."

"Don't they understand the obvious when it's as plain as the nose on your face?" Major Val Sevier said.

"Obviously not," John frowned. "I'm afraid the principles of regular warfare will get too many of us killed."

"That's not my idea of a fun-filled foxhunt!" Major Sevier said.

"Why don't they listen to you, John?" Robert asked.

"They say I have no experience. Without experience I get no respect, and without respect I have no influence."

"Nonsense, you've had plenty of experience that would make many a man respect you!" Sam Sherrill said.

John looked at Sam. "Give us an example."

"You had a town named after you," James Sevier said with a laugh.

"Yes, that was an unusual experience, but not the kind that earns great respect," John said.

"What about your experience with women?" Sam asked. "You have been married to two of the most remarkable women in America! And that's the kind of experience that most men can only dream about."

John laughed. "I think my colleagues are looking for military experience!"

"A successful marriage is greatly respected and envied by every man," Sam said.

"And not too different from military experience," Major Val added.

"You just need some help showing off your wealth of experience," Sam suggested.

"If only I could get through to the ranks of bright young officers below my fellow colonels, I think they would at least consider my tactics!"

The silence that followed allowed John to think of something else to discuss with

Charles McDowell. It allowed Sam Sherrill to hatch an idea that might help John get the attention he wanted. John left his kinsmen to seek a conversation with Colonel McDowell.

"Boys, I have an idea," Sam Sherrill said. "Colonel Sevier wants the attention, respect, and trust of the other officers so he can persuade them toward his ideas about how to fight this war; is that right?"

"That's what I heard him say," Robert Sevier affirmed.

"And the reason he needs their attention, respect, and trust is to save the many lives of our men from the waste of regular warfare; is that right?"

"That's why it is so important to all of us," Captain Val agreed.

Sam took a deep breath and laid out a plan for the men of the family that was so simple and yet so brilliant that even John Sevier would have to appreciate it—someday.

Chapter 14

The Quest for a General

At the patriot camp in South Mountain Gap, the rain continued all night and the next morning as well. The officers decided not to proceed with the day's march. The colonels had a more important reason to delay than the weather, and it was about command. None of the officers had any clear authority to take charge of the overall operation. In camp that wasn't a problem, but on the battlefield it could be disastrous.

Colonel Sevier started early by hosting a breakfast for the other colonels, again stressing the need for a battle strategy that would give his men the best advantage for success by ambush. Colonel McDowell insisted on a pitched battle in the open fields near Gilbert Town. A poll of the other colonels found only Shelby openly supporting John's idea, with Campbell, Cleveland, and Hampton skeptical that Ferguson could be lured into an ambush. McDowell left the breakfast more certain than ever that a respected general with about a thousand more troops would be needed to get the job done. He hoped that Colonel James Williams and Colonel Thomas Sumter, both of South Carolina, could be called upon to join the army of the mountaineers and supply the needed men. Then he would need his friend Governor Nash to help him find a general. It would likely take a week of travel to and from Hillsborough to arrange it all. Charles McDowell felt that his own influence with the governor would be the single most important ingredient to the expedition's success.

After breakfast John and Isaac began a tour of the camp to discuss the situation with every officer down to lieutenant in an attempt to present Sevier's ideas and generate support among the junior officers. As John Sevier was introduced to companies and men of the Virginia division and the eastern Carolina counties, he was generally warmly greeted with grins and looks of admiration. His natural outgoing nature responded to their attentions and cemented strong relationships. John and Isaac both were surprised at how eagerly the men had listened to John's battle plan.

"It's him, the fellow we heard about this morning!" a captain of Colonel Cleveland's regiment announced to all his men.

"Are you sure?" someone asked.

"They said it was the colonel with the big feather in his hat! It's him for sure!"

John smiled modestly. "Yes, I'm Colonel John Sevier, of Washington County."

The men crowded around and listened as he described how a battle could be fought from ambush without risking too many lives of the smaller attacking force. When he finished the men grinned.

"Colonel Sevier, we want to thank you for coming over and talking to us today," the captain said. "I think my men have some questions, if you would humor us."

"Certainly," John said.

"Is it true you rescued Bonny Kate Sherrill from the Indians at Watauga Fort?" asked one of the soldiers.

"I believe Miss Sherrill had the character and the ability to scale the wall herself, but I consider it my good fortune to have been present to assist her and at the same time make her acquaintance."

"Is it true you named her Bonny Kate after your favorite tavern song, *The Bonny Lass of Fisherow*?" another soldier questioned.

John laughed, "That's what I called her then, and what I still call her."

"So you really did marry the same girl you rescued?"

"I most certainly did!" John smiled.

"Is it true you broke the bed on your wedding night?"

John reddened, but maintained his polite composure. "Where did you hear about that?"

"Some fellows that say they are relatives of Bonny Kate's have been telling that all over camp, Colonel. Is it true?"

"The fellows that told it ought to know better. Please excuse me, gentlemen."

The men seemed pleased with his answers as he stormed away looking for his Sherrill in-laws. Isaac trailed after him laughing. "You broke the bed?"

"No, not exactly."

"Then *she* broke the bed?"

John stopped and confronted his friend. "A gentleman does not discuss the private details of marital relations."

"But John, this is brilliant! Did you see how they hung on your every word, how they hungered to make your acquaintance? You held their attention like I've never seen any man do. I think by now they would go along with anything the great lover had to say. It's your romantic passion that makes you so attractive as a leader. This is a stroke of genius!"

"What? Do you think I would spread malicious gossip about my own wife, just to gain attention for my opinions on how we ought to conduct a military campaign?"

Isaac shrugged. "Why not? If the end justifies the means, it worked beautifully!

Now you have men in every part of the army who desire nothing more than to be counted among the friends of John Sevier, the country's greatest lover!"

"Shut up," John snapped.

"Did the Sherrills do this?"

"If they did, I'm going to demote the whole lot of them!"

"The Sherrills are already privates; you can't bust them any lower."

"Oh, if word of this ever got back to poor Bonny Kate, how could she stand the embarrassment?"

"John, she's done things that if all were known, would eternally embarrass the both of you. I think she'll manage this one just fine."

A fight broke out in the camp, but John and Isaac were near enough to stop it. "You men break it up," John ordered. "Get back to your companies and stay there. I know it's hard to sit around camp all day waiting for the rain to pass, but we can't tolerate this breakdown of discipline."

"Yes, sir," the men answered. They obeyed John immediately without any question or explanation.

"John, are we ready for some organization and discipline now?" Isaac asked.

"I think everyone is about ready. Isaac, I want you to bring up the question of a commander for the expedition at the officer's staff meeting tonight."

"It's about time!" Isaac rejoiced.

"Yes, Isaac, it's about the *right* time. Now if you will excuse me, I have the unpleasant task of disciplining my father-in-law and his co-conspirators for sabotaging my reputation."

"Don't be too hard on the old man. He may have done you a lot more good than harm!"

That evening the officers gathered around a campfire for a staff meeting that included all the colonels, majors, and company captains. Colonel Charles McDowell had a large audience to work with when he called the meeting to order.

"Gentlemen, let's get started," Colonel McDowell said. "I want to begin by thanking you all for assembling your various commands into a considerable force in a very short time. You have answered the call to arms for the state of North Carolina and in defense of the interests of Virginia to repel the invader from our soil. I especially want to thank Colonel Sevier for hosting my people at Watauga when our own lands were overrun. He has shown his friendship repeatedly over the past several weeks with much good advice." The officers cheered John and clapped in appreciation for his recently enhanced reputation.

John bowed in acknowledgement.

"We have decided a plan of operations is necessary to maintain order and ensure our success," McDowell said.

"We need a commander," Isaac shouted. "Someone needs the authority over all of our forces, and it must be someone we can all eagerly follow into battle." The officers expressed their support for Isaac's proposal.

John stepped forward and motioned for quiet. "Gentlemen please, let's proceed in an orderly fashion. Colonel McDowell has an idea to share. Let's hear him out." Charles McDowell looked at John, who encouraged him to continue.

"It has been suggested that we send a formal request for General Gates to appoint a general officer to command us," McDowell continued.

"Just as long as it's not Gates himself," Colonel Cleveland bellowed. The men all laughed in derision, having no respect for the shameful behavior General Gates exhibited after the disaster at Camden.

Charles McDowell had great difficulty getting them quiet again. "Please, gentlemen! Gentlemen, let's come to order!" Finally the noise subsided enough for him to continue. "Having a general appointed is the only way to unify our command."

Isaac Shelby interrupted again. "A messenger to Hillsborough would take three days. Finding a general like Davidson or Morgan and dispatching him here could take up to a week! We can't wait that long! Even now the Indians prepare to attack our homes and families on the frontier. Colonel Sevier, you, of all people, should feel the great urgency."

"Indeed I do," John said in a voice strong and full of authority. He moved toward McDowell to deliver his message. "I left my beautiful bride and my dear little children in the most imminent danger. I risked their very lives to come to the rescue of North Carolina. If any harm comes to my beloved ones because of devotion to my country, I could never forgive myself. Yes, I feel the need for urgency in concluding this business. So I say to all of you, decide quickly, and let Colonel McDowell leave immediately for Hillsborough to procure us a general!"

"What's this?" Isaac asked in surprise. "Did you say Colonel McDowell is going to Hillsborough?"

John bowed politely and yielded the floor back to Colonel McDowell. Then he returned to his place at the edge of the circle.

"That's correct," McDowell said. "Colonel Sevier has convinced me that only my influence with the governor and with General Gates can accomplish the speedy appointment of a proper general. Therefore I'm going to Hillsborough myself." There was a moment of silence. Then the officers cheered him heartily and warmly applauded. Colonel McDowell acknowledged their affection until John finally brought the assembly back to order.

"Gentlemen, we have drafted a letter for Colonel McDowell to carry to General Gates, and I read it now for your approval: *From Rutherford County, Camp near Gilbert*

Town, October 4, 1780, to General Gates. Sir, we have collected at this place about fifteen hundred good men, drawn from Washington, Surry, Wilkes, Burke of North Carolina, and Washington County, Virginia, and expect to be joined in a few days by Colonel Williams of South Carolina with about a thousand more. As we have at this place called out militia without any order from the executives of our different states, and with a view of expelling out of this part of the country the enemy, we think such a body of men worthy of your attention and would request you to send a general officer immediately to take the command of such troops as may embody in this quarter. Our troops being militia, and but little acquainted with discipline, we would wish him to be a gentleman of address, and be able to keep a proper discipline without disgusting the soldiery..."

The men laughed. Colonel Cleveland stood up and strutted his two hundred fifty pounds. "Do you think Gates will understand we don't want him?"

"I don't think we could make it any plainer," John said with a grin. "I continue the letter: *Every assistance in our power shall be given the officer you may think proper to take command of us. It is the wish of such of us as are acquainted with General Davidson and Colonel Morgan (if in service) that one of these gentlemen may be appointed to this command. We are in great need of ammunition and hope you will endeavor to have us properly furnished. Colonel McDowell will wait on you with this, who can inform you of the present situation of the enemy, and such other particulars respecting our troops as you may think necessary. Your most obedient and very able servants* ... and now I need you gentlemen to come forward and sign your names."

The colonels lined up to sign the letter. Charles McDowell put on his riding cloak, his spurs, and his hat. When they finished signing, John folded the letter, put it in a courier pouch, and handed it to Colonel McDowell. The other officers shook his hand, thanked him, and wished him Godspeed. He mounted his horse and waved his hat as the men cheered him again. Then Colonel Charles McDowell disappeared into the darkness, followed by a small escort detachment.

John Sevier quickly found Joseph McDowell and took him aside. "Major McDowell, I need to explain some things that went on here tonight."

Joseph looked John in the eye, "No need to explain, Colonel Sevier. I know my brother Charles better than anyone, and I know why none of the others wanted him to command. I am grateful to you for the kind way you arranged the change in command."

John smiled and shook his hand. "Then the Burke County boys are still with us?"

"We are with you all the way!" Major McDowell grinned. "I like your idea about the Indian play. It's the only way we can win."

"Thank you, Joe!" John Sevier returned to the center of the council circle and motioned for quiet. "Gentlemen, there is one more item of business to consider tonight. Colonel Shelby, I believe you have a motion for us to consider."

"Yes, Colonel Sevier. Our last intelligence indicates that Ferguson waits at Gilbert Town. If that is the case, we shall most likely meet him tomorrow. I move that we elect a commander to lead us into battle...that is, until General Gates sees fit to send us a general." The other officers laughed, all knowing that they were now completely on their own.

"If Ferguson is so near, let's be up and at him!" proposed the impetuous Colonel Cleveland. "I second the motion to elect a commander!" The men all expressed their approval.

"We seem to be unanimous," John declared.

"What about a man so universally admired, both in the east and the west!" Cleveland shouted. "Colonel John Sevier!"

The men began chanting, "Sevier...Sevier...Sevier...Sevier!"

John rose to speak and quieted the crowd. "Thank you, Colonel Cleveland, but I decline that honor. I must remain free to detach my regiment and fly to the relief of the over-mountain settlements at the first report of Indian attacks. Besides that, because of a political aberration in my home county, I am, after all, only a humble Lieutenant Colonel."

The men were somewhat disappointed that their new darling, a man known to all as "Lover Boy," had declined the post, but understood his concerns for home and family. They appreciated his desire to return to his threatened home, especially when they thought of the legendary charms of the woman that awaited him there. It was completely understandable, noble, and excusable.

Then Isaac Shelby stood up. "Gentlemen, there is a fine commander among us, a man of good sense, and sincerely devoted to the cause. In fact, he traveled the farthest to be here and commands by far the largest contingent of the army. I nominate Colonel William Campbell."

"I'll second that!" Cleveland shouted.

"Hold on just a minute," Campbell shouted. "May I confer privately with Colonel Shelby?"

"Certainly, Colonel Campbell," John allowed.

"You too, Colonel Sevier," Campbell said.

John addressed the group politely. "If you gentlemen would excuse us? Does anyone know any campfire songs?" The men laughed as Colonels Campbell, Shelby, and Sevier walked a short distance from the council circle.

"I ask that my name be withdrawn," Campbell said. "I have the same concerns for the security of the western settlements as Colonel Sevier. If you gentlemen will remember, I was a reluctant participant in this campaign from the start. Why not let Shelby command?"

"I am the youngest colonel, and was the most outspoken against McDowell's leadership," Isaac explained. "It would offend the McDowell party and the men of Burke County further to have me succeed him."

"Please, Colonel Campbell, Isaac and I have done our parts to make this thing work. Now we need your help. These Carolinians are ambitious men, squabbling on their home turf for personal gain and glory. They will gamble with the lives of our men if we don't elect a strong leader with the good of the whole country at heart."

"I agree with your reasoning," Campbell responded.

"We can still meet in council each evening and make the strategic decisions together," Isaac offered. "We just need a strong leader to enforce discipline and carry out our plans each day."

"Besides, it's just until McDowell returns with the general," John said with a grin, which brought smiles to the other two colonels.

"I see there's no use arguing with you. I'll accept the post."

John clapped the Virginian on the shoulder as Isaac shook his hand. They all returned to the council circle to complete the election of the new commander. William Campbell was humbled by the trust placed in him by the officers and men of the western army, made up entirely of citizen soldiers, armed only with tomahawks, and their own odd assortment of hunting rifles.

Chapter 15

The Work of the Scouts

Augusta, Georgia, was occupied by British and Tory forces and used as a supply depot for channeling muskets and ammunition to Creek and Cherokee war parties. In exchange for the weapons, the British expected their Indian allies to make war on the white settlers of the frontier, to harass and distract the rebel governments of the American states so a British invasion of the South could roll unopposed north through the Carolinas into the Commonwealth of Virginia. Colonel Elijah Clarke recognized the British strategy and decided to stop it if he could. Clarke's determined little army of Georgia patriots attacked Augusta and laid siege to it for three days beginning on September 14, 1780. Clarke's attack very nearly succeeded in overcoming the Tory occupation forces of Colonel Thomas Brown until a band of Chickamauga Indians arrived at Augusta for the promised gift of British muskets and ammunition. With the arrival of the Indians, and a Tory relief column from South Carolina, Elijah Clarke was forced to evacuate the patriots of upcountry Georgia. Colonel Clarke allowed his force of three hundred men to return to their homes and collect their wives and children. Colonel Clarke, like a modern-day Moses, led over seven hundred people north out of Georgia into the wilderness, seeking a place of safety. Trekking far to the West to avoid British forces occupying South Carolina, Colonel Clarke's Georgia refugees came under vicious attacks from the Indians of that mountainous country.

Major Patrick Ferguson, the British commander at Gilbert Town, had received information on September twenty-fourth that Clarke's Georgia rebels were moving in his direction. He was alerted to be on the lookout for them and apprehend them if possible. Major Ferguson had swept away all resistance in western North Carolina as far as the passes of the wild mountain country. He felt confident enough to not only send patrols towards the southwest to locate the Georgians, but to also grant furloughs to many of the Carolina Tories in camp to allow them visits home to their families. On the twenty-seventh Major Ferguson moved his camp from Gilbert Town to the Green River region, hoping to intercept Clarke if they could find him.

In the evening, Sevier's scout Anthony Twitty sat on his blanket eating a cold meal when he heard someone moving through the brush not far from his position. All his senses strained to make out the nature of the threat. He took another drink from his canteen and washed down his mouthful of parched corn. He felt for his loaded pistol, moved it closer to his right leg, and waited. When the sound of the other human being was close enough for a sure shot, he called out. "Whig, Tory, or Indian, don't make no difference to me. I never let politics spoil a good dinner in a pretty place like this."

The bushes parted and revealed the grinning face of another bearded frontiersman with his rifle at the ready. Twitty made the split-second decision not to shoot the fellow just yet.

"Care for some dinner? Good nourishing food is hard to come by, so far from civilization."

"That's right neighborly," the man answered. He uncocked his rifle and stepped over to where Twitty was and sat down. "I reckon I know you, now that I see you up close."

"How's that?" Twitty laid out some jerky and parched corn for the man to eat.

"Musgrove's Mill; you was a Carolina scout with Colonel Shelby. I rode with Major Candler in Colonel Clarke's brigade."

"Then I reckon we's both patriots. I'm Anthony Twitty." Both men breathed a sigh of relief as they shook hands.

"I'm Lewis Musick."

"I thought you Georgia boys went back to Georgia."

"Georgia is lost for good," Musick reported sadly. "We nearly took Augusta from the damn Tories, but the Indians showed up and drove us away. Then a British relief column came to Augusta, and there was nothing for Colonel Clarke to do but evacuate the whole region."

"Evacuate?"

"Yes," Musick said. "Men, women, and children marched off into the wilderness to escape Tory cruelty, but the Indians were even worse to us, all the way through north Georgia. Our people have suffered terribly."

"Where are they going?"

"Colonel Clarke knows about a place where there is peace and security from Tory atrocities because the leaders up there are good patriots and have used the rule of law to suppress the enemies of mankind. They have a strong army, a home guard that constantly watches for Indian trouble, and a generous colonel who is famous for his good works and hospitality."

"What is this place? Maybe I've heard of it."

"It's called Washington County, and it's away across the mountains in a beautiful land of milk and honey. If only our women and children could reach that heavenly place, our men would sacrifice everything to defend it from the Indians."

"I know a little about that place," Twitty said. "I'm scouting for that generous colonel you mentioned. His name is John Sevier."

"Yes, that's the name our women and children pray for every day. He promises to be the salvation of our people."

"They won't find Colonel Sevier at home. He is now at the head of his army in the east, hunting down Major Ferguson."

"We learned that the other day from a scout named Ed Hampton," Musick replied. "Colonel Clarke sent Major Candler and thirty of our best men to join Colonel Sevier and render whatever service we can to the glorious cause. I am working as scout for Major Candler."

"Good, why don't you send Major Candler on to Gilbert Town to meet Colonel Sevier, and join me in a scout of Ferguson's camp? I could use your help."

"Much obliged," Lewis Musick agreed. "I'm eager for that kind of action."

Early in the morning at Green River, Major Ferguson's breakfast was delayed as his cook struggled to start the fire after a night of hard rain. Major Ferguson went out to drill his troops and receive the returns of the daily muster rolls. Two hunters came into camp with a sack of fresh killed quail. The cook looked up at the two scraggly-looking back country bumpkins and noticed their homespun clothing, hunting rifles, and leather accessories for living off the land. They might be powerful, tough, independent men who seemed at ease coming and going as they pleased, but they rarely made good soldiers. These two looked hungry and took great interest in what was cooking. One even opened the porridge pot.

"Here, you fellows leave that alone," the cook protested. "That's Major Ferguson's breakfast."

Anthony Twitty stepped back. "The major's breakfast is it? Did you hear that, Mister Musick?"

"I did, Mister Twitty. Major Ferguson's breakfast is what he said."

"Why aren't you two at muster? They are taking roll. You will be missed."

"We're on special duty," Musick answered.

"So move on. The major doesn't care to have people such as you in officer's camp. And he will return soon."

"I reckon we better move on then," Twitty said calmly.

The scouts helped themselves to some fresh baked biscuits and walked away. As they ate, they strolled around counting the horses, tents, and wagons. They surveyed the field pieces in the artillery park and watched the companies drilling in the field.

"Nice of them boys to line up like that so we can get an accurate count for Colonel Sevier," Twitty remarked.

"Hello," a woman's voice spoke up behind the men. They turned to see a pretty little redheaded woman walking up from the river with a basket of wash.

The men removed their hats politely. "Good morning, ma'am."

"Are you the new volunteers?" She smiled as she looked them over.

"No ma'am, we are just a couple of old scouts. This is Mr. Twitty, and I'm Mr. Musick."

"I'm Virginia Sal," she replied. "If you need to speak with Major Ferguson, he will be coming back in a few minutes. He's the one on the white horse out there. He's a fine gentleman."

"We recognized him immediately as an officer of quality," Anthony said.

The lady smiled as she watched the gallant commander of the king's western forces. "I think I'm in love with him, but I haven't told him yet."

"Your secret is safe with us, ma'am," Lewis said, and he smiled at the lady.

She laughed. "I should take greater care with my confidences, shouldn't I?"

"Yes, ma'am, you should," agreed Anthony. "We brought some quails for the cook to fry up. Would you deliver them for us?" He offered the sack to the lady.

"Certainly," she said cheerfully. She took the sack of game and walked toward the cook fires. She happened to glance back at the strangers, but they were gone so quickly and quietly that they reminded her of spirits in the fairy stories.

The drums on the drill field rolled and the fifes blew a shrill tune as the soldiers turned in their ranks and files, marching into the road at the far side of the open ground. Men were packing up the baggage wagons and pulling out, following the horse-drawn artillery. "Come on," Twitty urged his friend. "Colonel Sevier wants to know which way the redcoats are headed today." They mounted their horses and rode down to the Green River, crossing at a place unknown to most travelers on the main road. Anthony Twitty flew through the woods with Lewis Musick right behind him for about ten minutes and drew in his horse at a burned out farmhouse.

"Where are we now?" asked Musick.

"Twitty's Ford they used to call it, before the troubles broke out." Anthony looked at Lewis with a sad expression. "This was my home where I grew up."

"Where are your folks?"

"Buried nearby; my sisters married, and my brothers are scattered all over the country in various units of the service."

"I'm sorry for you, Mr. Twitty," Lewis said. "Take all the time you need for a memorial."

Twitty laughed. "It won't take long. We just need to stay out of sight. If my guess is correct, we should see some redcoat cavalry soon."

Musick steadied his horse at the sound of approaching riders. As Twitty had predicted a troop of redcoats splashed across the ford and rode on past the ruins and east on an overgrown farm road.

"What does that tell us?" Musick asked.

"Those riders were Ferguson's flank guards. There's only one reason they would come through here. Ferguson took the left fork of the river road. He is heading east."

Twitty wheeled about and rode back the way they had come. When they reached the Green River at the redcoat camp, Musick again questioned his companion. "What are we doing here again?"

"I still haven't had my breakfast. Let's capture that cook and see if he knows anything."

Musick and Twitty observed the camp until it was almost empty. The cook was among the last to leave, because it had been necessary for him to allow his cast iron cookware to cool down and be washed. The scouts prepared a little ambush for the cook and his servant along the road.

Twitty jumped out from behind the foliage of a fallen tree and grabbed the reins of the servant's horse. Musick stepped out with his gun leveled at the British cook. "Halt! Don't make a move or I'll shoot."

"Damned if you're not a rebel!"

"Damned if I won't shoot you," Musick answered. "Now get down!" The cook climbed down as ordered. The servant put the spurs to his horse and pulled the reins away from Twitty. He made a clean getaway with the pots and pans clanging as he went.

Twitty grinned, "We don't need him anyway. We got the one with the major's breakfast. Let's get off the main road." They walked their prisoner some distance from the road along a quiet country lane into the woods where they had left their horses.

"You won't get away with this," the cook said in a loud voice. "Major Ferguson will send search parties after me day and night until I am found."

"Shut up," Lewis prodded him roughly.

"Major Ferguson is a bear when he hasn't had his breakfast. He's probably sending out the dragoons right now to accomplish my rescue."

"Shut up, I say," Lewis repeated.

"Help! Help!" the cook screamed. "These rebel buggers have captured me, and I am supposed to serve the major his breakfast."

Anthony Twitty grabbed the cook's shirt and pulled a hunting knife to the startled man's throat. "Tell me what the Major is doing so far to the west!"

"I won't tell you," the cook said. He struggled as Lewis Musick tied his hands securely behind his back.

"Use your tongue, man, for liberty's sake, or we'll it fry in the pan with the Major's breakfast."

"Barbarian!"

"Answer quickly. Why is the Major so far west?" Twitty persisted, pressing the knife persuasively at the soft flesh of the captive.

"He was looking for Georgia rebels escaping to the north," the cook revealed.

"Where is he going next?"

"I don't know. Now let me go!"

"Sit down and shut up," Twitty ordered. Lewis Musick gagged the cook and tied him securely to a tree. The two scouts enjoyed a leisurely breakfast compliments of Major Ferguson and rifled through the cook's belongings. Anthony found a writing kit and wrote a letter to Major Ferguson which he shared with Musick.

"To Major Patrick Ferguson: Dear Sir, We captured this Red Coat trespassing on our land and determined that he belongs to you. We are convinced by his arguments that you cannot well dispense with such an important personage in the conduct of the retreat of your army. Therefore we have paroled the fellow and trust to your kindness that you will restore him to his butlership without reprimand for his waywardness. Your most obedient servant, Yankee Doodle."

"Sounds good," Musick approved. "Here's something I found in the saddlebag that might be of interest to your colonel." He handed Twitty a piece of heavy paper.

"This is a recent notice: *To the inhabitants of North Carolina*...Yep, the colonel's going to be mighty interested in this. Mister Musick, take the gag off that fellow. I have more questions." Musick did as he was told.

"What do you know about this notice to the inhabitants of North Carolina?" Twitty asked.

"I operate a small press that Major Ferguson carries with him in the baggage train. He sent those notices to be posted in every town in North Carolina. The friends of the king will turn out everywhere to drive back the barbarians."

"Where did Ferguson learn about these backwater men?"

"Two of their deserters came into camp. They were vile, detestable men wanting to be paid for their information. Major Ferguson clapped them in irons after they told all they knew."

Twitty folded the paper and stuffed it into his hunting bag. "Mr. Musick, we have some traveling to do. Release that redcoat and let's be on our way!"

Chapter 16

Gilbert Town

On the morning of October 3, 1780, the patriot army prepared to break camp at South Mountain Gap. Colonel John Sevier had called a special assembly of all the men to hear the plans of their officers and listen to some inspiring speeches. Lieutenants were sent throughout the camp, calling the men to assemble at the center of camp. "Old Round-About is fixing to give us a speech! Come to assembly!" the lieutenants announced.

Sam Sherrill and Major Val Sevier caught up with their popular leader and walked with him to the assembly.

"Who is Old Round-About?" Sam asked. He still felt hurt that Colonel Sevier had scolded him so roundly for his efforts to promote the colonel's reputation.

"That's the affectionate name the soldiers use for Colonel Cleveland," John answered. "The same way they now call *me* Old Lover Boy!"

Sam winced. "I told you I was sorry."

"You were too harsh with us yesterday, Johnny," Major Val told his son. "I remember a certain colonel of Washington County telling me that applying nicknames to their officers is one of the favorite sports in the dreary life of the common soldier. I advise you to grin and get used to it."

John stopped and grinned at the two older men. "Thank you, Major Sevier. I have always cherished your wise and well-considered advice."

"But you have not always taken it."

"True, but today is a new day, filled with promise. I forgive all wrongs done me in the last couple of days by well-meaning kinsmen. And I will grin and get used to the nickname."

"There Mr. Sherrill, all is forgiven," Major Val declared. "I told you my Johnny never holds a grudge."

"The last two days of rain and camp idleness have hurt morale," John continued. "So I asked Colonel Cleveland to speak a few words of encouragement this morning as we prepare to march."

"This ought to be good," Sam said as the trio continued their brisk walk to the assembly.

When they reached the circle of men, John made his way to the center where all the officers had gathered. Colonel Benjamin Cleveland, the big man, began speaking as soon as John gave him the signal.

"Now, my brave fellows, I have come to tell you the news. The enemy is at hand, and we must up and at them. Now is the time for every man of you to do his country a priceless service...such as shall lead your children to exult in the fact that their fathers were the conquerors of Ferguson. When the pinch comes I shall be with you, but if any of you shrink from sharing in the battle and the glory, you can now have the opportunity of backing out and leaving...and you shall have a few minutes for considering the matter." Colonel Cleveland scanned the faces of the men as he paced around the inner circumference of the circle.

Major Joseph McDowell stepped forward to speak next. "What kind of story will you, who back out, have to relate when you get back home?" Fighting Joe McDowell let his words sink in during the next moment of silence.

Isaac Shelby stepped forward next. "You who desire to decline, will, when the word is given, march three paces to the rear!" Isaac allowed another moment to pass as the men quietly talked among themselves.

Colonel Campbell stepped forward and with the voice of ultimate authority gave the order, "Make your decisions now!"

Nobody moved. They looked around and grinned. Then they proudly applauded each other's bravery. Isaac Shelby called for their attention again, and they quieted down for him to speak. "Men, when we encounter the enemy, don't wait for the word of command. Let each one of you be your own officer and do the best you can. If in the woods, shelter yourself and give them Indian play. The moment the enemy gives way, be on the alert and strictly obey orders." Isaac stepped back and nodded to Colonel Campbell.

"This is the day you've been waiting for," shouted Campbell, the acknowledged new commander of all. "We march within the hour. Let's move!"

The men cheered and sprung into action. Colonel McDowell, before his departure, had acquired several large barrels of whiskey to use as a special treat for the men at an appropriate time. These he left in the care of Colonel Cleveland. Old Round-About figured with spirits running so high, this morning would be an appropriate time to distribute the distilled spirits. As the men completed their preparations to march, they stopped by Cleveland's camp and raised a mug to each of the colonels of the command, and as if that weren't sufficient, they toasted the majors and captains, too. About the time the men were down to toasting their lieutenants, Old Lover Boy Sevier,

Isaac Shelby, and William Campbell got wind of the festivities and tried to put a stop to it. But the damage was already done.

"What were you thinking?" Colonel Sevier scolded Colonel Cleveland. "Today was to be the day of battle!"

"Exactly the point. I've got these boys raring to go! Hell, they'd tangle with lions bare-handed if we ordered them to!"

John could tell Colonel Round-About had received a sufficient share of his own generosity. He turned away from the giant in disgust.

"John, these men will be good for nothing by midafternoon!" Isaac said. "It's irresponsible to get the men in such a condition with Ferguson just a few miles away."

"More than irresponsible, Isaac, it's dangerous!"

Colonel Campbell was not amused either. "McDowell's whiskey and Cleveland's poor judgment have ruined our day!"

"Welcome to your new command, Colonel Campbell," John said with a grin.

"Is it too late to back out?"

"Yes, sir. We have already promised the men a march to glory, and a march they shall have. With your permission, Colonel, I would suggest we march anyway, but no man will be allowed to sit a horse. Everyone walks to clear their heads and get the whiskey out of their systems. We won't arrive at Gilbert Town until tomorrow, but by then we will all be in much better shape."

"Sounds like a good plan," Colonel Campbell agreed.

The army marched down Cane Creek on foot, leading their horses, slowly advancing on Gilbert Town. About mid-afternoon the sober officers stopped the progress of their staggering army and ordered the men to eat a cold meal and sleep in the formation of their companies on their firearms. That way they would be ready immediately if attacked during the night. Colonel Sevier posted the pickets at a safe distance to warn of any approaching danger.

Better progress was made that day by Colonel Charles McDowell, miles away to the east on his way to Hillsborough to get the mountaineers a general. At Flint Mountain he and his two companions found a camp of South Carolina patriots and were led by a picket guard up to the commander's tent. Colonel William Hill and Edward Lacey were there to meet them. Colonel Hill appeared to be suffering from a shoulder wound.

The guard saluted and announced, "These men showed up on the perimeter this morning. This one claims to be Colonel Charles McDowell of Burke County."

"Good morning, sir," Colonel Hill saluted, but he eyed the stranger warily. "Now what would Colonel Charles McDowell be doing riding east with the enemy invading the western counties?"

"Who am I addressing, if you please?" Colonel McDowell responded.

"Excuse me, sir. I'm Colonel William Hill, and this is Colonel Edward Lacey. We are the South Carolina battalion of Colonel Thomas Sumter."

"Is Colonel Sumter in camp?"

"He's gone to Hillsborough to consult with Governor Rutledge," Colonel Hill replied. "Where is your command, Colonel McDowell?"

"I left them in capable hands. I have over fifteen hundred men under the various commands of six different militia colonels. We have decided to request a general officer to command us, so I'm on my way to Hillsborough to deliver that request to General Gates. If your men want to see some action, you ought to join us."

"We are eager for action, that's for sure," Colonel Hill spoke up with great interest despite the pain of his shoulder wound. "But since we don't know you, Colonel, I'm obliged to verify your story before I can let you proceed. Would you join us for breakfast?"

"We need a good breakfast. We rode all night and are ready for a rest."

Colonel Hill turned to the guard and gave him an order, "Go bring in Colonel Williams. He can identify Charles McDowell."

"Colonel James Williams?" McDowell asked.

"Yes, sir."

"Why, he served in my command back in the summer," McDowell said. "He can vouch for me."

"I just need you identified, sir," Colonel Hill said sternly. "I'm afraid Colonel Williams hasn't the credibility to vouch for anybody."

"I don't understand," McDowell responded.

"Colonel Williams was our commissary officer back in July," Colonel Hill explained. "When he went out west to join your command, he stole all our provisions and left Sumter's battalion to starve! Then Williams claimed the credit for the victory at Musgrove's Mill when he delivered the prisoners to Hillsborough. For that big lie Governor Rutledge gave him a general's commission."

"Why, that old scoundrel," McDowell exclaimed. "Shelby and Clarke deserve equally the credit for the victory at Musgrove's Mill, and they were all under *my* command."

Colonel Lacey delivered a plate of food to McDowell and said, "You can understand Colonel Sumter's indignation when *General* Williams presented his commission and tried to assume command of all the South Carolina militiamen."

"I can imagine," Colonel McDowell replied.

Colonel Hill continued, "Well Tom Sumter, that Fighting Gamecock, threw the rascal out of camp and gave strict orders for us not to pay any attention whatsoever to *General* Williams. Then he hurried right up to Hillsborough to clear the air with Governor Rutledge."

"So Colonel Williams is trying to take over the command of your outfit?"

"Yes, he's camped out yonder with about seventy recruits, the sorriest bunch of brigands you ever saw," Colonel Hill said. "He can come over and identify you, but then I want the pleasure of kicking him out of camp again."

Charles McDowell laughed. "It sounds like he deserves whatever he gets."

"Didn't you say *you* were looking for a general to lead your army?" Colonel Lacey grinned. "It just so happens we have a spare general you can have."

"I'm sorry, Colonel Lacey, but General Williams wouldn't last a day trying to command that tough bunch of wild mountaineers." Colonel McDowell ate his breakfast hurriedly, thinking about his long ride to Hillsborough. He decided his testimony might help Colonel Sumter clear up the injustices done by Colonel Williams.

The sentries escorted Colonel Williams into camp. Colonel McDowell put down his breakfast plate and stood beside Colonels Lacey and Hill.

Williams sported the uniform of his new rank. "Well, if it ain't Colonel Charles McDowell. I thought you were hiding out in the over-mountain country."

"I went there to get help. I brought back a thousand mountain men to hunt down Ferguson. Cleveland and others have assembled five hundred more."

"Where is your force, Colonel McDowell?" Williams questioned.

"They are waiting for me at South Mountain Gap, planning an attack on Ferguson's headquarters at Gilbert Town. I'm on my way to confer with General Gates about appointing a general and consolidating our western command into a better organized army."

"I'll organize them for you, Colonel McDowell," Williams offered. "I'm newly commissioned as a general by the state of South Carolina, and I have the authorization of Governor Nash to recruit an army in North Carolina."

"That will be all, Colonel Williams. You may return to your camp," Colonel Hill dismissed him rudely.

"Colonel Hill, come to your senses, man! McDowell's mountain men will not find Ferguson at Gilbert Town. The Tories have fallen back to Fort Ninety Six. We all need to join forces and pursue them to upland South Carolina."

"That will be all, Colonel Williams!" Hill repeated more forcefully.

"What about you, Colonel Lacey?"

"I take my orders from Colonel Sumter," Lacey replied. "I suggest you work it out with him when he returns from Hillsborough."

"And I take my orders direct from Governor Rutledge with a general's commission. The people of South Carolina deserve better results than they have been getting up to now."

"Good day, Colonel Williams," Colonel Hill said sternly. He turned his back on Williams and returned to his tent.

Williams glared at Lacey as he too turned away. "What do you say, McDowell? I have the authority and the ability to take command of your western army and whip them into shape."

"You would be whipping Colonel Isaac Shelby," McDowell warned.

"I can handle that whipper-snapper."

"And Colonel William Campbell of Virginia," McDowell added.

"No Virginian can equal my courage in battle," Williams boasted.

"Then there's John Sevier," McDowell said.

"Who has ever heard of John Sevier?"

"John Sevier's men revere him and will follow him anywhere he leads them. They obey his every command and carry out his every wish. He is a man of great discernment who can recognize the obvious, detect the fraudulent, and steer clear of the ambush. He will not place his men under a command that does not suit his purposes."

"I'll deal with him and make him like it," Williams replied. "Let's be up and going, Colonel McDowell."

"Like I said, I'm going to Hillsborough to consult with General Gates and Governor Nash."

Colonel Hill returned with his pistol in his good hand and leveled the piece at Colonel Williams. "Leave this camp at once, Colonel Williams."

"Address me as General Williams."

"Get out, you bastard general! That's how we will address you; General Bastard! You lied to secure an illegitimate commission."

Williams turned and marched away without another word.

"What's got into him?" Charles McDowell wondered.

Colonel Hill uncocked his pistol and tucked it into his belt. "I suspect he plans to plunder Tory property in upland South Carolina while the Tories are away with Ferguson invading North Carolina. He just needs more men to accomplish that."

McDowell breathed deeply and took a last drink of the coffee he had been provided. "Gentlemen, thank you for the breakfast. With your leave, I will be on my way."

"Godspeed you, sir," Colonel Hill said. "If you happen to see Colonel Sumter, tell him to hurry back. Williams keeps trying to steal our men with promises of abundant food and regular pay. It's hard to maintain discipline with such lies flying about."

"I'll tell him that," McDowell promised. "Good day, sirs." Charles McDowell nodded to both Colonel Hill and Colonel Lacey and climbed back on his horse. He and his escorts continued on their way.

On the afternoon of October 4, 1780, Colonels Campbell, Sevier, Shelby, and Cleveland stopped their horses in the little hamlet known as Gilbert Town.

"Mr. Ferguson seems to be long gone," John observed.

"This is a curious thing," Isaac mused.

"Do you suppose Ferguson knows about our approach and is circling around to trap us?" Colonel Campbell asked.

"We can't rule that out, Colonel Campbell," John said.

A farmer walked out to them from his house in the hamlet. "Good day, gentlemen. If you have come to join Ferguson's army, you are too late. Major Ferguson marched out to capture a band of rebels from Georgia."

"Is that right?" John acted surprised.

"Yes, sir. If you catch up with him, I'm sure you will see some action," the man replied.

"I'm sure you are correct," John replied. "When did Major Ferguson pull out?"

"It's been about a week ago," the farmer replied. "But I'm sure if you leave today you can still join up with him."

"No, I think we will just camp here for the night," John said dismounting. "The day we find Major Ferguson we will have to have more daylight left and a brilliant battle strategy firmly fixed in our minds."

The farmer became uncomfortable with the realization that the military host before him were not the friends of King George.

"Then, you men are not looking for Ferguson to join him?"

Isaac leaned down on his saddle horn to address the farmer. "We came to whip his ass."

"Major Ferguson called you barbarian bandits," the man said nervously.

John Sevier laughed aloud. "Sir, you will find us a much better sort than the men that follow Ferguson. We will pay for any provisions we require."

"I can't trust anybody's promises these days," the farmer complained. "Ferguson sent out some Carolina boys to round up rebel cattle. Ferguson's men feasted mightily, until they learned they'd been tricked into eating Tory beef."

"Yankee Doodle strikes again!" John declared as the patriots laughed. "Can there be any doubt now who will win this war?"

"Gentlemen, pass the word to your companies," Colonel Campbell ordered. "We will stay here in Gilbert Town to eat and get some rest, at least until we find out where Ferguson went."

"I'll post the pickets," John volunteered. "No one will enter or leave this town without me knowing it." The officers dispersed to attend to their men.

The late afternoon sun was a welcome change from the recent days of rain. The men tried to dry out their clothing and gear the best they could after they set up their camp. The officers gathered under a spreading oak tree to discuss what to do next. John Sevier's pickets escorted in a young scout named Jonathan Hampton, the son of Colonel Andrew Hampton. Father and son had a warm reunion before Colonel Hampton introduced his boy to the other colonels in the council.

"Jonathan, do you know the whereabouts of Major Ferguson?" John Sevier asked.

"He headed south from here a week ago and camped at Green River," Jonathan reported.

"What have you learned of his intentions?"

"Don't know that, Colonel Sevier. Some of the country folk say he's trying to catch Colonel Clarke and his Georgians."

"That doesn't make sense, if he knows we are chasing him. I would be inclined to believe he is laying a trap for us," Isaac Shelby reasoned.

"It does seem strange that every patriot militia in North Carolina can find their way into camp to join us, and Major Ferguson acts like he is completely unaware of our presence," John said with a puzzled expression.

The officers thanked young Hampton and returned to the shade of the tree where they continued to confer. It wasn't long before young Joseph Sevier rode up and saluted his father.

"What is it, Joseph?" Colonel Sevier asked.

"We stopped a force of thirty men at the picket line. They say they are here to join up with Sevier. Their leader is Major William Candler."

"Am I supposed to know this William Candler?" John asked.

"The Georgia boys," Isaac Shelby identified the unit. "William Candler is one of Elijah Clarke's men."

"All right, Joseph, bring them in," John said with a grin. "The more the merrier."

"Yes, sir," Joseph saluted and turned to carry out his father's order.

The Georgians rode into camp with much rejoicing all around. Riding among the Georgia troops John noticed his scout Anthony Twitty. When John caught the eye of the scout, Twitty grinned and saluted him. "Isaac, look who rode in with our friends from Georgia."

Isaac saw Twitty and turned to John. "I told you he was a resourceful man."

"Let's interview him in private before we bring him before the other officers. I need to question him thoroughly and take time to assess what he's learned."

When Twitty dismounted, he walked over to address Colonel Sevier quietly.

"Have a good trip, Mr. Twitty?" John asked.

"Very productive, Colonel Sevier."

"We will confer privately, in due time," John promised.

"I appreciate that, Colonel. I don't do public speaking. In my line of work it is *not* an advantage to become well known."

Isaac Shelby introduced the officers of the Georgia company, and they were warmly welcomed. As William Candler shook John Sevier's hand, he grinned.

"It's a pleasure to finally meet you, Colonel Sevier. We have heard glowing reports about your management of Washington County."

"I've heard much about the bravery of Colonel Clarke's men at Musgrove's Mill," John said.

"I hope the report of our more recent activities will be just as pleasing to you, sir," Major Candler said.

Colonel Campbell called to order the officer's council, and the discussions resumed. "Let's hear your report, Major Candler. Tell us how you found us, and where the devil is Ferguson?"

"Well, sir, we lost Augusta to a superior force of British regulars, Tories, and their Indian allies. Colonel Clarke decided to remove our women and children to a place of safety, so we headed north through Indian territory with hopes of finding refuge at Colonel Sevier's place. After weeks of hardship and Indian attacks, some of Colonel Sevier's mountain scouts found us and directed us to safety. At that time Colonel Clarke sent thirty men, all he could spare, to find Colonel Sevier and offer whatever assistance we could. Meanwhile Colonel Clarke and the Georgia families should be arriving at the Sevier farm any day now. Colonel Sevier, I hope our Georgia families are no burden to your wife while you are away."

"She'll take care of them," John predicted confidently. "Don't worry about a thing."

"Thank you, sir," Major Candler said.

"Tell us about Ferguson," Isaac Shelby said.

"We haven't seen any sign of Ferguson. All we saw was Indians."

"That confirms my suspicions," Isaac announced. "Ferguson's move to the southwest was a ruse to cover his attempt to rejoin Cornwallis in Charlotte."

"Or he will continue his move due south for the safety of Fort Ninety Six," Colonel Campbell theorized. "Gentlemen, I suggest we rest and resupply tonight, and in the morning we'll march south and see what we can find."

The meeting broke up, and the officers dispersed. John and Isaac went off to look over some horses at the edge of camp, and they were joined by Anthony Twitty and Lewis Musick.

"Colonel, this here is my assistant, Lewis Musick. He was with me at Ferguson's camp." John shook hands with the assistant scout. The two scouts laid out their entire knowledge of Ferguson's army, including the artillery, the horses, the eighteen baggage wagons, the fifteen hundred men, fifteen hundred stands of muskets, the bayonets, the training drills, the washing of Ferguson's laundry, and firsthand information about what the major eats for breakfast.

"So where is Ferguson?" John asked when he had absorbed all the details.

"We saw him leave Denard's Ford on Green River the morning of the second, heading south, but the army took the fork in the road leading east."

"What does that mean?" John asked.

"I'd say by the look of it, Major Ferguson is running scared."

"Why do you say that?"

"Because of this," Twitty said, removing the paper notice from his hunting bag and presenting it to Sevier and Shelby.

"Well done, Mr. Twitty! Isaac, pay this man double what we agreed, for he has delivered double what we expected!"

"Thank you, Colonel Sevier!" Twitty and Musick smiled with pride.

"Let's show this to the others right away, Isaac," John said, and they went looking for Colonel Campbell to reconvene the officers' meeting.

Isaac addressed the assembled officers. "Listen to this notice from Ferguson printed on October first:

To the Inhabitants of North Carolina. Gentlemen: Unless you wish to be eat up by an inundation of barbarians, who have begun by murdering an unarmed son before the aged father and afterwards lopped off his arms, and who by their shocking cruelties and irregularities give the best proof of their cowardice and want of discipline; I say, if you wish to be pinioned, robbed, and murdered, and see your wives and daughters, in four days, abused by the dregs of mankind—in short, if you wish or deserve to live and bear the name of men, grasp your arms in a moment and run to camp. The backwater men have crossed the mountains; McDowell, Hampton, Shelby, and Cleveland are at their head, so that you know what you have to depend upon. If you choose to be pissed upon forever and ever by a set of mongrels, say so at once and let your women turn their backs upon you and look out for real men to protect them. Signed, Pat Ferguson, Major 71st Regiment."

"He can't possibly be referring to us, can he?" Colonel Cleveland reacted.

"This sort of language is preposterous!" Colonel Hampton declared. "Ferguson is no gentleman. He's a liar and a dishonorable scoundrel."

"Well, I'm glad he didn't include my name on that list," Colonel Campbell said with mock relief.

"Neither you nor Colonel Sevier even got a mention." Isaac laughed.

"That shows the state of his intelligence," Sevier observed. "His force is no larger than ours at the present time. If we can just maneuver him into an Indian-style ambush, we could finish this business quickly."

"Still too risky," Campbell cautioned. "We could sure use Sumter's thousand-man South Carolina regiment that McDowell told us about. If they would just show up, I would order the attack on Ferguson immediately!"

"I say we go now, before the fox escapes," John proposed.

"Take it easy, Jack," Campbell said. "Let us not rush to our destruction before we have had our dinner and a good night's sleep."

Chapter 17

Peril on the Frontier

Monday morning, the second day of October, Bonny Kate rose early for some quiet Bible reading and reflection as she watched the sunrise from her bench on the porch at Plum Grove. Betsy Sevier, her lovely twelve-year-old stepdaughter, joined her on the bench and rested her head on Bonny Kate's shoulder. Bonny Kate looked down at her sweet face and planted a kiss on the girl's forehead. Betsy lifted her blue eyes to look into Bonny Kate's and said, "Good morning, Mother."

"Good morning, Betsy." No greater compliment could have been paid the stepmother than to hear those precious words. "Did my stirring around wake you, my dear?"

"I was already awake. I was thinking about all the things that have happened to us since Mother died, how you came and helped us, how Father stayed home from the summer campaign because of you, and now that you and he are married, he has gone away again."

"These are extraordinary times, Betsy. I have great faith the men will be victorious and bring peace and freedom back to our land."

Betsy reached over and placed her hand on the Bible on Bonny Kate's lap. "Your faith comes from here, doesn't it?"

"Yes it does, Betsy. So much of what I have to offer the world comes from the pages of this Bible."

"Like the fancy words you use, and the strong, confident way of speaking that make the men stand back and respect you?"

"Yes, Betsy. My manner of speaking and my vocabulary both come from my familiarity with, and regular reading of, the Word of God."

"Mama didn't read us those Bible stories the way you do."

"Please don't compare me to your dear mother, for I will always come up short in every measure."

Betsy laughed. "You *are* taller than she was."

"I might have married earlier if I hadn't been so tall. Most men won't look twice at a tall woman."

"I'm glad you didn't marry anyone else."

"Me too." Bonny Kate hugged her stepdaughter.

"Bonny Kate, I want to be able to stand tall and speak out like you do. I so admire that."

"Then start here," she advised, placing the Bible on Betsy's lap. Betsy sat up straight. "Now dear girl, close your eyes, and open the Bible to whatever page it opens to naturally. Point to the page and open your eyes."

Betsy did as she was told. "Proverbs, Chapter 31," she announced.

"Yes, that's a good passage. Now, read your lesson for today."

Betsy began reading in a sweet and clear voice. "These are the words of King Lemuel, the prophecy that his mother taught him. What, my son? And what, the son of my womb? And what, the son of my vows? Give not thy strength unto women, nor thy ways to that which destroyeth kings. It is not for kings, O Lemuel, it is not for kings to drink wine; nor for princes strong drink: Lest they drink, and forget the law, and pervert the judgment of any of the afflicted. Give strong drink unto him that is ready to perish, and wine unto those that be of heavy hearts. Let him drink, and forget his poverty, and remember his misery no more. Open thy mouth for the dumb in the cause of all such as are appointed to destruction. Open thy mouth, judge righteously, and plead the cause of the poor and needy."

"Slow down now, and pronounce every word you read," Bonny Kate advised.

Betsy continued. "Who can find a virtuous woman? For her price *is* far above rubies. The heart of her husband doth safely trust in her, so that he shall have no need of spoil. She will do him good and not evil all the days of her life. She seeketh wool, and flax, and worketh willingly with her hands. She is like the merchants' ships; she bringeth her food from afar. She riseth also while it is yet night, and giveth meat to her household and a portion to her maidens. She considereth a field, and buyeth it: with the fruit of her hands she planteth a vineyard. She girdeth her loins with strength, and strengtheneth her arms. She perceiveth that her merchandise *is* good: her candle goeth not out by night. She layeth her hands to the spindle, and her hands hold the distaff. She stretcheth out her hand to the poor; yea, she reacheth forth her hands to the needy. She is not afraid of the snow for her household: for all her household *are* clothed with scarlet. She maketh herself coverings of tapestry; her clothing *is* silk and purple. Her husband is known in the gates, when he sitteth among the elders of the land. She maketh fine linen, and selleth *it*; and delivereth girdles unto the merchant. Strength and honour *are* her clothing; and she shall rejoice in time to come. She openeth her mouth with wisdom; and in her tongue *is* the law of kindness. She looketh well to the ways of her household, and eateth not the bread of idleness. Her children arise up, and call her blessed; her husband *also*, and he praiseth her. Many daughters have done virtuously, but thou excellest them all. Favour *is* deceitful, and beauty *is* vain: *but* a woman *that* feareth the LORD, she shall be praised. Give her of the fruit of her hands; and let her own works praise her in the gates." Betsy stopped when she reached the end of the chapter. "This describes you!"

"I always thought of your mother whenever I read it," Bonny Kate laughed as she stood up. "And someday, soon, that will be you. I'm leaving you in charge of Plum Grove today, because right after breakfast I'm riding over to Salem Church to visit Esther Doak."

"Yes, ma'am," Betsy answered.

Bonny Kate let the horse run on the five-mile ride to visit Reverend Doak's wife, Esther. She knew her visit would be appreciated, because it was the pastor's practice to always visit the sick and needy on Mondays, leaving Esther, daughter Julia, and baby John Whitfield home alone. She left the Jonesborough road at the place they always turned west to follow a buffalo trail and pass through the gap at the head of Onion Creek. Bonny Kate admired a parcel of land her brother Adam was planning to buy for a farm on Onion Creek until the campaign came along and disrupted his plans. She followed the trail along the creek until she came to the valley that led north to Reverend Doak's Salem Church.

The north wind brought the scent of wood smoke as she began the last mile of the journey at a full gallop. Soon she could see a column of smoke that indicated a larger fire burning than that required by any form of home industry. Bonny Kate became concerned. As she entered the clearing where the log church and pastor's humble cabin stood, she saw the Doak family belongings ransacked and strewn about the yard and the cabin well involved in flames. There was no sign of life. She jumped off her horse, ran up to the porch, and peered in through the open door. She could see through the cabin to the open rear door, but could not enter because of the thick smoke. "Indians!" she concluded by the look of things. She immediately returned to her horse and gained the saddle. If the Indians were still nearby she wanted to be mounted and ready to fly as soon as they showed their grotesque war-painted faces. She guided her horse to the rear of the cabin.

"Esther?" she called. "Esther, where are you? Please, dear Lord, protect Esther and her children!" Bonny Kate looked all around warily, feeling the heat from the flames. Suddenly, at the edge of the clearing, the bushes parted and Esther appeared holding her baby close to her.

"Bonny Kate, take cover!" she called in a hoarse whisper. "The Indians are still nearby!"

Bonny Kate rode over to her friend. "Then we shouldn't stay here! Come, get on my horse." Esther came out of her hiding place. Bonny Kate received the baby and helped Esther climb up behind her. "Where's Julia?"

"She went visiting about with her papa this morning. I pray they are safe!"

Bonny Kate urged her horse to a gallop and away they went along the valley trail toward Onion Creek. Bonny Kate returned home the same route she had taken earlier, hoping to avoid any contact with the dusky fellows of Chickamauga. "How many of them were there, Esther?" she called over her shoulder.

"Eight or ten," Esther answered. "They came up mighty quick, but I was quicker!"

As soon as the women crossed the gap and landed on the Jonesborough road, they came up with a company of light horse led by Charles Robertson. "Major Robertson," Bonny Kate hailed the leader of the troopers. "Ten Indians burned Esther's cabin at Salem Church this morning. No telling where they might show up next!"

Major Robertson turned in his saddle and called forward Isaac Thomas, a well-known Indian trader and dear friend to John Sevier. Bonny Kate immediately felt safe to have such a trusted expert on Indian ways available at that moment to render assistance.

"Howdy, Mrs. Sevier," Mr. Thomas greeted her. "Hello, Mrs. Doak. Did you say it was ten Indians?"

"Yes, Mr. Thomas," Esther answered. "They ransacked my house and set fire to it, but Mr. Doak will be pleased to learn they didn't burn the church."

"We will track them down and stop them if we can," Mr. Thomas assured the ladies. "They didn't harm anybody, did they?"

"No, sir. I thank the Lord I saw them coming in time."

"Take two dozen of the men and leave us a small escort to see the ladies to safety," Charles Robertson directed. Isaac Thomas selected his detachment and led them over the Onion Creek gap. Bonny Kate continued her progress home with Charles Robertson and his men.

"I need to send word to my husband that I'm all right," Esther said.

"Where is he this morning, Mrs. Doak?" Major Robertson asked.

"He left in the direction of Jonesborough."

"We'll find him," Robertson assured her, and he detached two more men north to Jonesborough to find the worthy pastor.

Several minutes later Bonny Kate's rescue party arrived at Plum Grove, where they dismounted and secured their horses to the hitching rail near the house. Grace Bowman, Eliza Miller, and Mary Sherrill rose from chairs on the porch to meet them.

"Indians burned Esther's house!" Bonny Kate announced.

"Oh, how awful!" Mary Sherrill exclaimed. "Where is Pastor Doak?"

"He rode into Jonesborough this morning," Esther replied. "I was there alone with the baby when the Indians came. I saw them coming and ran out the back door. We hid in the woods until Bonny Kate came to the rescue."

"Oh, you poor dear," Mary Sherrill said. "Come into the house." The pastor's lady was gently escorted into the house by Grace and Mary.

Major Robertson turned to Bonny Kate. "Mrs. Sevier, I have grave concerns about the safety of our community."

"I know, Major Robertson, but I will not set the example of cowering within the walls of a fort while the enemy lays waste to our homes. The wife of John Sevier..."

"Knows no fear... yes, ma'am, I've heard that before," Charles interrupted. "But you have to understand, I can't protect every family in the community with the few men I have."

Bonny Kate stood straight and tall, her black hair tumbling out from under her lace cap. "I understand that, and I do not blame you for what happened today. I believe those who burned Esther's place were a small party of marauders and not the persistently rumored invasion."

"Still, I could do my job better if everyone were gathered into the forts."

"And my job is here on this plantation until my dear husband comes home the victor. I do hope that happens soon."

"It has been my experience in military matters that anything that can go wrong, will go wrong."

"Stop that! I won't hear that kind of talk!"

"Then I suppose you should know the rest of the news," Charles continued. "I received a letter from my nephew, James Robertson, colonel of the Cumberland settlements."

"I know him well. He is one of my husband's dearest friends."

"James reports that the Cumberland settlements are besieged by Indians and are now desperately short of powder and shot. The crops waste in the fields because they can't get out and harvest. They appeal to Colonel Sevier hoping he has the means at hand to save the lives of every man, woman, and child on the western frontier. Bonny Kate, you have a new emergency to deal with, my dear. I hope you are equal to the task of making some hard, life and death decisions."

Bonny Kate looked at the Major in charge of the Washington County militia. "Why don't you send him the help he needs?"

"It is not my decision, it's yours."

"Why do you say that?"

Robertson sat in a porch chair and took a deep breath. "Colonel Sevier supplied the North Carolina enterprise with all the powder and shot we had. All the production of Mary Patton's powder mill and Sevier's lead mine for the next two months was bought up, and paid for in full, for delivery...to Mrs. John Sevier."

"Me?"

"Yes ma'am, you own it all."

"Why would John have done that?" She was confused.

"Jack has a strange way of doing things sometimes," Charles laughed. "He probably figured the county couldn't afford to buy the supplies so he paid for the purchases himself, and probably borrowed the money to do it. If Mrs. Patton and Mr. Embree can produce the goods fast enough, you may have the means of salvation in your hands!"

"Then I shall send those supplies to Fort Nashborough as soon as I receive them!"

Charles shook his head. "I don't recommend that, ma'am. We have a desperate need for those munitions right here, in defense of Washington County."

"But the people at Fort Nashborough are friends and kin. My dear friend Ann Robertson Johnston is there!"

"Well, like I said, it's your decision. I'm glad I don't have to choose, but I urge you to consider carefully and choose wisely. Give me your answer tomorrow. That's a hell of a responsibility for Jack to put on a twenty-something-year-old girl, without even telling her."

"Oh dear, much is required of those to whom much is given."

Charles Robertson and his militiamen mounted their horses and rode down the lane to continue their patrol.

A brilliant sunset illuminated the cabin at Plum Grove with a golden orange light, as warm as the glow of the fireplace. Bonny Kate and the children cleared away the dishes from a satisfying supper. Esther Doak, Grace Bowman, Eliza Miller, and Mary Sherrill seemed lost in their thoughts and concerns of the day as Reverend Samuel Doak stood at the door gazing at the colors of the sunset.

"Pastor Doak, it is a rare privilege to have as our guest, a man so learned in the Word of God," Bonny Kate said. "Won't you please lead us in our evening worship?"

"I'd be delighted, Mrs. Sevier. I'm feeling so blessed that Esther and the baby escaped, and that you came to the rescue today."

"Yes, sir, we all have much for which to be thankful. But please include in your prayers James Robertson's people of the Cumberland, the soldiers on the campaign we love so much, and the difficult decisions I face here at home."

"I will." The pastor walked to the fireplace, picked up three candles from the mantle, and placed them on the table. He lit the first candle. "In the Name of God, the Father, Almighty..." Then he lit the second candle. "And in the name of the son, Christ the Savior..." He lit the third candle. "And in the name of the Holy Spirit, the Comforter, our Advocate, and unfailing Companion, hear now the Word of the Lord," he pronounced solemnly. Then he sat at the table and opened the Bible.

"Now this is the scripture concerning Christ the Lord, and it clearly tells us his purpose in the earth." Pastor Doak took a deep breath and began reading with voice clear and strong. "And he came to Nazareth, where he had been brought up: and, as his custom was, he went into the synagogue on the Sabbath day, and stood up for to read. And there was delivered unto him the book of the prophet Esaias. And when he had opened the book, he found the place where it was written, *The Spirit of the Lord is upon me, because he hath anointed me to preach the gospel to the poor; he hath sent me to heal the brokenhearted, to preach deliverance to the captives, and recovering of sight to the blind, to set at liberty them that are bruised, to preach the acceptable year of the Lord.* And he closed the book, and he gave it again to the minister, and sat down. And the eyes of all them that were in the synagogue were fastened on him. And he began to say unto them, *This day is this scripture fulfilled in your ears.* This is the Word of the Lord."

The ladies answered in unison, "Thanks be to God."

Sam Doak looked up from the Bible. "Let us pray. Heavenly Father, we thank you for sending Jesus to live and work among the peoples of the earth. We thank you for the great price he paid, even his very life, his blood, to free us from our sins. We claim the blood of Jesus to wash away our sins and protect us from the evil of the enemy in every perilous day. Come Holy Spirit, and stay beside us, to teach us, and to guide us in our daily walk with Jesus. Be with the soldiers in far Carolina, and with the settlers of far Cumberland, and with the wives, and the mothers, and the children who need your special protection. Also send your spirit among the enemy to confound their evil designs and correct their understanding of the truth. For you are the God of truth, the God of liberty, the God of righteousness, and the God of your people. In the name above all other names, Christ Jesus, we pray. Amen."

"Amen," the women answered.

Several minutes passed as the words of the pastor were remembered, appreciated, and taken to heart by the women and children, resident and refugee in Bonny Kate's cabin.

The hostess at long last rose to speak. "Thank you, Pastor Doak. It is clear to me now what I must do. Dear friends, James Robertson and the people at Fort Nashborough have requested our help. They need powder and shot immediately to be donated from our dangerously depleted supplies. I realize that such action on my part would endanger the people of Washington County and Sullivan County in two circumstances. If the Indians attack us, or if our army is defeated and forced to retreat back here, pursued by the British, we would be powerless to defend ourselves. But right now, it is within my power to save the people of Fort Nashborough and supply them enough to get them through the winter."

"Major Robertson has advised against that, Bonny Kate," Pastor Doak warned.

"Do you agree with him?" She earnestly sought the advice of the only mature male in the group.

"Not necessarily," the pastor said.

"What action would you advise, Pastor Doak?"

"I advise you to follow the leading of the Holy Spirit, and go on faith," he replied.

Bonny Kate felt encouraged. "I'm going to do just that, and trust to Divine Providence that we soon receive good news from the East or some great sign of favor in answer to our prayers. James Robertson will have his powder and shot."

Grace Bowman looked up at Bonny Kate and said, "Amen!"

Everyone joined in and repeated, "Amen!"

"Bonny Kate, I think we should sing a hymn!" Mary Sherrill suggested.

"Yes," Bonny Kate agreed. "Mama, you brought the fiddles from home. You and Esther can play, and the rest of us will all sing along."

Chapter 18

The Georgia Refugees

Bonny Kate bathed little Nancy in the great room of Plum Grove. Nancy splashed the bath water in her oak tub, soaking her stepmother's apron. Grace Bowman worked nearby dressing her little daughter for the day, and Mary Sherrill did the same thing for her year-old son Aquila. Eliza Miller cared for her two little girls, Sarah and Mary. Esther Doak was feeding her son, John Whitfield, his breakfast, and Kesiah Sevier held her three-month-old Valentine against her shoulder trying to get him to burp.

"This place is starting to look like a baby mill!" Bonny Kate declared.

Grace Bowman laughed. "This *is* a baby mill, Bonny Kate. We are grinding out the next generation of citizens to carry on the revolution!"

"I hope the war doesn't last *that* long. There is already too much heartache on all sides of the conflict." Bonny Kate thought about something she had been putting off for several days, and the neglect of it had built up tremendous anxiety for her. The object was a visit to Mary Dyckes, the woman who had saved not only her life, but the lives of every member of the Sevier family. The loss of Mary's own husband in the heroic effort was a sad business that weighed heavily on the heart of Bonny Kate.

"Bonny Kate, this is more important work than anything the men are doing," Grace declared. "The flame of liberty has been ignited here on this continent for the first time in the history of mankind! The generations to follow must carry on the work our husbands started. This will go on until the entire world has been liberated from the tyranny of kings and placed under the rule of popular law. I believe that is the purpose of Divine Providence revealed in our own time by the grace of God."

Bonny Kate had nothing to add to such a visionary speech as she lifted Nancy from the tub into a towel and carried her to the bed for dressing. Her friend Mrs. Dyckes had been burned by that flame of liberty and desperately needed healing. She wondered how her outreach might be received by the victim of the tragedy. Perhaps if she took Pastor Doak along on the visit, he might provide some comfort.

When Nancy was dressed and playing happily on her blanket in the pen they had improvised to keep her from wandering, Bonny Kate removed her wet apron and made ready to travel.

"Where are you off to?" her mother asked as she watched Bonny Kate prepare.

"I have to go see Mary Dyckes today. I can't put it off any longer."

"Shouldn't you leave well enough alone?"

"Mother, she lost her husband for trying to help me. I am not going to desert her when she needs a friend as never before!"

Esther Doak looked up from where she had gone to tend the cook pots at the cooking hearth. "Take Reverend Doak with you. Mrs. Dyckes needs a friend like Jesus, especially if she rejects your offer, Bonny Kate."

"My offer?"

"Yes, my dear, you are going to invite her to join our little congregation here at Plum Grove. Nothing would help the poor woman more than the company of this group of exceptional Christian women!"

"It crossed my mind," Bonny Kate admitted. "Do you think she will accept?"

"We won't know until you ask," Esther said.

"Would you all support me in my efforts to help Mrs. Dyckes?"

"No," objected Kesiah. "She is the widow of a Tory assassin! Let her stew in her own miserable juices for the wickedness her husband was certainly about."

Esther looked sternly at the vindictive wife of Tory hunter Captain Robert Sevier. "Kesiah, we need to have a discussion about that uncharitable attitude."

"Grace, what do you think?" Bonny Kate asked the visionary Mrs. Bowman.

"I do not know the woman; but if she is a friend of yours, Bonny Kate, I shall do all I can to help in her rescue!"

"Eliza, you don't know this woman either; but her situation deeply disturbs me, and I am compelled to reach out to her."

Eliza Miller smiled. "No frontier woman is a stranger to me. She is a sister, and this one sounds like a lost sister who needs to be found."

"Mother?" Bonny Kate turned to the woman who had always stood beside her.

Mary Sherrill smiled. "You never take the easy way, my dear daughter, but I'm so proud of you and your accomplishments. God bless you!" She hugged her daughter in approval. "Be home by dark."

Mary Dyckes sat on a bench outside her cabin and brooded over dark thoughts. Fate had been so unkind to her, all because of her husband's political ideas. She was nearly out of food, and the farm was a ruin. She hadn't seen a living soul for days, except for that county lawyer who had brought her a letter, the meaning of which she couldn't make sense. When she asked what it was about, the man told her she had been served. Earlier in the month she had received the news of her husband's hanging with shock and despair.

Shouldn't there have been a trial? She didn't understand why Colonel Sevier couldn't have prevented the destruction of her husband's life, especially after she had taken such great risks to warn Bonny Kate and her family. As she thought about her wretched condition and contrasted it to Bonny Kate's apparent happiness, two riders appeared in the clearing of her homestead, and one of them was Bonny Kate Sevier.

"Good morning, Mrs. Dyckes," Bonny Kate said dismounting without being invited. She breezed past the idle woman and entered the cabin and surveyed the condition in which her friend was living. The place was a filthy mess.

"Get out of my house!" Mrs. Dyckes called after her. "You are not welcome here."

Pastor Doak stepped down from his horse and politely removed his hat. "Mrs. Dyckes, I am truly sorry about the misfortune that befell your husband. If there's anything we in the community can do to help you in your present circumstances, please call on us to provide it."

"You can get that tornado of a woman out of my house!"

"I'll just clean up a little and be on my way," Bonny Kate called out. "Mary, do you have any wash rags and soap? Oh yes, here they are, and a bucket of water, just what I need."

"Mrs. Doak sends her regards to you and would like to call upon you someday soon to see how you are getting along."

"Thank her for her kindness," Mary replied. "But I'm not receiving visitors just now. And that goes for you too, Bonny Kate. Leave my house alone!"

"I'll only be a minute," the tornado of a woman called out. "You just talk to Pastor Doak, my dear lady, and I'll have your house put in order directly."

"Are you eating regularly, Mrs. Dyckes?" the pastor asked kindly.

"As regular as ever," Mary answered with little energy.

"She hasn't eaten anything today," Bonny Kate announced from the doorway. "The fireplace is as cold as stone."

"You shut up, you tattletale. I don't feel like eating."

"That's because your cupboard is empty, my dear! You can't continue to live here like this."

"I'll live as I bloody well please. Leave me alone, Bonny Kate."

Bonny Kate shook out her dust rag and returned to her work.

"There is nothing wrong with grieving for a lost loved one," Pastor Doak spoke comfortingly. "It is perfectly natural, but it always works best when you are surrounded by a loving community of others."

"If Mother hadn't passed with the pox last year, I could have gone home to her."

"I'm so sorry about your mother," the pastor continued. "This has been a really hard year for you."

"Yes sir, it has been a hard year for many of the Tory persuasion."

"Jesus doesn't care about our politics," Pastor Doak said. "He loves us all and wants to gather us all together under his protection like a mother hen gathers her chicks."

"I hardly think anyone would welcome me to a gathering," Mary said sadly.

Bonny Kate had reappeared in the doorway with a letter she found in Mary's cabin. "That's the reason we came to see you, Mary dear. I want you to come live with me at Plum Grove."

"No. You betrayed Jacob to a rebel lynching. I trusted you and warned you to save yourself from destruction, and for all my trouble, you killed my husband."

"No, I didn't. Mr. Dyckes and Mr. Holley were murdered by persons unconnected to Washington County justice. There would have been a fair trial when Colonel Sevier returned home, and he planned to present the special circumstances and plead for the merciful treatment of Mr. Dyckes."

"Then who killed my Jacob?"

"We don't know yet. Major Robertson suspects it was the Regulators."

"I don't believe you! If I ever leave here I'll stay at Pastor Doak's."

"Esther and I would be pleased to have you, Mrs. Dyckes, but the Indians attacked us the other day and burned our house to the ground."

"Indians? Is Esther safe?"

"Yes," he replied. "We moved to Plum Grove for safety. It is built like a fort and can easily be defended. I urge you to go with us today."

Mary Dyckes looked at Bonny Kate suspiciously. "Why would you take me under your roof?"

"You are my friend." Bonny Kate turned to Pastor Doak and gave him a letter. "I found this on her table. It's not good news."

"Stay out of my business, Bonny Kate."

Pastor Doak looked at the letter quickly and sighed. "It's the Confiscation of Tory Lands Act. Mary, do you know what this says?"

"No, I can't read."

"The State of North Carolina passed a law that allows counties to take away the lands of convicted Tories and sell the property at auction," he explained. "This letter is ordering you to surrender your home to the county and move off the premises."

Bonny Kate protested. "That is so unfair! Jacob Dyckes never had a trial and therefore was never convicted as a Tory." She remembered her conversation with Judge Carter when she had told the judge where Mary Dyckes lived. She now had one more reason to feel guilty about the calamities befalling her friend, and one more reason to distrust Judge Carter.

"I'm sure we could help her fight this thing," Pastor Doak said. "But she needs a safe place to stay while we inquire into the matter. We need to move her to Plum Grove."

"Please, Mary," Bonny Kate appealed again. "Come with us. I'm cooking chickens tonight."

The mention of food finally brought Mary to her senses. "I'll come for the chicken."

"Good," Bonny Kate said. "I'll help you pack a few things now, and we can come back later for the rest of your possessions. Where is little Isaac?"

"My sister has been keeping him at her place on Buffalo Creek."

"Who is little Isaac?" Pastor Doak asked.

"My three-year-old son," Mary replied. "He doesn't understand what's happened to his daddy."

"I want him to come to Plum Grove, too," Bonny Kate said. "I'm sure he needs to be with his mother."

"I don't know if I'd be any good for the boy. I've had some very dark thoughts, Pastor Doak."

"Then it's time to let the light of God in," the pastor said. "The best way to see God's light is through the eyes of a child. Little Isaac should live where you live, Mrs. Dyckes."

"I reckon we'll go to Plum Grove, then."

The next day Plum Grove had another visitor, a handsome young Quaker named Thomas Embree. For over a year now, Thomas, and his even more talented father, Moses Embree, had been working for Mr. Sevier building the grist mill, constructing an iron forge, and developing the lead mine. Young Mr. Embree tied his horse to the rail and stepped up on the porch, politely removing his black wide-brimmed hat. All he could see out front were some children, each engaged in some sort of home industry. Dolly Sevier churned the butter, Mary Ann Sevier carded the wool, Little Val showed Dicky how to wash the vegetables from the garden in a tub of water, and Johnny Sevier cleaned one of the few rifles left in Washington County since the men had gone to war.

"Good day to you, children," Mr. Embree addressed them politely.

"Good day, Mr. Embree," Dolly replied.

"Look at all this good industry. May the Lord maketh ye all to prosper. Is your good stepmother hereabouts? I have some news for her if you would be good enough to tell me where to find the good lady."

"Yes, sir. The good lady and Betsy are making candles today, behind the cookhouse," Dolly reported. "Do you have any news of our father?"

"No news of thy good father have I heard," he replied. He bowed politely, taking leave to proceed. "Thank you, Miss." He glanced into the parlor where he heard the voices of many women and some crying babies, obviously guests of the lady of the house. He then made his way around the outside of the house to the wood yard, back of the cookhouse, where he found Bonny Kate and Betsy Sevier working beside a large rendering pot. Again he swept the plain black broad-brimmed hat from his head and bowed politely. "Good day to you, Mrs. Sevier."

"Good day to you, Mr. Embree," Bonny Kate greeted him. "How are things at the lead mine?"

"Very good, ma'am; your shipment of shot and powder left for the Cumberland settlement yesterday in the care of Captain Casper Mansker, consigned to Colonel James Robertson."

"Thank you, Thomas. I'm praying for a miracle!"

"Well, ma'am, somebody's prayer got answered last night. About dusk, I entertained some visitors who descended upon us from the hills."

"Visitors?"

"Yes, ma'am. It was a large group of refugees from Georgia; men, women, and children, seeking the protection of Colonel Sevier."

"They asked for my husband by name?"

"Yes, ma'am, and you should have seen the relief and joy on their faces when I said they had arrived on Colonel Sevier's property. They were rejoicing and praising the Good Lord!"

"Who could they be, Thomas?"

"The leader is Colonel Elijah Clarke."

"Oh..." Bonny Kate said thoughtfully. Elijah Clarke was an unfamiliar name to her. Her expression must have communicated her confusion, because Mr. Embree was quick to explain further.

"Colonel Clarke says he has never actually met Colonel Sevier, but he has placed his entire hope on finding refuge here. His people have suffered most horribly at the hands of Tories and Indians as they retreated from the onslaught. He obviously admires your husband's good reputation for hospitality."

"Well, Thomas, whatever hospitality these good people hoped for, we will provide tenfold! How many shall we prepare for?"

"Colonel Clarke tells me there are about seven hundred; four hundred of them are women and children. They are starved, sick, and some badly wounded. They will arrive here around noon today."

"Seven hundred you say; oh my goodness!" Bonny Kate's mind went to work immediately. "Well let's see...if Colonel Clarke has a family, they will stay here with us. Then I can get Reverend Doak and Major Robertson to organize the community to take in the other families."

"You'll have to act fast to save as many lives as you can," Thomas warned. "These pilgrims are in poor condition."

Bonny Kate turned to Betsy and spoke rapidly. "Betsy, we are done with candle-making for today. Let's get the cooking started. I'm sure I have a recipe somewhere that feeds seven hundred!"

"Bonny Kate, is this the miracle from Divine Providence that you were praying for?"

"We will see, Betsy. Thomas, I imagine you could use a good breakfast before you head back to the mine."

Thomas Embree smiled. "Yes, ma'am. I would be most grateful to you."

About noon that day, a long procession of exhausted refugees crossed Sevier's Ford of the Nolichucky and approached the house at Plum Grove. Tired men led tired horses carrying women and children too tired to walk. The sick and wounded were carried in stretchers. Grace Bowman, Esther Doak, and Mary Dyckes watched from the front porch as Sam Doak and Johnny Sevier ran down to meet the refugees. Esther called into the house. "Bonny Kate, they're coming up the lane!"

"I'll be right out!" A moment later Bonny Kate appeared in the doorway, removing her apron and hanging it on a peg by the door. She squinted in the bright midday sun and shaded her eyes with her right hand as she looked down the lane. "They are in worse shape than I imagined. Betsy?"

"Yes, ma'am?"

"Gather the children of your bucket brigade, and bring up the water like we planned. Let the folks drink and wash, and then we can start serving them dinner."

"Yes, ma'am." Betsy flew into action, giving orders in a tone that would have made her father proud. "Bucket brigade, take up your buckets and follow me to the spring!" She organized the small Seviers to carry buckets down to the spring to fetch cool water for the guests.

Colonel Elijah Clarke rode up to the porch, dismounted, and removed his hat as a bedraggled band of refugees streamed up the lane and into the yard. "Which of you beautiful ladies is Mrs. John Sevier?"

"I'm Mrs. Sevier. And this is Esther Doak, our pastor's wife, and Grace Bowman of Burke County, and my friend Mary Dyckes."

"How do you do, ladies? I am Elijah Clarke from the state of Georgia, and I have come seeking refuge for the families of my men."

"You are welcome, Colonel Clarke. What brings you so far from your home?"

"The British and the Tories have completely overrun the fair state of Georgia. They hanged our leading civil and military authorities, burned our homes, and left us destitute. Then they used our town of Augusta as a place to meet and arm the Indians with muskets, powder, and shot for continued attacks on the people of the West. We tried to take Augusta and prevent that from happening, but we failed in the attempt. So, I gathered all our families and came here to warn you and help you prepare for the Indian War that we know is certainly coming."

"Oh dear, these are bad tidings."

"We chose this place because of your husband's reputation for hospitality and the peace he has brought to this area," Colonel Clarke continued. "If we can successfully prepare you to defend your lands from the Indians, we might all have a chance of survival."

"I hope we don't disappoint you, sir. Please settle your people under the shade trees. Our children are bringing buckets of water for your refreshment and for washing. Then we will serve dinner."

"We're much obliged, ma'am." The colonel bowed politely.

"Colonel Clarke, you and Mrs. Clarke will be my guests here in the house. Where is Mrs. Clarke?"

"Here I am," answered Hannah Clarke. She and her children stepped forward from the crowd and walked up to the porch. Hannah Clarke was an older woman possessed of indomitable courage and great life wisdom under a rather plain but pleasant appearance. Bonny Kate liked her immediately.

"Please come in, Mrs. Clarke," Bonny Kate invited. "Your family will have our parlor room on the right of the hall. Wash up, get comfortable, and dinner will be served in a few minutes." The entire farm became a beehive of activity to welcome, settle, and feed the seven hundred refugees.

At lunch, Hannah Clarke was getting to know the other ladies better and noted that Grace Bowman and Mary Dyckes, seated next to each other, both wore black. "These young women have seen some recent tragedy," she said sympathetically.

"Yes, ma'am," Grace answered. "We are war widows. Our husbands died bravely for what they believed was right." Grace reached for Mary's hand and squeezed it tightly. "But we are like sisters, and we will come through these dark days to a brighter future. That's what Christian women do, isn't it, Mrs. Dykes?" The Tory widow managed a smile, the first one Bonny Kate had seen on her friend in all the years since the day of her wedding to Jacob Dyckes.

The luncheon honoring Mrs. Clarke, their new acquaintance, was short for the women of Plum Grove. Mary Sherrill and her daughters Mary Jane and Susan Taylor were the first to excuse themselves, followed by Esther Doak, Grace Bowman, Eliza Miller, and Mary Dyckes. They were all soon among the sick and wounded, making them comfortable and caring for them the best they could.

Bonny Kate completed her rounds from group to group more quickly than the others and went looking for Colonel Clarke to discuss the situation.

"Mrs. Sevier, you amaze me. The dinner was so much more than anything we had imagined."

"Thank you, Colonel Clarke. I've been surveying your sick and wounded. Even as we speak, Pastor Doak and Major Robertson are arranging shelter for everybody with neighboring families. Of course, we'll treat the most serious cases here at Plum Grove.

Unfortunately, Dr. Cozby accompanied my husband on the eastern campaign, but we do have several women that know how to properly dress a wound."

"I'm much obliged," Colonel Clarke responded. "It seems you have thought of everything. How can we ever repay you?"

"Actually, Colonel Clarke, your presence here is payment enough. While our men are chasing the British out of Carolina, the Chickamaugas will most likely attack us. The news you brought about the British supplying them with arms and ammunition just confirms my worst fears. Maybe together we can mount a spirited defense if it becomes necessary."

"Certainly," the colonel agreed. "My army, such as it is, will be at the service of your community. I wonder if you could supply us with powder and lead. Our stocks are nearly exhausted."

A dread realization overtook Bonny Kate at that moment. She had risked the destruction of everything in her own community to save Fort Nashborough. All the lead and powder she could find was on its way to the Cumberland settlement, consigned to Colonel James Robertson. She didn't want to admit the vulnerability of the home guard that she had caused, so she evaded the issue. "That is something we can discuss with Major Robertson tomorrow."

"Bonny Kate, Bonny Kate," Mary Ann Sevier called from the house. "Nancy is crying for you."

"I'll be right there," she answered. "Nancy is our baby girl. Please excuse me, Colonel Clarke, while I tend to her."

"Of course, Mrs. Sevier," Colonel Clarke said as he tipped his hat and bowed politely. Another officer from Georgia was nearby and approached his colonel.

"So that's Bonny Kate Sevier," he said admiringly. "She's a pretty thing. You know, Colonel, she's practically better known than her husband. They say she can outrun, outjump, outshoot, and outtalk any living soul west of the Blue Ridge."

Elijah Clarke laughed. "I would not be surprised if that proved to be true."

The evening progressed with another meal provided from the household of Colonel Sevier for the seven hundred guests from Georgia, prepared with love by the hands of the colonel's lady and her ladies of mercy. The healers continued their important work under the leadership of Esther Doak, and so effective was the ministry that no person among the sick and wounded died that night. The Georgia children enjoyed some delightful diversions provided by the hostess and the Sevier children, who shared their games and entertainments.

"When can I have my men resupplied with powder and shot?" Colonel Clarke asked his hostess later that night.

"Major Robertson will be here tomorrow to discuss strategy," Bonny Kate dodged with a disarming smile. "Tonight we will have a hymn sing and a sermon from Reverend Doak. We have much to be thankful for, Colonel Clarke."

"Indeed we do!"

Chapter 19

Considerable Troubles at Home

Bonny Kate rose before dawn and quietly packed for a half-day trip to Sinking Creek for a consultation with Major Charles Robertson. She had not seen Major Robertson since she sent word to inform him about the Georgia refugees. She hoped to catch up with him before he left home for the day. It had occurred to her in the night that Washington County now had two armed forces in the area that were unacquainted with one another, and if she and Major Robertson didn't quickly coordinate the patrols, either the home guard or the Georgians might attack the other force by mistake. Mary Sherrill heard her daughter moving around and rose to observe by candlelight the preparations being made.

"Where are you going at this hour of the night?" Mother Mary asked.

"I haven't seen hide nor hair of Major Robertson since I sent him word of the arrival of the Georgia people. I have to make sure he got my message and is acting in response to it."

"Why not send one of his men to follow up?"

"This is too important and too urgent to trust it to any man."

"Your work here is too important to leave to anyone else."

"Mama," Bonny Kate spoke seriously. "In ten days, seven hundred Georgians will eat up Colonel Sevier's entire annual food supply. If we don't resettle these families on neighboring farms, starting today, my mismanagement of this crisis will ruin the fortunes of my dear husband. That is no way for a wife to begin a marriage!"

"I suppose that's a good enough reason to go gallivanting about in the dark of night."

"Colonel Clarke has posted pickets all around the plantation. If the home guard doesn't get the word that the army occupying Plum Grove is a friendly force from out of state, we could find ourselves in the middle of a shooting war before the mistake is discovered."

"That's an even better reason to go gallivanting! What shall we do for breakfast?"

"Ham and eggs, and biscuits, ought to satisfy them. You, Mary Jane, and Susan had better get the fires going. It could take half the morning to get everybody fed."

"Be careful on the road. Do you have an armed escort?"

Bonny Kate grinned. "There's not another horse that can keep up with mine. Colonel Clarke's horses are still pretty much broken down after the hard usage of the retreat."

"I don't like it, Bonny Kate," Mary said worriedly.

"I'll be fine. I'll be back with a plan before midday, so our friends won't eat us out of house and home!"

On her way up the river road, she was stopped by the home guard sentries who knew her well and let her pass. Then a short time later, she ran into the Georgia pickets who didn't know her at all.

"Halt!" the Georgia trooper called out. "Who goes there?"

"Bonny Kate Sevier," she answered as she reined in her powerful horse.

"What would Mrs. Sevier be doing riding alone at this hour of the morning?"

"I have county business to discuss with Major Charles Robertson, and I wanted to catch him this morning before he leaves home."

"We have orders not to let anyone pass in or out of this farm," the trooper said.

"Those orders do not apply to me. I am the mistress of Plum Grove Plantation!"

"As I live and breathe, my orders apply to all God's creatures," the man said stubbornly. "Now, I'll have you climb down off that horse and wait while we get you a pass from the captain of the watch."

Bonny Kate knew better than to argue with loaded Georgia muskets, but she could not disguise her irritation at the unexpected delay. "Who is the captain on duty?"

"Captain Benjamin Few."

"Where is Captain Few?"

"He checks in with us every *few* minutes," the trooper laughed. "He'll be along directly."

"I hope so," she said impatiently. "My business has to do with a *Sevier* emergency."

"Ha, ha, ha," laughed the Georgian. "That was good, ma'am."

Thirty minutes passed, and the captain of the watch did not appear at the picket post. Bonny Kate became angry. "You said that Captain Few would be along in a *few* minutes. Where is he?"

"Can't say, ma'am," the soldier answered. "He might have stopped in at the big house for breakfast. I wonder what they are cooking."

"Eggs and ham, served with my special fluffy biscuits. Now, if you will just call Colonel Clarke down here so he can authorize my release, I'll see that you get some butter and honey to go on that mouthwatering hot biscuit."

"Ma'am, you don't want to do that, now," the guard said quickly. "Colonel Clarke is not to be disturbed. He's right ornery in the morning."

"I don't care what he is," she snapped. "You get him down here and get him now!" One of the sentries ran for the big house to do her bidding and to see personally if she was telling the truth about the biscuits.

Another half hour passed as the Georgians learned about the wonderful breakfast being served and lined up for plates of the best breakfast they'd had since evacuating Georgia. When word finally reached Colonel Clarke that the pickets had captured a haughty lady on a thoroughbred horse in the early morning hours, he saddled his horse and rode down to investigate.

"Good morning, Mrs. Sevier," Colonel Clarke greeted her. "Where are you headed so early in the morning?"

"I have to go see Major Charles Robertson about getting your people cared for and settled today," she said impatiently.

"Since your mission involves my people, please allow me the privilege to ride escort for you this morning," Colonel Clarke offered.

"I hate to take you away from your breakfast, Colonel Clarke."

"I've had my breakfast, and it was a fine one!"

"I'm glad you enjoyed it, sir," Bonny Kate said as she mounted her horse. They rode up river at a pretty brisk pace.

"Mrs. Sevier, I understand you control the production at the lead mine," Colonel Clarke began. "I want to ask you about replenishing our supply of powder and shot."

"Not today, Colonel Clarke. My immediate concern is getting your sick and wounded back into service. If I continue to provide for all your needs from my own resources, I will very soon ruin my husband's fortunes."

"I'll send out foraging parties as soon as my men have ammunition. That's how an army feeds itself. Just tell me where the Tory farmers live, and we will confiscate *their* livestock and foodstuffs first."

Bonny Kate had lived innocently, in ignorance of how an army feeds itself, and the idea of despoiling the farms of her neighbors—even her Tory neighbors—to sustain the Georgia refugees was unacceptable to her. She now understood the challenges she faced and desperately needed men with the experience and the authority to deal with a man like Colonel Clarke. She urged her horse to a faster pace, and within the second hour of travel they dismounted at Major Charles Robertson's home on Sinking Creek. Susannah Robertson came out to greet them, followed by her three-year-old grandson, Charlie Sevier.

"Hello, Bonny Kate."

"Good morning, Mrs. Robertson. Is the major here?"

"No, he went up to Kesiah's tavern this morning to help her reopen."

Bonny Kate knelt down, and little Charlie ran into her arms. "Good morning, Charlie! Oh, you are such a big boy now! Are you helping your dear granny run this big farm today?"

"Yes, ma'am," the boy answered. "I-I-I-I did all my chores already!"

"I'm so proud of you," Bonny Kate beamed. "When are you coming to see me again at Plum Grove?"

"I-I-I-I want to come with you now."

"I would love to have you, Charlie, but I'm traveling on to Jonesborough today with Colonel Clarke, and I'm not going home for a long time. Get your mother to bring you down for a visit soon and bring your granny too!"

"Who is this little fellow?" Colonel Clarke asked.

"This is Charlie Sevier, the son of Captain Robert and Kesiah Sevier," Bonny Kate introduced.

"It's a pleasure to meet you, young man." Colonel Clarke shook hands with the boy. "I served with your father at the battle of Musgrove's Mill. He is a very fine officer."

"Bonny Kate, I have some woman's business to discuss with you," Susannah said. "Would you excuse us for a moment, Colonel Clarke?"

"Certainly, ma'am. I'll just entertain this little lad with stories of his brave father's exploits in South Carolina," Colonel Clarke replied.

The women retreated to the privacy of the Robertson cookhouse. "Bonny Kate, you are going to have your hands full with this infestation of Georgia patriots! Did you know that Elijah Clarke was a North Carolina Regulator in his earlier days?"

"No, ma'am."

"He would have been hanged with the worst of them if he hadn't escaped to Georgia!"

"He seems nice to me."

"Watch out for him. The Regulators revolted back in '71 because of the corrupt practices of the county governments and courts under the king's provincial government. The rebellion was crushed at the Battle of Alamance."

"I remember those days. I was seventeen and living at Sherrill's Ford, but we didn't know anybody involved in that."

"Well, be careful of the Regulator mindset. They take the law into their own hands and dish it out according to their own purposes. They take what they need or think they need without regard to legal process or payment. They commandeer all your resources and pay little heed to the liberties and rights of others. You might end up a prisoner on your own farm."

"Oh dear!" Bonny Kate recalled her experience with the Georgia pickets that very morning.

"That's why Charles is so worried about you and the other ladies at Plum Grove."

"Was he worried enough to come help me yesterday?" Bonny Kate reacted angrily.

"Was he worried enough to send the home guard to my rescue? Was he worried enough to call out the reserves? Or was he worried enough to help Kesiah reopen the tavern, the first time a couple hundred new customers come stumbling into the county?"

"Bonny Kate, that's not fair to Charles," Susannah defended her husband. "He needs some time to work on the problem, and helping Kesiah will help him get focused on the priorities."

"Priorities," Bonny Kate repeated in disgust.

"Yes, we do have priorities. Bonny Kate, I didn't tell you this to anger you. I just thought you needed to know!"

Bonny Kate realized that Susannah Robertson was not the one who deserved the reproach she was so ready to inflict. She walked over to the open door and gazed out to find Elijah Clarke standing beside the stock pen counting the hogs in Major Robertson's herd of swine. The colonel's strange actions alarmed her even more. "Mrs. Robertson, thank you for the information. You have helped *me* get focused on my own priorities."

Charlie Sevier ran in and clutched Bonny Kate's skirt in another affectionate gesture. He looked up into her beloved face. "Don't be a stranger to us!"

"I'll try not to be, Charlie," she laughed, patting the little fellow on the back. She looked at Susannah again and smiled. "Good day, Mrs. Robertson."

"Take care, Bonny Kate."

Little Charlie Sevier had expressed it very well, Bonny Kate thought. She had become a stranger to all those she loved ever since she became Mrs. Colonel John Sevier. She had even become a stranger to herself. The change had been as sudden as the calamitous events that had forced themselves upon her in the past two months. Her life was careening out of control like a runaway horse packed with powder kegs. That image brought to mind *her* powder kegs, and sacks of shot, packed on horses bound for the wilderness road that led to the Cumberland Gap. She wished she had that decision to make over again, but at least Colonel James Robertson of Fort Nashborough would be pleased with her. She mounted her horse quickly and waited while Colonel Clarke came running to mount his.

"Colonel Clarke, we have room for forty of your people on Sinking Creek," Susannah called from the doorway of her cookhouse. "The hunting is good up this way, and we have several families willing to shelter your people. Send them up first thing in the morning, and I'll see that they get settled."

"Thank you, Mrs. Robertson," Colonel Clarke responded, tipping his hat. "That is very kind of you. I'll make the assignments this evening."

The ride to Jonesborough was fast, and it was all Elijah Clarke could do to keep up with the woman who rode a racehorse. He had observed the rifle, the tomahawk, and the bullwhip she equipped her saddle with and knew a woman would not carry such equipment if she were not well skilled at using them. He admired her sense of purpose and her quiet determination. She was not unnecessarily talkative as were many women he had known, and he appreciated that.

Bonny Kate was in a near panic as she pushed her horse faster and faster. Based on Mrs. Robertson's revelations, she could not trust Colonel Clarke, the Regulator, to respect her property and her liberties, so she thought it best to reveal as little as possible about the community and not even speak to him. It would be awkward to have him with her when she addressed her concerns to Major Robertson. She stopped her horse to drink at a branch of Little Limestone Creek.

"Where in the world are we?" Colonel Clarke asked.

"This branch runs into Little Limestone Creek. My husband owns a grist mill farther down, and I should be running it night and day since the corn harvest. But I've been so busy dealing with other emergencies since Colonel Sevier went away that I have sadly neglected that important industry."

"I have a family of millers among my people," Colonel Clarke offered. "Maybe they could be put to work until your husband returns."

"I would pay them handsomely in Continental notes," she said with a grin. "I wish I had silver instead of promises."

"Mrs. Sevier, the good food and the respite from Tory atrocities is payment sufficient for us." Clarke smiled back at her.

"The valley of Little Limestone Creek would support at least one hundred of your people, Colonel Clarke. Pastor Doak's church and school are there, so it would be a good place to settle the men who brought their families."

"Excellent! We are making fine progress."

Bonny Kate hoped for more progress once she could catch up with Major Robertson. Her anger toward him had not lessened, and neither had her apprehension about hosting a family, or perhaps several families of Regulators at Plum Grove.

Robert Sevier's Tavern was open for business when Bonny Kate and Colonel Clarke arrived there about noon. Bonny Kate marched right in, and Colonel Clarke followed. Rum kegs and whiskey barrels lined the wall of the tap room, newly arrived in a shipment from Virginia. She glanced at her companion and caught him with his index finger up, quietly counting the inventory! Charles Robertson walked over to greet them.

"Hello, Bonny Kate," Robertson greeted her. "Are you showing Colonel Clarke the most important places of the community? How are you, Colonel Clarke?"

"I'm in much better circumstances than I have seen since the British came back to Savannah." Colonel Clarke grinned and shook hands with the major.

"Bonny Kate, did you know that Colonel Clarke and I were both wounded by British cavalry sabers at Cedar Springs? Did you know that he was actually captured by two burly redcoats and was being led away when he came to his senses, threw those fellows to the ground, and ran back to rejoin us to continue the fight? It was a glorious action!"

"Major Robertson," Bonny Kate began. "I sent word that all the sons of liberty from the entire state of Georgia had arrived at Plum Grove yesterday, with all their families, a great many of which were starving, sick and wounded. Why did you not respond?"

"I was out patrolling when the news reached me late yesterday. I answered your note this morning. Did you receive it?"

"Obviously not," she replied. "I left the house before first light and rode all the way up to your place only to find you away in Jonesborough attending to business that is unrelated to the defense of Washington County."

"Now Bonny Kate, you have to understand. Kesiah needs me to help her get set up again. We have an opportunity at making a considerable profit here."

"I have a crisis developing at Plum Grove, and all you can think about is a filthy profit?" Bonny Kate's rage had returned after being suppressed for the better part of the morning.

"Bonny Kate, I have my priorities. Besides, I sent you the note."

"Your wife told me some disturbing news this morning," she continued.

"About...?" Major Robertson finished his question with a quick nod of the head in Colonel Clarke's direction.

"Yes, and what are you going to do about the command and control issues we have looming before us?"

"How would you like a tankard of rum, Colonel Clarke?" Kesiah offered. "I'm Kesiah Sevier, the proprietress of this ordinary. Welcome to our community."

Elijah Clarke gave Kesiah his full attention at the bar as Charles Robertson drew Bonny Kate aside and spoke with her in hushed tones.

"Well, you see Bonny Kate, I'm outranked here, even in my home jurisdiction, so there's very little I can do without the proper authority."

"Have you thought about Colonel Carter's authority? He holds the actual title of Colonel and Judge of Washington County. Go get him!"

"Now Bonny Kate, I don't think we should trouble Colonel Carter. He's much afflicted with the palsy these days."

"This is an emergency," she insisted loudly. "Either you fetch Judge Carter down here to Plum Grove, or I'll take the law into my own hands!"

"Now there's a lady after my own heart!" Colonel Clarke noticed her animated speech and raised his tankard in appreciation of her spirit.

Bonny Kate reacted harshly. "You stay out of this!" Colonel Clarke was somewhat taken aback, but not understanding the issues chose from then on to remain quiet and watch.

"Simmer down, Bonny Kate," Charles cautioned. "There's no need to lose your temper."

"No need you say? No need? My farm is covered up with people in need!" Her shrillest voice rose to a volume rarely exceeded in the wildest revelries of the tavern's busiest days. "Those Georgians are starving, wounded, and sickened with all manner of maladies.

Their clothes are tattered and filthy. They have no shoes, no tobacco, no blankets, and no medicines, and you say there's no need? Their soldiers have bravely faced the Tories and the Chickamaugas without supplies and ammunition and lost their loved ones to the noose and the cruel tomahawk, and you say there's no need?"

"Why don't you get out of here and go do something about it?" Kesiah suggested.

"I'm doing all I can do, but I need your father's help, and I need it now!"

"Bonny Kate, you stupid clodhopper, you ruined us all when you sent our powder and shot to the Cumberland!" Kesiah Sevier fired her salvo from a position of safety behind the bar.

"It was within my power to save Fort Nashborough! I made that decision and I will always believe it was the right thing to do. James Robertson, your own cousin, sent the request for our help."

"So you chose the destruction of your own community," Kesiah charged. "You are a traitor to your own people!"

"Be quiet, you fribble!"

"Now Bonny Kate is harboring a Tory spy within Colonel Sevier's own household," Kesiah accused.

"Silence, I say!" There was fire in the blue eyes of the tall lady.

"You can't silence me in my own place of business, you fastidious frump!"

Bonny Kate went after her tormentor and chased her out the back door of the tavern. Behind the tavern, Kesiah took refuge in the cabin where she lived. She slammed the door and managed to bar it before Bonny Kate could force entry. She didn't have time to close the shutters, however, and Bonny Kate slipped over the window sill to stand in Robert Sevier's parlor and confront her troublesome critic.

Colonel Clarke and Major Robertson walked to the back door of the tavern and listened.

"Get out of my house, you bitch!"

"Don't ever call me that again!"

"Oww...You're hurting me!"

"That's going to be one hell of a catfight, Major Robertson," Colonel Clarke observed.

"They just recently became sisters-in-law," explained Charles Robertson. "There are a few things they need to work out between them."

"Are you a betting man, Major?"

"I will always bet on a sure thing, Colonel," Charles replied.

"Get away from me!" Kesiah shrieked. The sounds of tin plates and cups being thrown reached the ears of the men.

"Kesiah is a thrower," explained her father. "That's why Robert had to lock up all the china, crockery, and blown glass. They use nothing but wood, tin, and pewter. It sounds worse in there than it really is."

"What about a little wager on the outcome?" Elijah persisted.

"I wouldn't take advantage of a newcomer to our community," Charles grinned. "Everybody around here knows that the colonel's wife outranks the captain's wife in almost every way." The sounds of scuffling continued for another minute before peace was restored.

"Ohhh, Bonny Kate, that's gross!" Kesiah wailed in disgust.

The door opened and Bonny Kate walked out closing the door behind her. She walked up to the back door of the tavern and washed her hands in the wash pan at the door. She straightened her hair and clothing and calmly stepped inside.

"I thought you were going to Sycamore Shoals to fetch back Colonel Carter," she said to the major.

"Aren't you going to tell us how it turned out?" Major Robertson asked.

"She picked up a chamber pot I wasn't expecting. Before she could throw it at me, I helped her empty it. She has a lot of cleaning up to do. Now Major Robertson, you can stay here and help your daughter wash her hair, or you can go fetch Colonel Carter."

"I think I'll ride up and have a visit with Big Chief John Carter." Major Robertson escorted Bonny Kate and Colonel Clarke to the front door of the tavern and closed the tavern for the day.

"Major Robertson, would you also place an order for me at Patton's Mill?" Bonny Kate requested.

"The mill is shut down, Bonny Kate. All Mary's workers went on the campaign. The last order was completed as a special favor to Colonel Sevier by Mary Patton herself."

"I'm placing an order for thirty kegs to supply the home guard and Colonel Clarke's men. I'll pay her in horses as soon as my horses come back from the war."

"How do you expect her to produce such quantities all by herself?" Robertson asked.

"Colonel Clarke, do you have any men experienced in the delicate art of milling gunpowder?" Bonny Kate asked.

"I believe I can find the men." He smiled at Bonny Kate.

"Will they take orders from a woman?"

"If the Patton woman is as forceful as you seem to be, the men will have little choice."

"I am confident she manages far better than me. Mary Patton has been milling powder since she learned the trade from her father. She has continued in the business even after losing her husband in an unfortunate work-related accident. She carries on a remarkable trade that ensures the safety and independence of Washington County."

"She sounds like an amazing woman," Colonel Clarke said.

"I'll place the order today, and tell Mary to expect some Georgia men to help her reopen the mill," Major Robertson promised. He mounted his horse and was quickly on his way to Sycamore Shoals.

Bonny Kate and Colonel Clarke left Jonesborough and turned their horses south toward the Little Limestone Creek community where John Sevier's gristmill was located. Bonny Kate's activity of the morning had warmed her up. She felt some conversation might help clear the air.

"I had hoped Kesiah might have prepared us a lunch, Colonel Clarke, but she chose instead to involve herself in county politics."

"I like the way you play your politics, Mrs. Sevier."

"I'm sorry you had to witness such an unseemly hullabaloo, but sometimes it takes such an effort to motivate others to action."

"Now that girl you rough-housed with is Robert Sevier's wife?"

"Yes, and Charles Robertson's daughter, and she is little Charlie's mother. She just had another baby this summer, and they named him Valentine after my husband's father."

"Everybody seems to be related to everybody else up here in the mountain country."

"For better or for worse, we are all woven together, like an intricate fabric."

"You sure got old Major Robertson to jump up and go," he said with a laugh.

"He displeased me in the way he set his priorities this morning. And Kesiah angered me when she shot off her mouth about our supplies of powder and shot. That is supposed to be a military secret."

"A secret you were desperately trying to keep from me."

"Yes, Colonel Clarke. I don't yet know whether I can trust you or not."

"I wasn't surprised about the powder and shot."

"You knew?"

Colonel Clarke nodded. "I asked your Quaker friend up at the mine if he had any shot, and he told me where it went. Today I was going to order a search of your farm to see if you had kept any in reserve."

"You would have searched my plantation?"

Colonel Clarke laughed. "Plantation, is it? Mrs. Sevier, your pretty little farm is hardly a plantation! Why in Georgia, plantations are thousands of acres, tended by thousands of slaves."

"Don't think that I will tolerate your arrogance and your presumption that you can order a search of my farm, or any other farm in Washington County. Nothing has been withheld from your people in hospitality, sustenance, and support, and nothing will be. You are not going to take the law into your own hands, commandeer my resources, forage on the farms of my neighbors, take anything without paying for it, or keep me prisoner in my own home. If you entertain such thoughts, let's settle our differences right here and now!" Bonny Kate pulled her rifle and primed the pan while guiding her horse away to create some space between them.

"Whoa, Mrs. Sevier, take it easy!" Colonel Clarke looked shocked. "Please, never consider me your enemy. Why would you suspect me of such dark motives?"

"I know you and your people are Regulators, and I saw you counting hogs at Major

Robertson's and counting inventory at the tavern. And you just admitted you were going to order a search of my farm!"

"I can explain the counting," he replied calmly.

"The only thing you can count on is my hospitality and the generosity of Colonel Sevier. I never invited you here, and I don't believe he did, either."

"That is true, but when we were surrounded by Tories and harassed by Indians down at Augusta, the stories of your generous and peaceful country became our only hope."

"Explain the counting, then."

"It's a habit of mine. I count things. I amuse myself with mental calculations. I estimate distances, weights, volumes, livestock feeding requirements, and the like. I'd say you are about five-foot-eight and one hundred ten pounds. Am I right?"

"I'm not saying," she snapped. "You're still a Regulator."

"I *was* a Regulator, as was Charles Robertson, as was Jacob Brown, as was Adam Sherrill."

"That's a lie! My grandfather was too old to be mixed up in that."

"Too old to fight at Alamance, but not too old to believe that what we were doing was the right thing for the country. You might say we were the first patriots to rebel against a corrupt royal system of government."

Bonny Kate lowered her rifle. "I still don't know whether I can trust you or not."

"And I don't know that I can trust you, either. Your sister-in-law said you are harboring a Tory spy. Can these charges possibly be true?"

"Mary Dyckes is the widow of a man accused of being a Tory, but he was lynched before the charges were proved in court. Before Mrs. Dyckes married we were friends, so I'm trying to help her recover from an unpleasant past. I don't believe she cares anything about the politics of her deceased husband, and I don't believe she will betray my hospitality. Now, Colonel Clarke, how are we going to make this arrangement work?"

"We can seek to understand each other before we make decisions, just as we understand each other now."

"That seems reasonable. Let's move on; I'm starving for something to eat." She returned her long rifle to its sheath on the saddle and urged her horse back onto the trail.

The gristmill at Little Limestone Creek was in full operation when Bonny Kate and her escort arrived and stepped down from their horses. Moses Embree, the old Quaker gentleman and father of Thomas Embree, greeted them.

"Bonny Kate, I'm doing my best, but I could sure use some help," Moses told her. "Half dozen boys with strong backs could really make this operation pay handsomely."

"Moses, this is Colonel Elijah Clarke from Georgia. He knows some people that can help you, if you let them live in the stone house."

"Sure they can," Moses agreed. "I always sleep in the mill. I love the sound of the water wheel at night."

"There's a piece of furniture I want moved to Plum Grove."

"Is it Sarah's desk?" Moses guessed.

"Yes, sir," she smiled.

"I figured you'd eventually want that. I'll deliver it down there tomorrow."

"Thank you, Moses. I think I'll just walk through the house if you don't mind."

"Help yourself, Mrs. Sevier. You own it."

The men watched her stroll up the hill, and Colonel Clarke turned to the talented old mill builder and operator. "Mr. Embree, there goes one hell of a woman!"

"Hell's got nothing to do with her; Divine Providence guides her steps. She may look like a girl, but she acts like a lady, thinks like a man, works like a horse, and has the temper of a tornado!"

Elijah laughed. "Well said, Mr. Embree, that's exactly what I've seen today. I wonder what her husband is like."

"You don't know Jack?"

"Never met him," Elijah admitted.

"He's every bit the equal of her. It was a match made in heaven. You won't know him long before you'll feel like he's the best friend you ever had."

Bonny Kate walked up to the stone cabin and stepped inside. She looked around at the deserted rooms and tried to imagine the sound of Sarah Sevier's voice speaking words of wisdom and encouragement to her dear children in happier times. She found the neat little desk Sarah had used to run the colonel's businesses so effectively. She wondered if Sarah ever imagined that the family businesses would become so complicated. She appreciated the solid construction of the house and thought the family must have been warm and cozy in the great room last winter. She looked at the room where she supposed Sarah had given birth to little Nancy. As Bonny Kate turned to leave, the room started spinning and she felt her sick stomach return with a cold sweat and everything went black.

"Mrs. Sevier, Mrs. Sevier!" she heard Colonel Clarke saying as her eyes fluttered open. "There, she's coming around." The wet handkerchief was cool against her tingling face. She felt weak in the stomach and drained of energy.

"What happened?"

"You've apparently fainted," Colonel Clarke answered. She focused on the Georgia officer's concerned face as he propped her head up slightly with his folded coat to get her off the hardwood floor. "You've been out several minutes."

"You want some water, ma'am?" Moses Embree hovered above her, and she remembered she was in the stone house at Sevier's mill.

"Pass me that canteen," Colonel Clarke directed. "She said she was starving some time ago. It's been a long time since breakfast." He helped her take a sip of water.

"I never got any breakfast," she said weakly. "I felt sick to my stomach."

"Good Lord, ma'am," Colonel Clarke exclaimed. "You've overdone. I've never seen such activity and nerve; and all without the benefit of a good breakfast. You continue to amaze me! Mr. Embree, do you have something we could feed her to get her back on her feet?"

"Corn muffins and corn whiskey," Moses replied.

"Just a muffin and water for now," the colonel recommended. "I have to get her home to Plum Grove." Moses made a pretty quick passage to the mill for a man his age to fetch back a midafternoon breakfast for the boss lady.

"I don't know what came over me," she said as Elijah fanned her face gently with his hat. "I was thinking about when the family was living here and having the baby."

"Who is having a baby?" Elijah asked.

"Sarah—I mean Sarah had her baby right here in this room."

"Do you suspect that *you* might be having a baby?"

"Me? Noooo. I'm not having a baby. I've got all I can handle right now. There is no way I could be having a baby." She was emphatic about that.

"Well, I reckon you know your own business better than anyone else," Colonel Clarke concluded.

She sat up and felt a loosening of her bodice and discovered the laces were undone. "Why Colonel Clarke, you have taken liberties with my attire."

"You seemed a little tight-laced," he explained. "I didn't want you turning blue."

"I was *not* about to turn blue, and you must not trespass beyond the boundaries of Colonel Sevier's hospitality."

"I shall make every effort to learn those boundaries and respect them," he promised.

"Please do not speak of this little rest period to the other ladies. It would unnecessarily cause them concern."

"Your secret is safe with me, Mrs. Sevier."

Chapter 20

Washington County Politics

Bonny Kate made her rounds among the sick and wounded the next morning still somewhat sick herself. She had again prevailed upon Colonel Clarke to not mention her fainting spell to the other ladies by promising to eat a good breakfast, a promise she found difficult to keep. It wasn't until midday that Colonel John Carter and his venerable lady, Elizabeth, came down to Plum Grove for a fact-finding visit. The Carters were accompanied by William Tatham, a talented scribbler and corresponding clerk in Colonel Carter's employ.

"Why, Mr. Tatham," Bonny Kate greeted the newcomer. "What a pleasure it is to see you again. What's it been, two years since you went away?"

"Three," Tatham replied, grinning at the beautiful lady. "I left for Virginia right after the harvest gathering of '77 when we passed so pleasant an evening as dance partners."

"Yes, sir. I remember it well. You spoke so long and so lovingly about your fiancée back in England."

"She was never my fiancée, and it wasn't long after our dance that I received word she had married far above her station."

"Oh, Mr. Tatham, I'm so sorry. I understood then how deeply you esteemed the lady."

"I have become wiser about women in the last three years."

"Well, I heard your business had prospered."

"Briefly, but the war interrupted the flow of English goods. I had not the resources to establish new trade with French or Dutch factors, so I am back with my old friend, Colonel Carter."

"And we are very pleased to have him return to the firm," Colonel Carter declared. "He has also agreed to serve again as county clerk until your husband comes back."

"Oh," she reacted aloud, but in her mind, she resented how easily John's office could be transferred to someone else so Washington County could continue to operate as though the men of the militia had never left.

"It seems you have married well, Lady Sevier," Mr. Tatham continued. "When was the happy event?"

"Almost two months ago." She turned to Colonel Carter and spoke icily. "I have experienced all of the responsibilities of marriage but very few of the pleasures, Colonel Carter."

"Don't complain to me, Bonny Kate. Your pleasures are none of my business."

"I beg to differ, sir. The business of Washington County took my husband away from me, and I want him back, safe and sound, do you understand?"

"God willing, we want our entire company home safe and sound," the older man answered. "You know they went to defend the mother state, so this is a bigger business than just Washington County."

"I realize that, sir, but when I call you for help, I would really appreciate an immediate response."

"Ah, the impatience of youth," he replied with a patronizing grin. "Well, Bonny Kate, I can see you have a problem."

"Colonel Carter, if I can't get these Georgia people settled throughout the community on farms that can support them, I shall very quickly impoverish my dear husband's estates."

"I see clearly your dilemma," he empathized, completely appalled at the condition of the refugees and amazed at their numbers. "What would you have the Watauga Association...uh...the county, rather, do to remedy the situation?"

"I need someone in authority to direct the resettlement of the refugees. Susannah Robertson offered to resettle some of them on Sinking Creek, and they were to leave this morning, but as you can see they are still here and expecting another midday dinner!"

"Why didn't they leave this morning?"

"They are quite satisfied to camp in my yard and enjoy Sevier hospitality."

"I shouldn't wonder, with your reputation as a passable good cook. What's on the menu today?"

"Beef, potatoes, and greens, served with my mother's sweet corn muffins."

"Excellent," he approved. "I wouldn't miss it for the world!"

"What about exercising some authority to resettle these families?"

"Excellent idea, Bonny Kate. I grant you that authority."

"Me? How am I supposed to get these people to take orders from me?" Her hot blood was rising at Colonel Carter's lack of concern.

"That's easy. Just tell them when and where the next meal is being served. These people will go wherever the food is. You lead, and they will follow."

Bonny Kate thought about it for a moment, and sure enough, Colonel Carter in his wisdom had solved the problem. She, and her mother and sisters, could move the community kitchen to Sinking Creek that very afternoon, and serve the evening meal there. She began to work on the plan in her mind as she took Colonel Carter to meet

Colonel Clarke. Bonny Kate wanted to be able to overcome any objections that the Georgia commander might have to splitting up his command and dispersing their families into more comfortable temporary homes. She felt confident that she could do that with the authority of Washington County's Colonel Carter behind her recommendations. They found Colonel Clarke in conference with Major Charles Robertson under a shade tree.

"Colonel Clarke, this is Colonel John Carter of Washington County," she introduced the officers. "He is the chief military officer, judge, and president of the Washington County committee."

"Your servant, sir," Clarke responded politely. "We are greatly obligated to you and your community for providing so generously to our needs."

"Until today, Mrs. Sevier has been the primary provider of your relief, but we will soon activate the rest of our fair community to share more equitably the burdens of support." Colonel Carter spoke politely and diplomatically.

"Our greatest concern is the powder and shot supply." Colonel Clarke repeated his familiar theme. "My men must be resupplied before the Indians attack us again."

"We have a bit of a shortage in those commodities," Colonel Carter admitted. "The same spirit of generosity that has so kindly attended to your needs has very recently provided powder and shot to Colonel James Robertson and the Fort Nashborough community."

Major Robertson grinned at Judge Carter's diplomatic words. "That's a polite way of saying that Bonny Kate mismanaged our war supplies and put us all in the perilous situation of being completely defenseless."

"Those supplies were the property of Colonel Sevier, and he intended me to act as stewardess of them for the greater good of the country," she defended.

"Everybody knows you screwed up," Major Robertson charged. "Why don't you just admit it?"

"I made a decision with the resources and information I had at the time." She tried to control her temper, but her ire was rising. "How could I have known that seven hundred refugees from Georgia would show up at my door seeking protection from the Chickamaugas?"

"Chickamaugas? How do you know it was just the Chickamaugas? The Creeks and Cherokees are just as likely to put on war paint these days. We can't trust any of them!"

"Trust is what it all boils down to, Major Robertson. You don't trust me to manage my husband's own property. Well, I don't trust you, and I don't trust him either." She pointed her finger at Colonel Clarke. "You are nothing but a couple of old Regulators!"

"Well, that's a fine how-do-you-do, Colonel Clarke. We have just been called Regulators by a girl cousin of Ute Perkins, the man who made horse thieving the profession that it is today!"

"This gets more interesting by the minute!" Colonel Clarke laughed.

"Hold on, now!" Judge Carter intervened when saw the discussion was leading nowhere fast. "Let's not antagonize one another. Bonny Kate, you need to calm down and refrain from the name calling. And Major Robertson, please don't criticize the difficult decisions Mrs. Sevier has had to make in the first month of her husband's absence. All in all I'd say she has done a remarkable job, considering the challenges she has had to face. We shouldn't be second guessing our decisions in front of our friend from Georgia. He might get the wrong idea about how things get done in Washington County."

"I do wonder why you have this woman involved in your military decision-making. Perhaps you could explain that to me," Colonel Clarke requested.

"Yes, Colonel Carter, I'd like to hear the explanation myself," Major Robertson chimed in.

"I'd be interested to hear that as well," Bonny Kate said. "I certainly can't explain how this came to be."

Colonel Carter shifted uneasily as he began. "Well, it's all about leadership, love, and money."

Charles Robertson sat down under the shade tree. "It sounds like a long story." Colonel Clarke joined him, and so did Bonny Kate.

"When I first met John Sevier, about eight years ago, I was surprised at how easily I came to like the young fellow," Judge Carter said. "He was polite, honest, respectful, and ambitious. Now, his ambition was different from most men who put self first. He was ambitious for the success of other fellows ahead of his own interests. I'd call that noble ambition. He was a dreamer, filled with hope and good will toward others. You would think that such an idealist would wise up, as other men would always disappoint him and take advantage of his generous nature, but not Jack Sevier. He has never lost faith in the good nature of his fellow man."

"That's true," Charles Robertson affirmed.

The judge continued. "Rare was the man who met him, that didn't come away with the feeling he had just made a new very good friend. Now that is a remarkable talent that he applies to all his acquaintances, and that is why he has become such a great and popular leader."

"His reputation for friendship and hospitality has spread even as far as Georgia," Colonel Clarke noted.

"And rightfully so," Colonel Carter said. "A man like him doesn't come along very often; am I right, Bonny Kate?"

"Once in a lifetime," she agreed. The men noted a look of satisfaction and fond remembrance on the lady's face that spoke volumes of her high regard for her husband.

"Look at her, gentlemen," Colonel Carter observed. "And you will see a woman smitten with the deepest kind of love, the kind that goes to the heart of the soul. She is joined spiritually, emotionally, mentally, and physically, to a man who completely reciprocates her love for him; am I correct, my dear?"

"You cause me to blush, Colonel Carter," she protested, but the expression on her face revealed all.

"I find this whole thing fascinating," Colonel Carter marveled. "Here is a lovely woman, confident, strong, independent, completely secure in her own talents, skills, and abilities, making a good living in her father's horse business and in no great need of relational ties to anyone. She had proved herself the better of many a man in competition, and had reached a stage in life where the expectation of marriage was all but gone; in fact most men would admit a certain intimidation about such a woman. Yet, this is the woman who won the heart of the most beloved man in our country!"

"Please, Colonel Carter," she objected, fanning herself with a kerchief. "Your misrepresentations embarrass me."

"While she alone possesses the deepest affections of Mr. Sevier, she is not alone in her affections for the man. Every man, woman, and child loves the hero of Washington County."

"I concede the point," Major Robertson said. "Let us not belabor the subject on such a warm morning."

"Is this discussion making you hot, Major?" Carter grinned.

"It's making me hot," Bonny Kate admitted.

"Get on with why the lady is involved in the county affairs," Colonel Clarke reminded the story teller.

"Very well," Colonel Carter nodded. "It's the money. Whenever Washington County needed a military solution to any of our problems with the Indians or the Tories, Colonel Sevier provided the money to finance the expedition and the leadership to make things happen."

"You mean he bought his appointment as lieutenant colonel?" Clarke asked.

"No, but his unselfishness was a factor I considered in my recommendations to the state commissioners," Colonel Carter explained. "We have always enjoyed military success because the people love him. The men will follow him anywhere, and the women adore him because he is very careful not to lose their husbands, sons, and sweethearts. Even though I outrank him, I have always let him do the military part of the job, because he loves the adventure and has proved to be very good at it. He has saved me and the county thousands of pounds by funding the campaigns himself."

"That explains a great many things," Bonny Kate sighed.

"Yes, my dear," Colonel Carter agreed. "The sacrifice affects his entire family. That's why I always gave Sarah Sevier an active role in directing military affairs in John's absence. Bonny Kate, you have inherited the authority and the responsibility, along with the financial interests in the Washington County militia."

"Where does Colonel Sevier get all his money?" Colonel Clarke asked.

"From the prudent management of his household and his businesses," answered Colonel Carter. "It seems to flow from a divine source at times, like an outpouring of blessings from heaven. Wouldn't you agree, Bonny Kate?"

"I can't say. I'm still pretty new at this job, and I haven't seen much of it yet."

"You'll get the hang of it," Colonel Carter promised. "Now gentlemen, Mrs. Sevier will present her settlement plan for distributing and sustaining the Georgia families. I suggest you listen to her and cooperate as best you can. I believe in her good sense and judgment, and lend her my authority to get the job done." With that endorsement, Colonel Carter repaired to the shade and comfort of the porch at Plum Grove. He was delightfully anticipating the midday dinner with Bonny Kate and her seven hundred guests.

"Colonel Clarke," Bonny Kate began. "This afternoon we will move fifty of your healthiest men, women, and children to Major Robertson's home on Sinking Creek. I will cook them their evening meal there, and tomorrow Major Robertson will find homes for them among his neighbors."

"You'll have to clear that with my lady Susannah," Major Robertson cautioned.

"She offered the invitation when I spoke to her yesterday," Bonny Kate assured him. "Colonel Clarke, you will choose the people we will take. Tomorrow afternoon we will take a hundred more to Little Limestone Creek, and the rest of them can be settled along the Nolichucky and up along the Watauga Valley."

"I'll organize the companies," Colonel Clarke promised.

"Now gentlemen, if you'll excuse me, I'll go and prepare another meal." The men bowed politely, and she walked toward the cookhouse. She knew she would have to organize her own household to operate more efficiently while she was away settling the refugees, but the talent was certainly available in the persons of Mary Sherrill, Grace Bowman, Eliza Miller, Esther Doak, Hannah Clarke, and Mary Dyckes. Many of the Georgia women were taking on greater responsibilities as their families recovered their health and vitality in the peace and security of Plum Grove.

Bonny Kate circulated among her guests as the lunch was enjoyed. She marveled at the different types of people she encountered, all as dedicated as she was to the cause of liberty.

"Honey, I'll have some more of that sweet cawn bray-ad," drawled an old man of the Savannah volunteers.

Bonny Kate looked at the filthy old man as he smiled up at her with missing teeth. She thought about telling him she wasn't anybody's "honey" but Colonel Sevier's, but that would have sounded inhospitable. She returned his smile and decided to have some fun with the old geezer. "I'll see if my dear old mother has any more."

"Tell yore mama, she sho' runs a fine fahm hyeah," the man complimented.

"Actually sir, I run this farm," Bonny Kate said with a grin.

"Why, you ain't nuthin' but a young gull!"

"Don't be misled by my looks, sir. I am the mistress of this farm, and I have ten children!"

"You don't mean it!"

"Yes, sir," she insisted. "I am a very old lady."

"Go on! Why, you don't look a day over seventeen!"

"Thank you, sir, but you are a flatterer, I think," she winked at the man. "I will share the secret of my ageless beauty if you promise not to tell a living soul."

"Please tell me, ma'am!" He leaned forward, listening eagerly.

"When I found this place not too many years ago, the Indians told me about a spring that runs into the river down yonder that has wonderful restorative properties. They said if I would bathe in the river once a day, it would do wonders for an old hag like me." She grinned at him as she continued. "Well sir, I started bathing every day, and before long my gray hair turned black, and the wrinkles in my face went away completely; my back straightened up, and I could see clearly again. My missing teeth even grew back when I drank the spring water, and nobody in the world would ever guess that I am the mother of ten children!"

The man looked excited. "You know, ma'am, the Indians always know best about such thangs. Thank ye for the information."

"Remember, don't tell a living soul," she cautioned. "Now I have to find you another piece of that sweet cawn bray-ad."

"Never mind about that," said the Georgian. "I'm takin' my wife down to that river for a bath!"

"Get one yourself, while you're at it," she called after him, laughing at how fast he moved.

After lunch Colonel Carter found his hostess at the wash pot directing the children as they washed the dishes. "Oh, Bonny Kate, I need to speak with you privately if I may."

"Yes, sir," she answered. "Would a stroll through the plum orchard be private enough?"

"That would do fine."

When they had walked beyond earshot of the busy household and surrounding encampments, Judge Carter began. "I'm in a legal dilemma, Bonny Kate, and I need to borrow the county clerk's record book immediately."

"Mr. Sevier keeps that under lock and key. I have never in my short tenure as his wife been allowed access to the county records."

"Under the circumstances, I would not imagine you could have had time to concern yourself with the legal business of Washington County."

"That's a fact, Colonel Carter," she replied with a smile.

"Just show me where the books are, and I will absolve you of any responsibility in this."

"You make it sound as though I would be doing something wrong by giving you those books."

"This is an emergency, Bonny Kate, a life-and-death matter!" The judge seemed agitated at her hesitance to comply with his request. "I don't want any harm to come to you or your family."

"Now what do you mean by that?"

"Why do you suppose those Tories tried to hang your husband just before he went campaigning?"

"Wasn't it to stop our men from defeating Ferguson?"

Judge Carter laughed. "My dear, you have a charmingly naive view of the world. Our men don't stand a chance in the world of defeating Ferguson in a pitched battle."

Bonny Kate straightened up and took a deep breath. "My husband believes they can!"

"Do you suppose those rabble-rousing, backwoods militiamen, without discipline or proper weapons, can stand up against the infantry, cavalry, and artillery of the finest military establishment in the world? That's highly unlikely."

She glared at the judge. "Why *did* the Tories ambush my husband?"

"The county took away their farms under the Confiscation of Tory Lands Act passed by the General Assembly. They tried to kill John out of revenge."

"I don't understand why they would target the county clerk in an act of revenge."

"He is one of the dozen or so trustees of the county who were awarded title to the Tory lands until the cases can be decided in my court. As clerk, John recorded the names of all the trustees, and the Tories could have forced him to reveal the names before they hanged him."

She was shocked at the judge's information. "John is too honorable to have betrayed his friends."

"Perhaps, but he might have betrayed his friends to save you and his children. All men have difficult choices."

"I know John Sevier would not have told!"

"I'm glad you discovered the plot in time to save him, but the danger from Tories has not passed. Why, at this very moment you have a Tory woman lodged in the bosom of your family. Watch her like a hawk, Mrs. Sevier. Lock up your tomahawks and meat cleavers before you put out the lights each night."

"It was a bad law. I heard John complain about it."

"Yes, my dear, but we don't make the laws; we just have to carry them out."

"They need to repeal it before too many people get hurt by it on both sides of this horrible war."

"I'm sure the state assemblymen will figure that out, but I need to take custody of the county record books just in case anything happens to the lieutenant colonel of the rabble-rousers."

"Nothing will happen to him! The Lord will not allow anything to happen to him!"

"The military expedition is a dangerous business, Mrs. Sevier. Now please hand over the books."

Bonny Kate was deeply disturbed by the judge's information and how he presented his views of the political and military realities. She realized at that moment she might have some political leverage with Judge Carter to correct the two injustices that she believed needed to be corrected. "Judge Carter, I will give you those record books if you agree to two conditions."

"Mrs. Sevier, you are in no position to bargain with me about this. Now give me those books or I will declare you in contempt of court."

Bonny Kate saw that she would have to turn up the charm. She smiled as she reached out and placed her hand on his arm.

"Dear Judge Carter, I'll give you the books, but hear my plea in the name of justice. I have but two requests. Could you ever hold little me in contempt after the useful service I gave your dear wife in her struggle with the camp fever during the siege at old Watauga Fort?"

Judge Carter was always sensitive to the fact that as colonel he had left Watauga Fort in the hands of subordinates when the Indian attacks suddenly came in 1776. He never liked to be reminded of the glory of a spectacularly successful defense carried out by Captain James Robertson and Lieutenant John Sevier while he was away in the state assembly on business.

"I'm listening," he replied.

"I want you to review the case of Mrs. Jacob Dyckes. John and I both believe that her warning saved John's life. We think her case should be reconsidered."

"If John were to propose it and present compelling new evidence, I would allow it to be placed on the docket."

"Thank you, Judge Carter," Bonny Kate said, smiling with satisfaction.

"What is your other request?"

Bonny Kate knew her next request would be very difficult and politically dangerous if the way she asked it displeased the judge. "Did you enjoy your dinner, Judge Carter?"

"Very much, and so did my wife."

"Well, reflect on that pleasant memory and imagine a future of always being an honored and welcome guest at the Sevier family table as I describe my next request."

"Please, get on with it, Bonny Kate."

"Well sir, you must understand that in my humble opinion, my husband is the most talented and adept military commander on the entire continent."

Colonel Carter smiled at her unqualified humble opinion, but he let her continue without challenge.

"He has tirelessly devoted himself to the cause we all hold dear, throughout the years of the war, except for a brief time this past summer when he took leave to grieve for the loss of his wife, Sarah."

She looked the good judge in the eye as he nodded in agreement.

"Well, sir, when we assembled at Sycamore Shoals it became painfully evident to John that his inferior rank of lieutenant colonel hurt his ability to get his ideas heard and considered in the council of officers. None of the full colonels would listen to him. Even young Isaac Shelby outranks him. That's just not fair to the men of Washington County. We are the oldest county in the west, and the most supportive of the army in men, horses, equipment and supplies, yet our lieutenant colonel has to take orders from all the other colonels who, when all taken together, don't begin to measure up to him in talents and ability."

Colonel Carter reacted with stony silence, shocked that a woman would be the one to point out the deficiencies of the organization of the governing structures of Washington County.

"Don't you see that our men of Washington County will be at a dangerous disadvantage by not having a full colonel in command? My father and brothers are threatened by this inequity, as well as your own son, Landon!"

"I never could have foreseen such a circumstance," the judge admitted.

"Well, it is what it is," she declared. "You should have relinquished the title when you passed down the responsibility. Why didn't you?"

"I saw no reason to give up my colonel's compensation from the state when I had a willing and able lieutenant filling in for me. But now, even that money stream has dried up."

"If you had done the right thing back then, we wouldn't be having this discussion."

"This discussion is over." Colonel Carter started for the house, but she caught his arm and stopped him.

"What are you going to do about it?"

"I am going to get those county record books and go home."

"I'm not going to give them to you until we settle this thing."

"Mrs. Sevier, you are known to drive a hard bargain from your horse trading days. What is it you want from me?"

"I want my husband to be a full colonel as he deserves!"

"I do not deny he deserves it, and I have nothing but good will and warm feelings for the man, but Mrs. Sevier, I am going to be honest with you. Our militia is no match for the king's army. They will run like rabbits before the hounds of hell, and the gallant officers will be captured and taken to the prison ships in Charleston harbor, and I fear that's where they will die."

Bonny Kate pulled out her handkerchief. "Oh, Judge Carter, have mercy in your opinions. Would you make of this bonny bride a woeful widow in one turn of a phrase?"

"Well, it is what it is," he said sadly. He regretted his brutal frankness that had caused the lady to shed tears. "I'm sorry, Bonny Kate. Sometimes, with you, I forget I'm not talking to a man."

"You do not flatter me, sir," she wept.

"Aw, come now, my dear. Forgive this old, gruff bear of a man. I must deal harshly from the bench all the time, and sometimes that spills over into regular conversation."

"Is there no better hope for the man who went off to war in your place, to fulfill the duties of your rank and title?"

Judge Carter sighed. "You have made your argument as well as any lawyer who has ever presented his case in my court, Mrs. Sevier. If your husband survives the fighting, and if we ever see him again, I promise I will resign my commission and write a letter to Governor Nash recommending his appointment to succeed me as full colonel."

She looked at Judge Carter through teary eyes and managed a smile. "Oh, thank you, Judge Carter. There is hope for my dearest John."

"Yes, ma'am," the judge said, patting her on the shoulder. "A wife can always hope for the success of her husband."

"Forgive my foolish tears," she replied, trying to dry her eyes with her handkerchief.

"Forgive my harsh words," he said. She nodded and led the way to the house to get for the judge the county record books.

When she had found the key to John's tall secretary, and located the desired books on one of the upper shelves, she took them down and handed them over to Judge Carter. "I suppose the judge of Washington County, and the president of the Washington County Commission, has the authority to review the records of the county clerk, but I shall require a receipt."

Judge Carter laughed. "You have learned your business well, Mrs. Sevier. Your husband would be very proud of you."

Out on the porch, Colonel Carter summoned William Tatham to take charge of the county records. "Put these in your saddlebags and prepare to leave at once."

"I'm surprised she gave them up so easily," Tatham marveled as the two men made their way to the corral.

"It wasn't easy," Colonel Carter corrected him. "I had to make certain promises and agree to certain conditions. She drives a hard bargain."

"I would expect that of her," Tatham said. "She and Jack both are mighty high-minded about what's right and what's wrong."

"Never mind about that," Judge Carter said. "Your handwriting is so close a match for Jack Sevier's, no one will ever be the wiser. As soon as you get those land entries recopied, I'll hide the originals. No matter what the General Assembly decides to do with the confiscated Tory lands, our people will be protected. We'll make damn sure of that."

Chapter 21

A Dangerous Move

Amy Sevier, the whip-cracking wife of Captain Valentine Sevier, drove a herd of cattle from her home at Stony Creek to the Plum Grove home of her new sister-in-law, Bonny Kate. She accomplished the twenty-four-mile feat in just two days with only the help of a pair of cattle dogs and her six eldest children. Her mother, Jemima, rode their only farm horse and carried Amy's two youngest children, three-year-old James and two-year-old Jemima. Amy and the cattle-driving children, Elizabeth, Jack, Ann, Valentine, and twins Robert and William all had to walk. The enterprising cattlewoman had heard the news about the Georgia refugees and their pitiful plight and wanted to do something to help. That's when she rounded up all the cattle she had and began the cattle drive. On the second day, she drove her cattle through the mud streets of Jonesborough and as the cattle kept moving, she stopped in at the Sevier Tavern for a visit with her other sister-in-law, Kesiah Sevier.

"Why do you want to spend any time with her?" Kesiah asked Amy.

"Haven't you heard? Bonny Kate's farm is infested with uninvited Georgia refugees. She needs our help."

"I'm not lifting a finger to help that haughty bitch."

"Kesiah! How dare you disparage our sister in her time of greatest need!"

"Let her stew in her own miserable juices for all of her transgressions."

"How has Bonny Kate transgressed?"

"She sent all our powder and shot to the Cumberland settlers; she took in a Tory spy to live in Jack's house; she gave away all our food supplies to those Georgia people; and now she's trying to settle those locusts on everybody else's farms. Bonny Kate will be the ruin of Washington County, you can mark my words!"

"Come now, Kesiah. When it comes to the truth, I think you are shooting a little wide of the mark. I know you are angry with her for visiting here the other day."

"How did you hear about that?"

"A little bird told me," Amy replied sweetly.

"Did the bird tell you what that Viking Amazon did to me?"

"Yes, I suppose she acted rashly in the heat of the moment. She's under a great deal of stress, which puts the greater responsibility on you to be civil and accommodating."

"Amy, you know me better than you know her. Why are you trying to make excuses for that horrible harpy?"

"The name calling has got to stop, Kesiah. I suspect that is what got you into trouble the last time. What did you call her?"

"I called her a stupid clodhopper, a traitor to her own people, a bitch, and a fastidious frump."

"Oh, that last one was unforgivable," Amy said with a laugh. "It's no wonder she flew at you. If you ever expect to get along with Bonny Kate, you'll have to curb that tongue!"

"If she ever expects to get along with me, I demand an apology for her trespassing into the sanctity of my own home and soiling me with the chamber pot."

With such graphic imagery of the recent action, Amy had a hard time holding back a horse laugh she knew was building up in her. She had to refocus quickly on something sad, like the imminent peril her husband risked on the far away campaign. "Kesiah, haven't you been told your whole life to clean out the chamber pots first thing in the morning so your house doesn't stink all day?"

"So I missed a day. Does that give Mrs. High-and-Mighty the right to come in and empty it in my hair?"

"No, I suppose not," Amy admitted. "It *was* an unsisterly thing to do, and she *does* owe you an apology. And for the wrongs you committed against her, I know Bonny Kate has a kind and forgiving nature. The two of you just need to patch things up."

"I suppose you are right, Amy. Since Sarah died, you are now the oldest and wisest of the Sevier wives."

"Except for me," Jemima Sevier called from the door. "Who could be older and wiser than me?"

"Jemima!" Kesiah exclaimed and rushed to embrace Amy's mother. "Come in and visit. Can I offer you some strong drink?"

"Not today, Kesiah dear. We are in the midst of a cattle drive, and I need Naomi back out here if you are finished with her."

"What's wrong, Mother?" Amy asked.

"These cattle are loose in town, getting into the kitchen gardens and crapping all over the place. The dogs have completely lost control. I told you it was a bad idea to drive them through town."

"Good-bye, Kesiah dear," Amy said. "Be sweet to Bonny Kate when next you meet. Guard your thoughts and hold your tongue as a favor to me."

"Yes, dear Amy, I will do it as a favor to you," Kesiah promised.

The sheriff's wife was a wonder in her rapid response to the cattle catastrophe.

She quickly restored order with a whistle to her dogs, who became her deputies in rounding up the bovine bandits. The deputy dogs drove the troublemakers out of town. Then, the sheriff's wife borrowed a shovel to collect and remove all the fresh reminders of their visit.

As the cattle drive progressed in the direction of the Little Limestone community, Amy Sevier encountered three riders approaching from the opposite direction. She quickly recognized her neighbors, Judge John and Elizabeth Carter, accompanied by Mr. William Tatham.

"Good day, Judge Carter, Mrs. Carter, Mr. Tatham," Amy greeted the travelers. "I'm bound for Plum Grove with food for the starving refugees."

"That's mighty good of you, Mrs. Sevier," Judge Carter said, tipping his hat. "Let me warn you that your sister-in-law is suffering from a bad humor today. Try to avoid the raw nerve, so to speak."

"Now, John dear, I didn't see any bad humor," Mrs. Carter contradicted him.

"You didn't have to transact any business with her. Bonny Kate's in a foul temper, I tell you, the foulest I've ever seen."

"Perhaps the cause has something to do with women's business," Mr. Tatham suggested with a grin. The two men were more amused at that idea than the women.

"Mrs. Bonny Kate Sevier has good reason to be sore, with seven hundred uninvited guests and very little help from the county, I'm sure," Amy said. "I am well acquainted with the stinginess of Washington County from my husband's long-suffering service with it. As sheriff he is constantly collecting your fees, taxes, and fines from the citizens least able to afford them. The office weighs heavily on a man who, by nature, is so sweet, empathetic, and kind toward his fellow man."

"I don't believe stinginess is quite the proper word for describing the county's financial obligations to the war at a time of continental emergency. The appropriate word is prudence."

"Call that what you will, but when a grateful nation honors those who made the greatest contributions to the cause of liberty, the name Sevier should be at the top of every list," Amy declared.

Judge Carter desired to change the subject so he turned to Jemima and said, "Mrs. Sevier, I was sorry to learn that your husband took an unauthorized leave for a tour of duty with the central command of the Washington County militia. It was my understanding from Lieutenant Colonel Sevier that his father's honorary commission of major was to be used in the service of the home guard. Please accept my sincere condolences if any harm befalls the old gentleman. Take comfort in the fact that no legal consequences await Big Val upon his return, since his commission was only honorary."

"Thank you, Colonel Carter. I intend to exercise complete jurisdiction in this case, since *I* was the injured party," Jemima replied.

"John dear, our neighbors are busy driving cattle," Mrs. Carter observed. "We should not detain them any longer from feeding the starving Georgians."

"Quite right, my dear." Judge Carter tipped his hat. "Good day, neighbors."

"Good day to you, Judge Carter," Amy replied. She ran after the herd to catch up, and her mother Jemima urged her horse forward.

On the porch at Plum Grove, a fair flock of frontier females worked at sewing clothes for the Georgia refugees. Hannah Clarke, Grace Bowman, Eliza Miller, and Mary Sherrill were producing goods as fast as their fingers could fly with needle and thread.

"That Pastor Doak amazes me with his active ministry and witness to the gospel," Hannah Clarke remarked. "He goes out every day to check on the wives of the soldiers and takes Mrs. Doak and their friend Mary Dyckes with him. He chops wood, cleans out barns, fetches water, and tends their farm animals..."

"He's a good shepherd," Mary Sherrill nodded with satisfaction.

"Georgia needs pastors like him," Hannah said. "He has even organized some of our Georgia men to help with the late season harvesting. It's good to keep our fellows busy like that instead of allowing them to waste time and money at Jonesborough's tavern."

Mary Sherrill laughed. "Not too loud, Mrs. Clarke. Colonel Sevier's brother is the owner of that tavern, and Major Robertson has a part interest in it too."

"Thank you for warning me, Mary," Hannah laughed. "Outspokenness has always been my only imperfection, but it covers a multitude of sins." The ladies all laughed.

"I wonder what Bonny Kate is up to?" Mary asked.

"She said she was feeling tired and went down for a nap," Hannah reported.

"She would sleep in the middle of the day?" Mary was surprised. "That's not the Bonny Kate I raised. She has more energy than any dozen women I know."

"I noticed she didn't eat her breakfast," Hannah said.

"She normally eats like a horse."

"She has no fever or weakness, but the smell of food makes her sick," Hannah diagnosed. "What does that sound like to you, Mrs. Sherrill?"

"Oh my goodness!" Mary took a deep breath. "It's so soon after the wedding!"

"That's what I think it is," Hannah decided.

Bonny Kate appeared in the doorway and slowly walked to the edge of the porch where she leaned against the post.

Hannah looked up from her sewing. "Good afternoon, Mrs. Sevier. Are you feeling any better?"

"Some," Bonny Kate answered. "But I have no appetite for food."

Hannah winked at Mary Sherrill. "Your mother tells me this is so unlike you."

"That's true, I'm never sick or tired, and of course, unfailingly cheerful."

"Perhaps the burden of so many uninvited guests has taken its toll."

"Nonsense! We are much safer surrounded by friends like you. Did you know that Colonel Sevier had to draft enough men to stay home and serve in the home guard? Then the Tories came out of the woods like skunks in a drought."

"How frightening," Hannah exclaimed. "But your hospitality has been truly legendary."

Bonny Kate turned and Hannah looked into her face where she saw a woman about to faint. She rose quickly to steady her and helped her to a chair. "Better sit, dear Mrs. Sevier. You look like you are fading."

"Thanks, it comes and goes," Bonny Kate said. "I'll be all right."

"A private talk with your mother might reveal the cause of your malady," Hannah suggested.

"I've had that talk, and I don't see how that could be. News of the war came so soon after the wedding, and we worked day and night to get the men ready to go."

"Are you telling me you never...?"

"No—oh no. We had a few nights together."

"It only takes one, you poor dear."

"I have no regrets, Mrs. Clarke. Those few nights were the happiest nights of my life!"

"She broke the bed," Mary revealed.

"Mother! Don't tell that!"

"The bed was an heirloom. It had been her Granny Sherrill's," Mary added.

"The cording was old and frayed."

"And put to hard usage on the wedding night. My Katie has always possessed a passionate nature."

"Mother!" she groaned. "I didn't want that told. If such conversation ever got back to Mr. Sevier, he would be mortally embarrassed."

"I shouldn't wonder," Hannah said. "So, Mrs. Sevier, may we safely assume that you could be in the family condition?"

"I don't know, but the thought of it thrills me!"

"Really? Don't you have enough children to care for already?"

"Love is infinite, Mrs. Clarke. We can always make room for another baby; and this one, my very own. If only it were true, John would be so pleased with me!"

Hannah laughed. "I hope so, my dear, I sincerely hope so."

"Oh, I'm fading again. Excuse me, ladies." Bonny Kate rose and went into the house.

"So much excitement out here in the wilderness," Grace Bowman said. "I have not missed Burke County a single day since I've been here. There has been too much going on to be homesick."

"I wonder who that could be," Mary said, gazing out to the west. "That is a fair-sized herd of cattle moving down the hill toward the river. Bonny Kate, you better come out here and take a look at this!"

Amy Sevier directed her herd of cattle beyond the branch west of Bonny Kate's place and arrived at Sevier's Ford without disturbing the campgrounds of the refugees that surrounded the big house at Plum Grove. The cattle were brought to rest and pastured across the Nolichucky on the green grass at the foot of Mount Pleasant. Amy directed her dogs to cut out a half dozen milk cows and drove them up to the house to provide milk and butter for the children.

Bonny Kate ran to meet her sister-in-law and flew into an emotional embrace. "Oh Amy, it's so good to see you!"

"I brought back your cattle and brought all mine, too. I figured if Washington County is going to starve, we might as well starve together."

"Amy, I can't begin to tell you what a comfort it is to have you here with me. I have been beset by problems upon problems every day since John has been gone."

"I understand, and we need to begin to face those problems and solve them one by one."

"Thank you, Amy. I so love your calm confidence. It helps me to know that everything is going to be all right."

"Why wouldn't everything be all right?"

"Look at me, Amy, I'm pregnant!"

"Oh my goodness, so am I!"

"Really? When?" Bonny Kate could not believe the news.

"It had to be August, when Val came back from the summer campaign."

"I'm August too, probably the night of the wedding!"

"Count forward then, and we will deliver in May!"

"May babies," Bonny Kate exclaimed.

"How sensible we are, sister, to get the job done before the weather gets too hot!"

The next day Bonny Kate put into motion her resettlement plan. Colonel Clarke seemed pleased and was very cooperative in the operations to resettle the families. When all the resettlements were complete several days later, Bonny Kate was left with only about fifty of the most seriously wounded and of course, the Clarke family. She arranged for Reverend Doak's cabin to be rebuilt by Georgia soldiers, had Mary Patton's powder mill back in operation and the grist mill grinding out the corn. Her efforts soon had the community buzzing with useful industry, but her own children were the ones who felt most acutely the effects of her preoccupation.

"Bonny Kate, you never read to us anymore," complained little Dicky Sevier, the spokesperson of a small delegation of dissatisfied customers.

Bonny Kate looked up from her desk strewn with letters of requisition and business correspondence she had been struggling over the better part of the morning. Standing before her were Dicky, Becky, Mary Ann, Val, and Dolly. "Oh precious, I have to read all these business letters, and they are dreadfully dull!"

"It's making you dreadfully dull," Dolly said.

"I must agree. Have you all completed your morning chores?"

"Yes, ma'am," the children answered.

"Then I think we could slip away for a picnic with our cousins at Mount Pleasant," Bonny Kate suggested. "What do you think about that?"

"Do we have to invite the Georgia girls and boys?" Mary Ann asked, always mindful of the obligations of hospitality.

"No, dear," Bonny Kate said in a low voice. "It will just be us Seviers. I'll have Sister Betsy and Cousin Betsy fix us lunches, and Johnny can saddle the horses. Then we can leave as soon as we are ready."

The children could hardly contain their excitement, but promised not to tell any of their Georgia guests where they were going. Only Amy Sevier's children could go on the family picnic with them. The outing was necessary and overdue as Bonny Kate once again embraced her cherished role as stepmother to Sarah's precious children. The hours passed pleasantly on the hilltop known as Mount Pleasant as they ate, conversed, and enjoyed the view of the valley. Bonny Kate revealed her ideas for the Mount Pleasant dream house they would build in happier times to come. She led them in games, told stories, and sang silly songs until the little ones reclined on their blankets for an afternoon nap. Bonny Kate picked up her knitting during the quiet time, and her slender fingers flew through the yarn as she skillfully managed the needles without even watching what she was manufacturing. Out of her work came thoughts of John, and she imagined all the noble things he was doing for the good of the country. A sad song rose to her lips, and she sang softly into the October breeze that rustled the gold, red, and orange leaves.

Here I sit on Buttermilk Hill
Who could blame me cry my fill.
Every tear would turn a mill.
Johnny has gone for a soldier.

Oh my baby, oh my love,
Gone the rainbow, gone the dove,
Your father was my own true love,
Johnny has gone for a soldier.

Me, oh my, I loved him so,
It broke my heart to see him go,
And only time will heal my woe,
Johnny has gone for a soldier.

Oh my baby, oh my love,
Gone the rainbow, gone the dove,
Your father was my own true love,
Johnny has gone for a soldier.

I sold my flax, I sold my wheel,
To buy my love a sword of steel,
So it in battle, he may wield,
Johnny has gone for a soldier.

Oh my baby, oh my love,
Gone the rainbow, gone the dove,
Your father was my own true love,
Johnny has gone for a soldier.

I'll dye my petticoat, dye it red,
And through the world I'll beg my bread,
For the lad that I love from me has fled,
Johnny has gone for a soldier.

From her hilltop perch she observed a rider she recognized as her brother Billy Sherrill, come rapidly from the direction of Daisy Fields. He crossed the ford and galloped up to Plum Grove. Several minutes later she saw Colonel Clarke and several of his men take the river road toward Daisy Fields, and she knew something was stirring. She stood up, put away her knitting and went to saddle her horse, which had enjoyed munching on the lush grass found at Mount Pleasant. Betsy and Johnny Sevier had seen her reaction.

"Are you leaving us, Bonny Kate?" Betsy asked.

"Colonel Clarke is lightin' out for Daisy Fields, and I have to know why."

"I reckon you'll know soon enough. Here comes your brother Billy," John Jr. observed. She turned in the direction of Plum Grove and led her horse down to meet the rapidly approaching messenger.

"Bonny Kate, it's Indians!" Billy Sherrill arrived all out of breath. "They are approaching Horse Creek by foot. One of the Georgia scouts saw them and reported it to Captain Few. They sent me up to give the news to Colonel Clarke. Mama told me where to find you. We figured you would need to know."

"Thank you, Billy." Bonny Kate turned to her sister-in-law and spoke calmly. "Amy, take the children home and fortify Plum Grove. Johnny is very responsible, and the younger ones listen to him. He will keep you all safe."

"I'm going with you, Bonny Kate," Johnny declared stubbornly. "I'm a member of the home guard."

"Then you'll follow orders. Fortify and hold Plum Grove!"

"Father made me promise to protect you. If there's going to be an Indian war, I go where you go."

"There's not going to be any Indian war if I can help it."

"Why not?" Billy Sherrill asked.

"We don't have any powder and shot."

"We all know who to blame for that," Billy said grimly.

"Thank you, dear brother, I love you too." She turned back to Johnny Sevier. "Johnny, when you have secured Plum Grove, I want you to send word to Major Robertson and have him bring all units of the home guard forward to Daisy Fields at once."

"Where will we find the major?"

"Uncle Robert's tavern in Jonesborough; the Major is no doubt trying to make a profit there."

"Yes, ma'am," Johnny said. He was his father's son and bred for heroic action, so he was eager to get started on his mission to alert the home guard. Bonny Kate fully intended to stop the Indian trouble before it started. She and Billy spurred their horses down the hill and across the meadows toward the land they knew so well as Daisy Fields.

Betsy and Johnny watched them go. Baby Nancy awoke from her nap on the quilt, and Betsy picked her up. Betsy sang to her nine-month old sister.

"Oh my baby, oh my love,
Gone the rainbow, gone the dove,
Your father was my own true love,
Bonny Kate's gone for a soldier."

"What are you planning to do?" Billy called ahead to his elder sister as the horses flew across the open meadow.

"Get close enough to see what kind of Indians they are. I'm hoping it's a hunting party of friendly Cherokees."

"What if they are hostile Chickamaugas?"

"Then we will be forced to rely on stratagem!"

Billy knew his sister well enough to realize she had no earthly idea how to head off an Indian war and that she would make up her stratagem as the emergency developed. It was useless to question her further about it. His only comfort as they approached the menacing prospects lay in the fact that sister and brother rode fast Sherrill horses and the Indians were reportedly on foot. Half an hour of riding brought them to the upper reaches of Horse Creek where the Indians had reportedly been seen. They were still some distance from their family home, Daisy Fields, where Bonny Kate guessed the Georgians were assembling their forces.

Bonny Kate and her brother Bill stopped, looked, and listened for signs of Indians passing through. They proceeded down Horse Creek cautiously, but one does not overtake Indians in the wilderness completely undetected. They crossed a meadow beside the creek where Bonny Kate had often, in the past, tended her father's sheep. It was a peaceful place where she could lay in the soft green grass with her faithful sheepdog, Bounder, and watch the towering clouds pass over the lofty mountains to the south of the Nolichucky Valley. Not a bird rustle disturbed the afternoon peace as they rode their horses at a slow walk through the long grass. As they approached the end of the meadow, their progress was arrested by the sight of one Indian as he stepped out of the woods into the sunlight. Another appeared and then another as Billy Sherrill turned in his saddle to plot their escape. His heart sank when Indians appeared all around the meadow, and he knew they were surrounded. Bonny Kate sat taller in the saddle and looked straight ahead.

"Billy, they are not wearing war paint. Don't make any sudden moves, and we can talk our way out of this." She looked for the leader of the party with whom she might parley. Her voice had been strong and steady despite the sickness she felt stirring in her belly.

"They may not be wearing war paint, but each one carries a new British musket," he replied in a low voice.

Bonny Kate's father had many times in the past scolded her for taking initiative aggressively while using poor judgment concerning the consequences. Now in her latest misadventure, she had left her husband's children unattended and led her brother into an ambush, endangering the entire community once again by being absent from her post.

Chapter 22

Western Deception

A voice of authority spoke from the forest shade. "Swift Running Doe! Beloved Woman of the Hunakas!" It was a woman's voice, clear and confident. The woman emerged from the forest, tall and proud, holding the swan's wing, her badge of authority.

"Nancy Ward, Beloved Woman of the Cherokee, I welcome you to Daisy Fields, the home of my father," Bonny Kate answered. She breathed a sigh of relief. John Sevier was always quick to say there was no better friend to the white settlers than Nancy Ward, a powerful and influential female of the Cherokees.

"Where is Chucky Jack?" Nancy asked.

"He is here in my heart and always in my thoughts," Bonny Kate replied.

Nancy approached, and Bonny Kate thought it might be a more diplomatic gesture to dismount and greet the great woman for whom she had so much respect. They embraced, and Nancy kissed her on both cheeks in the French fashion of greeting. "It is good to see you looking so well, and you glow like the woman with a secret, no?" She placed her hand on Bonny Kate's tummy, but she recoiled from the ticklish touch and blushed.

"No, I haven't any time for secrets."

"Did the Spirit Warrior tell you of my coming? I told no one of my journey, yet you are here to welcome me."

"Yes, the Spirit guides me."

"Did he tell of my purpose?"

"No, he has given me the honor of hearing you tell it." Bonny Kate smiled.

"I have come to see the daughter of Chucky Jack that he named to honor me."

"Oh," Bonny Kate said. She began to realize the awkwardness of a visit from the Cherokee queen. Diplomacy and deferential treatment would be required for her and her entourage, which numbered twenty-two armed warriors, and two women attending the Beloved Woman. How would she host them properly, with her lands infested with

Georgia refugees who still had fresh memories of cruel atrocities at the hands of the Chickamauga and Creek Indians? A sort of panic began to overtake her as she realized it had been several days since she had scoured and scrubbed the floors, walls, and tables of Plum Grove. No one had ever found deficiencies in her housekeeping, yet now the world seemed to be crowding in on her home and hospitality faster than she could deal with it. She wondered how John would handle this unexpected pleasure. She didn't have long to consider it as she remembered the Georgia army assembling at that moment near Daisy Fields to annihilate the Indian threat. She turned to her brother Billy and introduced him to the Beloved Woman. "This is my brother Billy. He will carry the good news of your arrival to Daisy Fields, then to Plum Grove, and he will tell the good news to Charles Robertson at the tavern in Jonesborough, and he will go and get Colonel Carter and bring him to Plum Grove immediately."

"Bonny Kate, that's a full day of travel," Billy protested. "It's well after noon already."

"Then I suggest you get started," she ordered sternly. "You have to stop Elijah Clarke right now or we will have a catastrophe, do you understand?"

"Yes, ma'am. Where will you be?"

"I'm taking our honored guests to the sacred campground and meeting place at Mount Pleasant, where they will be comfortable and safe."

"I understand," Billy said. He eased his horse toward Daisy Fields, watching the warriors warily as he was allowed to exit their encirclement. He took one look back and shuddered to see his favorite sister surrounded by heavily armed Indians.

"Mount Pleasant sounds so romantic," Nancy said.

"It has more than lived up to its name," Bonny Kate agreed.

That evening the Indians built a bonfire on the hill at Mount Pleasant while Bonny Kate entertained Nancy Ward in the parlor at Plum Grove. Hannah Clarke, Esther Doak, Grace Bowman, Eliza Miller, Amy Sevier, and Mary Dyckes spent their evening in the cookhouse. They were all suspicious of the presence of Indians at Plum Grove and purposely stayed away. Colonel Clarke had posted pickets and guards all over Plum Grove and uneasily strolled from picket post to picket post, carefully watching the Indian camp on Mount Pleasant.

"She is such a beautiful baby!" Nancy Ward smiled broadly as she held and admired her little namesake. "Your husband did me a great honor in naming her after me. When did her mother die?"

"Only a few days after giving birth," Bonny Kate answered.

"So you are the only mother she has ever known?"

"It has been my great honor to care for her and become her stepmother."

"I can see the love you have for her," the Cherokee lady sighed. "If anything happens to you, I would take her to live with me at Chota."

Bonny Kate didn't like the thought of that and chose her words carefully. "The Beloved Woman is very kind, and I would trust her with any of my children; but my husband has a very large, loving, and caring family that would all want the same honor."

"Yes, I am sure Chucky Jack has his own plans for each of his children. When will your man come home?"

"He is away hunting with some of his friends. He will be home soon."

"How many days must I wait to see him?" Nancy pressed for the information.

"You might sooner see him at the council ground at Chota," Bonny Kate answered with effect. "I cannot predict his movements."

Nancy looked concerned. "What do you know, Beloved Woman?"

"What do you know, dear lady? Are your people going to attack us soon?"

Nancy laughed. "A question for every question, and you never give me an answer!"

"A splendid game, don't you think? We could play at this all night if you like."

Nancy gave her a dark look that unsettled her. The Cherokee princess rose from her chair and delivered baby Nancy back into the care of her stepmother.

"I do not want war with Chucky Jack. I want to talk with him."

"I do not want war either. War has always been a great inconvenience to me, but for the defense of my children and my beloved man I would fight to the death."

"I have children also. My children of Kingfisher are Catherine and Little Fellow. Brian Ward has given me Betsy and Nannie."

"We have much in common. Where are your children now?"

"Little Fellow has taken the warrior's path and gone to the camp of my cousin Dragging Canoe. Catherine married among my people, and wants to live in peace with many children of her own. Betsy married among her father's people, a great chief named Joseph Martin."

"I know Major Martin," Bonny Kate said. "He is a brave officer in the Sullivan County home guard."

"Nannie, my precious girl, will marry soon, and I think I might find her a husband from among the sons of Chucky Jack. They are proving to be warriors of great promise, are they not?"

"I am very proud of both Joseph and James."

"I should like to see them; are they close by?"

"I hold them close in my heart and in my prayers, but you cannot see them now for they have gone with their father on the hunt."

"Chucky Jack would not make war on his own family. We can make peace with marriage."

"I have never heard of any marriage that ever brought peace!" Bonny Kate laughed. "It only brings passion!"

Nancy grinned. "I'm sure you could tell me much about that, but the night is short and I have much to learn about the fate of nations."

"You won't learn it from me, Beloved Woman," Bonny Kate replied softly.

Nancy Ward paced the floorboards in the fire-lit room as Bonny Kate settled Baby Nancy into her cradle and covered her with a little blanket.

The Cherokee woman continued. "My daughter has told me that the Sullivan County men have gone with the Virginia men to fight the British over the Yellow Mountains. The British have promised us they will destroy the Hunakas as soon as they emerge from the mountains."

"Men make promises all the time they cannot keep," Bonny Kate countered. "Even honest men, who believe their promises, cannot know the direction of the winds of God."

"Did Chucky Jack go with the men who will be destroyed?"

"I think not," Bonny Kate replied sitting in a chair by the fire. She turned to her Bible on the stand beside her and paged over to Psalm 57 and read aloud in the candle light:

"Be merciful unto me, O God, be merciful unto me: for my soul trusteth in thee: yea, in the shadow of thy wings will I make my refuge, until these calamities be overpast. I will cry unto God most high; unto God that performeth all things for me. He shall send from heaven, and save me from the reproach of him that would swallow me up. God shall send forth his mercy and his truth. My soul is among lions: and I lie even among them that are set on fire, even the sons of men, whose teeth are spears and arrows, and their tongue a sharp sword. Be thou exalted, O God, above the heavens; let thy glory be above all the earth. They have prepared a net for my steps; my soul is bowed down: they have digged a pit before me, into the midst whereof they are fallen themselves. My heart is fixed, O God, my heart is fixed: I will sing and give praise. Awake up, my glory; awake, psaltery and harp: I myself will awake early. I will praise thee, O Lord, among the people: I will sing unto thee among the nations. For thy mercy is great unto the heavens, and thy truth unto the clouds. Be thou exalted, O God, above the heavens: let thy glory be above all the earth."

Bonny Kate looked up from the Bible and fixed her gaze upon the woman standing before her.

Nancy stood tall and proud; she spoke with the authority of a prophetess. "You are crafty like the cougar, but there are other ways to learn where the great wind blows." Nancy walked across the room and turned. "The news from the nation is not good. My uncle, Chief Attakullakulla, is dead, and Oconostota is very old. There is no wisdom in the council to oppose the talk of war. If they make Dragging Canoe the new War Chief, all is lost. The war will come, Bonny Kate. Prepare yourself. The warriors with me now are not men of talk, but men of war. They came to see your defenses and to discover the place where Chucky Jack makes his bed."

The words of Nancy Ward sounded to Bonny Kate more like a personal threat than a friendly warning, but she understood Nancy's precarious standing among her own people. She had warned the white settlers of attacks in the past, and her friendship with John Sevier could be looked upon by her own people as traitorous.

"I'm sorry about your uncle. He was a great and wise chief. I admired him very much."

"Call your man home, Bonny Kate. The warriors are looking at your lands to possess them again."

"If they look closely, they will see that I am prepared for war. I have an army of warriors all around me."

"The Council knows about your Georgia army of runaway soldiers and they laughed to hear the stories of how they fled before the Chickamaugas."

"They did not run away from Chickamauga warriors. They ran to me, in obedience to the call of the Holy Spirit, for I called them to me in my day of distress," Bonny Kate said calmly. "They will not run away when Chucky Jack directs them in battle."

"I wish I could see him and talk with him."

"I wish you could too," Bonny Kate sighed. "I expect him home from the hunt any day now."

Nancy sighed too. The designs of nations and her desire for peace imposed upon her greater burdens than any leader should ever have to bear.

The next morning the Indians on Mount Pleasant were gone. They had melted into the forest and slipped beyond the reach of Colonel Clarke's patrols. Not even the best trackers could determine their direction. Nancy Ward did not seem concerned about the movements of her escort warriors. At breakfast she announced, "I am leaving this morning to go home."

"I have a gift for you, Beloved Woman," Bonny Kate said. "I know you are very interested in dairy cattle providing milk, butter, and cheese for your people. I am sending four cows and a bull for you to take back to Chota. I wish for you the blessings of peace."

Nancy smiled. "Thank you, Beloved Woman of the Hunakas. We are friends forever. I left a gift for you at the camping place you call Mount Pleasant."

Major Charles Robertson had great sensitivity and extensive experience with Cherokee diplomacy. He provided horses for Nancy and her two female companions and organized the honor guard to escort the great woman back to the crossing of French Broad where her own party awaited her.

Later that morning one of Colonel Clarke's men brought down the gift that Nancy Ward had left. It was the Sherrill race horse that a gang of Tories had stolen the previous year and taken to Indian country. Bonny Kate was ever so glad to have the horse returned. As she examined the condition of the gift horse, Billy Sherrill rode up to Plum Grove from the direction of Jonesborough. He and his horse were exhausted from the long trip to and from Colonel Carter's mansion at Sycamore Shoals. He dismounted and delivered a letter from Colonel Carter. She read it immediately and laughed.

Billy grinned, "Colonel Carter was not in a good humor last night when he wrote that. What did he say?"

Bonny Kate read it aloud. *"Dear Mrs. Sevier, I cannot leave my demanding post at the head of a continental mercantile consortium every time you spot a small hunting party of peace-loving Indians. The last time I attended one of your emergencies, I was chagrined to discover that there was no emergency at all. You do not need my permission or participation to dispense your husband's hospitality, or give away his property, any more than you need my permission to change your baby's diaper. Handle it, I say, just handle it, as I'm sure by now you already have. The consequences and expenses of your decisions you can settle between yourself and your husband as soon as he comes home. Until that happy occasion, should you discover an opportunity for genuine profit—and not the sort of sorry enterprises you have heretofore presented—please notify me and consider me your most obedient and humble servant, Colonel John Carter, Esquire."*

Billy laughed. "You are on your own, dear sister! The county does not want to soil its hands in the changing of your baby's diapers."

"I have never found the government to be particularly helpful in any of my public or private business," she declared haughtily with a toss of her head that caused the morning breeze to caress her long silky hair.

"Colonel Carter doesn't want to share in the blame for you giving away all the powder and shot, harboring Tory spies on Colonel Sevier's plantation, letting these starving Georgians help themselves to all our food stocks, and letting those Indians come up here to spy on us. By the way, where did the Indians go?" Billy Sherrill had accurately catalogued her mistakes, adding guilt to the burdens she already carried.

"They all went home, I reckon. Here Billy, take this horse back to Daisy Fields. Nancy Ward returned it to me, and Mama and Mary Jane will be so glad to see it."

"Hey, it's the one the Tories stole the night they made off with you."

"Don't ever mention that to me again. It was a night of unspeakable terrors."

"You came through it without a scratch," Billy said.

"The wounds are upon my soul, and I don't ever want it discussed around Colonel Sevier's children. If it hadn't been for Jacob Dyckes, the Tories would have killed me."

"So that's why you have been so kind to the Widow Dyckes."

"Twice they saved my life and see what it got them; Jacob is dead and Mary lost the farm."

"Sister, your life is too complicated."

"Don't I know it."

Billy Sherrill left Bonny Kate with her reflections on the complications of life and the state of affairs in Washington County. Her thoughts soon turned to yearnings for John.

She counted the days since he left and tried to guess how many more days it might be before he returned. She longed to tell him everything that had happened to her since he left and share with him the secrets that only she could tell.

With Nancy Ward and the Indians gone, the household returned to normal. The women and children went about their business as before, but Colonel Clarke's officers remained on alert and increased their patrol activity. Colonel Clarke himself slept much of the morning, having stayed up all night watching the Indians. At noon Bonny Kate prepared another lunch for her guests and the remaining sick and wounded of Georgia. Attending also was Major Charles Robertson, who had come to investigate the Indian activity. As Amy Sevier and the other women washed the dishes and cooking pots, Bonny Kate met with Colonel Clarke and Major Robertson in the parlor.

"Colonel Clarke, we had a close call yesterday," Major Robertson began. "I wish you had consulted me before assembling your troops for action."

"There wasn't time," Clarke replied. "We discovered those Injuns just a mile from Sherrill's place. We could not have known their intentions."

"Nancy Ward is a princess of the Cherokees and the best friend we have among the nations," Bonny Kate said.

"That's the delicate nature of our situation out here," Robertson explained. "There are many different kinds of Indians, some friendly and some hostile. We always have to look before we leap. Yesterday's visitors were our friends, but they represent the most populous division of the Cherokee Nation. If they ever turned on us, they could bring twenty-five hundred warriors down on our isolated frontier outposts."

"I'm glad Bonny Kate rode to the rescue," Colonel Clarke said. "But it was a very dangerous thing she did, fetching them Injuns right into her home."

"I did what John would have done," she replied.

"I'm not sure he would have invited those warriors to camp on the mountain where they could spy out the whole valley," Major Robertson said.

"It was the first place I thought about to ensure their safety."

"So what did Nancy Ward tell you?" Robertson asked.

Bonny Kate sat down and frowned, "The news from Chota is not good. Our old friend, Chief Attakullakulla, is dead. Oconostota is powerless to stop the younger chiefs from ousting him and making Dragging Canoe the new War Chief of the Cherokees."

"Thunderation!" Major Robertson jumped to his feet.

"What does it mean?" Colonel Clarke asked.

"Indian war for sure," Robertson answered. "Dragging Canoe is chief of the Chickamaugas, the bloodiest band of Injuns on the continent. They broke away from the Cherokees when we made our peace treaty with Attakullakulla. If the Cherokees are reunited under Dragging Canoe, the civilization of the white man, west of the mountains, is finished!"

"How soon could this happen?" Clarke asked.

"Days, weeks, months; you never know with Injuns," Robertson said. They have their warrior rites, with the black drink. They'll work themselves into a frenzy of rage and hate; then nothing will stop their cruel onslaught."

"Colonel John Sevier can stop them," Bonny Kate declared. "All we have to do is hold on until he returns."

"*If* he returns," Robertson said.

"Hush that kind of talk. I won't have it in my house."

Elijah Clarke stood up and paced. "Charles, the two of us saw plenty of action last summer, and we whipped the British at Musgrove's Mill. They *can* be beaten with the correct strategy, and I trust that Isaac Shelby and John Sevier will achieve what they set out to do. All we have to do is focus on the correct strategy for dealing with this Indian threat. What does John Sevier usually do when the Indians get stirred up?"

"He sends Isaac Thomas, the Indian trader, down to Chota with a load of gifts and trade goods," Major Robertson answered. "Nancy Ward sends her warnings through Mr. Thomas. I'll arrange that with Thomas as soon as possible."

"Good," Clarke approved. "The next problem is getting Colonel Sevier and his men released from state service once Ferguson is defeated."

"Won't they just come home on their own?" Bonny Kate asked.

Elijah Clarke laughed. "Mrs. Sevier, you are refreshingly naïve about the way the military world works. Once Colonel Sevier proves his usefulness on the field of battle, there will be no end to the demands for his services until the last battle is fought, on the last day of the war!"

"I didn't realize that. I thought he could just come home."

"He will, if the citizens of the West send urgent pleas for help against a very real threat of Indian War. But the requests have to be made by a western authority like Colonel John Carter. I would recommend he get the letters going immediately and not stop until somebody close to the governor listens."

"Bonny Kate, I think you should go up and motivate Colonel Carter to action," Major Robertson suggested. "You have a talent for that."

"You certainly do, Mrs. Sevier," Colonel Clarke agreed.

"I'm afraid I've burned my bridges with Judge Carter. His last letter to me was decidedly icy."

"I recommend you rebuild the bridges, and quickly," Robertson said.

"I've no time for Judge Carter. My work here at Plum Grove is all-consuming."

"That will all go away when we move you to the safety of Watauga Fort," Major Robertson predicted.

Bonny Kate drew a deep breath. "I would as soon die by the tomahawk and scalping knife as by famine! I put my trust in that Power who rules the armies of Heaven, and among men on earth. If God protects him whom duty calls into danger, so will He those who trust in him and stand at their post. Who would stay out if Colonel Sevier's family forted?"

"That's the spirit!" Robertson grinned. "Speak like that to Colonel Carter, and you will light the fires that need to be lit!"

The next morning Bonny Kate prepared for a journey to the Watauga community. As traveling companions she had Amy Sevier and her mother, Jemima Sevier, and Colonel Clarke as their escort. Major Robertson had left the previous evening and ridden as far as the Jonesborough Tavern, where he spent the night in the home of his daughter. The Sevier sisters, Betsy, Mary Ann, and Dolly, rose early to help with the breakfast and took issue with Bonny Kate's travel plans.

"Why do you have to leave us again?" Dolly asked.

"Major Robertson needs my help to light a fire under old Judge Carter," Bonny Kate replied.

"You are going to burn the old judge?" Mary Ann asked. The nine-year-old still wondered at such figures of speech and tended to visualize them as she heard them.

"No, Mary Ann, lighting a fire under someone is a way of saying I'm going to urge the gentleman to action."

"I don't want you to go," eleven-year-old Dolly spoke her mind. "Betsy always makes me change Nancy's diaper, and then she's still a little cry-baby."

"Nancy is cutting teeth," Bonny Kate explained. "It hurts her and makes her fuss and drool a little more than usual. Just give her a wooden spoon to chew on, and she'll calm right down."

"Bonny Kate, what do we do if the Indians come back and you're not here?" Betsy asked.

"Listen girls, I'm depending on you to take charge around here without any complaining. I'm leaving you with Mrs. Clarke, Mrs. Doak, Mrs. Miller, and Mrs. Bowman, and they possess such capability and wisdom that you will never miss me. Judge Carter has to be informed about the unrest among the Cherokees, and I have to persuade him to write letters to Governor Nash so he will send your father home to us."

"So this is about getting Father to come home?" Betsy asked.

"Yes, that's exactly what this is about."

"Then I suppose we can spare you for a few days," Betsy said. "But it will be a challenge to make these little children understand why you left us again."

Bonny Kate smiled. "I'm sure you girls are equal to the challenge." She hugged each child as they said good-bye. "Have no fear, you were born a Sevier!"

The Jonesborough road led first to Little Limestone Creek, where Sevier's Mill operated under the management of Moses Embree. Bonny Kate was surprised to find that a construction crew of Georgia men was adding a wing onto the mill house.

"Mr. Embree," Bonny Kate greeted her independent contractor. "I did not authorize any such alteration to the mill house."

"Colonel Sevier did," Moses explained. "He paid me in advance, in full, to have it built nearly a year ago. I'm just now getting around to it, now that I have some skilled builders in this community."

"But that addition was a promise he made to Sarah."

"I sure am sorry she didn't live to see it," he replied. "Wait until you see the new kitchen. You are going to love it, with every modern convenience for today's woman."

"No," she protested. "This expenditure of money and effort is *not* necessary."

"I appreciate the thriftiness of your home economics, Mrs. Sevier, but with your standing in the community and your obvious plans to expand Colonel Sevier's family; you are going to need the room. We heard the news. Congratulations on your blessed event."

"Did you hear my news?" Amy chimed in. "I'm going to have a baby the same month as Bonny Kate."

"Well now, that's the best news I have heard all day!" Moses smiled. "I offer my congratulations to you too, Mrs. Sevier. I expect you will need a good builder to add a wing onto *your* house."

"Well, now that you mention it," Amy replied thoughtfully.

"Stop the building," Bonny Kate interrupted.

"Speak for yourself, Bonny Kate. If John Sevier can add onto his house for his family, there's no reason why Valentine Sevier can't do the same."

"I *am* speaking for myself. Stop this construction project immediately. We still have homeless people from Georgia exposed to the elements, and each night gets a little colder. You should be building cabins for the needy."

"The homeless can move into Plum Grove when you move in here, Mrs. Sevier," Moses suggested.

"That sounds like a splendid idea," Jemima exclaimed.

"No, I'm not leaving Plum Grove. Stop the building!"

"I can't do that, Mrs. Sevier," Moses replied. "My contract is with Colonel Sevier. He has fulfilled his obligation to me by paying in full and allowing me all this time to accomplish the work. It is my sacred duty to complete the work, now that Providence hath provided these good craftsmen. Now if you will just look over the layout here, and imagine that view of the mountains from your kitchen window, I think you will appreciate what we are doing for you."

"No! I don't want to live here. Sarah didn't want to live here either!" She broke down and began to cry.

"I thought you would be pleased, Mrs. Sevier," Moses said.

"She *is* pleased, Mr. Embree," Amy said cheerfully, putting her arm around Bonny Kate. "She's very pleased."

"She doesn't seem pleased in the way I'm used to seeing a woman pleased." Mr. Embree's disappointment in her reaction was evident.

Amy guided Bonny Kate back to their horses. Jemima smiled at Moses. "Don't worry Mr. Embree, she really is pleased. It's just the morning sickness. Carry on with your good work. Any woman would be pleased with all this!"

Colonel Elijah Clarke rode ahead of the three women, confused by what he had seen and listening for some explanation for the strange behavior.

"It's all about Sarah, isn't it?" Amy guessed.

"I can't talk about it," Bonny Kate spoke through her tears.

"I know," Amy said empathetically. "None of us could deal with a loss like that. It would have killed John if you hadn't been there for him."

"She was my best friend, and as she lay dying, she asked me to care for her children until John remarried."

"Mission accomplished," Amy declared.

"But I feel so guilty for my happiness, my own true love, my own baby, my own destiny at long last realized. It is a cruel circumstance that Sarah had to die for all that."

"No, you must never feel guilty about that, Bonny Kate," Amy said. "It was all in God's good Providence. Sarah would have died on that same day even if Bonny Kate Sherrill had never walked the face of this earth. Then what would have become of John Sevier and his children?"

"Amy's right," Jemima agreed. "John would have been much worse off with any of those Jonesborough widows who lined up to take Sarah's place. There were some mean women in that bunch. Sarah knew what she was doing when she chose you to care for her children."

"If anybody should feel guilty, let it be Sarah Sevier," Amy said.

"What do you mean?"

"She took you away from a perfect girlhood, loving family, and successful horse breeding business, and put you to work in Colonel Sevier's baby mill. She left you with full responsibility for baby number ten, and now you have the entire burden for baby number eleven and Lord knows how many more. She left you all the work, all the pain, all the risks, and all the mistakes that she would have made."

"Sarah never made mistakes."

"Ha, Bonny Kate, how little you know! Look at what Sarah escaped with this

Carolina war and this infestation of Georgia refugees who came down on us like the plague..."

"I resent being compared to the plague," Colonel Clarke spoke up.

"Excuse me, sir, but I'm trying to make a point here," Amy continued. "Sarah doesn't have to give a thought to the next Indian war, the financial ruin you'll face with John's farm and businesses. She won't have to worry about losing him in battle, and she never had the tragedy of having to bury a dead child. Don't ever tell me you feel guilty for taking on all that heartache in her place. She lives forever in the joyful presence of God Almighty, where she never again has to worry about what to fix for tonight's dinner."

"You have said enough, Sister Amy."

"Enough to make you realize, you are *not* feeling sorry for Sarah Sevier? I think you are just feeling sorry for Bonny Kate Sevier."

"I'll stop feeling sorry when I stop feeling sick to my stomach," Bonny Kate replied.

"Shall we stop a moment and let you throw it all up?"

"No. I can endure it."

"Good, because our next stop is a visit with Kesiah Sevier. And I want you to behave yourself and take a step toward reconciliation."

Bonny Kate looked again at her strong, confident sister-in-law. "If you can endure it, I can endure it."

Chapter 23

Letters to the Governors

At the Jonesborough Tavern there was much activity. Major Charles Robertson had called his home guard officers together for a staff meeting, where they discussed the Indian situation and worked on plans for patrolling the frontier. Several of the Georgia men were also using the tavern as a meeting place to discuss the health and healing progress of their own people. When Colonel Clarke and the three Sevier ladies arrived at the tavern, they were welcomed and given refreshment by the tavern's hostess, Kesiah Sevier.

"Kesiah, let's have a private visit, just you, me, and Bonny Kate," Amy suggested.

"I'm busy," Kesiah answered truthfully.

"Mother can tend the business for a few minutes," Amy said. "She had plenty of experience helping Big Val run the original Sevier Tavern, Inn, and general store."

"All right, let's get this over with," Kesiah said.

"Oh, Mrs. Sevier," a man called out.

The four ladies turned and all answered in chorus, "Yes?" They looked at one another and laughed.

"Which Mrs. Sevier are you addressing, sir?" Bonny Kate asked.

"You, Bonny Kate," the man removed his hat and bowed politely.

"Should I know you?"

"I reckon you should, ma'am. You recommended daily bathing in the Nolichucky River for me and my wife. My name is Clark, John Clark, of the Savannah Volunteers."

"I wouldn't have recognized you, Mr. Clark."

"The waters did everything you said they would, except for my teeth."

Bonny Kate grinned. "Some treatments take longer than others, Mr. Clark. Are you a relative of Colonel Clarke?"

"No, ma'am, we're the Savannah Clarks, no kin to the Colonel."

"What can I do for you, Mr. Clark?"

"I want to make you an offer for ya fahm.

"My what?"

"Ya fahm, the plantation," Mr. Clark repeated.

"Oh, my farm!" Bonny Kate laughed. "I'm sorry, Mr. Clark; Plum Grove is not for sale."

"I don't mean right away," he continued. "I mean after you move yo' family up to that fine big house at the mill."

"I'm not moving, Mr. Clark, and I'm not selling Plum Grove."

"Why would you order all that work on yo' house at the mill and not move there? It's going to be the finest house in the West and much closer to town."

"It's a long story, John," Elijah Clarke interrupted. "Mrs. Sevier is very sensitive about it, and I don't think she wants to discuss it."

"I'll pay top dollar for it, in silver, if she would consider selling. You know I can pay it, Colonel."

"I know you can, John," Colonel Clarke said. "But Mrs. Sevier can't consider it right now."

"Why not?" Mr. Clark asked.

"Because she doesn't own it," Kesiah spoke up. "She doesn't own any of it; her husband does. If anything happens to John Sevier, she might get her filthy paws on it briefly, but not without a fight, I'll tell you. John's children ought to have it all, by right of inheritance, and she should get nothing!"

Amy grabbed her two sisters-in-law by the hands and guided them toward the back exit of the tavern. "Hush, you troublemaker. Today is a very special day, and I'm not going to let anybody spoil it. Bonny Kate, don't say a word. I know you were provoked, but just ignore it."

The women arrived at Kesiah's cabin behind the tavern and entered for their visit.

"Why is this a special day?" Kesiah asked.

"This is a day of covenant peace between three sisters-in-law. All past wrongs will be forgiven and promises will be made for perpetual peace."

"Why can't I defend myself from her outrageous lies and slanders?" Bonny Kate protested.

"And why can't I defend myself from her bad temper and physical abuse?" Kesiah countered.

"Because your behavior is not dignified, and it disgraces the family," Amy said. "If you don't believe me, just look toward the tavern door." Bonny Kate and Kesiah looked out the windows and saw what Amy was talking about. All the men in the tavern were gathered at the doors and windows, listening eagerly for the anticipated action. They held paper money in their fists and were prepared to bet it all on a favorite.

"Now what in the world are they doing?" Kesiah asked.

"I'll show you," Amy replied. She opened the door and called out. "Major Robertson, what are the odds?"

"Even money, Miss Amy," he replied.

"Well, save some of that action for me. It won't take me long to go over the rules and get them started."

"Will do, Miss Amy," Robertson answered with a grin.

"My own father," Kesiah said with a huff. "I'll wager he's betting on Bonny Kate!"

"How embarrassing," Bonny Kate responded with disgust. "I would have expected better odds than even money."

"Val, John, and Robert are as close as brothers can possibly be," Amy said. "They love each other in the same way they were loved by their mother Joanna, God rest her soul. We should model the same kind of love and respect for each other as our dear husbands do. Anything less dishonors our beloved men."

"You are right, Amy," Kesiah exhaled, "right as rain."

"I'm sorry, Kesiah, for every mean thing I ever did to you," Bonny Kate said.

"For soiling my hair?"

"Yes, I'm especially sorry for that."

"And I'm sorry for every mean thing I ever said."

"Well, that's fine," Amy approved. "Can we promise to never say or do anything like that again?"

"All I can promise is, I'll try," Kesiah replied.

"We are women, Amy. Please don't make this impossible," Bonny Kate said with a grin. "But I'll tell you this: I don't ever want to give those tavern men the satisfaction of seeing me involved in any more catfights!"

"And take care not to hurt that baby," Amy cautioned.

"What baby? Bonny Kate, are you pregnant?" Kesiah asked with surprise.

"Yes, and so is Amy. We are both going to deliver in May."

"Oh, sisters, that's wonderful news!" Kesiah was delighted and sincerely pleased for both her sisters-in-law. The ladies continued to visit peacefully for a long time, and the men in the tavern, one by one, gave up on the prospect of a catfight and drifted away to find other amusements.

After lunch at the tavern, Colonel Clarke, Major Robertson, and Bonny Kate set out for Watauga Valley to complete their mission to motivate Colonel John Carter to write the governor and get the over-mountain army released from service in the eastern part of the state. Jemima Sevier and Amy Sevier stayed in Jonesborough for a longer visit with Kesiah.

Mr. John Clark was at the hitching post to see the travelers off. "Mrs. Sevier, please seriously consider my offer to buy your fahm. Discuss it with your husband, and let me know what he says."

"Plum Grove is not for sale at any time, or at any price, Mr. Clark," she answered. She was glad to be moving again on that beautiful October afternoon. The sun was warm and the air was cool as they made their way over the ridge north of Jonesborough and into the watershed of the Watauga Valley. It was a more settled region of the backwater country than the Nolichucky Valley with pretty farms of pasture land, cornfields, wheat fields, and vegetable gardens. The harvesters were busy in every field, and Colonel Clarke frequently stopped to speak to various Georgia men and women helping in the fields.

The travelers finally arrived at the Sinking Creek farm of Charles Robertson. His wife, Susannah, warmly greeted them and built up the fires in the cook house for a fine dinner.

"Bonny Kate, did you see Kesiah today?"

"I did indeed, and she was very kind to me."

"Amy Sevier was there, no doubt," Susannah guessed.

"Yes," Bonny Kate replied. "Blessed are the peacemakers, for they will be called children of God."

"So, you and Kesiah have patched things up?"

"Yes, ma'am. All that passed between us is forgiven. We had a wonderful time talking about having babies and all the changes that come with that."

"Who is having a baby?"

"I am, and so is Amy, the same month as me."

"Well, Bonny Kate that is truly a blessing. A baby changes everything in a woman's life."

"Most of the changes I am already acquainted with, caring for baby Nancy and Rebecca, Dicky, Valentine, Mary Ann, Dolly, Betsy and Johnny. They are all such sweet children. I love every one of them."

Susannah smiled. "And now you will have one of your own. That was mighty fast work, Bonny Kate."

"You know what they say about the Sherrills; we never do anything halfway."

"I wonder how Jack will take the news."

"He was always so pleased and excited each time Sarah got pregnant."

"Then he will be the same with you," Susannah predicted with certainty.

"We have been apart more than we have been together since the wedding," Bonny Kate said sadly. "My remembrance of him fades a little more each day. This war is a cruel thing for families."

"It doesn't get any easier with the years, Bonny Kate. When Charles was gone this past summer, I had the same feelings you just described."

"I have to meet with Judge Carter in the morning, and I'm not looking forward to it," Bonny Kate admitted.

"It's about your visit with Nancy Ward, isn't it?"

"Yes, ma'am. Nancy thinks there will be more trouble as the Cherokee leadership transfers to the younger chiefs."

"I was afraid of that. We sure need to get our men back home from the eastern war mighty quick."

"I hope I can get Judge Carter working on that tomorrow," Bonny Kate sighed.

Two Georgia families were staying at the Robertson farm, and when they came in from their labors, they were delighted to see that the lady from Plum Grove, their first hostess on the frontier, was visiting and spending the night with the Robertsons. Pleasant dining and interesting conversation made it a very fine evening for all.

Judge Carter was still in bed when Bonny Kate and her military escorts, Colonel Clarke and Major Robertson, arrived for the business of the day. The Judge's secretary, Mr. William Tatham, entertained them while Mrs. Carter roused the Judge and helped him dress.

"Colonel Carter doesn't sleep well these nights and compensates by staying in bed later than normal," Mr. Tatham explained.

"Is he sick with something catching?" Clarke asked.

"No, I think he worries too much about the administrative details of his civil and military offices. Then, his business concerns and his investments in times such as these all combine to work great stresses upon the man's constitution."

"In our last meeting, I prescribed a remedy for that which distresses him," Bonny Kate said. "He should delegate some of his offices and titles to those who have already relieved him of the commitments and responsibilities. Then he could put his mind at rest about the military portion of the county's business."

Colonel Carter called from the hall where he was making his progress toward the parlor. "Is that sweet songbird, Mrs. John Sevier? She is singing a song I have heard before, and I know that tune!"

"Yes, Judge Carter, it's me," she called back. The next instant he appeared in the doorway smiling as he leaned on his cane.

"Good day, madam," he bowed.

"Good day, sir," she replied.

"Gentlemen, thank you for attending." The judge acknowledged the two officers as they stood and saluted. "Please be seated. We observe no formalities here, do we Bonny Kate?"

"Very few," she answered.

"Can I offer you gentlemen some rum, or a pipe of tobacco? Mr. Tatham, serve our guests, if you will, and the lady too."

"No, thank you, Judge Carter, nothing for me," she said.

Tatham prepared rum and tobacco pipes for the officers and served them as directed.

"Madam Sevier has been smoking the peace pipe and treating with the Cherokees, but declines to smoke with us, Mr. Tatham. What do you think about that?"

"I don't smoke with anybody, Judge Carter. You know that."

"She held a talk with the Queen of the Cherokees, without notifying the proper authorities."

"Not by choice, sir, but out of necessity. The circumstance came upon me like an emergency, and I called for your help immediately."

"She negotiated a treaty with Nancy Ward and exchanged gifts to seal the deal. Now she wants to explain the terms and ask for our approval after the fact."

"That's not true, Judge Carter."

"Listen to me, young woman. Only the governor of the state has the authority to appoint commissioners to make treaties with the Indians. Even now, the Continental Congress argues that only *they* shall have that authority. You have meddled in something that does not concern you."

"Listen to me, you pompous windbag..." She rose in a rage and approached the judge. Colonel Clarke and Major Robertson intercepted her in midstride.

"Whoa there, Bonny Kate," Major Robertson said. "Let's not do anything we will regret later. Calm down, now. There has been a misunderstanding."

"I'll say there's a misunderstanding. I didn't make any treaty with the Cherokees, and he has no right to accuse me when he was advised of events and did nothing to help me."

"I was indisposed," Judge Carter said.

"Bonny Kate, why don't you sit down and tell the whole story, calmly and rationally," Colonel Clarke suggested. She sat down and communicated her displeasure with the judge by frowning.

"Nancy Ward showed up on Horse Creek with an escort of about twenty warriors and some kinswomen of hers. I rode down and stopped them from walking into Daisy Fields, where a troop of Georgia horse soldiers was waiting. I prevented a killing that would have immediately plunged the whole frontier into deadly war."

"That's a fact," Colonel Clarke agreed. "We were ready to attack them as soon as they showed up."

"I took Nancy and her Indians to Plum Grove and provided food and hospitality, while I learned from Nancy the purpose of her visit."

The judge adjusted his spectacles on his nose. "What was her purpose?"

"She said she wanted to see the baby that John had named in her honor, but what she really wanted was to talk to John and warn him about the situation in the Cherokee Council."

"How did she describe that situation?"

"Very dangerous," Bonny Kate answered. "Attakullakulla is dead, and Oconostota will be replaced by Dragging Canoe as War Chief. Nancy says that nothing can stop the war from coming."

"Anything else?"

"She desperately wanted to know where my John was so she could talk to him about an arranged marriage between one of his sons and a daughter of hers."

"What information did you give her?"

"Nothing she could use for a military advantage. I kept all my answers purposefully vague."

"No promises were made?"

"No, Judge, I never make promises I have no way of keeping."

"What about these reports of gifts being traded?"

"Nancy returned a stolen horse that belonged to my father, and I gave her some milk cows and a bull."

"Are these the same cattle that were donated to Washington County for the eastern campaign?"

"Yes, sir," Bonny Kate answered.

"Giving the Indians county cattle that were donated for a state campaign, and later returned, might be a legal problem for you, Mrs. Sevier," the judge advised.

"But you told me that the cattle belonged to Colonel Sevier," Bonny Kate said.

"That's true, Judge," Mr. Tatham confirmed. "I see that journal entry right here."

"And I have since discovered that Colonel Sevier has yet to pay the original owner for the cattle," Bonny Kate shared.

The judge continued his examination. "Who was the original owner?"

"Amy and Valentine Sevier," she answered.

Judge Carter looked perplexed. "So the wife of the lieutenant colonel, took possession of the cattle donated to Washington County for use by the State of North Carolina when it was determined that said cattle were surplus property of the State and returned to the county. The county judge ruled the cattle to be the property of the lieutenant colonel until said lieutenant colonel settles a debt owed on the cattle to the sheriff of the county and his wife."

"Yes, but I left the cattle at Amy's until I could decide what to do with them."

"That constitutes a return of these particular cattle to the rightful owners," the judge ruled.

"But then Amy brought the cattle to me the other day to feed the Georgia refugees, and I gave four milk cows and a bull to Nancy Ward so she can start a dairy farm for the Indian children to have fresh milk, butter, and cheese."

"Mrs. Sevier, please don't tell me anything else about these transactions. I don't want to hear about it, and I don't want to know about it. Just have Colonel Sevier and his brother settle their accounts when they return from the campaign."

"What about the legal problems you mentioned?"

"Mrs. Sevier, there's not a lawyer on the continent that can untangle the mess you have

242 | Bonny Kate's Honeymoon

created concerning these confounded cattle," Judge Carter decided.

"I glad that's settled," Bonny Kate breathed a sigh of relief. None of the men who were present believed that anything had been settled.

"Mrs. Sevier, it seems we owe you a debt of gratitude for preventing the death of Nancy Ward, the Beloved Woman of the Cherokees, and by so doing you postponed a Cherokee War that would have been disastrous to the country!"

"Thank you, Judge Carter," Bonny Kate answered. "Now if we can just get Colonel Sevier and his men to come home and reinforce the western frontier before the Cherokees *do* attack, we may have a fighting chance at survival."

"Ever the optimist," Judge Carter said.

"She's right, sir," Charles Robertson spoke up. "We must prevail upon the governor to release the over-mountain men as soon as possible to return and protect their own homes and families."

"Well now, let's not be hasty," Judge Carter cautioned. "We don't want to recall the troops before they have accomplished the mission they set out to accomplish. That would be wasteful of the funds already expended."

"If we write the governor today, the release would arrive at just about the time the thirty-day enlistments run out. That is not hasty. I call that perfect timing," Robertson said.

"He knows what he's talking about, Judge Carter," Colonel Clarke entered the discussion. "We both have experience in McDowell's command, and we discovered that McDowell moved too slowly. He would want to keep your troops in his service over there for the better part of a year!"

"We can't spare our men for a whole year, not with an Indian war just over the horizon," Bonny Kate said.

"I understand your impatience, Mrs. Sevier, but not one single report has returned from Colonel Sevier concerning their progress."

"Send him a courier, and see if we can learn anything," she suggested.

Colonel Carter stood up with difficulty and turned to Major Robertson. "Charles, communicate the situation, here on the frontier, directly with Colonel Sevier. I'll send the governor a report about the Indians and request the release of our men. I guess this is a good time to include my letter of resignation as Washington County Colonel and recommend the promotion John Sevier."

"Oh, thank you, Judge Carter!" Bonny Kate flew into an embrace with the feeble gentleman.

"Whoa, Bonny Kate, don't knock me down!"

The officers moved into action. William Tatham wrote out the letter to Governor Nash as Judge Carter dictated it to him. As they finished the first letter, Judge Carter recommended they write a similar letter to Governor Rutledge of South Carolina just in case the action had moved south into another jurisdiction. He knew that both governors had been conducting their state business from the same North Carolina town of Hillsborough.

"Bonny Kate," a sweet feminine voice called from the drawing room. Bonny Kate left Colonel Carter's office, crossed the hall, and entered the drawing room.

"Yes, Mrs. Carter?"

"When the courier rides to Colonel Sevier, I know your husband will be expecting a letter from you, dear girl. Use my desk and get started."

"Thank you, Mrs. Carter." Bonny Kate curtsied. She found everything she needed at Mrs. Carter's well-organized corner desk and went right to work. "There's so much to tell him about everything that has happened to me. I hope he has time to read it all."

"Are you telling him the really big news?"

"No, ma'am," she replied. "Some things can only be told in whispers, between long loving kisses."

"That's the spirit, my dear, bonny girl," Mrs. Carter approved. "Tell him like that, and you will never run out of interesting things to say."

Some time had passed as Bonny Kate drafted her letter, and Mrs. Carter pursued her needle work. "A pompous windbag, did you say? I must take issue with your assessment of our good judge."

"Oh, Mrs. Carter, I'm so sorry," Bonny Kate replied. "I owe your husband my deepest apology."

"Well now, let's not be hasty," Mrs. Carter imitated her husband's manner with a sparkle in her eye. "I would agree he certainly can be pompous, but the dear man is not windbag enough to outtalk the average woman, let alone a woman like you!"

Bonny Kate laughed at Mrs. Carter's joking, but still felt bad for losing her temper. She resolved to patch things up with Judge Carter before leaving for home.

Upon Bonny Kate's recommendation, her brother, John Sherrill, was chosen to ride the communications to Hillsborough on a swift Sherrill horse. He was honest, reliable, efficient, and knew well the route over the mountains and through the Catawba River Valley to Sherrill's Ford, then east on Sherrill's Path to the more settled areas of the state. Bonny Kate also wanted a man who could make a good impression on the governor representing the character of the western people, and John Sherrill could certainly do that.

In the afternoon, when all the communications were complete, Colonel Clarke escorted Bonny Kate home. As they approached Jonesborough, Bonny Kate saw a familiar sight in the road ahead; it was the big Conestoga freight wagon that was a Sherrill family heirloom. The canvas sides were rolled up for the comfort of passengers, and Billy Sherrill drove the oxen. Bonny Kate recognized Amy Sevier and all her children, Jemima Sevier, Eliza Miller, and her two daughters.

"Hello, Bonny Kate," Billy called to his sister.

"Hello, Bill," Bonny Kate responded. "You have quite a precious cargo today. Where are you headed?"

"Stony Creek," the young man replied.

"I was hoping to meet you along the way, Bonny Kate," Amy said. "I wanted to thank you for your hospitality and kindness. We so much enjoyed our visit."

"Why end it so soon?" Bonny Kate asked.

"We don't want to become a burden to you, and since Billy was heading up to Powder Creek to pick up a shipment, we thought we could ride along," Amy explained. "This surely beats walking."

Bonny Kate looked at Billy, "Powder Creek?"

"Yes, ma'am. Mrs. Patton has your order ready for delivery. And yesterday, Tom Embree brought a load of lead shot down to Plum Grove."

"Praise the Lord!" Bonny Kate felt great relief knowing that the resupply of ammunition would allow for the defense of Washington County.

"I have decided to use the stone house at Sevier's mill as our temporary Washington County armory," Bonny Kate said. "Deliver the powder there, if you will, and put Moses Embree in charge of it."

"Yes, ma'am."

"Are you leaving too, Mrs. Miller?"

"Yes, Bonny Kate, and I'm so grateful to you for your kind hospitality. I believe our men are coming home soon, and I think they will arrive at Sycamore Shoals first. I want to be there."

"She's staying at my place," Amy explained. "Esther Doak has moved back to New Salem and taken Mrs. Dyckes with her. Now you won't have so many guests to feed. How did your visit with Judge Carter turn out?"

"Very well, I think. I believe we have done all that we can do to defend the frontiers and hold this community together until our men get home. All that's left now is to pray and wait for Divine Providence."

The wagon continued on its way, and Bonny Kate turned to Colonel Clarke. "Well sir, this is a great day! You can now supply your men with the ammunition they need."

Colonel Clarke laughed. "This is a most unlikely place of refuge. You have Indians as your neighbors, Tories as your friends, a judge who thinks he's a colonel, women running the militia and milling the powder, Quakers in charge of the ammunition..."

"And Georgians doing all the hard labor," she said with a grin. "This is a most unlikely refuge indeed, Colonel Clarke. What in the world ever induced you to seek protection in such an upside-down place?"

"It must have been your friend, Divine Providence!" He grinned back.

Chapter 24

Eastern Confusion

John Sevier's army of backwater men along with their friends from North Carolina and Georgia marched south from Gilbert Town with no clear idea where they were headed, and no idea about the kind of battle they were seeking. They still had no experience in fighting a pitched battle in open fields against artillery, massed musketry, bayonets, and cavalry. The problem with the country they passed through was the fact that it was well settled land with open croplands and abundant pastures. They were leaving behind their beloved mountains and heavily forested valleys where Indian fighting experience gave them the greatest advantage. Only Isaac Shelby and John Sevier expressed concerns about that.

Colonels Sevier, Shelby, Campbell and Cleveland rode at the head of the column that filled the main road to Green River. John recognized his tall impressive young scout Joseph Greer waiting in the road ahead.

Greer saluted. "Colonel Sevier, more volunteers are waiting to join up about two hundred yards down."

"Who are they Joe?" Sevier asked.

"The leader says he is Major William Chronicle. He leads twenty mounted men from the South Fork of the Catawba."

"Let's make their acquaintance," John said urging his horse ahead. The other officers followed to meet the new volunteers. They found them dismounted and resting near a deserted farmhouse belonging to a Mr. Probit, beside the Broad River.

"Good day, gentlemen, which of you is Major Chronicle?" John asked.

A tall, slender, twenty-five-year-old man of distinguished bearing stood up and spoke. "I'm Major Chronicle. Who are you?"

"Colonel John Sevier, and this is Colonel Isaac Shelby, Colonel Benjamin Cleveland, and the leader of our expedition, Colonel William Campbell. We are looking for the enemy force under Major Patrick Ferguson. Would you have any news of his whereabouts?"

"Nothing certain," answered William Chronicle. "But I think you will find our services most valuable. We know all the country between here and Charlotte. Ferguson will most certainly pass through this area on his way to join Cornwallis."

"That's not the way we figure it," Colonel Campbell spoke up. "Our reports indicate Ferguson went to Fort Ninety Six. We are marching south."

"That doesn't make much sense, if the Colonel will pardon me for speaking plainly." Major Chronicle was an intelligent, thoughtful officer, considerably wise to be so young.

"Please, go on," Colonel Campbell encouraged the man to speak his mind.

"Well sir, Cornwallis has occupied Charlotte for two weeks, waiting for his supply trains to catch up," Chronicle explained. "Tarleton covers his right, and Ferguson his left. Only if Cornwallis were retreating would it make sense for Ferguson to withdraw to Fort Ninety Six and leave his commander's left wing uncovered. I can assure you, Cornwallis has met very little resistance and has no intention of retreating."

"Finally, we have a fellow that talks sense," Isaac Shelby said.

"Not so fast, Isaac," Colonel Campbell cautioned. "Although Major Chronicle presents a good theory, the facts still indicate Ferguson is escaping from us to the south. We are wasting precious time debating this issue."

"The movement south troubles me too, Bill." John Sevier weighed in on the matter. "Every mile takes us farther from home and increases the peril to our families from Indian attacks we know are being planned."

The attention of the officers was immediately drawn to a field on the east side of the road, where two officers in South Carolina uniforms approached them. No one spoke up to identify them until they arrived and introduced themselves.

"Good day, gentlemen. I am General James Williams, and this is Colonel Thomas Brandon. I was sent by Governor Rutledge to command the South Carolina troops on this campaign. I'm looking for the army of Colonel Charles McDowell."

"General is it now?" Isaac Shelby recognized him, as did several of the men from the summer campaign. "Since when did you become a general?"

"Well hello, Colonel Shelby," Williams said. "It's good to see you."

"And what makes you a general?" Isaac pursued his inquiry.

"Governor Rutledge was *very* grateful for our victory at Musgrove's Mill. I am prepared and authorized to serve as general of this campaign."

"Colonel Campbell is our leader," Shelby declared. "He brought four hundred men, and we have all agreed to follow him."

"Well, I have four hundred and fifty men, a general's commission, and in South Carolina, you are now operating in my jurisdiction," Williams said to assert his claim.

"You can't just ride in here and start giving us orders!" Isaac Shelby protested.

"Hold on, Isaac," Colonel Campbell said calmly. "Now listen, General Williams, we didn't come here to get involved in your politics or serve in your army. We came to get Ferguson. He insulted us and threatened our families. If you know where he is, tell us, and we will be on our way."

"You'll find Ferguson at Fort Ninety Six at the head of a large army of regulars and Tories," Williams informed them. "With our joined forces we can reduce the fort and take Ferguson."

"Where are your four hundred and fifty men, General Williams?" Colonel Sevier asked.

"We are camped only twenty-five miles to the northeast."

"I think you should bring your men along, and we will reorganize according to our combined resources," Colonel Campbell suggested. "Do you have artillery and a sufficient commissary to support us all?"

"I remind you, sir, I am a general of the South Carolina militia. What we need, we will find at Fort Ninety Six."

"We need artillery to reduce the fort and force the garrison to surrender," Colonel Cleveland pointed out.

"We will get it," Williams insisted.

"Very well, General Williams, bring your men up and join our line of march," Colonel Campbell said.

"I suggest we meet at the Old Iron Works on Lawson's Fork," Williams said.

"That's too far to the south if you intend to catch Ferguson," Major Chronicle objected. "Hannah's Cowpens would make a better camp. There's water, plenty of room for the horses, and we may find some beef."

"The Old Iron Works," General Williams insisted. "I'll be there tomorrow night."

"Very well, General Williams, we will see you then." Colonel Campbell saluted. Williams returned the salute, and the South Carolina officers galloped away to round up their men.

"Hold on, Colonel Campbell. You can't turn over command to him without a vote in officer's council," Isaac protested.

"I wasn't going to," Campbell said. "I just want to see his four hundred and fifty-man army with artillery and commissary. With those kinds of resources, we could really give Ferguson a proper battle in any kind of terrain."

"I'll wager Williams is lying about his resources," Isaac said with conviction.

Major Chronicle spoke up again in warning. "It would be a great mistake to take your men to the Old Iron Works. Ferguson will get away scot free if you do that."

"We are camping at Green River tonight so our scouts can report in," Colonel Campbell said. "Do you know the way to Green River, Major Chronicle?"

"Yes, sir! Mount up men; we're in a real army now. What may come of it, God only knows!"

That night, along the banks of the Green River, the patchwork army rested while the officers listened to the conflicting reports of the various scouts who reported their findings. The men rested secure in the knowledge that Old Lover Boy's pickets were guarding the camp that night. Those ever-alert pickets detected the approach of two riders feeling their way along the dark road.

"Stop right there and identify yourself!" Sam Sherrill Jr. called out.

"I'm Colonel Edward Lacey of Colonel Thomas Sumter's South Carolina Battalion."

"All right, Colonel, state your business."

"I'm looking for the army of mountaineers who came with Colonel Charles McDowell. Have I come to the right place?"

"Maybe. Come in real slow-like so I can see how many is out there." Sam Jr. was cautious and fully aware of his fellow sentries coming up to support him.

"It's just me and my guide," Colonel Lacey answered. "I need to talk to your leader." Lacey and his guide walked in leading their horses. The other sentries took control of their horses.

"Sit down, Colonel," Junior motioned toward a fallen log at his sentry post. "It will be awhile before the officers can see you."

"It's urgent that I see your commander."

"What's the password?"

"I have no idea."

"Well, who do you want to see?"

"The commander of the mountain men who came with Colonel McDowell," Lacey replied.

"What's his name?"

"Hell, I don't know, but I must see him!" the South Carolina colonel was becoming impatient.

"How do I know you are not a spy?"

"I rode all night to deliver information about the British army under Ferguson, and you will not even show me the courtesy of calling an officer?"

John Sevier appeared from the darkness of the surrounding woods. "What seems to be the problem, my dear brother-in-law?"

"Colonel, this fellow wants to see our commander, but doesn't know the password or the name of the person he has come to see. I'm thinking he's a spy."

"What's your name, sir?" John asked politely.

"I'm Colonel Edward Lacey, of Sumter's South Carolina Liberty Boys."

"I'll take him in, Junior. Thank you for your vigilance. Blindfold the fellow."

"Listen, John, I'm sorry we got the whole camp calling you Old Lover Boy."

"Forget it," John laughed. "I've been called a lot worse."

"Don't tell Bonny Kate what we done."

"She'll likely hear about it from someone in the community."

"She'll be powerful mad at the embarrassment."

"More than likely," John agreed. He took charge of Colonel Lacey and guided him toward the center of camp, where the officers were gathered discussing the options of what course the army should take. "Forgive me for this treatment, Colonel Lacey. We just can't be too careful. By the way, I'm Colonel John Sevier of Washington County."

"Old Lover Boy?" Lacey asked much amused by what he had heard. "What was that about?"

"A family matter, Colonel Lacey," John answered, but he would say no more.

At the center of camp a fire burned cheerfully on the cool night in early October. Colonels Campbell, Shelby, and Cleveland conferred with Major Chronicle, Captain William Lenoir, Major Joseph Winston, and Major Joseph McDowell. Colonel Campbell called out to Old Lover Boy when he appeared with the blindfolded Colonel Lacey.

"John, these gentlemen have worked most of the night to select the best men and horses for the final dash to catch Ferguson. I just need your report to complete the night's work."

"I'll have one hundred twenty fit for duty, sir," John reported. "Do you need a list of names?"

"That's all right, John," Colonel Campbell answered. "That's about half your original force. Have you lost that much capability?"

"The horses suffer more than the men; but I assure you, the ones I have selected are all battle ready. We came to get Ferguson, and we will." He removed the blindfold from Colonel Lacey.

"Who have you got there?" Campbell asked.

"I'm Colonel Edward Lacey of Sumter's South Carolina Liberty Boys. Who am I addressing, sir?"

"I'm Colonel William Campbell of Virginia. Where is Colonel Sumter?"

"He's in Hillsborough conferring with Governor Rutledge, but if there's opportunity for action against Ferguson, we will join you." Lacey was forthright and obviously game for a fight.

"Do you know where we might find Ferguson?" Isaac Shelby asked.

"He is moving east toward Charlotte," Lacey answered quickly.

"That's not what we heard," Campbell challenged. "We think he's headed south for Fort Ninety Six."

"No, sir; our patrols have repeatedly intercepted Ferguson's couriers on their way to Charlotte with requests for reinforcements from Cornwallis. Ferguson is moving toward Charlotte." Edward Lacey spoke with a confidence that encouraged those officers who agreed with his assessment.

"Well, just hours ago a general from South Carolina told us with great certainty that Ferguson is going to Fort Ninety Six," Colonel Campbell argued. "He is meeting us today with four hundred and fifty men, artillery and a commissary."

"Would that be General Williams?" Lacey asked.

"Yes, do you know him?"

"I know him," Lacey said with obvious disdain. "He's a liar. He lied to get that commission from the governor, and he lied about his four hundred and fifty men. He hasn't got any artillery, and if he has any commissary he probably stole it, like he stole General Sumter's commissary back in the summer."

"It sounds like General Williams has a colorful history," Colonel Sevier judged.

"Williams has only seventy men camped near us up at Flint Hill, and we have one hundred and fifty," reported Colonel Lacey. "And I assure you he is lying about where Ferguson went!"

"Why would General Williams lie to us?" Colonel Campbell inquired.

"*Colonel* Williams needs an army to reduce Fort Ninety Six so he and his men can recover their own property and plunder their Tory neighbors," Lacey explained. "Don't you see it's a trick, to use your army for his own purposes?"

"And in the process he's going to make it possible for Ferguson to get away!" John Sevier realized the full consequences of the deception that Colonel Williams was promoting.

"Damn!" Colonel Campbell said angrily. "Who can we believe?"

"I believe Colonel Lacey," Major William Chronicle volunteered. "It just makes sense that Ferguson would move closer to his commander and the source of his reinforcements." A heated discussion broke out among the officers as the various points of view were argued.

"Hold it!" Isaac Shelby called out above the tumult. "Come to order! Quiet, men! This doesn't settle anything." The men quieted again as Isaac took center of the circle. "I served with Colonel Williams in the summer campaign, and I don't trust him either."

Colonel Campbell turned to Colonel Lacey. "You see, Colonel Lacey, there is a great difference of opinion as to where we think Ferguson may be moving. Tonight we will meet General Williams at the Old Iron Works on Lawson's Fork."

"That's no good," Lacey said. "You would be marching directly out of the way from Ferguson!"

"That's where the general will bring his four hundred and fifty-man army."

Colonel Lacey was angered. "That's bullshit! Williams hasn't got any four hundred and fifty men. And I'll make damned sure he doesn't show up at the Old Iron Works."

Colonel Campbell considered the options. "What about that other place, the cattle market?"

"Hannah's Cowpens," Major Chronicle said, supplying the proper name.

"Yes, the Cowpens," Campbell said. "We will meet there and settle, once and for all, the matter of what course we should take. Colonel Lacey, can you guarantee that the South Carolinians will meet us at the Cowpens later today?"

"Yes, sir. I'll be there with Colonel Hill, Colonel Hambright, Colonel Graham, and all the South Carolina men," Colonel Lacey promised.

"Good man," Colonel Campbell approved.

"One more thing, sir," Lacey shared. "Ferguson will get his reinforcements in about two days. If we don't catch him soon, the opportunity is lost forever."

"Godspeed, Colonel Lacey," Colonel Campbell dismissed the officer. Colonel Lacey saluted and left the council circle.

John Sevier took him back to where he left his horse and his guide. "Colonel Lacey, thank you for riding so far on a dark night to correct what would have been a terrible mistake."

"I'm not sure I convinced them all," Lacey expressed his concern.

"Have no fear; John Sevier will take over from here," John said grinning.

Edward Lacey laughed at the clever rhyme. "You are a fascinating character, Colonel Sevier."

"So I've been told. Would you like some breakfast before you go?"

"No, thank you. I need to get back to camp and get our men moving before *General* Williams steals them for his stupid attack on Fort Ninety Six."

"Make sure Williams comes with you," John said. "We will put him to some useful purpose and keep him out of trouble."

"You'll have your hands full!" Colonel Lacey laughed as he mounted his horse and noticed the eastern sky beginning to lighten. "I'll see you this evening." The men saluted and Lacey rode away.

Chapter 25

The Council of Cowpens

At dawn on October sixth, the patriot army was moving again after breaking camp at Green River. John Sevier, Isaac Shelby, and the other officers had worked tirelessly through the night reorganizing the army and deciding which men and horses would bear up for the final push to catch Ferguson. Older men like Major Valentine Sevier and Samuel Sherrill would have to be told they were being left behind with the foot soldiers. John struggled to find the words that would no doubt hurt his close kinsmen and rehearsed in his mind how to explain his decisions. Sam Sherrill rode up beside him and provided a lively narrative that in any other circumstance would have been highly entertaining; but lack of sleep and strategic concerns about the campaign distracted the lieutenant colonel into an uncharacteristic sullenness.

"Hannah's Cowpens used to be a great gathering place for the people of both North and South Carolina in the peaceful days before the war," Sam said. "I remember the cattle drives. We would ride miles through the forests rounding up those free ranging cattle and sorting out who owned which ones. Then, all the men would drive them to market at Hannah's Cowpens while the women would ride together in the wagons talking, visiting, and planning their purchases at the fairgrounds. And we weren't just trading cattle either. There were horses, sheep, and hogs a-plenty. Livestock traders from Charleston, Savannah, and Richmond were all there looking for bargains, while we were there hoping to get top price. Old man Hannah made a fortune in those days just selling whiskey. The war ruined everything for us."

"Yes, Sam, the war has become a great personal inconvenience," John agreed.

"Interferes with your love life, doesn't it?" Sam grinned as he went on with his remembrances. "John, I tell you, that wife of yours was a game girl. She would enter just about any kind of contest at the big gatherings. I remember how small she was when she entered her first greased pig contest. She was so sure she could catch that greasy pig, she put up her own entry fee and stepped into the pen with boys twice her size. Yes, sir, she had a word for every bully who tried to discourage her by saying the contest was for boys only. She wasn't about to be told she couldn't play. I think it made her work all the harder to catch that pig. Of course the pen was a muddy mess, but she didn't seem to mind. She got right in there and really mixed it up. She moved quicker and shoved harder than any boy did to get at that pig. The pig liked to dart away between the legs of those boys, but that strategy wouldn't work with Katie. She caught him up in her petticoat and fell on him. That pig was wrapped up and pinned to the ground in the wink of an eye. It was the most amazing thing I ever saw. I was mighty proud of her."

John laughed and was lifted out of his gloom. He loved such stories about the early experiences of his beloved wife and imagined every detail of Sam's story. "So you know this part of the country pretty well?"

"Like the back of my hand. We used to go on hunting trips all around these parts after the stock trading was done. The hunting was good back then, before all these farmers came in and cleared the land. I'm getting to feel like the Indians do every time I see another tree cut down."

John reconsidered and reversed his decision to leave Sam Sherrill with the foot soldiers. Sam Sherrill's horse was among the best on the expedition, and his knowledge of the landscape surrounding the Cowpens would be too valuable to leave behind.

In the evening the patchwork army of the West arrived at the big open fields of the Cowpens, where they found two separate armies of South Carolinians already dismounted and resting. General Williams commanded seventy mounted men, and Colonels Hill and Lacey commanded one hundred fifty men of Sumter's battalion.

The mountain men were told to build fires and cook a meal, but not to do anything about setting up a camp. The North Carolina officers found the South Carolina officers outside a small cabin trying to question a Tory resident to see if he had any knowledge about British military movements. The cabin was shut up and very quiet.

"The man's name is Saunders, but he's a Tory," General Williams warned. "I think we should burn down the house around him."

John Sevier walked right up to the door and knocked.

"Go away, I'm sick," called a man's voice from inside.

"Can we get you anything to help comfort you? What about some chicken soup?"

"No, thank you," the man called back.

"Can I offer you the services of our good doctor? He's a horse doctor, but I've seen him work wonders on people as well."

The door opened a crack for the occupant to see what sort of fellow would be standing on his porch politely asking about the welfare of a sick man. Colonel Cleveland pushed his way in and roughly pulled out a man in his night shirt shivering with a chill.

"Easy, Colonel Cleveland," John cautioned. "The man said he is sick, and I believe him."

"He's a damned old Tory, and sick or not, he ought to be hanged."

"No man wants to be a Tory, any more than he wants to be sick," John said. "I'm here to offer him a cure for both conditions."

"Go ahead then, Sevier," Colonel Cleveland said. "I'll be interested to see how you cure a Tory."

"We are looking for a large army of British soldiers commanded by a fellow named Patrick Ferguson," John explained. "He offended the good people of North Carolina, and we intend to hold him responsible for the damages he has caused."

"I haven't seen him," the sick man declared. "I've been sick with the fever for three days, and nobody has passed through this place but a few small parties of hunters."

"Have you been boiling your drinking water?" John asked. "I believe that would prevent the occurrence of water-borne diseases of the stomach."

"No," the man answered. "It's not my stomach. It started like a cold, in my nose and throat, and went to my chest."

"Either way, a good chicken soup would help you feel better," John decided. "Go back to bed and rest. I'll have my men prepare you a chicken from your coup and bring it in to you."

The man looked uneasily at Colonel Cleveland and entered his cabin.

John walked away with Cleveland beside him.

"Well, Sevier, did you find out what you wanted to know?" Cleveland asked.

"Ferguson hasn't been here," John answered.

"You believe that confounded Tory?"

"Look around for yourself, Benjamin," John replied. "The British officers would have camped right here next to the house. Where do you see the campfire remains, the horse litter, the empty chicken coup, the trampled grass, and the tracks of an army the size of Major Ferguson's?"

"They could have hidden the evidence and left that fellow behind to lie about it," Cleveland insisted.

"They could have, but they didn't. The British are not that clever."

John Sevier and Isaac Shelby walked over to South Carolina officers to make their acquaintance. They found Colonels William Hill and Edward Lacey.

"Welcome to the Cowpens, gentlemen," John said.

"Colonel Sevier, I want you to meet Colonel William Hill," Lacey introduced his companion.

"My pleasure, Colonel Hill, and this is my good friend Colonel Isaac Shelby of Sullivan County."

"Is this the Old Lover Boy you told me about?" Hill grinned as he shook John's hand.

"Yes, sir. He's the only one who welcomed me and showed me any respect last night."

"We will have to know more about this Lover Boy story," Hill said.

"Ask any man in camp," Shelby said. "The story spread like wild fire."

Traveling with the South Carolinians were the men of Lincoln County, North Carolina, commanded by Colonel William Graham, and Lieutenant Colonel Fredrick Hambright, a recent emigrant from Germany. John and Isaac spent some time welcoming those officers as well.

"So Colonel Campbell is in charge of this campaign?" Colonel Hill asked.

"Yes, and we intend to keep it that way until we can catch Ferguson," John informed the newcomers.

"Colonel James Williams showed up in our camp with a general's commission signed by Governor Rutledge," Colonel Hill said. "He's going to cause trouble for your Colonel Campbell. He's trying to take control of your army for a move on Fort Ninety Six."

"We have spent our fortunes, braved all hardships, and risked the destruction of our own homes and families to get Ferguson," John said. "Nobody is going to interfere with our purpose."

"What about his general's commission?" Lacey asked. "On South Carolina soil he has a legitimate right to command."

"Let me handle General Williams," Sevier volunteered. "Who are the officers directly under Williams?"

"Colonel Thomas Brandon and Major Samuel Hammond are his chief supporters," Lacey said.

"Have your men relax and cook dinner while the officers are meeting," John directed the other officers.

"But don't let them get too comfortable," Isaac said. "We leave tonight with our best men mounted on the best horses, making the dash to catch Ferguson."

"So which direction are we dashing?" Lacey asked.

"That is the question we are just about to decide at the officer's council," John replied.

John returned to his camp and found his father, Major Valentine Sevier.

"Special detail, if you are up to it, Major Reives," John told his father.

"Major Reives is always ready for action," the older man replied with a grin.

"Get me a dozen of the roughest-looking mountain men you can find and line them up behind the cabin near the woodpile," John ordered.

"Are you taking someone out to the woodpile for a spanking, Sonny?"

"I'm trying to prevent a change in command," John answered. "I'm going to deliver to you a high-ranking officer of South Carolina. I want you to escort him out to the west pickets and keep him quiet until I come for him. Threaten him with violence if you have to, but don't hurt him. And don't let him find out the names of any of your men. I don't want him bringing anybody to court-martial but me."

"It sounds serious," Major Val said.

"It is," John responded. "This fellow is trying to take over the army and lead us off in the wrong direction. He's going to let Ferguson get away if I don't stop him. I want you to hold him until the officers' meeting ends, and then I'll come take him off your hands."

"I'll get the men rounded up," Major Val said. "We'll be waiting for you."

John found General Williams in his camp with the officers of his command.

"Everything's arranged, General Williams," John announced with great enthusiasm. "The change of command ceremony is just about to begin. I need Colonel Brandon and Major Hammond over at the council right away. Now Colonel Brandon, when I give you the signal, you nominate General Williams commander of the expedition, another officer will second, and the officers will vote."

"What's this about?" Williams asked.

"Colonel Campbell was a reluctant leader right from the start. I think he's very relieved to welcome our new general to the position of commander of the expedition. Now, the election is just a formality, but a necessary one in the minds of our western men. All militia officers serve at the pleasure of those beneath them in rank. We call that militia democracy."

"I'm ready, let's go," Williams said.

"That's the part we need to rehearse," John explained. "The general will enter the meeting escorted by his honor guard just after the election. That's why I need Colonel Brandon and Major Hammond and your other officers over at the meeting right away. They are just about to start." Colonel Brandon and Major Hammond hurried off to the meeting with their junior officers.

"What about the honor guard?" Williams asked.

"It's all arranged," John told him. "Just follow me."

"I'm glad you and Campbell have come to your senses."

"Think nothing of it," John replied.

General Williams was surprised at the rough treatment he received from the *honor guard* as they escorted him out to the edge of camp. He swore at the mountain men, he swore at Major Reives, and he swore he would get even with Colonel Sevier. The mountain men bound his hands and put a gag in his mouth to keep him from swearing anymore.

John Sevier joined the other officers at Colonel Campbell's campfire just as the meeting began. William Campbell received all the new officers and the introductions were made.

"Gentlemen, welcome," Colonel Campbell began. "You are just in time to help settle the matter of which way we might go to catch Ferguson and his army."

Colonel Thomas Brandon spoke up immediately. "Fort Ninety Six is where Ferguson is going. Catch him at Ninety Six, and we can win the war!"

"Don't listen to him," Isaac Shelby warned. "The scouts say Ferguson moved east toward Charlotte."

"That's right," Major Chronicle agreed. "He's going to join Cornwallis and link up with Tarleton, too!"

The men began arguing the matter again, and Colonel Campbell was still trying to restore order when Major Joseph McDowell entered the circle escorting a crippled beggar. Major McDowell helped the man over to Colonel Campbell and spoke quietly to Campbell about him. Campbell called for silence. "Be quiet, men! We have new information. Major McDowell has new information!" The noise died down, and all attention turned to Joseph McDowell.

"Gentlemen, a few minutes ago I received confirmation that Ferguson is indeed moving east."

"Where is the proof?" Colonel Campbell asked.

McDowell placed his hand on the beggar's shoulder. "This is Mr. Joseph Kerr, a scout in the service of Colonel James Williams. He just arrived in camp and reported Ferguson's location. Go ahead, Mr. Kerr, tell us what you have seen."

"Thank you, Major McDowell. I serve my country, limping about from place to place begging for food and drink. I gather information that will help us in our great cause. Today at noon, I took my dinner at the camp of Major Ferguson. The soldiers told me they were marching to join up with the main British army at Charlotte. They are recruiting anybody and everybody who will take up arms for the king."

"Where did you see them?" Colonel Campbell asked.

"It was at Peter Quinn's plantation east of the Broad River," Kerr answered. "But they left there and marched to Little King's Mountain. There they will camp and wait for reinforcements from Cornwallis."

"What are their numbers?"

"Not above fifteen hundred men."

"Is the enemy well mounted?" Colonel Sevier asked.

"No, sir, only the officers are mounted. The rest are foot soldiers; some Provincial regulars in uniform, but mostly loyalist militia."

"Where is this King's Mountain?" Sevier asked.

Major Chronicle stood to speak. "I know the place very well. It's about thirty miles due east of here. We camp there on hunting trips. It's really just a heavily wooded hill."

The report had brought about an intensity of focus in John Sevier. "Is there plenty of cover for Indian-style fighting?"

"Yes, sir. The place is ideal for Indian play," Major Chronicle replied.

Colonel Campbell nodded at Sevier. "There it is, lads. Mr. Kerr has given us reliable firsthand information about the enemy's intentions. Major Chronicle has described the place where the enemy is camped tonight as ideal for Colonel Sevier's Indian-style strategy. We have the horses to deliver seven hundred men fast enough for a surprise attack. All in favor of going to King's Mountain, say aye."

The men all voted in one voice, "Aye!"

"Very well then, prepare your men for a thirty-mile ride," Colonel Campbell ordered. "We leave within the hour and ride through the night. Send out your scouts. God be with you, each and every one!" The officers hastily dispersed to their various commands.

Colonel Brandon caught Colonel Sevier by the arm. "I think you have played a trick on General Williams. He'll be mad as hell. How am I supposed to explain what happened here tonight?"

"I'm sorry, Colonel Brandon," Sevier replied. "I realize I put you in a bad position with your commanding officer, and I take full responsibility for that. How was I to know that catching Ferguson was a more important issue than the issue of who commands?"

"I see your point," Brandon admitted. "I believed General Williams when he declared with great certainty that Ferguson was withdrawing toward Fort Ninety Six. Now General Williams' own scout comes into camp and reports to the contrary."

"Don't be discouraged," John said. "Come with us and share in the glory."

"General Williams has sworn an oath that if he doesn't get to be commander of this campaign, he will go take Fort Ninety Six without the rest of you."

"How will he do that with only seventy riflemen and no artillery?"

"I don't know."

"Let me reason with him," John suggested. "I think I can persuade him to come along, but he'll have to get used to the idea of being a colonel like the rest of us."

The delegation that reached Colonel Williams consisted of Colonel John Sevier, Colonel Thomas Brandon, Major Samuel Hammond, and Scout Joseph Kerr.

"Sevier, this is an outrage! I demand an explanation."

"I'm sorry, Colonel Williams, they didn't vote to make you their general; they voted to go catch Ferguson at a place called King's Mountain."

"I told you Ferguson will be found at Fort Ninety Six!"

"That's not true, Jimmy," John replied. "Mr. Kerr, your own scout, arrived in camp not thirty minutes ago. He had lunch in Mr. Ferguson's camp very close to King's Mountain."

"Is that true, Joseph?" Williams demanded.

"Yes, sir, true as the gospel!"

James Williams was dumbfounded. His strategy was completely discredited and John Sevier had the upper hand. "But I'm still the general, and I claim my right to command!" He reached for the papers in his coat pocket but they were gone. "My commission, my papers; they stole my papers!"

"Major Reives?" John called.

"Yes, Johnny?" Major Val walked over with a grin.

"Where are the papers that belong to Colonel Williams?"

"We could drop them in the fire if that would simplify matters," Val suggested.

"No, I don't think that will be necessary," John smiled and held out his hand. Major Reives produced the papers and gave them over. "Colonel Williams, if you promise to keep these papers in your pocket for two more days, you might just earn the right to take over as a South Carolina general. All we want to do is whip Ferguson in our own way. I'm inviting you to go with us."

"Let me talk to Campbell. He'll listen to reason."

"Colonel Campbell, at this very moment, is preparing to lead his mounted men out of camp on the way to King's Mountain. I'll do the same as soon as I receive your decision and your promise. Stay here or join the action." John Sevier waited.

"General Williams, our men are brave and true. I think they want to go after Ferguson too," Brandon said.

"The Old Wagoner never yet backed down," Williams declared stubbornly.

"General Williams, sir," Major Hammond spoke up. "It's not backing down to go after Ferguson. Colonel Sevier has only asked for two more days. Then you can take over as general and we will begin our campaign to Fort Ninety Six. I think we should go along with Colonel Sevier."

"I have twenty mounted Georgians that rode with Elijah Clarke," John said. "I'll transfer them to your command to bring your companies up to full strength."

"That sounds fair," Colonel Brandon urged his commander. "Take the deal, sir."

"Colonel Brandon, organize the command for a ride to King's Mountain," Williams ordered. "I'll play it your way for now, Sevier, but I don't approve of your methods."

"That makes us even, Colonel," John grinned as he handed the papers over to James Williams. "I don't approve of yours, either."

Williams and his officers left to organize their men for the night ride, and Major Reives dismissed his special duty volunteers. As John and his father walked back to their camp, Valentine Sevier spoke his mind.

"See how handy it is to have an experienced man along for the really tough special details?"

"Well done, Major Reives," John praised him.

"Take me with you, Sonny."

"No, your work as quartermaster has been vital to the operation of the army. I need you to continue that important role until we return."

"Come on, Johnny, let me see some action," Val insisted.

"Give all your energy and assistance to Major Joseph Herndon, of Cleveland's command. He is to bring along the foot soldiers as quick as they can march. After our fight with Ferguson, we will fall back and rejoin you. Bring all the food you can find, because we are only taking enough to sustain man and horse for a single day."

"I'm still a good soldier."

"And a good soldier follows the orders of his colonel, without question and without complaint. I never wanted to disappoint you, Papa, and I hate leaving any of my command behind, but this is the way it has to be for any hope of success. All I ask of you is to follow orders and do your best."

"Yes, Colonel Sevier, I will do my best."

John hugged his father, "Thank you, Papa. Don't forget to bring the food."

"Bless you, my son!"

"Where the hell have you been?" Isaac Shelby demanded. "Campbell has already pulled out, and Cleveland, McDowell, and I are mounted and ready to go."

"I had some last minute recruiting to do," John replied as he swung up into his saddle. "The South Carolina contingent is now at full strength and committed to our purpose. That brings the mounted force to just over nine hundred by my calculations."

"You got Williams to see things our way?"

"Sure did!"

"You didn't have to make him a general?"

"Colonel Williams is a reasonable man. I think it will all work itself out. What is Captain Lenoir doing lying down beside that campfire?"

"His entire company was foot soldiers," Isaac explained. "He was the only one who brought a horse."

John rode over to Lenoir's camp, where he also found Major Joseph Herndon. "Captain Lenoir, go fetch your horse. I need another good officer in my command, if Major Herndon can get along without you. What about it, Joe?"

"I think I can spare him if you clear it with Colonel Cleveland," Major Herndon answered.

"I'll tell him," John replied.

William Lenoir made ready quickly, and his eagerness for action shone brightly in his eyes. As they rode away Captain Lenoir expressed his thanks. "I'll forever be grateful for this, Colonel Sevier."

"I couldn't stand to see such a talent for leadership unemployed when our country suffers in greatest need."

"Can we go now?" Shelby asked impatiently. "It's already nine o'clock."

John smiled and raised his great feathered hat. He looked at the officers of his companies and their neatly mounted columns all ready to travel. "Forward, my boys. We ride to victory! Follow the white plume, and there you will find the glory!"

Chapter 26

The Fox Chase

A cold drizzle fell as the patriot army rode down dark lanes and rutted roadbeds in search of their dangerously deceptive foe. The men wrapped their flintlocks with hunting shirts and blankets to keep the mechanisms and flash pans dry for priming powder if necessary. It was the third storm they encountered since leaving home. Many of them were reminded of the first night at Shelving Rock and the two-day deluge at South Mountain Gap. Tonight's storm gave them much more concern as the drizzle became a steady rain on what they supposed was the eve of battle. John Sevier tried to calculate their hour of arrival at King's Mountain, factoring in the road conditions, the back-road routes, the incredibly inky darkness that slowed every move, and the frequent stops to await the all-clear signal from scouting parties working the road far out in front. He estimated that noon was the earliest hour they could possibly arrive. He wondered if the enemy would still be on the mountain and if the rain would persist until that hour.

Sevier's men had been following Colonel Campbell's force of two hundred riders churning up the mud ahead of them. When the only recognizable road turned suddenly south, Major Chronicle's men led the way ever eastward into a forested stretch of land where the columns made their own trails. John's men came up alongside Campbell's column, and they rode parallel for a time, a dozen yards apart. During a particularly heavy downpour, the Washington County riders lost sight of the Virginians. John called his men to a halt, which also stopped Isaac Shelby's Sullivan County men at the rear. Shelby came forward along the column to check in with Sevier.

"Why are we stopping?"

"Campbell was right next to me for a while," John explained. "When the rain let up he was gone. Have you seen him?"

"No," Isaac answered. "Maybe he sped up and pulled ahead of you."

"Not likely," John said. "The Virginia horses are more jaded than ours. If you didn't see him lagging back, then he veered off to the north."

"Campbell commands a full quarter of our force. Without Virginia we cannot attack Ferguson."

"Is anybody else missing back there?"

"No," Isaac replied. "I have Cleveland behind me, then McDowell, Lacey, Graham, Winston, and Williams. That's very careless of you, John, misplacing the Virginians like that."

Major Chronicle appeared out of the darkness ahead riding toward them. "Is anything wrong? Why are you stopped?"

"The Virginians are missing," John said. "They veered off in a northerly direction during that last heavy rain."

"They can't have wandered far," Chronicle reasoned. "Surely they'll backtrack when they notice that nobody is following them. I'll send out some of Colonel Graham's men to look for them. Keep your columns moving behind my scouting parties and don't lose anybody else." Chronicle moved toward the rear seeking Colonel Graham, whose men best knew the local country.

"Yeah, John, don't lose anybody else," Isaac said.

"Colonel Campbell is responsible for this, not me," John grinned.

"You should have been in charge. This whole expedition was your idea right from the start."

"Well, you were so all-fired quick to jump on the idea, the same minute I said it. Who's to say you didn't think of it first?" John answered.

"Who's to say it wasn't Bonny Kate's idea? She interfered with every decision we ever made."

"Don't bring my wife into this. Her sound judgment kept us from many a fool idea of yours."

"You were the one with all the fool ideas," Isaac argued. "Your officers may call you a creative genius, but I say it's all dumb luck!"

"I thought you two were friends," Captain Lenoir interrupted.

"We are the best of friends," John said smiling.

"We always have been," Isaac agreed. "I'm just pointing out to my colleague that he ought to be in charge of this campaign, now that Colonel Campbell has apparently taken leave."

"There you go again, with another fool idea," John replied. "How is a lieutenant colonel, with no conventional battle experience, supposed to take command of eight or nine full colonels and one South Carolina general and expect to prevail against the armed forces of the greatest empire on earth?"

"You should have thought of that before you brought us all out here in this torrential rain," Isaac replied.

"Return to your troops, Colonel Shelby, and keep their spirits high with your encouraging words," John ordered.

"Yes, sir," Isaac saluted.

"Column forward!" John commanded, and the night march continued.

Hours later Colonel William Campbell caught up with John Sevier at the head of the column.

"Where have you been, Bill?" John asked.

"We struck a good road and made excellent time for a long while, until we figured out it was leading off in the wrong direction. Now I have small groups scattered all over the Broad River basin. We are doing our best to find them all."

"I can't imagine the costs in time and energy to the men and horses that went so far out of the way."

"Your fellows don't look much fresher," Campbell observed.

"I've heard a lot of grumbling in the ranks on account of this rain."

They arrived at a bank overlooking the Cherokee Ford of the Broad River. Major William Chronicle was there to stop the army.

"Welcome back, Colonel Campbell," Chronicle said with a grin. "That road you were taking might have led you straight into Charlotte. What a surprise Lord Cornwallis might have had, if you had gone much farther."

"It was all I could do to get the boys turned around and back on the right path," Campbell replied. "We will most certainly have to stop and rest the horses until dawn."

"It's nearly dawn now," John observed. "Is this the Broad River?"

"Yes," Chronicle answered. "I sent Enoch Gilmer over to scout the crossing for enemy activity. If I were Ferguson covering my retreat, I would post a company at each of the three major crossings, Deer's Ferry, Tate's Plantation, and here at Cherokee Ford. It worries me that the river is rising high from all this rain."

"Is Gilmer your talented play actor?" John asked.

"Yes, sir, he can assume any character that the occasion might require. He can laugh and cry in the same breath and be equally convincing in both, and even plays the lunatic to perfection. He's a shrewd, cunning fellow, and a stranger to fear."

"I have a man in my command that can recite any character from a Shakespeare play," John revealed. "Perhaps on a happier day we can get those fellows together for some real entertainment."

"I hope we all live to see that happier day," Chronicle said.

John Sevier turned in his saddle and recognized his brothers Valentine and Robert behind him. "Val and Bobby, pass the word to all men. Take precautions to keep your rifles and your powder dry as we cross the river. If the powder gets wet, we will have nothing but tomahawks to fight with when we catch Ferguson."

"Yes, sir," Val replied, and the word was passed.

Across the river the exuberant Enoch Gilmer broke into song with the jolly refrain of the song "Barney Linn."

"There's the signal for all clear!" Major Chronicle announced. The soldiers of the army urged their horses down the river bank into the cold water, where such care was exercised that not a single rider suffered a ducking.

Three miles beyond the river crossing, the army arrived at one of Ferguson's former campsites, where they halted to rest the horses. The men ate a very spartan cold breakfast of parched corn and whatever they had. Some had stripped a cornfield to feed their horses as well.

Colonel Benjamin Cleveland sat on a fallen tree to rest and looked up at Sevier and Shelby. "Fellows, if we mean to have a battle, I wish we could engage in it and get it over with all the sooner."

John sat down beside him as they watched Campbell and the others ride into camp. "That was a fine speech you gave at South Mountain Gap, Colonel Cleveland. Perhaps we might hear you give us another."

Cleveland laughed. "That was the day you made us walk off the rum, Sevier. I'm not going to inspire another such punishment for my men, no matter how you try to persuade me."

"But the men are getting discouraged."

"Let Campbell do the speech and explain how he lost his way in the fog last night," Cleveland answered. "We must have lost two hours trying to round up all those wayward Virginians." They watched as Colonel Campbell dismounted and unsaddled his horse. He rubbed down the animal with a blanket to work off the rainwater.

"I'm not going to mention it to him again," John said. "He felt terrible about that."

"Have you ever noticed how much Colonel Campbell resembles his serving man, John Broddy?" Cleveland asked. "Let's have a little fun with him and lighten his mood."

Cleveland rose from his resting place and strolled over to where Campbell worked. John and Isaac followed to see what Cleveland would do.

"Nice work there, Broddy," Cleveland bellowed out. "When you are finished with Colonel Campbell's horse, you can do mine."

Colonel Campbell stopped and turned with a scowl. "I suppose you think you are such a clever fellow, eh Cleveland?"

"Ah, Colonel Campbell," Cleveland laughed. "I mistook you for your man, Broddy. You look and dress so much alike."

"As you can plainly see, I am not Broddy," Campbell responded.

"Then you should dress appropriately in the proper uniform," Cleveland said. "Look at Sevier there, all decked out in the newest style of the uniformed officer. He's not ashamed to dress the part of the militia officer. He even has the big feather in his hat!"

"I do not wish to be conspicuous for the enemy sharpshooters," Campbell said. "The age of chivalry is dead, and so are a good many of the best dressed officers."

"The statistics show that active duty officers leading troops in battle are equally as likely to be shot by their own men as by enemy fire," Sevier pointed out. "My men are excellent marksmen, so if my own men can recognize me, my risks have been reduced by fifty percent."

Cleveland looked up at the white plume and asked. "What sort of bird is that, Sevier; a peacock perhaps?"

"Quiet, Cleveland," Campbell ordered. "Sevier just gave me an excellent idea. These loyalist militia men in Ferguson's army dress and look just like our common soldiers. When the pinch comes and all our men are mixed up with theirs in hand-to-hand combat, wouldn't it be nice to distinguish friend from foe?"

"It would save many a life," Sevier agreed. "Let every man on our side wear such a feather!"

"There are no birds enough for that," Isaac Shelby said.

"No," Campbell continued. "But a piece of paper pinned to the hat of every man on our side would do the trick. Gentlemen, pass the order that as soon as the rain ends, I want every soldier identified with a paper badge upon his hat. When challenged, the men will identify themselves with the counter sign *Buford*, in remembrance of what that butcher Tarleton did to a fine Virginia officer under the white flag."

The officers acknowledged the order. Colonel Campbell resaddled his bald-faced black horse as John Broddy approached leading Colonel Campbell's other horse, which was a bay.

"They do strike a remarkable resemblance except for color," Isaac marveled.

"They are a well-matched team when hitched to a wagon or a plow," Campbell explained. "The bay is gentler than the black."

Cleveland and Shelby burst out laughing at what seemed to be a private joke. Campbell looked at Sevier. "What has so tickled those two jokers?"

"I am sure I cannot tell, Colonel Campbell," John replied. "Perhaps they are tickled with my feather, but it was a favor from a lady and I will not take it off."

"John, you lead out and take the van," Campbell ordered. "You and Major Chronicle seem to be working well together. I still have companies trying to catch up, so I'll be in the rear. Try to get the men better organized and marching in columns. I don't like seeing them separated in these small groups scattered everywhere. And pick up the pace; we have to move quickly if we are going to surprise Ferguson."

"Yes, sir," John replied.

The pace became as relentless as the rain for most of the morning. John was satisfied to leave the men spread out in companies over a broad front and not have them riding in narrow columns along a muddy road. He hoped that his men might sweep up any Tory partisans in the wide swath and gather as much information as they could from local residents. Major William Chronicle was satisfied with the arrangement as well and fell back to enjoy the company of John Sevier and his staff officers who rode in a group more like a party of hunters than a military unit. The conversation was likewise more like a hunting party, filled with humorously entertaining stories.

"John," called Captain Jacob Brown from the left side of the road. Colonel Sevier turned to see his old friend from the Nolichucky Valley riding toward him through the woods. "John, you ought to see what we found over here."

"Excuse me, gentlemen," John said to his company of officers. "Carry on."

John followed Jacob Brown to a campsite where a full company of grizzly-bearded, tough, over-mountain rangers held a dozen men and boys at gunpoint. The appearance of a well-dressed American officer was a relief to some and a concern for others.

"Good morning, gentlemen," John tipped his hat. "What are you fellows doing out here on such a miserable day?"

"Hunting," replied the obvious leader of the group.

"What a coincidence," John smiled. "We're out on a little hunting trip as well."

"They are Tories, John," Jacob warned.

"We will see about that. Arrest their leader and take him out of camp." Jacob's men took the man and removed him from the scene. John looked at the remaining men and boys. "Are there any Tories among these fellows?"

One of the boys pointed to a man who had been seated next to the man they removed. The man was seized as he struggled to escape, but to no avail.

"Take him out there with the other fellow," John ordered. "Are there any more friends of the King of England?"

"They forced us to join their army," one man complained. "They said they would hang my father and burn down my house if I didn't serve."

"That's right," another affirmed. "They rounded us up like cattle and gave us no choice. They threatened our wives and children."

"Where are you fellows from?" John asked.

"North Fork of the Edisto, near Orangeburg," replied one of the men.

"That's quite a distance from here, John, well toward Charleston," Jacob Brown commented.

"In the name of the Continental Congress of the United States of America, I grant you life, liberty, and the freedom to pursue happiness," John declared. "Now go home, raise good crops and big families, and never bear arms against your country again."

"Yes, sir," the oldest man answered for the whole group. They gathered their belongings and prepared to depart.

"Could you gentlemen spare us your powder and shot?" John requested. "We'll have need of it today."

The Orangeburg man looked around at the rough mountaineers still aiming their loaded rifles at the captives. "I reckon you'll just take whatever you want."

"Not without paying a fair price for it," John replied. "When you leave here, head due south as fast as you can walk. That will get you out of the way of a large western army coming through to destroy Cornwallis and free the entire country from the wicked ministers of the King of England."

John's officers settled accounts with the paroled Tories and sent them off, while he considered what to do with their recruiters. He walked over to where they were being held.

"What are your orders from Major Ferguson?"

"What do you care?" the Tory answered.

"A good soldier should always obey orders," John replied. "Now what are your orders?"

"To go throughout the countryside and round up every good man who can bear arms and deliver them to Ferguson's camp," the Tory answered.

"Then why not deliver *us* to Ferguson's camp?"

"Rebel bandits ought to be hightailing it for cover," the man answered. "Ferguson will soon have enough men to crush you."

"You underestimate the mood of the country, sir. The people of America want independence, and they are willing to fight for it in overwhelming numbers," John replied confidently.

"What should we do with these traitors, John?"

"Hold them here for Colonel Cleveland. He has a persuasive way that might get them to cooperate," John answered. Colonel Sevier rejoined his troops, and they continued their progress.

A Virginia rider caught up with Colonel Sevier just after mid-morning and saluted smartly. "Colonel Campbell requests that you halt your column while he and the other officers come forward for a meeting of the officers."

"Thank you," John returned the salute and gave the order to stop his companies.

"Can you direct me to Colonel Shelby?" the Virginia lad asked.

John turned to his right and pointed. "He's even with us about a hundred yards over."

"Thank you, sir," the rider saluted again and rode away.

Colonel Campbell arrived very soon after with Colonel Cleveland, Colonel Graham, Colonel Lacey, and Colonel Hambright. Major Chronicle was present with Colonel Sevier, and Major McDowell and Major Winston were there also.

"Where's Colonel Williams?" John asked.

Campbell grinned. "The general was invited, but refused to attend any officer meetings where John Sevier is present. He has threatened to have you arrested before you leave the state of South Carolina. What did you do to him, John?"

"I persuaded him to keep his damn general's commission in his pocket until we get Ferguson," John replied.

"Whatever you did seems to be working, John," Colonel Lacey observed. "But be careful of him when this thing is over."

"John, we have talked it over and reached a consensus," Campbell explained. "The men and horses are just too exhausted to go any farther in this blasted rain. A couple of hours to rest and let the rain clear out would be advisable."

"No telling what Ferguson might do if he's given time to discover our presence," John warned.

"I understand the risks," Campbell replied. "But if conditions don't improve soon, the men will be in no condition to fight."

Isaac Shelby rode over and joined the group of officers. "Why are we stopping?"

"We were thinking about giving the men a rest and a cooked meal," Campbell explained.

"We can't afford the time," Colonel Shelby insisted.

"Consider the men and horses, Isaac," John said. "Except for the short stop at the Cowpens, they have been in the saddle since yesterday morning. The dark night and the rain have dispirited them."

"By God, I will not stop until night if I follow Ferguson into Cornwallis' lines!" Isaac shouted in exasperation. His tone was so serious and so determined that none of the officers dared answer. Isaac turned and returned to his men.

"I had better go with him," John said. "I can't let a friend get himself into trouble."

"It's only about five more miles to King's Mountain," Major Chronicle informed them.

"I wish to God Almighty this rain would quit," one of the officers called out, and immediately the rushing sound of the heavy rain stopped altogether. A shaft of sunlight appeared through the clouds in the West.

John looked around him to see the speaker. "Who said that?"

"It was Captain Lenoir," Major Joseph Winston declared.

"Captain Lenoir, I'm mighty glad we brought you along," John said. "We may have further need of your influence with the Almighty before this thing is over." At that point all the officers resolved to push on.

John Sevier spent the next couple of miles speaking to his men and encouraging them now that the sun had come out and a light breeze was drying out their equipment. They struck a good road and followed it east, and in the distance a low ridge appeared before them. Major Chronicle told them it was King's Mountain. When they passed a neat little house beside the road, John spoke to his son Joseph Sevier, and Adam Sherrill. "Joseph, you and Adam talk to these people and see if you can get some information. I'll ride up to the next house where Colonel Campbell is going."

Joseph Sevier knocked on the door, and a man opened it to reveal his table set for a midday dinner. The man was shocked to see the over-mountain men dressed in hunting shirts and homespun clothing riding by so close to his house. They looked lean and hungry, sinewy and tough, grimly intent on their mission to destroy their enemy. It surprised him also to hear a young man who looked as tough as the rest speak so politely and courteously.

"Good day, sir. My name is Joseph Sevier. I'm sorry to interrupt your dinner, but we are looking for the regiment led by Major Ferguson. We heard he might be in the area."

"We haven't seen him and don't know where he is," the man answered warily.

"Please, sir. We have ridden so far and suffered much hunger and fatigue looking for him. Haven't you heard any rumors of his whereabouts or seen any of his soldiers out foraging?"

"Look here, son. We don't want any trouble from either side. I don't even want to know which side you're on. Please, leave us in peace."

Joseph bowed politely and spoke once more. "Then, I wish you a good day, sir." Joseph and Adam walked back toward their horses, but Joseph noticed a pretty girl coming around the corner from the rear of the house.

"How many of there are you?" The girl looked around warily as if to escape the notice of the man in the house.

"Enough to whip Ferguson, if we can find him," Joseph answered.

She smiled with the satisfaction of a Whig partisan and pointed to the distant hill. "He is on that mountain, with all his men." The boys looked in the direction she indicated and then grinned at each other. "The neighbor ladies took food to the Tories this morning."

"It looks like we can catch that old fox today," Joseph declared.

"Good luck, boys," she said. "Please be careful."

Joseph returned his focus to the pretty girl. She had brown hair, green eyes, and looked to be about his age. "Thank you kindly, Miss...?" He paused, hoping she would give him a name.

She smiled again, and he judged her face to be like that of an angel. "I'm Mary Finley. What's your name?"

"I'm Joseph Sevier, Miss Finley. We are much obliged for the information." Joseph paused and continued to look at her admiringly for a moment.

"Joe," Adam called from the gate.

"I have to go," he told her.

"Take care of yourself, Joseph Sevier," she replied.

Joseph had never felt that way with girls back home. He regained the saddle and rode away sitting just a little taller. He looked back to catch another glimpse of her, and she waved to him. He tipped his hat.

"She was a pretty one," Adam observed. "You liked her, didn't you?"

"Yes. I think she liked me too."

"She did," Adam agreed. "I could see it in her eyes."

"A girl like that probably has a lot of beaus."

"It's likely, but you captured her attention with your good manners and that nice-looking uniform Bonny Kate made you. A girl can't resist a soldier in uniform."

Colonel Sevier arrived at a cabin where Campbell, Shelby, and Chronicle had dismounted, leaving their horses with Colonel Cleveland who remained in the saddle.

"Enoch Gilmer is in there," Cleveland explained. "He's Chronicle's scout. The boys are going to have a little fun with him."

John dismounted and joined the other officers at the door of the cabin. Campbell knocked on the door and a woman answered.

"Good day, ma'am. We saw the horse tied to your gate, and we believe we know the owner."

"He's having lunch, but I'm afraid we don't have enough food for all of you," the woman said. Campbell stepped into the cabin, followed by the others.

"We have you, you damned rascal!" Campbell said loudly.

Enoch Gilmer looked up completely in the character he was playing. "A true king's man, by God," he declared.

Campbell reached into his haversack and pulled out a rope with a noose and looped it over Gilmer's head. Gilmer fell to his knees and begged for mercy in the performance of his life.

"Please don't hurt me," Gilmer cried. "I never did anything to anybody."

The woman of the house began weeping and interceding for her guest. "Please don't hang him. He's a fine gentleman."

"You heard the lady," Gilmer said. "You wouldn't hang a gentleman, would you?"

"The damned king's gentleman will hang from the lady's front gate," Campbell said, and roughly pulled Gilmer toward the door.

"What about a trial? What about justice and mercy?" the actor pleaded.

"I'll grant you the same justice your king provides the people of our country," Campbell promised. "Hang him immediately!"

"No, please, have mercy!" the women of the house cried.

Major Chronicle brought up another consideration. "Colonel, if we hang the scoundrel on this lady's gate, his ghost will haunt her house forever."

"Oh, mercy," the woman repeated.

"All right men," Colonel Campbell relented. "Take him down the road to the first convenient tree. We have troubled these ladies enough."

The men left the cabin and walked down the road with their captive. Colonel Cleveland followed, leading their horses. Some distance from the house, Colonel Campbell removed the noose from Enoch Gilmer's neck and the officers listened intently to what the scout had to say.

"What news do you have?" Campbell asked.

"The younger woman rode up to the mountain this morning to deliver some chickens to Major Ferguson. It's only three miles away."

"Have they fortified the mountain?" Colonel Sevier asked.

"They couldn't have done much," Gilmer answered. "They arrived at the camp only yesterday and had the same weather we came through. I asked if she had seen Lord Cornwallis or Colonel Tarleton. She said it's only Ferguson, but he's anxious for reinforcements."

"How is the lay of the land?" Sevier questioned.

"The camp lies on top of the ridge at the same place where the deer hunters camp. Major Chronicle knows the place."

"Indeed I do," Chronicle said. "Captain Mattocks and I camped there just last year. Listen, John, we have men enough to surround the high ground completely. And when we fire uphill like that, we won't be hitting our own men on the other side. The British will have to aim downhill and will tend to overshoot. Heavy woods will favor our Indian play and disadvantage their use of the bayonet. It's perfect!"

"I wish we knew how many men they have," John said thoughtfully.

"The lady was certain that no reinforcements had come in from Cornwallis or from Tarleton," Gilmer reported.

"Well done, Mr. Gilmer," Colonel Campbell said. He turned to his officers. "Let's line up the men by outfit and organize as we go!" The officers returned to their horses and continued their progress.

Joseph Sevier caught up with his father. "Colonel, I talked to a girl and she said that mountain up ahead is where Ferguson is camped. Some of the neighbors took him some food this morning."

"Good information, Joseph. Now all we need to know is Ferguson's numbers."

"Colonel, can you spare a man to help me scout the location of Ferguson's pickets?" Enoch Gilmer asked.

"Adam Sherrill is a good scout," John replied. "Adam, go with Mr. Gilmer and report back to me when you get the information."

"Yes, sir," Adam saluted and rode forward with Mr. Gilmer.

The officers rode a little farther when a messenger overtook them from the West riding hard.

"Colonel Graham! Colonel William Graham!" The messenger searched urgently.

"Over here," Colonel Graham answered. "I'm here!"

The young man arrived beside the group of colonels. "Colonel Graham, it's your wife, sir. She's near death with some kind of colic. You'd better go to her in all haste!"

Colonel Graham was greatly agitated by the tidings. "Colonel Campbell, I must take leave to attend my wife."

"Where is the lady?" John inquired.

"My home is at Armstrong's Ford on the South Fork, hardly sixteen miles to the north," Graham explained.

"Can I send my personal doctor to her at once?" John offered.

"No, you cannot," Colonel Campbell replied. "We are about to fight a bloody battle here, and I need everyone to stay—including you, Colonel Graham."

"But my wife's condition is critical," Graham said.

"All the more reason to stay and attend to your duty," Campbell declared. "If we are successful, the news you could take her would be as good to her as a dose of medicine!"

"Oh, my dear, dear wife; must I never see her again?"

John Sevier had empathy for a man with a wife so stricken, having lost his own dearly beloved Sarah just the previous January. "For heaven's sake, Bill, this is women's business. Give him leave to go!"

Colonel Campbell was clearly annoyed with Graham for asking and Sevier for interceding. "Major Chronicle, the burden of command will fall upon you. Shall Colonel Graham have his leave of absence?"

"It is, after all, women's business. I say let him go."

Colonel Campbell turned to Colonel Graham. "Colonel Graham, you may go."

"Thank you, sir. Might I be granted an armed escort?"

"One man," Campbell snapped.

"Take Dave Dickey," Major Chronicle offered, indicating a young private soldier in his company who rode close enough to hear all the conversation.

"I'd rather be shot in battle than to leave just now," Dickey protested.

"Dave, you must go," Major Chronicle urged him.

"I'd rather be shot here on the spot, but if I must go, I must go, I must." David Dickey sadly turned out from the column and followed Colonel Graham.

Colonel Campbell turned to Colonel Sevier with considerable wrath. "Colonel Sevier, I am trying to hold this army together just a few more hours, and I do not need you undermining my authority with your concerns about women's business. You shouldn't have interfered."

"I appreciate your position, sir, and I apologize if my concerns interfered with your authority," John answered with a soothing and reassuring grace. "But I will share this as a secret of my success. My attention to women's business has afforded me certain delightfully pleasing rewards." The officers laughed along with Sevier, and their reactions softened Colonel Campbell's demeanor to the extent that his good humor was restored.

"Colonel Sevier, there is no question you have been well rewarded," Campbell said. "Major Chronicle, you must take Colonel Graham's place. Colonel Hambright, have you any objections?"

Frederick Hambright, the German immigrant lieutenant colonel of the Lincoln County contingent, should have been the ranking officer to take Colonel Graham's place, but Colonel Campbell appointed Major Chronicle instead for his knowledge of the battlefield and his usefulness on the campaign trail.

"Dat is vhat I vish for," Colonel Hambright replied graciously. "Major Chronicle knows best zee place of attack."

In the next mile of travel, the officers organized the men by their respective commands and orders were sent back to apply improvised paper badges to the hats of the men for identification. Colonel Campbell also ordered strict silence in the ranks so that only the hoof steps and breathing of the horses could be heard.

Chapter 27

The Hour of Battle

Colonel Campbell was annoyed. "Confound it, Sevier! I told you to form up your men in columns. Now why haven't you done it?"

"My companies are taking in all the Tory spies and messengers in a broad net and preventing them from discovering us to Ferguson. I will not allow us to ride into an ambush. We have already taken sixteen of the enemy without firing a shot."

"Seventeen," Major Chronicle corrected him, pointing out another captured horseman in the road ahead. John pulled out his telescope and viewed the prisoner just taken.

"Why, he's just a lad, but he's riding a horse bred to run."

"May I see?" Colonel Hambright asked. John handed him the telescope. "It is John Ponder; he comes from a family of Tories! Search him well for letters."

Captain Jacob Brown rode up to the gathering of colonels, saluted Sevier, and handed over the papers found on the prisoner. Colonel Sevier found a letter from Ferguson to Cornwallis and read it quickly; then he gave the papers to Colonel Campbell.

"We have Ferguson for sure," Jacob Brown declared. "The boy said Ferguson is wearing a red-checked hunting shirt over his uniform."

Colonel Hambright turned to his junior officers and spoke. "Well, poys, when you see dot man mit a pig shirt over his clothes, you may know who him is and mark him mit your rifle."

"This dispatch is to Cornwallis, and Ferguson is begging him for reinforcements," Colonel Campbell said.

"He lacks confidence in his troop strength," Sevier observed.

"We can take him!" Isaac Shelby said.

The next moment Captain Valentine Sevier rode up to deliver another stranger taken by the advancing frontiersmen. The man rode double behind Val and jumped to the ground when he arrived before the colonels.

"My name is George Watkins. I'm a good Whig, just released on parole from Ferguson's camp."

"Who is your commander?" John asked.

"Colonel James Williams of District 96, South Carolina," the man answered. "I was captured last month while on furlough after Musgrove's Mill."

"Get the general up here, damn it," Colonel Campbell ordered. "This is ridiculous for him to hang back there like a whipped dog and not participate in our decision-making."

"You want me to go back and get him?" John offered.

"No, you have done enough, Sevier. Colonel Brandon can go and invite His Excellency to attend our conference."

"Yes, sir," Colonel Brandon responded, and rode to retrieve the absent general.

"Quickly now, Mr. Watkins, tell us how many men are present in Ferguson's camp," Colonel Sevier redirected the conversation.

"Eleven hundred, most all Tory militia, many coerced into service."

"Not the most dedicated and eager of the king's soldiers," Isaac Shelby remarked.

"We might be slightly outnumbered, but I like our prospects," Sevier said.

The army continued another mile when Adam Sherrill rode swiftly toward them. He reined in his powerful Sherrill horse and reported.

"Colonel, the enemy, with old Ferguson himself, occupies the hill just a mile ahead."

"Did you see where he posted his pickets?" John asked.

"Close in, sir, at the foot of the hill."

"Thank you, Adam," John said. "Well, Colonel Campbell, I think we are close enough now to divide up the men into various units and surround the hill."

"I agree," Campbell said decisively. "Men, the time has arrived. When things get all mixed up, don't shoot each other! Let all your men know that when challenged, the countersign is "Buford." The enemy will pay dearly for what Tarleton did to Colonel Buford."

The officers all expressed their agreement. Colonel Campbell spoke again. "Listen up! Officers, issue your men these orders: When you reach your position, dismount, tie your horse, roll coats and blankets and tie them to the saddle. Put fresh prime in your guns, and every man go into battle resolved to fight until he dies!" Campbell allowed a moment for his words to sink in and then continued with the orders. "Major Chronicle, since you know the area, you will lead your South Fork boys around the left to the far end of the hill. Watch for the right column led by Major Winston to link up with you to complete the encirclement. Begin now."

Major William Chronicle saluted. "Yes, sir. Come on, my South Fork boys!"Chronicle and Hambright turned their horses to the left. Chronicle signaled his men to follow, and they moved off.

"Colonel Hawthorne, you follow Chronicle, and Colonel Lacey will follow you. Go as quietly as you can until we all move into position."

Hawthorne and Lacey saluted and directed their men into formation.

"Colonel Cleveland, you and your men will go next, and then I want Williams to the right of Colonel Cleveland." Colonel Campbell turned to James Williams, with thoughts of how wrong the man had been about where the enemy would be found. "Is that satisfactory to you, *General* Williams?"

James Williams, serious, focused, and with all personal ambition set aside for the task at hand, saluted Colonel Campbell and replied, "Quite satisfactory."

"Isaac, your men will be next to Williams, and keep Sevier's men on your right flank—no gaps, understand?"

"Yes, sir."

"John, you will advance from right here," Campbell directed. "I see you already have your companies arrayed in battle formation."

"Very good, sir," John replied.

"Major Winston, you will have the farthest to go to meet Chronicle on the other side of the hill, so move quickly," Campbell ordered.

Major Joseph Winston's column moved off to the right. John Sevier turned to Captain William Lenoir and spoke. "Captain Lenoir, please go with Major Winston's group. Your task is to ensure they link up with Chronicle's column on the far side of the hill. Once that happens, we'll have the wild cat in the sack."

William Lenoir responded with great enthusiasm, honored to have such an important job. "Yes, sir, Colonel!" He galloped away to catch up with Major Winston.

Colonel Campbell continued the troop assignments. "Now, Major McDowell, you will move to effect a junction with Winston's left, and my Virginians will form on your left."

"Thank you, sir," Joseph McDowell saluted and led his men to the right, keeping closer in to the mountain than the way Winston had gone.

Colonel Campbell was left with only John Sevier and Isaac Shelby. "Well, gentlemen, the die are cast. What time is it?"

"Quarter of three," John replied, having just looked at his pocket watch.

"You think we can get this done before sundown?"

"It all depends on how soon they surrender," John said.

Campbell laughed. "I'll see you boys at the top of the mountain."

"Good luck, Bill!" They exchanged salutes. Campbell led his Virginians off to the right as the last of McDowell's men passed by.

"No alarms up there yet," John observed. "That's a good sign."

"I'll have my skirmishers silence their pickets," Isaac said.

"Isaac, I know you are eager to get this thing going, but don't alarm the enemy before Chronicle, Winston, and the others get to their places."

Isaac looked to his left and observed the last of Williams' men file by. He signaled his captains to follow on. "It's going to be one hell of a party up there, old friend. Take care of yourself."

"You do the same," John answered. He turned to his captains and quietly gave the order. "Dismount the men. Fresh prime your guns. We will advance on foot from here." All the men of Washington County, North Carolina, prepared for battle.

In the dense woods surrounding King's Mountain, Major Joseph Winston and Captain William Lenoir led Winston's men in a mad scramble to find their assigned position in the line of encirclement.

"Major Winston, I think we wandered too far to the right," Lenoir called out. Major Winston signaled his men to stop.

"Confound it!" Winston exclaimed.

"Hold on, somebody's coming," Lenoir said, pointing out an officer on a white horse, with sword drawn, approaching from their left.

The officer addressed them authoritatively. "Major Winston, turn your column to the left and come on quickly! You have no time to lose!" The dashing officer wheeled about and disappeared in the thick woods.

"Who the hell was that?" Winston asked.

"I've never seen him before, but he called you by name," Captain Lenoir replied.

"I better do what he says," Winston said. "Column left! Follow me, boys!" The men of Surry County followed their gallant leader in a new direction, which seemed to be a more correct course. After several hundred yards they arrived at the foot of a hill.

"This must be it!" Winston declared. "Dismount, secure the horses, and fresh prime your guns." The men jumped off their horses, secured them as ordered, and lined up for the charge. Major Winston drew his sword and ordered the advance up the hill. "Take the hill, boys! Take the hill!"

The men raced up the hill and breathlessly arrived at the top completely unopposed. Winston signaled a halt and turned to Captain Lenoir.

"Damn it, Will, we've taken the wrong hill."

"It looks that way, Major Winston, but we didn't lose a single man!"

"Where the hell is King's Mountain?"

The officers and men heard the sound of a horse crashing through the woods and the officer on the white horse reappeared. "Major Winston, Major Winston," the emissary called out to him. Winston was still breathless from his run up the hill, but turned toward the approaching officer.

Captain Lenoir answered for him. "Over here!"

As the mysterious officer arrived his head eclipsed the midafternoon sun, making it difficult for Lenoir and Winston to see his features for the glare. He spoke with the same authority and urgency as before. "Major Winston, mount your horses and push on. The enemy is but a mile ahead!" The officer pointed with his sword, in the direction he wanted them to go.

"Yes, sir," Major Winston answered.

The unknown officer turned and descended the hill in the direction he had pointed out. Joseph Winston surveyed the terrain for a moment and then spoke to Lenoir. "Look there, Will, we can circle this hill to the right and go up that draw where he's going. Go back to your horses, men!" The men raced back down the hill and remounted their horses.

Winston led the men around the steep hill they had just climbed and found the way the mysterious officer had gone. "Who is that fellow? How does he know me?"

Captain Lenoir shouted back, "Catch up with him and find out." They galloped as fast as fox hunters through the brushy woods, crossing hollows, splashing through creeks, climbing small ridges, on and on. Winston looked off to his left and saw the white horse officer riding a parallel course and pointed him out to Lenoir.

The Surry County men very soon arrived at the foot of a tall ridge where they could see Major Joseph McDowell lining up his men in battle formation.

"Here we are, men! Secure the horses and line up for battle!" Winston shouted. As the men dismounted they heard the first shots from somewhere in the distance.

"Look at this," Lenoir marveled. "McDowell's men are on our left, and we arrived in perfect position, in perfect timing!"

"Divine guidance," Winston declared. "And by the Almighty's hand, we'll have the victory!"

Captain Lenoir looked to the right and said, "I'll take the right wing to make sure we link up with Chronicle's South Fork boys."

"Good idea," Winston approved as he went to work lining up and encouraging his men.

Captain Lenoir ran toward the right end of the line searching intently for Major Chronicle. Drums rolled up along the ridge, and Lenoir could hear the shrill of an officer's whistle. The enemy loosed its first volley on command somewhere on the other side of the hill. Immediately Lenoir saw the elegant Major Chronicle marching toward him. With a grin Major Chronicle raised his hat in recognition of Captain Lenoir, and secure in the knowledge that they had successfully surrounded the enemy, he turned an about-face and stopped his column. Holding his hat high and pointing uphill with his sword, Chronicle shouted, "Face to the hill!" As Lenoir watched the South Fork boys swing into action, a volley from the mountain swept through their ranks and Major Chronicle fell along with several others. Lenoir ran to Major Chronicle and knelt beside him, finding him dead from a wound to the head. William Rabb, another of Chronicle's men, fell dead six feet away. Captain John Mattocks came over to render assistance to Major Chronicle, but a second volley killed him too. Captain Lenoir shouted encouragement to the Lincoln County men, and they pressed forward despite the terrible toll. They were intent on exacting revenge upon the Tory sharpshooters.

Isaac Shelby's men had been fired upon in the first moments of the engagement, even before they had reached their attack positions. They wanted to fire back immediately but Colonel Shelby stopped them. "Press on to your places, and your fire will not be lost! Get closer! See what you shoot and shoot what you see!" Isaac's men advanced steadily toward the hill.

On the other side of the hill, Colonel William Campbell rode his bay horse down the line of Virginians speaking words of encouragement and last minute instructions to his officers. When the sounds of firing erupted on the other side of the mountain, he stripped off his coat and twirled it above his head and let it fly. "Here they are, my brave boys. Shout like hell and fight like devils!" The frontier Virginians shouted the Indian war whoop and advanced on the run.

Colonel John Sevier pointed his sword up the mountain and shouted to his men. "Here they are, my boys! Here is the enemy that said they would burn our homes and lay waste our lands! Here they are, boys, here they are!" The men of the Watauga and Nolichucky Valleys raised the war whoop and advanced in good order behind the man with the white plume.

Colonel Benjamin Cleveland had run into a swampy piece of ground that delayed his advance. The Wilkes County men had gotten just clear of the obstacle when they heard the sounds of battle commencing. Colonel Cleveland, on horseback, organized his men into a line of battle and as they advanced gave them a speech to encourage them. "My brave fellows, we have beaten the Tories, and we can beat them again. They are all cowards. If they had the spirit of men, they would join with their fellow citizens in supporting the independence of their country. When you are engaged, you are not to wait for the word of command from me. I will show you, by my own example, how to fight; I can undertake no more. Every man must consider himself an officer and act from his own judgment. Fire as quick as you can and stand your ground as long as you can. When you can do no better, get behind trees or retreat; but I beg you not to run quite off. If we are repulsed, let us make a point of returning and renewing the fight; perhaps we may have better luck in the second attempt than the first. If any of you are afraid, such shall have leave to retire, and they are requested immediately to take themselves off." Cleveland's men encountered a picket of the enemy and drove the soldiers up the mountain as a wave breaking on the seashore.

Colonel Campbell's Virginians were the first to reach the crest of the mountain and unleashed a deadly volley at the enemy. Before they could reload Major Patrick Ferguson launched a counterattack of his provincial rangers, brandishing their bayonets. With empty rifles and no experience in fighting against the bayonet the Virginia frontiersmen ran back down the hill pursued by charging loyalists. Colonel Campbell and his officers risked their lives repeatedly in the effort to stop their men and get them turned around. The king's men answered a whistle signal from Ferguson that meant for them to halt the attack and return to the crest of the mountain. Campbell's men had left an opening in the line that endangered John Sevier's flank. Colonel Sevier had his men hold their ground and direct an effective fire on the flank of the enemy as they returned from their wild downhill charge.

During the bayonet charge on the Virginians, Isaac Shelby's men had fought their way up to the crest of the mountain moving from tree to tree, firing, reloading, running to the next tree, and firing again. Major Patrick Ferguson rode a white horse behind the ranks of loyalist soldiers, who were positioned to fire. He shouted the command, "Fire!"

The volley had little effect against Shelby's men, who fired back from behind trees. Ferguson stood high in his stirrups trying to see the enemy through the smoke. "Fix bayonets! Prepare to charge at my signal!" The men who had cleared the other side of the mountain of Virginians now had returned for the action against Shelby's men. Major Ferguson blew his signal whistle, and his men charged downhill.

Shelby's men fired from behind their trees and then ran from the bayonets. The western men reached the bottom of the hill in good order, keeping up a steady fire at the approaching loyalist rangers. Isaac Shelby reached his reformed lines in the safety of the denser forest at the foot of the hill. He shouted encouragement to his men as they prepared to fight with tomahawk against bayonet. "Turn and face them! Give them Indian play!"

The British reached the foot of the hill as Major Ferguson blew the signal whistle. The king's rangers turned and marched back up the hill. Isaac Shelby saw them turn and shouted to his men. "Now, boys, quickly reload your rifles, and let's advance upon them and give them another hell of a fire!" Shelby's men surged back up the hill moving from tree to tree, firing as before.

The return to the top of the mountain proved costly to the king's rangers as Shelby's men pressed hard on their heels and Sevier's men poured in a destructive fire on their flank. Major Ferguson was focused once more on Campbell's Virginians, who had returned to the attack. As the tiring rangers reached the top of the hill, Ferguson formed them up for another bayonet charge on the Virginians. "To the other side of the hill! The barbarians are here. Charge them like you did the others, and the day is won!" Ferguson blew his whistle, and the men charged down the hill at Campbell's men. Robert Sevier's company posted on that side fired a sharp volley into the king's rangers and thinned their ranks. The Virginians, having learned the game from the first bayonet charge, played it better the second time, yielded more stubbornly, and dealt their blows to the enemy more effectively.

Colonel Campbell again rallied his men and got them to stop at the bottom of the hill and reload their rifles. Ferguson blew his signal whistle again for his men to return to the top of the hill. Campbell rode his bay horse along the front of his men and called out to them. "Boys, remember your liberty. Come on, do it my brave fellows. Another gun—another gun will do it." The line pushed forward again with even greater resolve to finish the business or die. The Virginians were hard upon the heels of the exhausted king's rangers as they ascended the hill for the third time. Sevier's men poured in a destructive fire as before, weakening further Ferguson's ability to mount the bayonet charge. William Campbell's horse was completely exhausted by the efforts of the campaign and gave out during the third advance. The Colonel continued his activity on foot, looking more like the common soldier than ever.

John Sevier stood at the center of Robert Sevier's company, directing their fire and encouraging them to stay in their formations and advance slowly up the hill. Suddenly he noticed a group of Campbell's Virginians descending the mountain while Colonel Campbell and the rest of his men were advancing. He turned to Robert Sevier and said, "Now what's that about? Robert, take over and press the attack. Nobody is to give any ground!"

"Right, John," Robert answered.

John raced down the hill to where his horse was tied and quickly mounted. He overtook the men and called out to what seemed like an entire company. "Turn about there, men! Where are you going?"

A lieutenant answered. "They said Tarleton's dragoons are coming. We'll stand a better chance against him on horseback."

"No retreat has been ordered, so I suggest you gentlemen return to your places and press the attack."

"What about Tarleton?" the lieutenant asked.

"Bloody Ban is miles from here," John answered. "And he better be glad he's not taking the beating that Ferguson is."

"Are you sure?" The men were still concerned about the rumor.

"My scouts are watching all enemy units, and I tell you there is nothing to fear from Bloody Tarleton!"

"Very well, sir," the lieutenant replied. "Come on, men; let's get back to the fight." The Virginia company marched back up the hill, but John directed them to the left of a company commanded by Valentine Sevier, where he guessed Isaac Shelby's men were again about to be chased down the hill by the king's rangers. The sudden appearance of the Virginians would encourage and support Isaac's tired troops to rally and make their third attack on the summit. Meanwhile, John found other parts of his line and the Virginia line affected by rumors of Tarleton's eminent arrival.

He rode all along the line intercepting men who told the same story. "Word's out that Tarleton's coming."

"No truth to the rumor at all," John told the men. "Stay at your posts and do your duty! Press on, my boys. Press on to victory! There's nothing to fear from Bloody Ban Tarleton. He's miles away and glad of it, because today is our day of conquest! Nobody can stop us! Up the hill, boys, take the hill!" After riding the entire line and encouraging the men, John dismounted and climbed back up to rejoin his men, who were by now nearing the crest. "Forward, boys. One final push, and the day is ours!"

Colonel Cleveland's giant horse was shot out from under him, and the big man took a tumble. He struggled to get to his feet as some of his men tried to help him.

"I'm all right, boys, I'm all right. Keep going, boys. A little nearer to them, my brave boys, just a little nearer!" The Wilkes County men followed Cleveland as he continued the charge on foot. A replacement horse was found, and the men got their corpulent commander back in the saddle.

Isaac Shelby's men were just about to the crest of the hill when once more the bayonet men reappeared out of the smoke cloud that shrouded the hilltop. Shelby ordered the retreat again. "Fire and retreat! Same as before! Tomahawks at the ready! Don't give 'em much ground." Shelby's men retreated in better order, stopping at a safe distance to reload and fire again at the Tories. Once again the Tory bayonet men stopped at the sound of the signal whistle. They obediently, but wearily trudged back up the hill.

Isaac Shelby shouted with the same energy and activity at the turning of the tide. "Now boys, quickly reload your rifles, and let's advance upon them and give them another hell of a fire!" Shelby's men boldly pursued the Tories and continued to thin them out. "Shoot like hell and fight like devils!"

At the top of the hill, Ferguson lined up his men for another charge against Campbell's position. The signal whistle sounded again above the roar of battle, and the rangers descended upon Campbell's men. Campbell and his men gave ground again to the bottom of the hill, where they loaded and fired at the enemy with deadly effect. At the sound of the whistle, the loyalist rangers turned and marched back up the hill. They made one more desperate charge on Shelby's men, but the bayonet charge did not move the mountaineers as it had before.

The Tories fell back along the ridge before Sevier's onslaught, and there would be no more work for the bayonet. Major Ferguson had answered an alarm at the other end of the mountain, where Colonel Hambright's men, Major Winston's men, Major

McDowell's men, and Colonel Lacey's men had overcome the same kind of fierce resistance and were drawing close to the crest of the hill and sweeping it clear with incessant rifle fire. Ferguson rode along the crest and cut down with his saber every white flag his men raised. He loudly cursed them and ordered them to keep fighting. When his horse was shot out from under him, he was quickly provided another by his assisting officers.

Colonel James Williams, sword in hand, fought heroically at the head of his companies, shouting encouragement to his talented officers and men. "Come on boys, the old wagoner never yet backed out. I know you won't let me down when your country needs you the most."

Robert Sevier was reloading his rifle when he dropped his ramrod. He bent over to pick it up and was shot in the back. He fell, and his brother Joseph immediately rushed to his side. A few yards away, Sam Sherrill pointed out three mounted British officers charging toward them. A wounded man named John Gilleland aimed, but his rifle misfired. Gilleland shouted to fellow soldier Robert Young. "It's Ferguson! Shoot him!"

"Let's see what Sweet Lips can do," Robert Young said calmly as he shouldered the rifle and fired. Ferguson fell out of the saddle. His boot caught in the stirrup, and Ferguson's terrified horse dragged him all along the ridge of the mountain.

John Sevier ordered a charge on the enemy remnant from his sector. "Let's go, men! We all move up!" The men surged forward, forcing the dispirited enemy back toward the end of the mountain where the wagons and tents were.

John met the red-faced, profusely sweating Isaac Shelby at the top of the hill. "By God, Isaac, they have burned off your hair!"

"I'm burning up to be sure," Shelby answered. "I had to charge up this hill four times because of the damn bayonets."

"Well, we have their goose cooked now," John said. "My boys just dropped Ferguson."

"Where?" Isaac asked.

"His foot hung in the stirrup, and his horse dragged him back up the ridge somewhere!" Together they ran behind a line of Americans pouring fire into the mass of Tories huddled among the tents of Ferguson's camp. The Tories raised white flags, calling for quarter.

"Tarleton's quarter," shouted someone sarcastically. "Give them Tarleton's quarter like they gave it to Buford!"

John found his son James, angry and hurt. He was reloading his hot rifle.

"They killed my father! Shoot them all! Shoot all them sons of bitches!" John ran up behind his son and grabbed his rifle as he prepared to fire another round. "Let me go! They killed my father!"

"No, James, stop shooting!"

"But they said Sevier was dead."

"Look at me, I'm fine," John insisted. James turned, recognized his father, and embraced him.

"Oh, Father, thank God! I could never face Bonny Kate again if anything happened to you."

"I'm unhurt, but Uncle Robert's wounded. I want you to go tend to him."

Colonel Shelby tried desperately to stop the other men from firing. "Lay down your arms! If you Tories wish to live, lay down your arms!"

Colonel Williams arrived on horseback to the confused scene of men still shooting, men trying to find someone to accept their surrender, and men too afraid of being shot whether they surrendered or not. "Victory, my lads! Victory!" Williams shouted. A shot rang out from an unknown source, and Colonel Williams fell from his horse.

The untrained American militiamen renewed their fire as the remaining British commander Abraham DePeyster shouted out to Isaac Shelby. "This isn't fair! We surrendered under the white flag!"

"Stop! Stop! Hold your fire!" Shelby shouted as he bravely ran out between the lines.

"Take cover, James, this thing isn't over," John Sevier warned his son. Sevier joined his friend Isaac between the Tories and Americans holding up his hands and shouting. "Hold your fire! Stop this immediately!"

The men recognized the man with the white plume on his hat and stopped firing again, and a strange quiet settled over the mountain. Then the Americans shouted three loud cheers. "Hip-hip huzzah! Hip-hip huzzah! Hip-hip huzzah!"

Some distance down the hill, Colonel Campbell had begun to count the costs of the day's action. He knelt beside his dear friend, Captain William Edmondson. Life was ebbing from the gallant captain, who suffered two mortal wounds. He held tight the hand of his beloved colonel. Big Bill Campbell wept for all the brave men who had fallen obeying his orders, but especially for Captain Edmondson. When the men on the mountain had shouted their loud huzzahs, word arrived by way of a Virginian named John McCrosky that a great victory had been won. Captain Edmondson, with tears in his eyes, kissed the hand of Colonel Campbell, smiled, and died.

Chapter 28

The Aftermath

Colonel Campbell was busy taking up swords among the surviving Tory officers. His sleeves were rolled up, his collar open, and he wore neither coat nor waistcoat. Many among the enemy assumed him to be a common soldier.

Captain Abraham DePeyster had survived the closing moments of the battle still mounted on his gray horse. When Colonel Campbell reached up to take his sword, he withdrew it from him. The Virginia colonel's visage darkened at the affront. Evan Shelby Jr., a brother to Isaac Shelby, rode over to Captain DePeyster and received the officer's sword. "Captain DePeyster, meet our Colonel William Campbell of Washington County, Virginia. He is the duly-elected commander in chief of this here American army."

"So it's true," DePeyster said. "There is not a regular professional soldier in your entire expedition?"

"Not a damn one," Evan Shelby declared.

"No man ranking higher than a county militia colonel?"

"Well, we did have a South Carolina general but we didn't take no orders from him," Evan said. "Colonel Sevier wouldn't even let him show his commission."

"Colonel Campbell, it was damned unfair! It was damned unfair, I tell you!" DePeyster protested the failure to recognize the flag of surrender.

"Get down off that horse!" Colonel Campbell ordered. "Officers will rank by yourselves. Prisoners, take off your hats and sit down."

Colonel Campbell saw a Virginian by the name of Andrew Evins raise his rifle to his shoulder. He ran over to the man and knocked the soldier's gun skyward. "Evins, for God's sake don't shoot. It is murder to kill them now, for they have raised the flag."

"One of the prisoners has a loaded and cocked musket," Evins explained.

"Well, go over and take it up, but cease firing, for God's sake. Cease firing," Campbell ordered.

Isaac Shelby looked over the sea of faces that were prisoners. "Good God! What can we do in this confusion?"

"We can order the prisoners from their arms," suggested Captain Sawyers.

"Yes, that can be done," Colonel Shelby said, and he gave the orders through Captain DePeyster to march the prisoners to another place along the ridge away from their weapons. Then it was easier for the patriots to pick up and stack the enemy guns. They found many that were still loaded.

Sam Sherrill found his son George guarding the prisoners and embraced him. "Thank God, you're unhurt. Have you seen Adam?"

"Saw him way out front, in the thickest part of the fighting, Junior was there too."

"I'll search the wounded, then."

"Wait, Papa," George said. "Yonder is Adam helping a wounded man over to the tents."

"Can you go with me?" Sam asked.

"Yes, sir," George replied, and he went with his father.

They caught up with Adam, and he was relieved to see his father and brother safe and sound. Sam helped Adam with the wounded man and learned his name was William Moore of Colonel Campbell's regiment. "That's a pretty bad leg," Sam remarked.

"Might have bled to death if this fellow hadn't tied it off," Moore replied.

"I thought we could find a doctor up at the Tory camp," Adam said hopefully.

The camp was a scene of confusion, but they found Dr. James Cozby, John Sevier's friend and somewhat of a horse doctor. He evaluated the wounded as they were brought in and lined them up for surgeries.

"Can you fix up this fellow?" Sam asked.

"Set him down over here. I can patch them up, but I don't have the skill to dig out the lead," Cozby answered. "Dr. Johnson will do that. He was Ferguson's doctor."

"Where is he?"

"He's over with Colonel Williams right now," Cozby answered.

Sam Sherrill walked away from the field hospital with his two sons searching for the third.

"There he comes now!" George exclaimed. Sam Sherrill Jr. carried a bucket of water, which he set down as he saw his brothers approaching. The Sherrill brothers warmly embraced, and Sam Jr. had tears in his eyes as he realized they had all survived without a scratch.

"I've never seen you cry, big brother," Adam said.

"I've never seen tragedy on such a huge scale," Junior replied. "I can't help but weep for these dying souls. They all keep calling for water, so I found this bucket and I'm doing my best to quench their thirst."

"Keep at it, son," Sam encouraged him.

"What about Uriah and Uncle Bill?" Junior asked.

"I've seen them and they are unhurt. Leroy Taylor is safe too," Sam said.

"And Mary Jane's new beau?"

Sam smiled. "Isaac Taylor is good, and so is all of Bonny Kate's family, except for Robert Sevier. We saw him shot in the back near the end of the fight. I don't know what has happened to him. I'll let you know when I find out."

William Campbell, John Sevier, Isaac Shelby, and Benjamin Cleveland walked among the many dead and wounded to arrive at a tent where the South Carolina leader James Williams rested. The Tory doctor, Uzal Johnson, stepped out of the tent and shook his head. "No hope," he told the officers in a low voice and walked away.

Inside a young soldier tearfully tended the officer. "This is Daniel Williams, the son of Colonel Williams," Isaac told John.

John and Isaac stepped into the tent respectfully and found General Williams conscious and aware. Campbell and Cleveland watched from the entrance.

"Hello, Jimmy," John said kneeling beside the cot. "Has the doctor been by to see you?"

"Been here and gone," Williams replied. "Tell the boys to press on to victory. Hold the hill."

"We have taken the hill, by God, and Ferguson is defeated," Isaac declared.

In his hand, James Williams clutched a piece of paper. "What do you have there, Jimmy?" John asked.

"It's my commission from the governor."

"You're going to need that," John said. "I'm certain the governor will want you to lead the attack against Fort Ninety Six. You and your men fought bravely today, and we thank you."

"It was a great victory, wasn't it?"

"Yes it was, General Williams, yes it was."

Williams closed his eyes to rest. John rose to leave the tent.

"Sevier?"

"Yes, sir?"

"Will you be going to Ninety Six with me?"

"Our service in South Carolina is finished, General Williams. Our enlistments expire soon, and we have Indian trouble in the West."

"That's a shame; I could have used a good officer like you. I'm sorry about the misunderstanding last night. We could have been great friends."

"I feel the same way, Jimmy," John replied. "Get some rest now, and we'll visit again later."

John was very anxious about his brother Robert and soon had the Tory doctor tending him beside the spring where the Sevier brothers and John's sons had taken him. Robert lay on his side in great pain.

"Robert, I brought the doctor," John said.

"The pain is killing me."

"They shot him in the back," Valentine Sevier explained as Dr. Johnson knelt to examine the wound.

"It seems the ball entered a kidney," Dr. Johnson assessed. "Are you wounded anywhere else?"

"No."

"Hmm, the ball must still be in there somewhere." He probed the wound with a slender instrument.

"Can you get it out?" Robert asked.

"It's lodged deep beyond the kidney. I can't perform such a delicate surgery under these conditions. Night is approaching, and I have hundreds of wounded men in my care."

"I have to get home to Kesiah and the boys," Robert said.

"No traveling for you, sir," Dr. Johnson ordered. "You have to rest quietly and get the bleeding to stop. I'll check in on you later." Dr. Johnson stood and made his way toward the camp at the top of the hill with John Sevier beside him.

"Doctor, what can we do for him?"

"Bandage the wound, get the bleeding to stop, and make him comfortable. He needs a surgery to get the ball out within the week; otherwise it will inflame the kidney and sepsis will set in. If I were you, Colonel Sevier, I'd move him to a nearby cabin and keep him there until you can find a local doctor who can help him."

"Thank you, Dr. Johnson." John returned to his brother.

"That Tory doctor wasn't much help," Robert complained. "Where's Dr. Cozby?"

"Both doctors will be busy all night," John said. "We are going to get you to a cabin for a meal and a good night's rest."

"I know a cabin," John's son Joseph spoke up. "It's the Finley place, where that nice girl gave us directions. It's only three miles back."

"That is a good idea, Joseph," John approved. "You and your Uncle Joe and James will stay with Robert and see that he gets the care he needs. Maybe tomorrow we'll find a doctor who can remove that musket ball."

"We'll do it," Joseph Sevier replied.

"John, did we get Ferguson?" Robert asked.

"We got him! His command was completely surrounded, and we killed, wounded, or captured every one of them."

"How many men did we lose?"

"I don't know yet," John replied. "Even one loss is too much for me."

"I guess we need to get out of here before Tarleton shows up," Robert said.

"That's the idea," John said. "Robert, I want you to do what the doctors tell you to do. Our brother Joseph and my boys are staying with you until you are strong enough to travel. I'll check in with you tomorrow. God bless you."

"Same to you, brother," Robert replied.

The renowned scouts Anthony Twitty and Lewis Musick surveyed the scene at the top of the hill where the Tory dead lay thick. "Look here, Mr. Twitty, it's the woman that spoke to us at Green River," Musick called out as he knelt beside the body. She was sprawled out face-up with her eyes still open to the horror she must have seen at the turning tide of battle. A roll of bandages was clutched in her stiff hand. A ball had hit her in the side of the head, and the blood ran out and caked in her pretty red hair.

"It looks like she was helping the wounded like an angel of mercy," Twitty said. "Do you remember how cheerful she was and friendly?"

"I remember she told us her name was Virginia Sal and her secret was that she loved Major Ferguson," Musick replied.

"Poor thing let her heart choose the wrong side in a political squabble she never even understood. We ought to give her a decent burial, Mr. Musick."

A stranger came by. "There's a pretty trollop. What treasures are you hiding, my pretty?" He reached down to rip away her chemise, but Musick caught the man's hand and stopped him.

"Leave her be," Musick said sternly

"There's bound to be jewels on one as fine as this."

"Leave her be," Twitty reissued the command more forcefully.

The stranger backed away from the two tough scouts. Musick lifted the lady gently and carried her down to the spring.

The scouts found a crowd of men gathered to view the body of Patrick Ferguson. One of the major's young orderlies sat weeping nearby.

"What's going on here?" Twitty demanded.

"They stripped the body of Major Ferguson and pissed all over him," the orderly cried.

"This will stop immediately," Twitty ordered.

"Who says so?" The perpetrators had responded to the hateful "pissing" proclamation Ferguson had written to insult the mountaineers.

"Colonel John Sevier orders you to stop immediately, and if that's not good enough for you, Colonel Isaac Shelby and Colonel William Campbell will back him up."

"And if that's not good enough, we have the orders of the Continental Congress!" Lewis Musick added for good measure.

"What orders?"

"We are here to give Major Patrick Ferguson the honors of a Christian warrior's funeral."

"But he called us mongrels, barbarians, and backwater bandits. He's the one who ought to be pissed on forever."

"Enough! There is a code of honor among great warriors. Colonel Sevier understands it, and so do the other colonels. This conduct dishonors them all!" Anthony Twitty, a rough frontier scout, spoke with learned authority as Colonel Sevier most certainly would have. His words had their effect, and the offenders backed away.

"You men dig the grave," Musick ordered the miscreants.

"With what? We haven't got any shovels."

"With your hunting knives; there are men enough of you to make short work of it."

Anthony Twitty turned to the weeping orderly, Elias Powell, and spoke kindly to him. "Clean up your Major Ferguson and prepare him for burial. I'm sure all our colonels will attend the funeral of this fallen warrior."

Colonel Shelby rode up while they were bathing the body and assumed by the attention he received, he was still alive. "Colonel, the fatal blow is struck; we've Burgoyned you!"

"He's already dead, Colonel Shelby," Anthony Twitty said. "We are conducting his funeral soon."

"The others will want to be here," Shelby said. "I'll tell them."

Colonel Cleveland arrived and watched as the body was washed and laid upon a raw beef hide. Lewis Musick gently laid the red-haired maiden beside her professed true love. The other colonels arrived for the solemn occasion, and at the insistence of Colonel Shelby, the Tory officers were afforded the privilege to attend their commander's funeral. A few words were spoken about his bravery and his conduct during the battle, and then the rawhide cover was folded over the bodies and they were buried together in the shallow grave. Colonel Campbell ordered the men to gather stones to pile over the grave to serve as a monument and to keep the wild animals from disturbing the mortal remains.

Colonel Campbell called an officer's meeting immediately following the funeral.

"You have all turned in your casualty reports, and the totals are twenty-eight killed and sixty-two wounded. I think you gentlemen need to go back and count again. It's unbelievable that in so large a conflict as we have seen today that you would so greatly undercount your dead. The enemy dead have already surpassed one hundred and fifty, and we are still counting. Among the officers lost were Major William Chronicle, Captain William Edmondson, Lieutenant Reece Bowen, and we will likely lose Colonel James Williams. Where's Colonel Hambright?"

"He's up at the doctor's tent with a wound in the thigh," Colonel Edward Lacey reported. "His boot filled up with blood, but he fought on until the enemy surrendered."

"Will he make it through?"

"The doctor stopped the bleeding and said he'll recover."

The sun set on October seventh at King's Mountain to the most dreadful sounds of human suffering. The horses were tended, the night guard was posted, the wounded gathered into the hospital tent all without the benefit of an evening meal and without sleep for the victors in the previous forty hours. The night was clear and cold. The starry band of the Milky Way stood out clearly as the survivors bedded down among the dead and dying.

The work of the doctor continued without ceasing all night, by lantern light in the tent at the top of the hill. The campfire outside burned brightly to illuminate the waiting patients as Dr. Cozby had lined them up. John Sevier and Isaac Shelby took one last tour of the field hospital before bedding down around midnight. Inside the tent a man was howling in the most intense pain. John started toward the tent to see what could be done for the suffering man, but Dr. Cozby stopped him by grabbing his arm. Their eyes met.

"No, John, it's an amputation," Cozby warned his friend.

"God be merciful!"

"Private William Moore of Campbell's regiment," Cozby identified the victim. "There was so much damage; it never would have healed before the gangrene set in. Dr. Johnson knows what he's doing, and I agree with his decision."

"Is it his arm or his leg?"

"The leg below the knee," Cozby replied. "It was the only way to save his life."

John noticed a young woman sitting and staring into the fire, exhausted, her apron red with blood. The firelight illuminated her red hair and alabaster complexion, but her face was expressionless. "Who's the lady?"

"Virginia Paul, another of Ferguson's cooks. He had two redheads named Virginia working around his camp; isn't that a strange coincidence?"

"I saw them bury the other one, so young and pretty."

"She's been trying to help the doctor with treating the wounded, but I fear for her sanity. I made her sit down and rest; and she's been like that for over an hour."

"Give her a shot of brandy and bring her out of it," Isaac Shelby suggested.

"No, Colonel Shelby, brandy is not the remedy for her. She needs sleep, but listen to how noisy it is all over this mountain. How will anyone sleep to such a mournful chorus of pain and despair?"

"How many of the wounded will be able to travel tomorrow?" John asked.

"How are you going to convey them?" Cozby asked. "Most of them cannot sit a horse."

"We can rig up horse litters like the Indians use," John suggested.

"We'll need about fifty for our men; three times that for the enemy wounded. If you travel tomorrow you'll have to take it slow and stop often."

"There is a great fear that Colonel Tarleton will arrive tomorrow," Isaac Shelby said. "It would be disastrous to stay here any longer than absolutely necessary."

Dr. Cozby knew of Isaac's impetuous nature. "I urge caution, Colonel Shelby, if you expect some of these wounded fellows to survive a great deal of movement. I will support the advice of Dr. Johnson in the matter."

"A Tory doctor will make every effort to slow us down and see us caught by Tarleton," Isaac charged.

"The medical profession is above political concerns, Colonel Shelby," Cozby replied. "I believe Dr. Johnson's motive would be to prevent any further bloodshed and human suffering."

Isaac turned to John. "Colonel Sevier, your friend here has been deceived by that old Tory sawbones. His advice will get us all killed."

"Ease up, Isaac," John said. "I'll confer with Colonel Campbell in the morning, and we will temper our decisions with opinions from every quarter. Carry on, Dr. Cozby. You are a blessing to all of us."

John walked away and Isaac followed continuing a rant. "John, I have to tell you what I saw this afternoon concerning Colonel Campbell. It was a full fifteen minutes before he appeared after the surrender. If he had been where he was supposed to be, that whole bloody mess could have been avoided when our men opened fire again."

"Colonel Campbell was attending a dying friend at that moment. I have that on good authority."

"He should have been at the top of the mountain with us."

"I'm not going to start a squabble over who was where and what anybody did or didn't do. The whole affair was in the hands of Divine Providence, and we must be thankful that it wasn't any worse for us than it was."

"After the second bayonet charge, I saw Bill Campbell sitting on his bald-faced black two hundred yards to the rear, just watching the battle."

"That's not possible, Isaac. Colonel Campbell was at the head of his troops on every charge and the last one back with every retreat. He commanded six companies and lost thirteen of his junior officers, who all died bravely."

"John, he looked right at me, and I know it was Campbell, sitting on his best horse. Then at the end of the action he came up to me and said, *Colonel Shelby, I cannot account for my conduct in the latter part of the action.*"

"What did he mean by that?"

"He as good as admitted he left the field in the middle of the action."

"That's not what I saw, and what Colonel Campbell said could be understood in many different ways."

"That's the way I understood it."

"You are making a serious charge, Isaac. You better get your facts straight before you tell this to anyone else. You need witnesses."

"Well what did you see?"

"I saw Colonel Campbell mounted, at the head of his troops on every charge except the last one, and then I had to leave the front, myself, to round up a company of Virginians who were convinced that Tarleton was about to attack. I turned them around and sent them to support your right. That's how your men got all mixed in with the Virginians there at the end."

"You may have to take over command if my investigation reveals misbehavior on the part of Colonel Campbell."

"No, Isaac, I will not take command. I'm going home as soon as the North Carolina authorities release me from service. The only question I have concerning Colonel Campbell was his whereabouts at the surrender. Attending a dying officer and friend is excuse enough for me."

"What if another officer in your outfit saw the same thing I did, would you back me up?"

"No, I'm going to bed. It will take every ounce of energy and skill to get my men off this mountain and home safely. I'm going to need a congenial relationship with all the other officers to accomplish it. So Isaac, please, try not to cause a mutiny while I'm asleep, and do not cause any trouble at the officer's meeting in the morning."

Nightfall overtook a party of Seviers escorting wounded Robert Sevier three miles from King's Mountain to the home of John Finley. When eighteen-year-old Joseph knocked on the door, Mary Finley opened it. Her eyes lit up when she recognized the handsome blond lad she had met just that morning.

"Good evening, ma'am," Joseph said politely. "My uncle is wounded and needs care and rest for the night. Could we please tend to him in the shelter of your barn?"

"I'll handle this, Mary," said a man who stepped into the doorway. "We don't want any trouble with you people. I don't care which side you are on, please go away."

"Sir, my uncle is wounded and night is coming on," Joseph pleaded. "Could we be permitted to just camp in your yard? We have the means to pay you for any inconvenience we might cause."

"No," the man protested.

"Please, father," the girl spoke up as she touched the older man's arm. "These men need our help, and I believe they are good men."

The man looked down into her face and his demeanor changed. "I'll likely regret this, but all right, bring the wounded man in."

Joseph smiled at the angel of mercy and was struck by the beauty of her smile. She had light brown reddish hair, and green eyes that communicated a native intelligence, wisdom, and kindness that impressed the lad. Joseph addressed the father once more. "Thank you, sir. We are much obliged. My name is Joseph Sevier, and my uncle is Captain Robert Sevier. We came from Washington County to catch and defeat Ferguson."

A woman brought candles over from the cook fire to light the interior of the cabin. "I'm Anne Finley, Mary's mother."

"Pleased to meet you, Mrs. Finley," Joseph bowed politely.

"We just came back from the battleground," Mrs. Finley explained. "Mary insisted we go and help the wounded as long as there was light enough to see."

"We heard the battle raging all afternoon," Mary said. "When the shooting stopped, I had to know what happened."

"What was the outcome?" Mr. Finley asked.

"We killed or captured every man of the enemy," Joseph replied.

"What became of Ferguson?"

"He was killed on the mountain, and none of his men escaped," Joseph reported. He looked at Mary. "I hope you had no loved ones serving under him."

"No," she said. "My brothers were defending Charleston when the British captured the city. We don't know where they are being held. Today was certainly a great day for the sons of liberty."

"Mary, we don't discuss our politics with strangers," her father warned.

"My father's employer and landlord is a stingy old Tory," Mary explained. "He makes our lives miserable."

Abraham Sevier and James Sevier assisted Robert into the cabin. The girl went right to work making a place for him on the bed in the main room. "What kind of wound is it?" she asked with great concern.

"He was shot in the back," Abraham said. "The ball is still in there, but we have managed to stop the bleeding."

"Lay him on his side and keep him still," she directed. "I'll redress the wound and see what we can do to make him comfortable."

Joseph admired the girl's caring attitude and her willingness to help. He felt good that his uncles had agreed to his suggestion to seek shelter at the home of Mary Finley.

"Oh, Miss Finley, this is my uncle Abraham. And here is my uncle Joseph, we are about the same age and with the same name, so it's kind of confusing. And that's my brother James. My other uncle, Captain Valentine Sevier, stayed at the battlefield tonight with my father, Colonel John Sevier."

"Such a big family," she said with a smile.

"Yes, ma'am," Joseph returned the smile. "I have eight more brothers and sisters back home in Washington County."

"Your mother must be a very busy woman," the girl said.

"Mother died this past winter."

"Oh, I'm sorry, Joseph," she said.

An awkward silence prevailed as Mary worked on Robert Sevier's wound.

"Father, I'll need the herbal poultice we use for farm injuries. Do we have the makings for it?"

"Yes, that will do wonders for Mr. Sevier," Mr. Finley answered. "I'll prepare it while you fix these men some supper. Are you fellows hungry?"

"I'll say we are," James Sevier answered. "We haven't eaten anything since last night."

"Make it a big supper, Mary," Mr. Finley said. "These men have done our country a great service today."

After supper the men sat by the fire and talked. Mary cleaned up the table and then put on her cloak and picked up a bucket. "We need another bucket of water," she announced. "I'm going to the spring." She took down the lantern and lit the candle.

"Mary, it's not safe," her father warned. "After the battle, we will be overrun with stragglers and deserters desperate to prey upon defenseless citizens. You need an armed escort every time you go out."

"I'll go with you," Joseph volunteered. He put on his hat and coat and primed his rifle. The girl watched as he prepared and turned to look at her father when they were ready to go. Mr. Finley nodded his approval, and they moved silently out the door. The chilly night air was invigorating as Mary led the way down the spring path. She moved quickly and quietly about the business until she arrived at the spring and stooped to draw the water. Joseph scanned the still forest and observed no danger. She turned to face him for the return trip, and he politely stepped aside to let her pass.

When they reached the door of the cabin she put the bucket down and faced Joseph, placing her slender hand upon his coat over his young heart. "Thank you, sir," she said softly, looking up into his eyes.

"For what do you thank me?"

"For coming back to me this evening," she said with a smile. "And for all you did in the service of our country today. Was it dreadful?"

"Worse than dreadful; I was glad to leave the mountain tonight, and I thank you for taking us in."

"I looked for you on the mountain, Joseph. Mother and I patched up many a wounded man, but I never did see you."

"It was the scene of great confusion. I never saw you either."

"Will you go with me to fetch water in the morning?"

"I will go with you as often as you like."

Mary Finley, the seventeen-year-old maiden who had been forbidden by her Whig father to marry any man of the Tory persuasion, reached up and bestowed a quick kiss on the cheek of her hero. Then she picked up her water bucket and entered the cabin.

Chapter 29

The Blue Hen's Chickens

John Sevier awoke just before dawn on Sunday, October eighth. The nightmares from an unimaginable night of horrors mixed with fresh memories of the previous day all weighed heavily as he rose and rolled up his damp blanket. He remembered his many concerns, including his family at home, the impending Indian attacks, the wounded men on King's Mountain, the families of the dead soldiers, the threat of Tarleton and Cornwallis coming to the aid of Ferguson's men, and the preservation of life as the army moved in the direction of home. John was especially concerned about his brother Robert.

"John, you have to eat something," Sam Sherrill said, holding out an apple.

"Thanks, Sam." John took the apple and ate it quickly. "Call the captains together for me, will you? I want to go over some orders for the day before Colonel Campbell calls me to the staff meeting."

John's captains gathered quickly, and he saw the same concerns on their faces that troubled him. "Gentlemen, we know that Cornwallis has issued an order of summary execution for any citizen caught bearing arms against the king. It's happened in Augusta, Savannah, Charleston, Camden, and it will happen again in Charlotte. That's why we will leave no man of ours behind, regardless of how badly he's wounded."

"How are we going to move them?" Captain James Stinson asked.

"Horse litters, like the Indians use," John replied. "So we will need about a hundred poles cut from saplings and enough rope to lash them onto the horses."

"I'll get the poles," Jacob Brown volunteered his company.

"Thank you, Jacob. I'll also need a company to help guard the prisoners while we prepare to move out."

"I'll take care of that," Val Sevier spoke up.

"Thank you, Val."

"John, there's something you should know about the prisoners," Val said. "We found those deserters, Sam Chambers and James Crawford, among them. Colonel

Cleveland was all for hanging them last night, but Colonel Campbell would not allow it on the field of honor where the blood of brave men had been spilled."

"I wish those boys had just deserted for home," John said. "It would have been so much easier."

"I don't think you can save them, but I know you will try," his brother said.

John sighed and waited a moment. In the distance he heard a messenger calling the officers to the staff meeting. He turned to his able neighbor, Lieutenant George Russell. "Congratulations, Mr. Russell. Your bravery and meritorious conduct in battle yesterday has earned you the rank of captain. You will attend to your horses, prepare your company for patrol, and await my orders."

"Yes, sir. Thank you, sir," the young man answered.

"Major Tipton and I have to meet with Colonel Campbell and the others to coordinate the rest of our activities for today. Carry on, gentlemen."

Major Jonathan Tipton accompanied Colonel Sevier to the morning staff meeting. "Well Jonathan, this is where it begins to get complicated. Some of the other colonels are already proposing military ventures for our united command in places such as upland South Carolina, Georgia, and Virginia. A success like we had yesterday will fire the imaginations of even the most unimaginative."

"I wouldn't mind a few more victories like this, but I know what we risked by leaving our homes and families unprotected from the Indians."

"My only objective is to get us as far from King's Mountain as possible by nightfall. I want to make it impossible for Colonel Tarleton to track any of us down, even if I have to command the rear guard myself."

All the colonels and majors assembled upon a nearby hill a little ways removed from the mountain top. Colonel Campbell opened the meeting. "Good morning, gentlemen. I trust you all got some rest, because you will need it for a very difficult day. We have to bury the dead and transport the wounded as far as the Broad River before nightfall. I sent William Snodgrass and Edward Smith out this morning to find the foot soldiers we left behind and direct them to set up a camp for us at Buffalo Creek. I want every one of you there by dark. Is that understood?"

The officers nodded their agreement. Colonel Cleveland spoke next. "What about the prisoners?"

"They go along too," Colonel Campbell answered. "I'm leaving behind no evidence, no eye witnesses, no written papers—nothing that will give the enemy any information about who we are, our numbers, our plans, or our line of march. I'm even taking the enemy wounded."

"What if they are so badly wounded, that transport results in their death?" Colonel Sevier asked.

"I'll make exceptions," Colonel Campbell said. "But I'll make the decision who goes and who stays behind. I'll be in charge of the burial details with two of my own companies and some of the healthiest Tories. The graves will be dug right here on this hill, and we will keep the Tories separate from the patriotic Americans."

"What are the final numbers, Colonel Campbell?" Isaac Shelby asked.

"The reports came back on your losses, and I thank you for revisiting that. We lost twenty-eight killed; six officers, and twenty-two privates. Fifty-four were wounded. I am amazed at how few casualties we suffered. Colonel Sevier's strategy of making this into an Indian-style fight succeeded beyond every expectation."

"What about the enemy losses?" Colonel Cleveland asked.

"The documents we found in Ferguson's tent and the letters we captured yesterday indicate he had eleven hundred men in his command. Two hundred were out foraging at the time we arrived yesterday. Captain DePeyster has confirmed that in private conversation, so we whipped a nine-hundred-man force roughly equal to ours. One hundred fifty were killed, one hundred fifty wounded, and we have six hundred prisoners, not including their wounded. As you march today, stay together and be vigilant for their two hundred foragers. They are still out there somewhere."

"What about our next target?" Major Joseph McDowell asked.

"We got Ferguson, and that's what we came to do. Now we have to get away from Cornwallis and Tarleton's dragoons. They command superior forces; better equipped and better trained with entire companies of British regulars. We have no authority and no orders to seek other targets. The over-mountain boys came out on thirty-day enlistments. It is the practice of their commanders to honor the terms of service, and I understand Colonel Sevier is already enlisting for an Indian campaign to follow immediately the return to his home on the Nolichucky."

"No time for the missus?" Cleveland laughed. "I can hardly believe such news!"

"I'll always make time for the missus!" John replied with a smile as the men laughed.

"Bonny Kate is the one who named us the Blue Hen's Chickens and got us to save our fighting for Ferguson," Joseph McDowell remembered.

Colonel Campbell saw that one of the officers had been brought to the meeting on a stretcher. "How do you feel this morning, Colonel Hambright?"

"Sore, but happy to be alive," the Lincoln County colonel answered.

Colonel Campbell stepped over and shook the wounded officer's hand. "I'm releasing the Lincoln County militia from service, Colonel Hambright. Your men may return to their homes today and see to the safety of their families. Thank you for all you did to guide us to the battlefield and the sacrifices made in the name of liberty. The bravery of Major Chronicle and Captain Mattocks will long be remembered by the men who had the privilege to serve beside them."

John Sevier took his hat off to honor the memory of the fallen heroes of the South

Fork, and the other officers followed the example of his gesture.

Colonel Campbell continued. "Two companies from each command will be assigned to conduct the march of the prisoners. I've ordered the flints removed from all the captured muskets, and each prisoner will carry two guns in addition to his personal gear. No living prisoner shall be robbed or plundered, but we will take up their knives, their papers, and their writing utensils. No messages will leave any camp or be left along the way for Tarleton's spies. Are there any questions?"

"What about the wagons? Couldn't we use those to carry the wounded?" Major McDowell asked.

"Wagons can't go where we are going," Campbell replied. "We'll stay to the river trails and wooded ridges where Tarleton can't use his horses and sabers should he overtake us. The wagons will be pulled over the bonfires and burned as the last unit leaves the mountain."

"Colonel Campbell, there are some local women searching for loved ones among the dead and wounded," Colonel Edward Lacey reported. "What shall we do about them?"

John Sevier answered quickly. "Give the ladies assistance and show them every kindness in their distress."

Colonel Campbell smiled. "You heard it from the man who best knows women's business. Do as he says, but don't give them any information that Cornwallis or Tarleton can use to find us. All units will be packed up and clear of the mountain by ten o'clock this morning. God be with you!"

When the Washington County officers returned from the staff meeting, the men were prepared to conduct a funeral for their fallen comrades. The bodies of William Steele, John Brown, and Michael Mahoney were carried to the burying ground. Sam Sherrill, a good Presbyterian, read the words of comfort and resurrection from his Bible, and Colonel Sevier spoke briefly on the good qualities of his three lost friends and neighbors. A prayer by Valentine Sevier concluded the ceremony, and the Washington County militia made ready to move.

Colonel Sevier and his staff arrived at the home of John Finley, and the Sevier brothers dismounted to go in and visit their brother Robert. They were politely and warmly received by the family of the house.

"Joseph has entertained us all morning with stories of the great West," Mary exclaimed.

Colonel Sevier gave polite attention to the enthusiastic daughter. "So you have learned all about the beauty of our mountains, the refreshing waters of our clear rivers, the depth of our valley soils, the plentiful game, the mineral riches in our mountainsides, and the size of our stately trees?"

"Not yet, sir," the girl beamed. "He's told me about you and Bonny Kate, the parties and the dancing, the weddings and the feasting, the children of your family, and the beauty of your horses."

"All true, I'm sure, for my son Joseph is an honest man above all his other fine qualities."

"John, who did we lose?" Robert asked from the bed where he lay. The colonel went over to his brother and sat beside him.

"William Steele, Michael Mahoney, and John Brown," he said quietly. "Patrick Murphy and John Gilleland were badly wounded, but Dr. Cozby thinks they will likely recover. How are you feeling this morning?"

"Poorly used, John," Robert replied. "I've been watching men marching by the house for the last half hour. Did our foot soldiers catch up with us?"

"Those are the Tory prisoners, six hundred of them," John explained. "We took the flints out of their muskets, and they are carrying the guns for us. The wounded are coming along next."

"I'll be ready to go shortly. I think I can sit a horse."

"The doctor said you can't be moved until you have that ball removed from your back." John turned to Mr. Finley. "Is there a doctor in this community that can perform a skilled surgery?"

"The closest doctor is in Charlotte, and Cornwallis has quartered his whole army in that town."

"Cornwallis will move against us when he learns about Ferguson's defeat. Do you think the doctor could be fetched when the British army moves out?"

"Maybe," answered Mr. Finley. "I can hide your men in the root cellar or down by the spring until the danger passes, and then we'll bring the doctor from Charlotte."

"I'm not staying here," Robert protested. "I have to get home to Kesiah and my boys."

"You'll do what the doctor orders," John said sternly. "Dr. Johnson and Dr. Cozby agree on this course of action as your best chance for recovery."

"I can't stay here," Robert argued. "It's not fair to Mr. Finley and his family to be caught harboring a rebel. It's a hanging offense."

"He's got a point, John," Valentine said. "You are placing a great burden on these good Samaritans."

Captain Jacob Brown stepped up to the open door. "John, General Williams has arrived."

John stood and looked at Mr. Finley. "General Williams is another fellow who shouldn't be moved." He stepped out into the sun and put his hat back on.

"Father, these men have hard decisions to make," Mary said. "We could help them."

"Let me think about this, Mary."

The tandem horse litter carrying General Williams stopped in the shade of a tree across the road from Mr. Finley's yard. Young Daniel Williams was worried about his father and spoke to Colonel Sevier. "He hasn't said a thing all morning."

John put his hand on the young man's shoulder. "He needs to stay still and rest. I'm leaving a small detachment here to care for the most seriously wounded. We are going to get a doctor to come out here from Charlotte."

Dr. Cozby came up with another horse litter carrying William Moore, the Virginian who lost his leg. "John, is this the place you told me about?"

"Yes, but Robert is arguing with me. He's pointed out the perils we would impose on these civilians by using their home as a hospital."

"Private Moore and General Williams can go no farther; that's a medical fact," Dr. Cozby said.

"Doctor?" Daniel Williams called. "He stopped breathing."

Dr. Cozby rushed over to General Williams and checked the vital signs. He shook his head and embraced the lad. "He's gone, Daniel. I'm so sorry, he's gone."

Colonel Sevier removed his hat and came over to express his condolences. "General Williams died a hero of the Revolution, doing all he could to make a difference. *The old Wagoner never yet backed down.* That's how I will remember him."

"Thank you, Colonel Sevier," Daniel answered. John assigned a detachment to escort the general's body to camp, and the honor guard moved out immediately.

"We couldn't do a thing to save him," Dr. Cozby said.

"I know," John said. He turned and met Mr. Finley who had come out from his house.

"Colonel Sevier, you can leave all your men here that are too badly hurt to be moved. My womenfolk and I have talked it over, and we want to do our part to help win the war."

"Are you absolutely sure, knowing the risks involved?"

"Yes sir."

"Very well, Mr. Finley. I'm leaving a small detachment here to care for our wounded and to watch out for enemy activity. I'll pay you well for their expenses, and if you ever want to move to the West for open land and better opportunity, I'll stake you the survey and filing fees."

"Thank you, Colonel Sevier. I may take you up on that."

Colonel Sevier said good-bye to his brother and assigned three men to stay behind with him, James Sevier, Harmon Perryman, and William Robertson. They also left William Moore of Campbell's battalion who had lost his leg.

"Colonel," Joseph Sevier addressed his father. "I feel compelled to stay here with the wounded."

"No, Joseph. You are assigned to Captain Valentine Sevier's company. You will rejoin your unit and continue the march."

Joseph looked at Mary Finley and could see the same disappointment in her face that he felt in his heart. He resolved to follow orders and make a brave show of leaving the beautiful girl who had so recently and completely fascinated him. When he came near to her to speak his farewell, a surprising thing took place that he had not prepared himself to receive. Mary threw herself into his arms in a tight embrace and lingered there.

"Come back for me," she whispered as her warm tears wet his cheek. "Do not forget me."

It was an awkward moment as the stunned audience of battle-tested men watched. Joseph pulled away gently and looked at her face, but she would not look into his eyes. "Good-bye, Miss Finley. I will not forget your kindness." She turned and rushed into the house. Joseph turned to Mr. Finley. "Good-bye, sir. Thank you for everything." A firm handshake followed as the older man evaluated the younger man and approved of what he saw.

Captain Jacob Brown leaned close to Colonel Sevier. "It's that old Sevier charm. Joe's got it!"

"Poor fellow," John replied. "I know how that feels."

By early afternoon the victorious army was gone from the King's Mountain neighborhood. Robert Sevier and his three companions prepared to travel and planned a route to the west of where the main army had marched. "We will go back to the Cowpens and camp there tonight," Robert decided.

"Captain Sevier," Mr. Finley said. "Your doctor and your colonel both ordered you to rest until we can arrange the surgery. They provided me with the money to pay for it."

"Use the money for Private Moore's care," Robert replied. "I have to go home."

"But your condition..."

"My condition will improve each day I get closer to home."

"Captain Sevier, I must insist that you stay here for your own good."

"Mr. Finley, thank you for your hospitality and care, but I release you from any further responsibility or obligation to me. I hope we meet again under better circumstances."

The men shook hands and their eyes met. "God be with you," Mr. Finley said. The four horsemen rode west and left behind a patriot couple, their tearful daughter, and an amputee from over-mountain Virginia to fend for themselves in a war-torn land.

"I'm done for," William Moore said. "They left me here to die, and my dear wife shall weep buckets for the loss of me."

"Mr. Joseph Sevier will come back for me," Mary declared. "Then we will all set out for the mountain country and take you home."

"Mary, you hardly know that boy," her father said gently.

"The gangrene can take a man inside of a month," Moore said. "I heard the doctor say it."

"It was as if I'd known him all my life. He is the love of my soul."

"Mary, Mary, don't go on so. He was but a passing stranger. You'll never see him again."

"And I'll never see my dear wife again. Don't bury me beside the road. Put me out on a hill somewhere."

"I know he loves me, Father, from the kind regard he showed me."

"He made no promises when he left, my dear. Your hopes are without foundation."

"I never told my wife I loved her before I left Virginia. I wish I had said it a hundred times before I went away."

"It's more than a hope, Father. I have a feeling deep in my heart that he will be back."

"Our hope is gone. Without a leg, a man can do little else but die."

"Hush, Mr. Moore," she answered. "You are not going to die in *my* house. We have the herbal poultice that will keep you from getting the gangrene, and I will change your bandage every day. You mark my words: when Mr. Sevier comes for me, we will take you back home, safe and sound. By faith, you can believe every word of what I say!"

In the evening, when Colonel Campbell and his two companies of the burial detail arrived at camp on the Broad River, they received the same dinner of beef, sweet potatoes, and pumpkin slices that the other soldiers had enjoyed. The foot soldiers with the supplies and provisions were a great comfort to their comrades and listened with great interest to their stories of the battle. Colonel Campbell had his dinner with John Sevier.

"We finished the work on the mountain. I left some badly wounded Tories up there in the care of some of the local women, but all our people got away safely."

"Did you have any trouble with Tarleton?"

"Saw no sign of him, but we rushed through the work and made a bad job of it."

"We have another funeral to attend in the morning," John said. "General Williams died on the march. I've ordered full military honors for the ceremony."

"He would have court-martialed you if he had lived, and you make him out to be a hero."

"He *was* a hero. I made a bargain with him to keep his general's commission in his pocket until we defeated Ferguson. As a man of honor he kept his part of the agreement. My part is to give him the honor he deserves."

"He nearly had me talked into giving him the command of the army and attacking Fort Ninety Six. What a costly mistake that would have been."

"Divine Providence has a way of directing events, don't you think?"

"Sometimes that's the only way we can make sense of it," Campbell agreed.

On the afternoon of Monday, October the ninth, three of the South Fork boys of the late Major Chronicle's outfit rested on the front porch of Robert Henry's mother's cabin. Mrs. Henry had just finished redressing her son's wounds when they saw three riders crossing the South Fork. Robert's friends, Hugh Erwin and Andrew Barry, stood up and stepped over to where their loaded rifles leaned against wall.

"No gunplay in front of the young'uns," Mrs. Henry told them, herding her younger children into the cabin. "Speak boldly as the conquerors of Ferguson. Put the fear of God in them damn Tories."

"Yes, ma'am," Robert Henry answered.

The riders entered the yard, but remained mounted. "Howdy, boys. We heard the fellow that lives here got hurt in a little fight the other day."

"See for yourself," Robert answered. "Bayonet went through my hand and into my leg, but it weren't no little fight. We struck a great blow for liberty. Are you fellows patriots, too?"

"Neutralists, peace-loving men," the lead rider grinned. "But we are interested in any news you might have."

"Well, we have seen plenty," Hugh Erwin replied.

"Is it certain that Ferguson is killed and his army defeated and taken prisoner?"

Andrew Barry answered. "It is certain, for we saw Ferguson dead and his army defeated and taken prisoners."

"How many men had Ferguson?"

"Nearly twelve hundred," Hugh said.

"Where did they get men enough to defeat him?"

"They had the South Carolina and Georgia refugees, Colonel Graham's men, some from Virginia, some from the head of the Yadkin, some from the head of the Catawba, some from over the mountains, and some from everywhere else!" Hugh grinned as his friends nodded in agreement.

"Tell us how it happened."

Andrew spoke up. "We met at Gilbert Town and found that foot soldiers couldn't overtake Ferguson, and we took between six and seven hundred horsemen, having as many or more footmen to follow, and we surrounded him and defeated him."

"Ah, come now, that won't do," the Tory declared in disbelief. "You say, between six and seven hundred to surround nearly twelve hundred? It would take more than two thousand to surround and take Ferguson."

"But we did it," Robert insisted. "And we were all of us blue hen's chickens!"

"There must have been of your horse and foot, in all, more than four thousand. We see what you're up to—that is, to catch Lord Cornwallis napping."

The Tories turned their horses abruptly, guided them toward the river crossing, and rode off toward Charlotte, the village where the British commander Cornwallis had set up his headquarters.

Tuesday, the tenth of October, had been like any other day for the British regulars serving in Lord Cornwallis' army until wild rumors began to circulate. A junior officer crossed the yard to the house where Cornwallis had established his headquarters and spoke to the officer of the guard.

"Did you hear the news?"

"No. What news?"

"Ferguson is killed and his whole army defeated and taken prisoners," the officer spoke quietly and seriously.

"How can that be? Where did the men come from to do that?"

"Some of them were from South Carolina and Georgia, some from Virginia, some from the head of the Yadkin and the Catawba, and some from over the mountains. They met at Gilbert Town, about two thousand desperadoes on horseback calling themselves the Blue Hen's Chickens. They overtook Ferguson at a place called King's Mountain, and there they killed Ferguson and defeated his army and took them prisoners."

"Can this be true?"

"True as the gospel, and we had best look out for ourselves."

"God bless us!"

The home Cornwallis had occupied as his headquarters was elegant by American standards and had a parlor as well as a dining room on the main level. That morning Lord Cornwallis was dressed and performing his duties after several days of suffering from one of those recurring American fevers so prevalent in the Carolina lowlands. Lord Rawdon, his second in command, was present, as well as several other officers discussing the reports.

Outside in the yard there was a man crowing like a rooster. Cornwallis angrily rushed to the door and yanked it open.

"Cock-a-doodle-doo! Day is at hand!"

"Guards! Guards!" Cornwallis shouted.

The officer of the guard immediately came to attention. "Yes, my lord?"

"Who is that crowing like a rooster?"

"One of the rebel prisoners, my lord; he's a harmless simpleton by the name of David Knox."

"Get him away from here!" Cornwallis ordered. "Turn him out immediately!"

"Release him, my lord?"

"Yes, just get him away from this house." Cornwallis slammed the door and returned to his officers. "That harmless simpleton is no doubt a clever spy, listening at the doors and windows. First we have a patrol reporting rumors of a four-thousand-man rebel army calling themselves the Blue Hen's Chickens. Then they claim these rebels destroyed Ferguson's army. Now the village idiot stands outside my headquarters crowing like a rooster. This reeks of conspiracy!"

"Such rumors are heard daily and never a grain of truth to them," Lord Rawdon said calmly.

An orderly entered the dining room to announce that lunch was ready. "Lunch is served, my lord."

"What is it today?"

"Baked chicken, my lord," the man answered.

"Chicken!? Take it away! I've no stomach for chicken. You see, Rawdon, the conspiracy widens, even to my kitchen. This town is crawling with rebel spies, and nowhere can I find reliable intelligence!"

"My Lord, I've sent men after the deacon," Rawdon answered. "He's considered a reliable source of information about rebel troop movements. We shall know the truth of these rumors presently."

"I fear the worst for Major Ferguson," Cornwallis continued. "I've had no communication from him in nearly a week. My couriers seem to have vanished from the face of the earth. I am thinking of sending Tarleton's dragoons out west to find out what's happening."

"Tarleton reports suffering from the same fever that has afflicted you, my lord."

"If that is the case, I understand his inactivity. I should return to bed with this intolerable malaise." Cornwallis collapsed in a stuffed chair to rest.

"The deacon is coming across the yard now," Rawdon announced. He opened the door to an older, respectable-looking gentleman in plain clothing.

"My lord, this is the man I was telling you about," Rawdon said as the man entered.

"Good day, my lord," the man bowed respectfully.

"Do you know why my soldiers have summoned you here?"

"There is much talk in the town about the defeat of Major Ferguson. I suppose you would like an account of that."

"What do you know?"

"I frequently trade with people from the countryside where, despite greater distances, news travels more freely."

"Get to it man," Cornwallis said impatiently. "What do you know of Major Ferguson?"

"Defeated, my lord, in a great and costly battle," the deacon answered.

"Who defeated Ferguson?"

"The men from over the mountains, commanded by Campbell, Shelby, and Sevier," the deacon reported. "They also had men from the Carolinas commanded by McDowell, Cleveland, and Williams."

"What are their numbers, and where are they now?"

"My lord, I understand they are three thousand strong, and they are bearing down upon you. The townspeople are in a great state of consternation."

"What happened to Ferguson himself?"

"Killed and buried on the field at a place called King's Mountain. His entire force was surrounded, and none escaped being either killed or captured."

"What else can you tell me about the men who did this?"

"All three thousand men are mounted on over-mountain horses, bred for speed and endurance. Each one is an expert marksman with the hunting rifle. Major Ferguson threatened their homes and families, and they answered with ferocity."

"I'm sure Major Ferguson's men gave a good account of themselves and considerably weakened the attacking force."

"On the contrary, my lord, American losses were very light because they fired from behind trees and fought like Indians. They are still a very powerful, fast moving, and dangerous force."

"And who leads them?"

"Campbell, Shelby, Sevier, Cleveland, and Williams," the deacon answered.

A moment passed as Cornwallis thoughtfully absorbed the report. "That will be all." He dismissed the man with a wave of his hand. As the deacon left the house and crossed the yard, a smile of satisfaction and pride crossed his face. He thought of his brave sons somewhere off to the west actively fighting for home, country, and liberty.

"Who are those rebel leaders he named?" Cornwallis demanded.

Lord Rawdon knew something of the provincial leadership of North and South Carolina. "Campbell and Cleveland are Whig militia colonels with a nasty propensity to hang their captives. Williams is a South Carolina partisan, with no considerable following. I've never heard of the others."

"Militia colonels," Cornwallis repeated with disgust and disbelief. "Obscure men I've never heard of, commanding an army of three thousand strong? What madness! We can't accept these reports as true. The last dispatch from Ferguson said he had swept the country clear of rebels, all the way to the mountain passes."

"But what dangers lay beyond those mountains?" Rawdon asked. "Perhaps Major Ferguson's fondness for bullying the western people has come home to roost."

Cornwallis turned angrily to Rawdon. "Did you say roost?"

"Forgive me, my lord, it was an unfortunate choice of words."

Cornwallis summoned his communications officer. "Take down this order to Colonel Tarleton."

The scribe sat at his desk and picked up his quill. "I'm ready, sir."

Cornwallis rose and paced slowly as he dictated. "Dear Sir: Upon receipt of this order, immediately march to the Catawba with your light infantry, and the British Legion, along with your artillery. I have no certain intelligence on the whereabouts of Major Ferguson. You are to reinforce him wherever you can find him and bring his corps to the Catawba. If you encounter any rebel forces, take action, at all costs, to prevent their advance into South Carolina. End it there, and I'll sign it."

"Shouldn't we tell Tarleton what we have learned?" Lord Rawdon asked.

Cornwallis was annoyed with the question. "What have we learned? We've heard nothing but unconfirmed rumors." He turned back to the scribe. "Write what I said and post a rider to Tarleton's camp immediately!"

"Yes, my lord," the communications officer said, and finished writing.

"So what do we do now?" Rawdon asked.

"Discretion would dictate a removal from Charlotte for the present," Cornwallis answered. "If the rumored force is as strong and well mounted as they say, they could strike us suddenly from any direction, at any time. If we were back at Camden, we could cover any threat to Fort Ninety Six or to Charleston itself. Gentlemen, prepare the army to move. Until we are ready to march, double the patrols in the countryside, looking for any unusual traffic from the north or the west."

"Yes, my lord," the officers obeyed. They filed out of the house to prepare their men for action.

Cornwallis sank back in his chair. "Oh, Rawdon, the whole business almost breaks my heart to think Ferguson may be killed. I received his letter of promotion to the rank of lieutenant colonel in the last dispatches from London. He worked so hard to earn it, too."

"Your brilliant plan to invade North Carolina and Virginia will have to be postponed. General Leslie will be surprised when he lands in Virginia and we are not there to meet him."

"I can't believe it was militia colonels. That's impossible! It would take a military genius to contrive a victory such as we have heard described. Who could have done this?"

Chapter 30

Justice and Mercy

On Wednesday, the eleventh of October, the patriot army moved again with an early start. Lieutenant Colonel Sevier was assigned to the rear guard, so his men busied themselves breaking camp and erasing all vestiges of recent occupation. The prisoners on foot soon crowded the river road, still carrying the captured muskets and other captured gear. John Sevier, reunited with his father Major Valentine Sevier and the rest of the army, felt more urgently than ever the need for a speedy escape from the overwhelming forces of the empire. Major Val's fatherly concern and questions about Captain Robert Sevier's condition caused John to rethink the decision to leave his brother and one of his sons behind at the Finley home. When John's men were finally in motion, Sam Sherrill came along beside him.

"What's on your mind today, John?" Sam Sherrill asked.

"I'm wondering what in the world could be delaying Colonel Tarleton from overtaking us."

"I'm sure you have a strategy all planned out if that were to happen."

"Yes, but it's not a good one. The rear guard will hide behind trees giving a spirited defense while Colonel Campbell, Colonel Cleveland, and the others order the execution of the prisoners."

"That wasn't your idea, I'm sure."

"No, but I couldn't persuade them to consider any other options. I tell you, Sam, I'm weary of this army business. They finally listened to my ideas on battle strategy and profited greatly, but today I am once again only a lieutenant colonel from Washington County they jokingly call Old Lover Boy."

"I'm sorry about that, John. I had no idea a little camp fun would cause you such grief."

"The real grief is the emptiness of not waking up beside my beautiful Bonny Kate, and hearing the joyful expressions of my dear little children. Those are the simple pleasures of home which are being pushed to the back of my mind by more pressing matters. It's a good thing we haven't had much to eat, or time for rest these past six days, or my worries would have prevented a proper enjoyment of such comforts."

Sam laughed. "That's one way of looking at it."

"I hated to leave Robert and James to find their own way home, but it may be safer for them. Tarleton will most certainly follow the tracks of the main army. The challenge for Robert is to find a doctor to get that musket ball removed. Then the boys can head more directly west to avoid pursuit and capture."

"We made only three miles on Monday, but covered twenty yesterday," Sam calculated. "That should bring us back to Gilbert Town by tonight."

"Too slow to suit me; Tarleton's dragoons could easily catch us. We have to make better time."

Captain Valentine Sevier rode up accompanied by newly promoted Captain George Russell, who saluted smartly. "You wanted to see me, Colonel?"

"Yes, Captain Russell. I want you to take your company, draw rations for a five-day patrol, and leave immediately."

"Yes, sir, and where do you want me to patrol?"

"Cross the Broad River and proceed to the southwest until you pass unobserved by Colonel Campbell's forward scouts. Then turn due north to Colonel Wofford's Fort on the Catawba. From there proceed to Watauga Fort and report to Major Charles Robertson and reinforce him for defense against the Chickamaugas if necessary."

"We're going home?"

"No, that's not what I am ordering at all," John said. "I'm calling this a patrol, a very long patrol, because I have the authority to send men out on patrol. I do not have the authority to send anybody home. Do you understand the secret nature of this patrol?"

The officers riding together grinned at Colonel Sevier's reasoning. "That's why you want us to proceed unobserved," Captain Russell replied.

"That's right, George." John drew from his haversack a bundle of letters. "Here are my dispatches to Major Robertson, Colonel Carter, and to my dear Bonny Kate." John paused and looked at the pouch of letters in his hand. "You can see how important this mission is to me, can't you George?"

"Yes, Colonel. I will not fail you, sir."

John grinned and handed over the letters. "I have one more thing I want you to do for me, George. Take Joseph Greer with you and escort him safely as far as Watauga. One of those letters is for him to take to the Congress in Philadelphia. I want them to hear the story straight from a tall Watauga lad who lived through the campaign and actually did the work of defeating Ferguson. Every governor and continental general between here and Philadelphia City will try to claim credit for our victory. The Congress deserves to hear the unvarnished truth, and Joseph Greer will tell it straight."

"I'll make sure he gets through."

"Thank you, Captain Russell. God speed you."

The young captain saluted and turned his horse to the accomplishment of his mission.

"Gentlemen, we won't discuss this with the other colonels until Captain Russell's patrol is well beyond the possibility of a countermanding order. Colonel Campbell has much on his mind these days, and I don't want to trouble him with the concerns of Washington County safety. Thirty good fighting men with news of our victory will lift the spirits of our courageous home guard and give comfort to our beloved women."

"I wish I could have been the one to bear the glad tidings," Captain Valentine Sevier said.

"We all are ready to go home, Captain Sevier," John said. "But I'm told the governor has the power to cancel the terms of our enlistments and keep us in service for the duration of the war. That was always the intention of Colonel Charles McDowell, and I am certain he has accomplished his designs by now."

"Serve under McDowell again? Not me, Johnny. Isaac Shelby won't serve under him either."

John looked at his brother and grinned. "Isaac is planning to persuade General Daniel Morgan back into the service. I would be content to serve with that good Virginian if I am forced to stay in the state service."

The men contemplated the sadness of never seeing home again as long as the king of Great Britain persisted in the madness of pursuing a war to take away American liberties.

Samuel Sherrill broke the silence. "I saw among the prisoners Chambers and Crawford, those fellows who betrayed us to Ferguson. They were disgusted by the way Ferguson treated them."

"Traitors are never welcome in any camp," John said. "They should have known better."

"I overheard Cleveland and Campbell talking about hanging the most notorious Tories. I reckon Chambers and Crawford will get the rope."

"I won't allow it," John declared. "I'll take them into custody and give them a fair trial in Washington County."

"Fine then, hang them in Washington County," Valentine Sevier said.

"Gentlemen, I am certainly not a petty-fogging lawyer, but I think I could argue the case that those boys helped our cause as much as anyone. Their information forced Ferguson to make mistakes that allowed us to catch him at a time and place that gave us all the advantages. No one should hang for that."

"We will see how well you can argue that at the hanging," Val replied.

At midday Captain William Lenoir and his Wilkes County foot soldiers rested beside the road as Major Joseph Winston's men rode by. Winston stopped and dismounted when he saw Lenoir and shook hands with his fellow officer.

"Good afternoon, Will. How are your wounds today?"

"I'm healing nicely, Joe. Sevier's Dr. Cozby has been kind enough to give me special attention."

"He's more of a horse doctor, I hear."

"And I'm more of a horse soldier, so I have no complaints."

"Have you seen that officer on the white horse, who guided us to the battle?"

"No, and I've been looking for him. I watched the burial details and helped with the wounded. I'd know that white horse if I saw it again."

"I haven't seen him either," Winston said. "There's only one explanation, Will. I think he was a spirit or something."

"Maybe it was Gideon!"

"I can't figure out the reasons why some died and not others. Take poor Major Chronicle. Everybody liked him. He was an honest fellow who spoke up boldly in the council of officers, helped plan the attack, took the place of Colonel Graham at the last minute, and paid with his life."

"He was the pure warrior." William Lenoir removed his hat in respect. "Joe, I'm taking my prayers more seriously from here on. I've seen the sword of the Lord and Gideon. I'm a changed man."

"Amen to that, brother, Amen! Take care of yourself, Captain Lenoir."

"You do the same, Joe."

Major Winston, the father of the triplets who thought a lot about his family, his farm, and his technique for tobacco production, climbed back into the saddle, saluted his fellow officer, and rode on.

Friday night, the thirteenth of October, the army was camped at Bickerstaff's Plantation. Mrs. Martha Bickerstaff had gone into mourning for the loss of her husband, Aaron, mortally wounded at King's Mountain. He fought bravely for Major Ferguson, and although Dr. Johnson had tended him closely throughout the night after the battle, he breathed his last Sunday morning and was buried with the others on the battlefield. Captain DePeyster and Dr. Johnson told Mrs. Bickerstaff the sad news about her husband, and she wept bitterly as the enemy host made camp on her lands. The Carolina colonels arranged a trial according to the laws of North Carolina, and Colonel Cleveland convened a rough court to hear cases against some thirty-three of the Tory prisoners.

"Come, Shelby, you'll want a part in this," Cleveland spoke loudly. "Some of the worst of these men are westerners from your over-mountain country. Will you sit on the board of inquiry?"

"No, thank you," Isaac replied.

"Well, where's Sevier?"

"He's the commander of the rear guard covering our trail and confusing Tarleton's trackers."

"I expected that of Gentleman Johnny to make himself scarce. Handy enough for women's business but not hard enough for man's business."

"Have another tankard of rum, Colonel Cleveland. You're not drunk enough to say that to his face."

"The law says I need two or three North Carolina officers on the bench to hear these cases. Campbell is from Virginia, so he can't serve."

"You have Colonel Hampton and plenty of majors to choose from."

"I'm going ahead then. The docket is full, and we need to get the business done while the witnesses to Tory atrocities are still in camp to give testimony."

Isaac Shelby took his concerns to Colonel Campbell, who was writing letters in his tent.

"I wash my hands of it, Isaac," Campbell said. "I have repeatedly issued orders concerning better treatment of the prisoners, but the atrocities I have heard described by some of the citizens and the petitions for justice that have been submitted seem to weigh heavily against some of those Tory officers."

"I don't care for the way Cleveland is dispensing justice from the rum keg."

"It's the business of North Carolina, Isaac. You and your fellow colonels have the jurisdiction to try these cases. My only involvement is to help carry out the executions. Where is Sevier?"

"Completing the work of the rear guard and placing the pickets for the night."

"I have to watch him now, like a hawk, so he doesn't desert. Did you know he sent one of his companies home without my permission?"

"I heard it was more like a long patrol."

"Desertion is what I call it, and Sevier will have to answer for it in court martial."

"You wouldn't bring charges against Old Lover Boy for sending a company on a long patrol, would you? That would really hurt morale in the army and ruin all our plans for consolidating the army under General Morgan and chasing Cornwallis back to Charleston."

"Well no, I wouldn't want to risk losing Sevier for that campaign, but he should tell me before he does anything like that again."

"I'm sure he will be more careful in the future. I'll talk to him about it and gain his assurances."

Isaac Shelby left the commander's tent to observe the court proceedings and all the while hoped for Colonel Sevier's eminent arrival in camp. The trials of the Tories proceeded long into the night by the light of torches. The charges leveled against the defendants were indeed serious. Before the tribunal many witnesses gave proof that heinous crimes had been committed in the name of the king against patriot women, children, and the elderly throughout Georgia, and the Carolinas. Thirty-three Tories were convicted and sentenced to hang. The tribunal moved to execute the convicts without delay. All men in camp were ordered to watch the hangings, and three Tories at a time were led to the gallows tree. Three groups were executed in this way and nine men dangled from the limbs of the oak in the flickering torch lights. The executioners prepared the next three convicts.

Suddenly there was movement through the ranks as a man with a white plume on his hat strode through the crowds and presented himself and his companion, Isaac Shelby, before the presiding officers. He pointed to one of the prisoners named James Crawford. "This man belongs to my regiment. I want him placed in my custody for the return to Washington County."

Colonel Cleveland rose from the bench and answered. "Now see here, Sevier. He is a convicted traitor, and he will hang with the others."

"No, I want him returned to Washington County to stand trial in a properly constituted court, before a real judge who understands the law and follows its due course."

"Where were you during his trial? You should have spoken up for him then."

"I was attending to the safety of the army so our men can sleep safely and soundly tonight, and I find to my amazement that you have prevented my men from receiving their well-deserved rest."

"This is a legal proceeding and that man has been convicted of treason. He is going to hang for his crime."

"Not tonight, Colonel Cleveland. I want that man released to my custody immediately, and I want the boy Chambers, as well."

"You can take Chambers, but Crawford will swing."

"No, sir; I'll stand here in your way all night if I have to, but I'm taking that man home."

"He warned Ferguson we were coming," Colonel Hampton said.

"I do not deny he gave Ferguson the information, but his warning caused Ferguson to make mistakes and hastily choose a place that gave us all the advantages. Mr. Crawford's communication to Major Ferguson did us more good than harm. Why should we now punish such a benefactor?"

"Take him for now, and we will deal with you later, Lieutenant Colonel Sevier," Cleveland said. "We have to get on with our work."

Sevier removed the noose from the neck of Crawford and pulled him out of the line of convicted prisoners. Sherriff Valentine Sevier came forward and escorted the prisoner away.

"John, we have to stop the whole thing now," Isaac said in a low voice.

"I know, Isaac. Any ideas?"

"Your boldness seems to be working. Let's try that again."

"Stay with me, then."

A Tory named Isaac Baldwin was among the next group to be hanged. Suddenly his young brother ran up crying piteously and embraced the man. The demonstration of grief touched many a patriot heart of the soldiers who stood in ranks four deep around the scene of justice. No one saw the young Baldwin lad produce the knife with which he sawed the ropes binding his brother's hands. The soldiers were startled when the prisoner removed the noose from his own neck and ran from the scene followed by the little brother, but no one raised a hand to stop them.

Colonel Cleveland shouted a curse and ordered the recapture of Baldwin, but at the same moment Sevier and Shelby captured the attention of all as they strode into the torch lit circle.

"We are sick of this business," Sevier said. "We have agreed upon it, and it must be stopped."

"Yes, stop this business at once," Isaac agreed. "We are sick of it."

The soldiers of the West were in agreement with their commanders, but the eastern North Carolina men were resolved to continue.

Colonel William Campbell entered the arena and approached Colonel Cleveland.

"Why didn't you hang all these damned rascals at once?" Colonel Campbell said angrily.

Sevier laughed and replied, "Why Colonel, if we had all been as much in earnest in the action, I think we should have killed more and had fewer of them to hang."

"Speak plain, man. You're on dangerous ground already."

John took Colonel Campbell aside and spoke quietly to him where only Isaac Shelby and a few officers could hear his arguments.

"The events of man need a strong hand to prevent the tendency toward chaos. We lost control at the conclusion of the battle, and I don't think we need to rehearse those same mistakes here."

"This is a properly constituted court of justice under the laws of North Carolina," Campbell said.

"Look at your judges, Colonel Campbell. They are in no condition to pass judgment, and the executions have taken place in the heat of the moment. That is not a proper context for the rule of law. I think we ought to incline ourselves toward mercy."

"Mercy!" Campbell shouted to the mob. "Colonel Sevier would have this assembly grant mercy to all these condemned Tories! What say you to that?"

"I agree with him," Isaac Shelby said.

Before the mob could respond, John Sevier stepped into the circle of light and spoke dramatically.

> "The quality of mercy is not strained;
> It droppeth as the gentle rain from heaven
> Upon the place beneath: it is twice blest;
> It blesseth him that gives and him that takes:
> 'Tis mightiest in the mightiest: it becomes
> The throned monarch better than his crown;
> His scepter shows the force of temporal power,
> The attribute to awe and majesty,
> Wherein doth sit the dread and fear of kings;
> But mercy is above this sceptered sway;
> It is enthroned in the hearts of kings,
> It is an attribute to God himself;
> And earthly power doth then show likest God's
> When mercy seasons justice. Therefore brethren,
> Though justice be thy plea, consider this,
> That, in the course of justice, none of us
> Should see salvation: we do pray for mercy;
> And that same prayer doth teach us all to render
> The deeds of mercy."

John Miller, the burley blacksmith, turned to Sam Sherrill and remarked, "Rare is the backwater man who knows his Shakespeare."

Cleveland in his imposing bulk swaggered toward the elegant, expressive Sevier, and the men around them feared an altercation. "Well, my erudite friend, we both have the mettle for making fine speeches! I think you mean to defend these wretches and prevent our just retribution upon their heads for the crimes they committed. Is that what you mean, sir?"

"Colonel Cleveland, my men are hungry and tired, and you have required them to stand here in ranks and watch your show of violent retribution, a practice that we found abhorrent in General Cornwallis. Many of these you now convict were just following the cruel orders of their British overlords. I am dismissing my men for some much needed rest. Goodnight, Colonel Cleveland." John turned to Captain Valentine Sevier. "Val, please dismiss the men."

"You can't do that, Lieutenant Colonel Sevier," Cleveland ordered.

"My men are dismissed also," Isaac Shelby said.

"Colonel Campbell, make them stay."

"This is a North Carolina matter, Colonel Cleveland. It seems your western counties are in revolt. I'm dismissing my men too. The rest of the hangings will be postponed until we can proceed in a more orderly fashion." Colonel Campbell turned and walked away.

"Damn, what's this world coming to?" Cleveland muttered to himself.

"What do we do with the rest of the convicts?" Colonel Brandon asked.

"Put them back with the other prisoners," Cleveland answered. "They have been granted a reprieve."

Saturday the fourteenth began slowly as the exhausted men slept beyond a cloud-obscured sunrise. Sevier's scouts were out early patrolling the hills south of camp, always watchful of the British counterattack. Sevier's officers met for a later than usual breakfast as Sam Sherrill and his sons cooked eggs and bacon they had procured from the farms of friendly families.

John received his breakfast with due thanks and asked his father-in-law about the trail ahead. "How far are we from Quaker Meadows, Sam?"

"More than thirty miles, John; it's farther than we can march in one day. I don't like the look of these clouds rolling in. A good October rain will flood the Catawba and keep us from crossing. I've seen days on the river where you couldn't even swim a horse across."

"Not even a Sherrill horse?"

Captain Val Sevier laughed. "John, to hear Mr. Sherrill talk, they usually just walk their horses over the top of the waters."

All the men laughed as Sam shook his head. "I just wish we were on the other side before the rain comes. We'd even be safe from Tarleton's horsemen."

"Sam, I appreciate your knowledge of the landscape, and your advice has been a treasure to me," John said.

"And you even took him to the battle, but you didn't take me," Major Reives groused. "You left me with the foot soldiers while the horse soldiers got all the glory."

"Papa, don't wear me out with that old song again. You weren't even supposed to be here."

"But I was a big help, wasn't I?"

"Yes, sir. I couldn't have run this camp without your experience and skill."

"And I helped you with General Pain-in-the-Ass, didn't I?"

"Don't talk about that, Papa; it was a secret deal between me and General Williams. He was an honorable man and died a hero of the revolution."

"Then what about the real heroes, who answered the call from you and the other officers and marched on foot all over this country, to carry the water, cook your meals, carry your baggage, guard your prisoners, and clean up your messes? There are two armies out here, Johnny; the men who rode to glory and the boys who had to walk.

You better consider the real heroes who get to go home with nothing much to tell."

John stood up and faced his father. "I consider all the men heroes who had anything to do with this King's Mountain campaign. But the opportunity for glory has not passed, and nobody gets to go home."

"What do you mean?"

"They mean to keep us in the field, Papa," John spoke quietly for only the officers to hear. "Any colonel, with a lick of talent and some recent good luck, is in this war for the duration. I haven't told the men yet, and I expect all of you the keep that under your hats."

"Bonny Kate will have something to say about that," the major said.

"I imagine she will." John sighed and sat down again.

"We have an Indian war starting up back home."

"The British invasion of North Carolina and the protection of the interests of wealthy eastern men are more important to the governor right now than a couple of hundred families on the western frontier."

"We don't need their permission. We can just pack up and go home."

"No, Papa, we can't. I sent Captain Russell home, and Colonel Campbell called it desertion. He said if I do that again I'll be court martialed."

"That's not fair."

"No, Papa, it's not, but now you know what I struggle with in my position as lieutenant colonel. I've got to patch things up with Colonel Cleveland and get this army moving again before the Catawba floods."

Captain Landon Carter arrived before his leader. "Colonel Sevier, that Tory DePeyster wants to talk to you. He says it's important."

John looked up and recognized the enemy commander accompanied by one of the convicted Tories who had been saved the night before. "Gentlemen, please sit with me. Can we share a breakfast?"

"No, thank you," they answered.

"What can I do for you?"

"Colonel Sevier, you seem like a decent sort of fellow who champions the cause of justice and dispenses it with mercy. We appreciate what you did last night."

"Thank you, Captain DePeyster."

"We want to warn you about some information we received this morning. Tarleton is on his way to defeat you and rescue all the prisoners."

"How do you know this?"

"The women you allowed into camp to care for the wounded have passed messages to some of the loyalist officers."

"Why are you telling me this? Don't you desire to be rescued by Colonel Tarleton?"

"I am not a traitor to my king, but a sensible man interested in saving lives. I know your Colonel Campbell has ordered that if we are attacked, the guards will shoot down all the prisoners. Then when Tarleton charges into the ranks, he will cut down everyone regardless of allegiance. Most of my men are dressed like yours, and forced to carry the captured muskets. We will appear to Tarleton's dragoons like enemy soldiers and be killed indiscriminately. That is not the outcome I desire."

"What do you recommend, Captain DePeyster?"

"Have Colonel Campbell rescind the order to shoot the prisoners and resume your march to safety as quickly as possible."

"Would you mind repeating this to Colonel Isaac Shelby? He holds a higher rank than I do and has preserved more of his political capital. I'm on the outs with Colonel Cleveland, and Colonel Campbell has expressed his displeasure at some of my recent decisions."

"I don't mind talking to Shelby, but you are universally admired by your men and by many of my men. Under different circumstances we might have become friends."

"Abraham, isn't it?"

"Yes, my friends call me Abe."

"I have a brother named Abraham, serving in my brother Val's company. Well Abe, let's go see Colonel Shelby and see if we can't get this army moving again. Preserving life is my top priority, too."

Chapter 31

Letters from Home

The march of October fifteenth began early in the morning in a light misting rain that became heavier as the day progressed. Many of the wounded, both Whig and Tory, had been left in the care of local families in the neighborhood of Bickerstaff's Plantation, allowing the army to move faster. Thirty-two miles were covered that day. At ten o'clock that night, the foot soldiers waded across the Catawba River Island Ford in chest deep water. Camp was pitched in the open meadows surrounding the McDowell home. Major Joseph McDowell encouraged fires to be built of his fence rails to dry out clothing and drive away the chill of the autumn night. Beeves were provided for a late night meal. Joseph McDowell also prevailed upon his mother's hospitality to take in some of the same Tory officers who had occupied her home in the summer. Her kindness toward the captives was remarkable considering the rude way they had treated her.

The Washington County men settled in quickly, and Sevier's staff of officers ate together in a festive mood despite the exhausting march that day. Captain Jacob Brown entertained with stories of old Carolina and the history of the local area.

"I knew Joseph McDowell Sr., who built this fine plantation, and I knew his brother John, too. In fact it was at John McDowell's plantation, Pleasant Garden, where I met the greatest chiefs of the Cherokee Nation and bought the entire Nolichucky Valley all the way down to the French Broad," Jacob Brown said. His son, Jacob Brown Jr., listened intently to his father. Junior had joined the campaign in the service of Colonel James Williams and been reunited with his father the night of the Cowpens dinner stop. He transferred to his father's company the day of the battle.

"How was the McDowell family involved in that?" Junior asked.

"Hunting John McDowell and I were equal partners with right of survivorship. Too bad the old boy kicked the bucket. The business has turned out very well indeed."

Major Valentine Sevier, another old boy, cleared his throat. "The McDowell heirs don't quite see it that way, Jake. They hold out for repayment of a considerable sum of borrowed money."

"Keep that quiet, will you, Val? The lawyers are going to work that out. I kept copies of everything in writing, and Judge Henderson tells me I have a good case for surviving partner takes all."

"Judge Henderson's own Transylvania land purchase may not hold up in court either," the elder Sevier said. "The State of North Carolina still has to decide whether all those land deals with the Cherokees were legal."

"Possession is nine-tenths of the law," Jacob said. "Persuading the chiefs was the hard part, and I did that all by myself."

John Sevier joined the group. "Tell them the story, Jacob. It's a good one."

Jacob Brown drew a deep breath and began his tale. "I came out with Boone in '69, but rather than playing that game of hide-and-seek with the Shawnee hunting parties of the north, I struck out on my own in a southwestern direction to find a group of Cherokees that an old Indian trader named Brian Ward told me about. Ward had lived among these Cherokees and married a princess named Nancy. I found those Indian towns all right just like Ward had described, and the land was beautiful, with tall trees, streams of clear tumbling waters, and rich game. I hunted with the leading chiefs and their sons; Attakullakulla, Oconostota, Dragging Canoe, John Watts, Abram of Chilhowie, just to name a few. I learned their ways, their lingo, and their beliefs about the spirit world. One morning Oconostota came to me and told me he dreamed that I had given him my hunting dog, my rifle, and my horse. Now Indians place a great store by the content of their dreams. And if a chief or a medicine man dreams it and tells you about it, you are honor-bound by the Great Spirit to comply with the outcome of the dream. Even though the old boy was running a game on me, and I knew it, I cheerfully went along with it and gave him all I had. I learned to use the bow and arrow that day on the hunt, but I was determined to get my trusty rifle back along with the rest of my property. That night I chanted some psalms that I knew and cooked a meal with some of their ritual herbs and made a show of praying to the Great Spirit before I went to bed. I think that kind of impressed old Oconostota, and Attakullakulla too. The next morning I told my dream, with the same seriousness and formal language the chief had used. I said I dreamed that good Chief Oconostota had given me back my dog, my rifle, and my horse; and in addition he had agreed to sell the Nolichucky Valley to me for a great wealth of trade goods. The chief looked at me a moment, and said, *It will be as the dream spirit has said, but between you and me, Brown, no more dream telling.*"

The men at the campfire laughed at Captain Brown's story. Major Tipton momentarily forgot that young boys were present and said, "Now tell us about Nan Henderson."

Captain Brown stood up and faced the major. "There's nothing to tell. She was a Cherokee princess who interpreted for me and taught me the language, that's all. Whatever else you're thinking is malicious gossip!"

"Gentlemen, please," Colonel Sevier interrupted. "It's been a long day and a happy night. Let's all have sweet dreams."

"We all know what the colonel dreams about, don't we?" Major Tipton grinned as the other men laughed.

Sevier looked at his friend, neighbor, and father-in-law, Sam Sherrill, and said, "Sam, have you been telling stories on me again?"

Sam grinned and shook his head. "No need for me to say anything, Colonel. You talk in your sleep."

"No, I don't!" The men had another good laugh at the colonel's expense.

A tired traveler led his Sherrill horse into camp and stopped at the cheerful campfire where there was heard the most laughter. He scanned the group of officers and saluted the colonel. "Good evening, Colonel Sevier."

"Why it's Johnny Sherrill!"

"Yes, sir. I rode hard today to find you. I have letters from Washington County and letters from Governor Nash, and Colonel McDowell at Hillsborough."

"Quick man, do you have a letter from Bonny Kate?" John asked.

"Yes, sir, I sure do."

"I'll start with that one. Come to my tent and I'll hear your report while I sort through those dispatches."

Sam hugged his son Johnny and declared to the happy group, "Colonel Sevier got a letter, boys. He will have sweet dreams tonight!"

The men slept serenely, confident that the raging Catawba River rushing past their camp would prevent a surprise attack by the demon Tarleton. The sky cleared and the twinkling stars shone on a night where every soldier was thankful for his blanket.

Colonel Sevier was up early for breakfast at Mrs. McDowell's dining room, conferring with Colonels William Campbell, Isaac Shelby, Benjamin Cleveland, Andrew Hampton, Thomas Brandon, Edward Lacey, William Hill, and all the majors who attended them.

"Gentlemen, this is the end of the expedition," Colonel Campbell announced. "We received word last night that Cornwallis has withdrawn from Charlotte and quitted North Carolina in great haste, abandoning his supply wagons and releasing all civilian prisoners taken in the invasion. He took that saber-swinging Tarleton with him."

The officers received the news with much good cheer, laughing and congratulating each other. They looked at all the official communication in the dispatches from Hillsborough that Johnny Sherrill had delivered in the night and began to realize the magnitude of their accomplishments.

"All we lack is an official report, which I will write with the help of Colonel Shelby and Colonel Cleveland. Colonel Sumter is now General Sumter and is resupplied to take the field once again. Colonel Hill, Colonel Lacey, and Colonel Brandon will join his command for operations back into South Carolina."

Colonel Lacey stood and addressed the group. "I speak for all the men of South Carolina when I say what a privilege it has been to serve with you. Rarely have I seen such dedicated officers, working together as brothers from various counties of three different states. You gentlemen from the West volunteered to help us in our greatest hour of need. You became witnesses to the ugliness of South Carolina politics; the jealousy and discord between certain officers of different regions of our state. Colonel Sevier handled a very difficult situation on the evening of October sixth that may very well have saved us from ruin. I shall ever be grateful for Colonel Sevier's strategy, wisdom, and skill. As you know the fair state of South Carolina still cries out in great distress. If it should ever please your home counties to send you back into service in our state, please call upon my service, and I shall again embrace you as brothers-in-arms."

"Thank you, Colonel Lacey," Colonel Campbell answered. "Now we have a letter from Governor Nash ordering Colonel Sevier's entire force back to Fort Patrick Henry, where he will join my cousin Colonel Arthur Campbell and Colonel Joseph Martin in a campaign to settle their differences with the Cherokee Nation. I hate to lose you, Colonel Sevier."

"I hate it too," Colonel Cleveland said as he rose from his chair. "I don't know when I've had so much good-natured fun. Jack, you are a delight and a pleasure when it comes to the practical joke, the amusing story, and your evening folics around the campfires. Whenever we wanted amusements we had only to listen for the liveliest portions of the camp and there we would find Sevier, in all his entertaining glory. I tell you lads, we ought to write a letter of protest to the governor about sending away the life of the party."

"Apparently the governor received some very strongly worded letters, indicating the need for Colonel Sevier's presence on the western frontier," Colonel Campbell reported. "Colonel John Carter wrote the governor about the Indian activity; Major Charles Robertson wrote of the burden on the community of some Georgia refugees; but what really moved the governor was a letter from Mrs. Sevier concerning her needs."

The room of officers erupted in laughter as Lover Boy John laughed along with the rest of them. When Colonel Campbell resumed control of the meeting, he closed by thanking all the officers and Major Joseph Winston offered a prayer of thanksgiving.

"Gentlemen, please leave camp by midafternoon, because Mrs. McDowell has already informed me that she's not providing any more food!" The men cheerfully began preparations to move on that very day.

John walked back to camp with Major Tipton. "Some surprise, eh Jack?"

"Yes, Jonathan. Let's clear out before they change their minds. I was afraid we could be stuck in this service until the end of the war."

"Do you think your wife really wrote such a letter to the governor?"

"It sounds like something she might do," John said. "We are lucky to be going home. They are keeping Isaac and the Sullivan County men in service."

"Hey, wait up, Jack!" The two officers recognized Colonel Campbell coming after them.

"Could he have changed his mind that quick?" Jonathan asked.

John waited for the Virginian to catch up. "Hey Jack, could you do me a favor? Could you take my foot soldiers with you?"

"I suppose I could, but don't you need them?"

"Mounted men are what we need for this kind of warfare. You have proved the value of mounted riflemen. We didn't even use our foot soldiers at King's Mountain."

"I'll see them home, Bill."

"Well Jack, I guess this is good-bye. I came on this little fox hunt because it was your idea, and you put me in charge of it. They are already celebrating my exalted name up in Richmond as though I am the hero of it."

"Enjoy the fame, my friend; you earned it. When you report to General Morgan, give him my regards."

"Thanks for everything, and good luck at the Indian War."

The two men shook hands warmly with mutual admiration and friendship, unaware that they would never meet again in the present life.

Isaac Shelby caught up with John at his camp. "John, will you take my wounded and sick boys home to Sullivan County?"

"Sure, Isaac; and if you have letters to the widows and mothers of the killed, I'll deliver those, too. I was kind of counting on you to help me take on the Cherokees."

"I don't have a wife to write persuasive letters to the governor."

"You need to work on that, Isaac. Start listening to your heart."

"You know my heart is firmly attached to the West, but if we lose our liberties in the seaboard states, what hope would we ever have for peace and progress?"

"Isaac, I admire your ability to see the broader scope. You are a man of long range vision, like me and Jamie Robertson."

"I wish you were going with us to join General Morgan. He might back out when he learns your regiment will not be part of the package."

"Nonsense. With you, Campbell, and Cleveland, General Morgan should be able to whip the redcoats all the way back to Charleston."

"Are you taking the Georgians, too?"

"Yes, Captain Candler is eager rejoin Colonel Clarke. Perhaps I can prevail upon them to help me on the Indian campaign."

"They are good men to have along in any kind of a scrape," Isaac said.

"We made friendships with many good men on this trip."

"Friendships that will serve us well our entire lives," Isaac agreed.

Major Joseph McDowell approached with his mother. "Couldn't let you leave without saying good-bye, Colonel Sevier."

John removed his hat and bowed to Mrs. McDowell. "Your kindness and hospitality have made a lasting impression on my regiment, Mrs. McDowell."

"And thank you for your hospitality to Mrs. Bowman. She sent me a letter with your messenger from the West and had many complimentary things to say about your wife and her friends and relatives. But I think Grace is homesick and ready to come home. How soon can you arrange her trip?"

"Immediately upon my return," John replied.

"Charles will be home soon on furlough, and it would be so perfect to have Mrs. Bowman return at the same time."

"I shall arrange everything for her safe journey."

"Colonel, I thank you for everything you did on the campaign, especially handling the issues of command and control," Major McDowell said. "I have learned so much watching you work your political skills. I shouldn't wonder that someday you could be governor."

"Thank you, Joe," John answered. "You and Charles have done so much for the cause; I hope Governor Nash remembers all the sacrifices. I really appreciate the chance to go home and defend the western frontier. I'm sure your brother's influence with the governor had much to do with that."

Joseph grinned. "The danger to Mrs. Bowman had as much to do with it as anything else."

"Tell Charles I approve of where he places his priorities. If any of you travel west again, I would be honored to host your visit."

The officers parted with deep feelings of friendship.

The march for home got underway at two in the afternoon. The men were in fine spirits, and very little complaining was heard. Colonel Sevier planned to camp the night at the town of Sevier, North Carolina. He wanted to see the place again, and perhaps present a captured sword to the mayor, so that's why the over-mountain men passed again through North Cove.

The next day they crossed the Blue Ridge marching hard through the mountains. Adam Sherrill and his brothers had learned the finer points of scouting in the service and were out front watching for signs of Indians. It had become the habit of Sam Sherrill to ride in the company of his illustrious son-in-law as a counselor and geographer. Major Valentine Sevier rode in that party as well, dispensing advice and wisdom to his son that was seldom solicited, but nonetheless freely given.

By late afternoon the horsemen were walking their horses and the foot soldiers were thinking about supper and the night's rest.

"We've pushed hard today," Colonel Sevier said. "We'll camp at Cathee's place on Grassy Creek."

Adam Sherrill, the talented scout, rode rapidly to meet the head of the column, and his face revealed that the content of his report contained some very bad news. He quickly saluted. "Colonel, your son James and the detachment we left at King's Mountain are camped just up the trace, but there's sad news."

"Is it Robert?"

"Yes, sir. I'm sorry to tell you, he won't be going home."

John leapt into the saddle and spurred his horse to a gallop. Major Valentine Sevier did the same. Sam Sherrill and his son Adam looked at each other sadly.

"I didn't know how to break it to him."

"You did right, son," Sam said. "The colonel is a man who likes his news served up hot and quick. Good or bad, he likes it hot and quick. You better go down the column and tell the other Seviers, Captain Valentine, the two Josephs, and Abraham. Let Major Tipton know about it too. There will be no happy campers tonight."

John and his father found the camp quickly and were soon embracing young James Sevier.

"My Jamie boy, I'm so relieved to find you safe and sound," the colonel said.

"Did you hear the news?"

"Yes. When did it happen?"

"Night before last," James reported with tears rolling down his cheeks. "We covered a great distance that day, and Uncle Robert seemed stronger. As we prepared our supper he became suddenly and violently ill. He was dead within the hour, despite our best efforts. I'll show you the grave."

At that moment the other Seviers rode into camp and dismounted. The story of Robert's last hours was repeated for them, and young James led the men of the family to a grove of trees where the body had been buried. The Seviers grieved and prayed as the rest of the army arrived and set up camp in the meadow.

A young foot soldier of Shelby's Sullivan County Volunteers approached Sam Sherrill as he was cleaning up after a dinner of venison steaks prepared especially for the officers. "I heard Colonel Sevier lost his brother. I thought I might offer some words of comfort in his hours of darkest grief."

Sam looked at the young man. "What's your name, son?"

"John Crockett."

Sam stopped what he was doing and stood up to give all his attention to the lad. "So you are John Crockett?"

"Yes, sir. Do you think Colonel Sevier might see me now?"

"I knew your parents. David Crockett was a good man and had a mighty fine family."

"Thank you, sir. Where is Colonel Sevier?"

"He's still out there at Robert's grave. He never came to dinner, and I fixed him a good one; venison steak, corn bread, dandelion greens, and stewed apples. There's his plate, untouched and unappreciated."

"I'll take it to him."

"Your company might be just what he needs tonight. Aren't you akin to him?"

"Sarah Sevier helped me get through my days of grief. She introduced me to her cousin Rebecca Hawkins, and we married last year."

"That makes you kin to Dr. Cozby, too."

"He married my wife's sister." Young Crockett picked up the plate of food and a flaming brand from the fire and made his way to the gravesite, where he found the grieving colonel sitting on the ground.

"Brought you some dinner," Crockett announced.

"I told them I wasn't hungry."

"I know just how you feel."

"How can anyone know what I feel?"

"Because I've been through the same dark valley, and I received some excellent help from a little lady named Sarah."

The colonel stood to face his unknown visitor and by the torchlight he recognized the man. "John Crockett!"

"Hello, Colonel Sevier. I thought I'd return a kindness to Sarah Sevier's next of kin. Your wife was sent to me by Divine Providence and she pulled me through all right."

"I'm feeling really bad just now, Mr. Crockett. I have to tell Kesiah Sevier I lost her husband and explain it to little Charlie. I have to do that, and I just don't see how I can find the words."

"I know what you have to do, so I'll just sit down here and listen, if you will allow me."

"This has been the hardest year of my life to lose Sarah last winter and now Robert. I left Robert in a safe place just like the doctor ordered. He needed an operation to remove the bullet before he could travel safely. That Dr. Johnson really knew what he was talking about."

"I learned all about the case from Dr. Cozby. He had those same worries about Captain Robert." Crockett pulled out a long stemmed clay pipe and prepared a smoke.

"Cozby supported my decision to leave the seriously wounded. I left some able-bodied men to help out; I left my own son, for Christ's sake. I paid Mr. Finley for all the expenses, and I provided for Private Moore in the same way. He had the good sense to stay there and heal; why couldn't Robert?"

"You can't blame yourself, Colonel."

"But I do. I should have given the orders more clearly, more forcefully. I should have known Robert would ignore the doctors and put himself in danger. He was always so stubborn."

"That seems to be a common family trait. Mr. Sherrill said you refused to eat your dinner. I think you hurt his feelings."

"What did Mr. Sherrill cook?"

"Venison steak smothered in dandelion greens with sweet cornbread and stewed apples. I'll tell you, Colonel, nobody in Shelby's regiment eats this good."

"So you think I hurt Mr. Sherrill's feelings?"

"It sure seemed that way to me."

"Give me that plate. I don't want Sam Sherrill to spread any rumors about me hurting an old man's feelings. He's already damaged my reputation beyond repair. I'm not about to give him any more reasons to assail my good name."

Colonel Sevier did justice to the plate of food so caringly prepared and so kindly delivered. John Crockett reflected on his own experience. "My brother William and I were riding patrol with Colonel Russell the day Dragging Canoe and his renegade warriors attacked our home. My mother and father were tortured and killed and so were all my younger brothers and sisters. We never did find little James. He's probably a captive."

The colonel stopped eating. "I thought my appetite had returned. Perhaps I was mistaken."

"I'm not going into any great detail, Colonel Sevier, but the point is this: I blamed myself for what happened. If I hadn't volunteered for the rangers, I would have been home to fight Dragging Canoe. I might have shot the savage bastard myself and saved hundreds of lives that still continue to fall victim to his cruel hate. Or, I might have been the first to fall in an attack I couldn't have prevented anyway. I will never know."

"We never know why things happen the way they do," Sevier agreed.

"Your wife helped me to understand that, and then along comes the greater good."

"Ah yes, the greater good," Sevier replied. "That was Sarah's idea about how Divine Providence works through the really bad things that happen to good people."

"For me it was meeting and falling in love with Rebecca Hawkins, and for you it was Bonny Kate."

"It's hard to recognize the greater good when you are sitting here beside the grave. Sometimes you have to take a long look back to see the Lord at work."

"But it's just like Sarah taught me. The greater good more than compensates for our losses along the way. It's all written out for us in the Book of Job."

Colonel Sevier finished his dinner. "So Mr. Crockett, are you enjoying the greater good up there in Sullivan County?"

"It's been tough. I couldn't go back to my father's farm. So I gave my share to William, thinking he could make a go of it. Then he turned right around and sold it. That wasn't very smart of me, was it?"

"I might have done the same thing for a brother under those circumstances. Where do you live now?"

"I lease my land from Colonel Carter."

"There's no future in that," Sevier replied. "Why don't you move down to the Nolichucky and be my neighbor? I'll stake you for the filing fee and the seed to get you started."

"I'm not looking for charity," the young man replied.

"This isn't charity. You are family, and tonight you have reminded me of the greater good. That's been a great comfort to me."

"I'll look you up when we get home, Colonel. I've heard that the Nolichucky land is very rich."

"I know just the parcel where you can build a fine farm."

"I better get some sleep. It's hard for us foot soldiers to keep up with you horse soldiers."

"I thought all of Shelby's volunteers were mounted."

"My old plough horse got me to King's Mountain, but he gave out on the way back. I had to put him down."

"Oh, that's a hard thing to do." The two men fell silent as the colonel thought about the hundreds of personal sacrifices made on the expedition that had gone unreported and unappreciated. "Mr. Crockett, you will transfer to the Washington County Volunteers first thing in the morning. I have a spare horse that you will ride home, and keep to work your new farm."

"I'm not looking for charity."

"And you'll not find any from me. I'm always looking for good men, and good neighbors. All you have to do is follow my orders."

John Crockett smiled at his kinsman and new benefactor. "I will gladly do that. Good night, Colonel Sevier."

"Good night, Mr. Crockett."

That night Colonel John Sevier slept on the ground, under the stars, and restlessly dreamed. In his dream the men were charging up the hill to the sound of drums beating and the Indian war whoop. A volcano of gunfire erupted all around him as he led the men in a charge into the enemy's bayonets.

"Here they are. Come on, boys!"

To his right he watched in horror as Robert fell wounded. A man next to him shouted, "There's Ferguson! Shoot him!"

John looked where the man pointed and suddenly he saw his dear Bonny Kate running for her life from a band of war-painted Indians. He heard the voice of Mary Sherrill shouting, "Run, Katie, run! Run, Katie, run!"

Bonny Kate struggled with the Indian, who caught her by the hair, and the savage raised his tomahawk.

"It's Ferguson, shoot him!"

John aimed his rifle at Bonny Kate's attacker, but just then the white horse dragging Ferguson's body blocked his shot. When the horse had passed and a cloud of gun smoke rolled away, Bonny Kate was nowhere to be seen. She and the Indian had vanished. John shouted out, waking himself as the dream faded to darkness.

"Bonny Kate! Bonny Kate!" The colonel sat up alarming the camp in the pre-dawn light.

"John, what's wrong?" Sam Sherrill answered.

The colonel hesitated unsure how best to explain. "Oh...I must be having a nightmare."

"A nightmare, about my daughter?"

"The Indians had her. I couldn't save her because Ferguson was there blocking my shot. Sam, it was terrible."

A sentry ran over from the edge of camp. "Colonel, what's wrong? We heard you shouting in the camp."

"It's all right. I just had a nightmare, that's all. What time is it?"

"Two hours before sun-up, sir."

"Thank you, Gabriel. You can return to your post."

John stood up and stretched. He put on his uniform, rolled his blanket, and began to gather his equipment.

"What are you doing?" Sam asked.

"I can't sleep anymore. What if that dream is a sign our families are in danger of attack? I'd feel better getting an early start. The horses are rested, and the men will do."

"That's fine with me," Sam replied. He roused his boys, and the camp began to stir with activity.

Chapter 32

Congress Receives the Report

At Independence Hall in Philadelphia City, the Congressional Sergeant-at-Arms paced the hallway outside the door where Congress was meeting in closed session. Two soldiers of General Washington's elite guard stood in front of the door as sentries. A road-weary courier from General Gates sat on the bench by the door. The Sergeant-at-Arms shook his head and commented, "You picked the wrong day to arrive, Captain. When General Washington makes his reports, it goes on for hours. The news has been nothing but ugly for three years."

"Well, I've got some news that will cheer them up; a great victory somewhere in the Carolinas," the courier reported.

"The Carolinas you say! Why there's not a single organized army unit south of Virginia since Gates lost his army at Camden."

"True enough, but somebody found a way to win. It's all right here in the dispatches," the courier said, patting the leather pouch he clutched at his side.

The great entrance door darkened as frontiersman Joseph Greer, the strapping seven-footer of Colonel John Sevier's command walked into the hall. He was covered in dried mud and road dust from the journey and still equipped with all the weapons and accessories of the active-duty militia soldier. He looked around and stepped over to where the sentries stood. They held their muskets before them to bar the way to all intruders.

"Is Congress in there?"

"Yes, but no one enters," the sentry said. "It's a closed session."

"Well, let's open it." Joseph grabbed their muskets and pulled the sentries off balance and then pushed them back against the double doors. The doors burst open as the sentries fell against them, and Joseph Greer admitted himself to the floor of Congress. He strode down the aisle toward the President of Congress, Samuel Huntington, with the surprised Sergeant-at-Arms chasing after him.

"Hey, you can't go in there," the sergeant shouted. "It's a closed session. Military matters are highly confidential."

Joseph arrived before the president's desk and saluted as President Huntington rose to restore order. "What's the meaning of this disruption?"

"Sir, I have news of a great victory!"

The Sergeant-at-Arms grabbed Joseph Greer by the arm and tried to pull him back. "You are out of order! You can't bust in here like this. Guards! Guards!"

The sentries rushed forward, but General Washington who had been making his report stepped over beside the president's desk, raised his hand, and stopped the sentries. "Just a moment," he ordered.

President Huntington turned to the general and said, "The chair recognizes General Washington." The room quieted, and Washington eyed the tall youth.

"What's your name, son, and where do you come from?"

"My name is Joseph Greer, and I'm from Washington County in the over-mountain settlements of North Carolina."

Washington reacted with pleasure to hear of a county named after him. He turned to the president and said, "Mr. President, I wish to present Mr. Greer of Washington County, North Carolina, for the purpose of hearing his report of a great victory."

"Thank you, General Washington," President Huntington said. "Very well, Mr. Greer, you have the floor." Joseph Greer was awed with the sudden realization that the man who had received him, and presented him to Congress, was the Commander-in-Chief of the American army. Joseph hesitated.

"Go ahead, son, give your report," General Washington prompted him.

"Yes, sir," Joseph answered. "Colonel Sevier sent me to say that he, and Colonel Campbell, and Colonel Shelby send their compliments to the Congress. It was on October seventh that we caught up with the British army of twelve hundred men led by Major Patrick Ferguson, at a place called King's Mountain. We surrounded them and killed or captured the entire force."

The members of Congress enthusiastically cheered the news, making such a commotion they could be heard in the streets of Philadelphia. President Huntington pounded his gavel to restore order. "Order please, come to order! Come to order!" The assembly quieted again, eager to hear more. "Tell us the details, Mr. Greer."

"Yes, tell us who commanded the American army," Washington inquired. "Was it General Gates?"

"No, sir. There weren't no regular army soldiers there, just militia units, all militia."

"Where was General Gates?" General Washington demanded.

"At Hillsborough, I reckon," the young frontiersman answered. "We sent Colonel McDowell over there requesting a general to lead us, but we had to fight before he came back."

"How many men did you have to defeat Ferguson's twelve hundred?"

"We commenced the attack with nine hundred and ten men and completely surprised the enemy. We lost forty-eight men, but killed more than two hundred and fifty of the enemy. We captured the rest with all their supplies and ammunition."

One of the delegates of Congress stood to be recognized. "Mr. President, this Congress is no stranger to deceptive and exaggerated reports. Why should we accept this report from a stranger with no credentials and no proof of what he says?"

The courier sent by General Gates, who had been waiting all morning out in the hall, spoke up boldly from the doorway. "Because he is telling the truth!" Members of Congress turned to see the speaker.

"And who are you?" President Huntington asked.

"I'm the courier from General Gates, who sends his respects to the Congress along with the official report of the Battle of King's Mountain. I've been waiting all morning to deliver this dispatch from General Gates."

"Please come forward," the president directed. The courier walked up and delivered his dispatch to the president, who looked at the documents several moments and nodded with approval. He handed the report to General Washington. "It's true! The western militias have defeated the British, and killed or captured one third of Cornwallis' army. Cornwallis has withdrawn from North Carolina!" Congress cheered the news again.

General Washington put aside his usual reserve and gave full expression to his joy at the news. "By thunder, this is the break we have sorely needed. Congratulations, son!" He shook the hand of Joseph Greer and smiled. "Now, who is your colonel out there in Washington County?"

"Colonel John Sevier," the lad replied.

"I should like to know more about this Colonel John Sevier and the other officers who took part in this miraculous action against our enemies. You shall be my guest, and see the best that Philadelphia has to offer!"

Colonel Alexander Hamilton, the secretary of General Washington, came over to congratulate Joseph as well.

"Alex," the general directed. "I want you to find comfortable quarters for Mr. Joseph Greer of Washington County, North Carolina. I want to keep him in Philadelphia until we can arrange a meeting with General Greene. I think Greene will need a complete briefing on the situation in the South before we send him off."

"Yes, General," Hamilton replied.

"Find the boy a hot bath and some Philadelphia clothes before you bring him to dinner with my staff this evening," Washington said. "Look at him, Alex; with soldiers like him, it is no wonder that the frontiersmen won that fight!"

Alexander Hamilton led Joseph Greer through the crowds of congressmen who

342 | Bonny Kate's Honeymoon

reached out to shake his hand as he walked toward the door. There continued much celebration in the chamber until President Huntington brought them back to order.

General Washington addressed Congress again in a much improved state of mind. "Mr. President, this concludes my report on the progress of the war!"

Chapter 33

The Heroes Come Home

Captain George Russell's company arrived unexpectedly at Watauga Fort on October the sixteenth, and failed to find Major Charles Robertson on post. Before Major Charles Robertson and Colonel Elijah Clarke could be summoned from their temporary headquarters at the Jonesborough Tavern, Captain Russell had gone on to Colonel Carter's mansion to make his report. Colonel Carter suggested they ride on to Fort Patrick Henry on the Holston in hopes of finding the leader of the home guard there. Captain Russell later complained that Colonel Carter had sent him *migh' near to Virginia on a fool's errand.* Luckily the women were better organized for communication than the army was. Mrs. Carter asked if Captain Russell had any letters from Colonel Sevier addressed to his wife.

"Why, yes, I certainly do," answered the gallant young captain. "Colonel Sevier was most emphatic that this letter was to reach his wife as soon as possible."

"I'll make sure she gets it," Mrs. Carter offered.

"I appreciate that, ma'am." He searched through his pouch of letters and handed over the soon-to-be-treasured epistle.

"Tell me, George, did you see my son Landon after the battle? Did he look well?"

"Captain Landon Carter is the bravest fellow I ever saw. He fought brilliantly and came through without a scratch."

"Thank God!" Mrs. Carter was a relieved woman and immediately called the overseer of her plantation to dispatch a rider to the Sevier plantation to carry the letter to Mrs. Bonny Kate Sevier.

Several days later, at Plum Grove Plantation on the Nolichucky, the community had gathered to seek news about their loved ones. Bonny Kate carried her letter from John in her pocket at all times and had reread it countless times, pondering every word and expression. She longed to see him and hold him again, but knew the uncertainties of war and North Carolina politics might conspire against her fondest hopes and prevent his coming home anytime soon. The letters she and Judge Carter had written to Governor Nash became her only hope of influencing events in a world gone mad.

Major Charles Robertson, Reverend Samuel Doak, and Colonel Elijah Clarke conferred in the shade of a large tree in the yard at Plum Grove.

"Isaac Thomas just got back with another ominous warning of Indian attack," Charles Robertson said.

"Have your patrols seen any signs of the Indians?" Pastor Doak asked.

"None," Robertson answered. "But that don't mean nothing. They are masters of the surprise attack."

Pastor Doak was more sensitive to the dangers faced by frontier families since the burning of his own home. "What should we do, gather the families into the forts?"

"I suggested that weeks ago, but Bonny Kate was dead set against it. She wants people to stay on their farms and complete the harvest."

"My men are patrolling as far down as the French Broad," Colonel Clarke said. "We hope to repay, in some small measure, the kindnesses we received from your people."

"You have relieved our patrols from continuous duty, but the appearance of Nolichucky Jack and his two hundred riflemen is what we really need to turn the advantage our way."

"Nolichucky Jack?"

"That's what the Indians call John Sevier," Robertson explained. "They regard him as a great warrior, under the protection of the Great Spirit."

The ladies had circled their chairs in the yard, stitching together the squares of a large quilt. Bonny Kate, Mary Sherrill, Susan Sherrill Taylor, Betsy Sevier, Kesiah Sevier, Susannah Robertson, Ruth Brown, Hannah Clarke, Grace Bowman, Esther Doak, and Mary Dykes were all there working and conversing.

"This quilt is beautiful, Grace," the hostess exclaimed. "When you go home to Burke County, you can look at it and always remember us fondly."

"I appreciate it, Bonny Kate, and I will cherish my memories of you and this place."

"That goes for us too," Hannah Clarke declared. "Georgia will forever be indebted to you and your community, Mrs. Sevier."

Kesiah Sevier looked up and asked, "How far is it to Burke County, Mrs. Bowman?"

"Well, it took us about a week to travel to Watauga Fort."

"Bonny Kate, when did John date that letter?" Kesiah asked.

Bonny Kate took the cherished letter from her pocket and looked at it again. "Ten days ago."

"So today could be the day they arrive. Read the letter again, Bonny Kate."

Bonny Kate held the letter up and read slowly. *"My Dearest Bonny Kate: My thoughts are always with you, upon your waking, your rising up, your voice as you say good morning, your cheerful smile, your lovely face and form in the morning light as you lean over me and..."*

"Skip that part and get to the news," Kesiah interrupted.

Bonny Kate paused, and smiled dreamily. "My dearest man thinks of me."

Kesiah was irritated. "Well, go on with the news."

"I just love the way he writes. Well, let's see. *The weather was dreary, and downpours slowed our progress as the rivers rose and the road became a bog the night we rode to King's Mountain.*"

"Never mind the weather," Kesiah said.

"All right, skip the weather... *We crossed the Broad River in the gray dawn and I thought of you, for I was told Broad River descends to the Catawba, the river you told so many stories about from your childhood at Sherrill's Ford...*"

"Good grief! Can we get on with the battle?"

"Oh yes, the battle," Bonny Kate continued. "*We found that fox Ferguson, defending a hill called King's Mountain. We completely surrounded him and killed or captured every one of those Philistines. Our men and boys fought heroically, and each did his duty. Our casualties were much lighter than the enemy's, but even one loss is too much for me. Tell Mrs. Sherrill that all the Sherrills are safe, as are all Seviers except for Robert. He was wounded and suffers much pain. I left him in the care of a good patriot named John Finley, with our James and three other men to travel directly home as soon as Robert feels up to the rigors of the journey. I judged it a safer course for my brother and son than staying with me, being pursued and possibly attacked by the rest of the British army. I pray I was correct.*"

"Whenever will they get home?" Kesiah asked with frustration.

Bonny Kate sighed and continued reading. "*The other colonels, encouraged by victory, are planning new operations in the Carolinas, and I am uncertain of the necessity of Washington County's involvement. I continue to impress upon the other officers the urgency of my need to return to the western frontier and quiet the Indian threats, but not even Isaac Shelby supports my contentions. We are marching north as fast as men and horses can endure to escape the British counterattack. I trust to God's good providence that this letter finds you and the children happy and safe. And now my dearest, my most tender words, I write to you...*"

"You can skip that part, too," Kesiah cut her off.

"I blush every time I read that part."

"He doesn't share much, does he?"

"Oh, he shares much more on the last page; far more than he should. I can't let the children see that." She folded the letter and put it away in her pocket.

"No, I mean about Robert. I still don't know when to expect him home."

Young John Sevier Jr. rode shouting across the meadow and through the plum orchard on Bonny Kate's own horse. "They're coming! They're coming! The men are home!"

All stood up and looked east where Johnny pointed. Sure enough there were riders appearing from the woods at the far end of the meadow. At that distance the riders were unrecognizable, but the leading man sported a fancy white plume on his hat.

"Oh, dear God, it's them. The men *are* home. I can see my dearest John!" Bonny Kate ran through the plum trees to gain a better view and stopped at the six-rail fence that defined the orchard from the meadow. It was a long column of soldiers that rode into the meadow, and they just kept coming out of the woods. John must have brought the whole army to Plum Grove. She wondered what she would cook to feed all those guests. The mounted men progressed far too slowly to suit Bonny Kate. Placing her hand on the fence post in all her womanly garb, she vaulted the rail fence from a standing start and cleared it easily. She ran with all speed toward the approaching army.

"John! John!"

Colonel Sevier saw his lady love, waved his hat, and urged his spirited charger ahead as the excited women and tired men watched with fascination. They met in the middle of the meadow, and in her eagerness she reached for him. He pulled her up easily onto the horse and seated her side-saddle in front of him. She felt his strong arms encircling her waist as she looked into his blue eyes.

"John," she panted.

"Hello, my Bonny Kate."

Her eager lips found his, and she generously bestowed her kisses.

Many of the men were deeply impressed by her demonstration. Major Jonathan Tipton grinned at Captain Jacob Brown. "I wish my wife would do that."

"I wish my wife *could* do that," Jacob replied. "She'd still be trying to get over that fence!"

"Oh John, I've got so much to tell you," she said breathlessly. "So much has happened to me since you went away."

"A lot has happened to me too," he replied.

Major Tipton led the men in three cheers. "Hip-hip huzzah! Hip-hip huzzah! Hip-hip huzzah!" Then the horsemen galloped forward and dismounted in the yard at Plum Grove. Many men were surprised to find their wives and children waiting at Plum Grove with warm, welcoming embraces.

Kesiah Sevier, holding her baby Valentine with little Charlie at her side, searched the crowd frantically for her wounded husband. "Robert... Robert? Has anybody seen my Robert?"

John pulled his horse to a stop in the yard and said to Bonny Kate, "I have to get to Kesiah quickly. Come help me."

Bonny Kate knew something bad had happened by his urgent tone and jumped off the horse. John dismounted and walked quickly over to Kesiah. The look of dread in her eyes told John she expected the worst.

"John, where's Robert?"

With all the tender concern he could muster, he grasped her upper arms and looking directly into her eyes, delivered the sad news. "Kesiah, we couldn't save him. He made it as far as the mountains and died there."

"No, it can't be. No! Oh God, no," she wailed, sobbing uncontrollably.

"She's fainting," Bonny Kate warned. She reached out and caught Baby Valentine from Kesiah's relaxing hold as the mother sank into John's arms. The colonel swept her up and carried her into the house as the leading women came to the rescue with a bucket of cold spring water and damp rags to revive the Widow Sevier. She was taken to the master bed of Plum Grove in a deep swoon to be tended by her mother Susannah and the Reverend and Mrs. Doak. Dr. Cozby came in to offer his services, but there was nothing Washington County's most celebrated and brilliant horse doctor could have done for the stricken lady.

"Run along then, Dr. Cozby. Let nature take its course," Susannah Robertson advised. "The women can handle this business, and there shall be no fee involved."

"Mrs. Robertson, do not concern yourself with my fee if there's anything I can do for Kesiah. I remain in the service of the Washington County Volunteers, and I will present any bills to the county clerk over here." Dr. Cozby stopped at the door where John and Bonny Kate stood. He placed a comforting hand on the colonel's shoulder. "You did everything Dr. Johnson told you to do, and Robert knew the risks. I'm sorry for your loss. He was a dear friend to all of us who rode with him."

John shook the hand of the medicine man. "Thank you, Jim."

Little Charlie Sevier stood at his mother's bedside. "What happened to Mama?"

"She fainted, Charlie," Colonel Sevier answered. "She'll wake up after she's had a little rest. Why don't you come with me, and we can have a little visit." Uncle John spent quite a while with his nephew explaining what had happened and how the sad event would affect his family. The three-year-old showed remarkable understanding and bravery at the disastrous news.

The October afternoon cooled quickly as everyone at Plum Grove worked to care for the tired horses, set up an overnight camp, and prepared an evening meal. Colonel Sevier spent some time conferring with Charles Robertson and several officers from the state of Georgia. He met Colonel Elijah Clarke for the first time. They quickly became fast friends as they discussed alternatives for dealing with the enemy threats from all directions.

Bonny Kate moved among the people helping them get settled, but frequently looked for John. It was comforting to her to be able to look at him now and again. Many times she observed him watching her. Finally he excused himself from his military guests, walked over to his wife, and took her aside.

"I can't take my eyes off you. I can't think of anything but you."

She smiled at him. "I have that feeling too."

"Let's ride up to our special place."

"Do you mean now? John, there's so much to do. We have a yard full of guests."

"I'll get the horses."

"I'll get my cloak and meet you behind the smokehouse," she replied. They parted and discreetly went separate ways.

Mount Pleasant was catching the day's last golden rays of sunlight on the autumn leaves when John and Bonny Kate crested the high wooded hill overlooking the Nolichucky Valley, from whence they could look out and see Plum Grove and the camp city of guest families. They dismounted and eagerly anticipated a private moment together. She walked into the center of the clearing discussing her plans. "And eventually John, I'd want wide porches all the way around the house, so we can sit and enjoy the view from up here." He took her in his arms and held her close. "Oh John, I've dreamed so long of the day you'd come home and we could be together like this. So much has happened, there was so much to tell you, I haven't stopped long enough to ask how you feel about our baby."

"Our baby?"

"Yes," she nodded smiling broadly, "our own little baby."

"When?"

"I'll have it in May, at the same time Amy and Val have theirs."

"Praise the Lord!" His embrace lifted her feet up off the ground and spun her around. They were both a bit tipsy when he set her down. "Amy and Val are expecting too?"

"Yes. Isn't it wonderful?"

"My dearest, you have made me the happiest man in the world! If our baby is a girl, I want her named for her mother."

"That's sweet, John. What if it's a boy?"

"We'll name him George Washington Sevier."

Bonny Kate laughed. "I might have guessed!"

She took a deep breath as she stepped away and then turned to face him. "How long do we have?"

John knew immediately what she was asking. "A few days, and then we march against the Chickamaugas. I was ordered to coordinate my operations with the Virginians, Major Joseph Martin and Colonel Arthur Campbell, but I fear the Indians won't wait for them. I'm reluctant to leave you again so soon. What kind of marriage is this for you?"

"The kind in which we have to take full advantage of every golden moment," she replied. She stepped into his arms again tenderly, lovingly, and he gently guided her to a blanket he spread upon the meadow grass. She reclined and watched as he removed his uniform. She marveled that he had gone forth to battle in the face of a hail of bullets, the discharge of canister, the charge of bayonets, and the slashing sabers of the dragoons and had somehow survived. She soon discovered that she had suffered more cuts, scrapes, and bruises in a five-minute catfight at the tavern than he had received in a month of campaigning. She had been slapped and cruelly treated by Tories, reviled, cursed, burned at the cook fires, had her moccasin-clad foot stepped on by a milk cow, been butted by the nanny goat, pricked countless times by sewing needles, surrounded by Cherokees, and warned by the queen of the Cherokees about impending extinction by tomahawk. She had to contend with militia officers, civil magistrates, Regulators, refugees, renegades, and relatives who continuously challenged her right to manage her new husband's affairs. She had been fighting the War for Independence as actively as her husband. Now she had arrived at a moment of peace amidst the storms of life as she breathed deeply and received into her arms her beloved man, the object of all her deepest desires. The miracle of that moment was not lost upon the colonel's lady as she prayed a quick prayer of thanksgiving to Divine Providence, the author of life and the creator of the surrounding majestic mountains ablaze with the splendor of many autumn colors.

The next morning Bonny Kate cooked a big breakfast that honored the Sevier reputation for hospitality. She organized the feeding of nearly one hundred persons; but as the morning passed most of the families packed up and went home.

Late that morning Bonny Kate found John relaxed and talkative as he brushed and groomed his horses. She joined him to help with the work around the horse barn.

"I brought home a trophy for you, Mrs. Sevier," John said. He opened a saddle bag and pulled out the silk sash that Major Patrick Ferguson had worn the day of the battle.

"What is it?"

"It is a beautifully made silk sash that belonged to Major Ferguson."

She looked at it but did not reach out to receive it. "Was he wearing it when they shot him down?"

"Yes, but look at the fine work. I wish we could develop a silk culturing industry here in Washington County."

"Is that his blood on it?"

"I washed it the best I could."

"So that is what they call the spoils of war?"

"I suppose so, but the other colonels got to pick and choose. I was busy lending aid to the wounded."

"And they left you with the bloody rag; how thoughtful of them. What did Isaac Shelby get?"

"I don't know. Like I said, I was occupied elsewhere."

"Who got Ferguson's horse?"

"Colonel Cleveland got it because his horse was killed."

"And for all your hard work and worry and the expense of mounting the campaign, this is all they gave you?"

John folded the sash and put it back in his saddle bag. "I received some documents belonging to various other enemy officers. I thought they might contain some valuable intelligence we could use in future engagements with the British. I felt bad about taking anything from such a thoroughly defeated foe. I hope I never see that spectacle again in my entire life."

"John dear, I didn't mean to make you feel bad about bringing home that trophy. I just thought your friends would have reserved for you something useful, like a horse, a sword, or a brace of pistols. You deserved so much more than you got."

"I deserve no more than the least of these, my brethren. Think of all my good men who followed my orders, suffered the hardships, and stood bravely beside me in the heat of battle without ever once complaining."

She placed her hand on his chest. "There beats the heart of a great man."

John smiled and returned to his work shoveling out the horse manure. "I have to arrange a detail to escort Mrs. Bowman home. Charles McDowell's mother is very anxious to see her again, and Charles will be returning to Quaker Meadows from Hillsborough for the happy reunion."

"Grace has been a delight and a great help to me here at Plum Grove, but I think she has developed warm feelings for Colonel McDowell and longs to be with him."

"He's a good man."

"Father told me you sent him to Hillsborough rather than taking him to battle."

"Charles McDowell was more useful to us in a strategic role at the state capital. I simply put him where he could do the most good. I think he understood the necessity of it."

"I hope so. I want to always remain friends with Grace, even after she chooses to become a McDowell."

"I think it's safe to say the McDowells will always be our friends. And I'm pretty sure Charles will persist until Grace agrees to become his Mrs. McDowell. You and I can escort Mrs. Bowman as far as Watauga Fort if you wish to go along. I have to make my report to Colonel Carter and then go over some court business with him. We could spend the night with Papa and Jemima. I hope by now my parents have made peace with each other."

"Jemima was very distressed, but I knew you would take good care of your papa once you discovered he was in the ranks."

"He posed as a Virginian, calling himself Major Reives; that's Sevier spelled backwards. When I discovered his deception, I made Papa stay back with the foot soldiers, and he proved to be quite useful."

"And were you pleased with all the Sherrills?"

"That goes without saying."

"What goes without saying, John? I heard there was an incident of someone starting rumors about one of our most closely guarded secrets."

John grinned, "Which one of our closely guarded secrets?"

"The broken bed," she replied. "Which of our papas was responsible for that?"

"I think they were both involved. How did you find out?"

"I have seven brothers, John. They will find much amusement in teasing me about that."

"I'm sorry, my dear. I will insist on sturdier furniture in our new home. If it's any consolation to you, there was a greater good produced in all the good-natured fun. The other officers were more willing to listen to my ideas after the broken bed grabbed their attention."

"I can just imagine what soldiers would say about our unbridled passions."

"Let's not speculate on that today. At least our reputations remain unblemished among the women."

"John, I'm sorry, my dear, but my own mother let the cat out of the bag."

John sighed, "What's done is done, I suppose."

"Miss Bonny, you got any work fo' me today?" There was a white-haired man standing in the door of the horse barn. He quickly realized she was not alone. "Uh, scuze me suh, I'ze looking fo' work."

"No, Ezekiel, there's nothing for you today."

"Thank you, Miss Bonny. Thank you, suh." The man bowed and went away.

"Who is that?" John asked.

"Ezekiel; he belongs to Hannah Clarke. Some of the Georgia people brought their slaves with them."

"Why didn't you give him something to do? Everybody wants to contribute to the common good. Work gives every man dignity."

"Let Hannah Clarke keep him busy. I don't need him messing up my perfectly ordered world. The children do the work around here so they can learn to run their own farms. I don't want them to think they can just order a slave to do the work for them. We'd raise up a mighty sorry generation if that idea ever got started."

"You have given all the white Georgians useful work to do in the mills and on the farms of this community. What makes Ezekiel any different?"

"He is Hannah Clarke's responsibility, not mine."

"My dear Bonny Kate, if we made every injustice and inequality someone else's responsibility, there would never be any human progress. The only difference between

Ezekiel and me is our terms of employment. I own my own plantation, and he is bound under an obsolete and unfair employment contract called slavery."

"Oh, I understand. It's kind of like the marriage contract, isn't it? There's always plenty of work and responsibility and very few rights for women under the law."

John grinned. "It seems the human condition needs a lot of work before we find any perfection in it. I had better start right away." John put away his horse grooming tools and put on his waistcoat.

"Where are you going?"

"I'm going to ask Ezekiel about his experience, what he's good at and what he likes to do, and find him some work. Someday slavery will be abolished by law and every man will be his own master, working his own farm and his own business as an independent contractor."

She followed him out of the horse barn. "I love that idea! Can women become independent contractors too?"

"I'll have to give that more thought," he replied. "When it comes to women, things get very complicated."

That evening on the porch at Plum Grove, Colonel Elijah Clarke listened eagerly to John Sevier's report of the Battle of King's Mountain and learned all he could about the situation east of the mountains. "Colonel Sevier, I want to propose a project I've been planning for several weeks while my men have rested and recovered from the Augusta campaign. A renewed attack on the British from the west would continue to confuse them and hasten their retreat back to Charleston. My men are restless and ripe for action. The glad tidings from King's Mountain will really put an edge on their resolve."

"What do you need for your project, Elijah?"

"Your wife has already generously provided ammunition, blankets, and clothing for my horse soldiers. With ten days of food, for one hundred of my men, I could make it down to South Carolina and join forces with Colonel Sumter."

John nodded in agreement. "Thomas Sumter is a general now, and he is just as eager for action as you are. Two of his colonels, Edward Lacey and William Hill, rode with us to King's Mountain."

"Can you help me out with the provisions?"

"Certainly we can," a lady's voice responded from the doorway. Bonny Kate and Hannah Clarke stepped out with their wool shawls draped over their shoulders against the chilly night air. "We had a very good harvest this year because we stayed on our farms and worked instead of forting the families. The Georgia patriots patrolling the Indian frontier made that possible."

The gentlemen rose to welcome their ladies and found chairs for them. Bonny Kate scooted her chair as close to John's as she could get it and snuggled up to him as his arm encircled her.

"We can give you anything you might need in equipment and supplies, but I can't spare any men or horses with this Indian trouble likely," John said.

"Provisions are all I need, and of course your leave to go, sir," Elijah replied.

"You have my leave and my prayers for your success."

"And we will take good care of your women and children," Bonny Kate promised.

"I have no doubt about that!"

The Georgia volunteers mustered on the first day of November and rode to the relief of Sumter's South Carolinians. Clarke's men were warmly welcomed and rendered valuable service that month in South Carolina.

Early in November the entire John Sevier family went up from Plum Grove to the Watauga Valley for several days. Plum Grove was left under the capable management of Mrs. Elijah Clarke. Bonny Kate rode beside Joseph Sevier for a time, and he spoke freely about the King's Mountain campaign as the greatest adventure of his young life. They had fallen behind the rest of the family column for greater confidentiality as Joseph shared things very close to his heart.

"I met a girl living so close to King's Mountain that they could hear the rifles firing the afternoon of the battle. She was the prettiest girl I have ever seen. She had light reddish-brown hair, green eyes, smooth white skin, and such a beautiful smile. Her name was Mary."

Bonny Kate was very interested. "What do you know about her family?"

"Her father's name is John Finley, and her mother's name is Anne."

"Oh, he's the man who cared for Uncle Robert?"

"Yes, ma'am. Mary's three brothers were taken by the British at Charleston. She and her family struggle to put food on the table, but they were very generous to take us in. I first saw her when I stopped at her home to ask for information about how to find the enemy. She pointed out King's Mountain to us and told us Ferguson was camped there. Then she smiled at me and told me to take care."

"She sounds very sweet."

"That night she washed and redressed Uncle Robert's wound three times and applied an herbal poultice. I watched her in the candlelight, and each time I heard her say a quiet prayer. I went with her to fetch the water from the spring, and it seemed we fetched a lot more water than we needed, but each time she thanked me and gave me a kiss."

"Was she that bold with all the men, or only with you?"

"I was the only one she would fetch water with; only me."

"Was she loud and brassy to play the show-off like a tavern girl?"

"No, her voice was soft and low, polite, and I suppose modest."

"What sort of game is that?"

"Do you think it was a game?"

"Girls are very skilled at playing games on young men, but it's very hard to know how serious the game is."

"Did you play a game on Father?"

"No, that was different. He saved my life; I had an obligation to be kind to him and help him during the siege of Watauga Fort."

"It sounds no different to me. Did you fall in love suddenly, or does it always happen slowly?"

"Your father was a married man when I first met him, and I knew that right from the start. Maybe you should discuss this with your father. His experience with Miss Sarah Hawkins would be a more useful example than my romantic misadventures."

"I would prefer a woman's view to guide me in this. The day I left her, all the men of the regiment were assembled there in Mr. Finley's yard, watching us, and she suddenly flew into my arms and lingered there. I felt warm tears against my cheek, and what do you think she whispered in my ear?"

"Tell me."

"Come back for me. Do not forget me."

"What did you say to her?"

"What could I say in front of the whole company? I think I thanked her for her kindness, and nothing more."

"How do you feel about her?"

"She's enchanting, she's beautiful, she's sweet, she's kind, and I think... she loves me."

"Do you love her?"

"I think about her all the time. I remember everything she ever said. I remember the kisses, the smiles, the laughter, and the tears. I remember every time she ever touched me. I hear her voice when I'm alone. I imagine being with her and holding her again and laughing at the funny things she says. When I see how happy you and Father are, I imagine it is Mary and me. I have never felt this way about any girl in my whole life. I have to go back to King's Mountain. Can you advise me?"

Bonny Kate studied the serious resolve in her eldest stepson and marveled at the depth of feeling the young man had expressed. Joseph Sevier had the confusing and dangerous world of lifelong relationships all figured out at the tender age of eighteen. Many men and old maids live their entire lives and never get it figured out. "Joseph, what you need to be looking for is the genuine article, true love for a lifetime. Don't waste your time on frivolous girls who make sport of breaking a young man's heart."

"How will I know the difference between the true love and the frivolous girl? Can you tell the difference?"

"Before I can be sure I have to meet her and have a girl talk. Girls can fool a man every time; that's a business with us. But rare is the girl that can fool *me* for very long."

"How can I know if what I feel is real and forever? And how will I know if Mary feels the same way?"

"You have to spend time with her, and I mean lots of time. This is not just the plans of a man and the plans of a woman coming together; but it's the plan of Divine Providence that fulfills a predestined purpose. Prepare yourself Joseph, in prayer and scripture. Watch for opportunities. It could take years to find your way back to that girl. You could start by writing her a letter and see if you could find a courier going east."

"Can I count on your support when I present the matter to Father?"

"I could even prepare him for the shock if you would trust me."

"I trust you, Bonny Kate."

"He-yah!" she shouted and her horse bolted into a gallop. She passed all the Seviers and screamed like a wild woman.

Bonny Kate flew past Colonel Sevier and Mrs. Bowman at the head of the column. Mrs. Bowman remarked, "Her horse has gone mad. He's out of control."

Colonel Sevier saw things differently. "If it's a race she wants, it's a race she'll have!" He spurred his horse to a gallop in wild pursuit. A mile passed beneath the thundering hooves until Bonny Kate reached a clear little stream crossing the road. She stopped and dismounted to let the horse drink. John came up a moment later and reigned in his powerful racer. He spoke as he dismounted. "Another half mile and I'd have caught you."

"You couldn't have caught me in another half *dozen* miles," she boasted. "You weren't even gaining on me."

"My horse just got home from a very tiring campaign. He's practically broke down."

"Then why are you running him like that?"

"Mrs. Bowman suggested your horse had gone mad. I was coming to save you."

"Hah, that's a lame excuse."

"Well, what's your excuse?"

"We have to talk. Joseph is in love."

"I know that. He's aiming to marry Miss Charity Cawood at the next big gathering."

"Not Joseph your brother; Joseph your son."

"What? How can that be? He doesn't even know a girl!"

"He met a girl on the campaign, and he has fallen in love. He just confided that to me and John, he's got it bad."

"Nonsense! Who could it be?"

"John, you met the girl; her name is Mary Finley."

"Mary Finley took care of Robert and the boys for one night."

"She had all that Sevier charm in her house for one night? What's a red-blooded liberty-loving girl to do?"

"Mary Finley," John repeated.

"Joseph wants to go back to King's Mountain to see that girl."

"Impossible! It's too dangerous. The Carolinas are crawling with Tories in that district, and we only defeated a third of the British army. Tarleton and Cornwallis are still very much alive and well."

"Can you think of any good reason why he shouldn't go?"

"Cornwallis has issued an order of summary execution for any person caught bearing arms against the king. Capture could mean certain death by hanging."

"I mean a really compelling reason."

"He's young and inexperienced when it comes to girls. He can't begin to understand what it takes to provide a woman the things that she requires. He's only eighteen."

"And you were only sixteen when you married Miss Sarah Hawkins."

"Things were different then. The French and Indian War had ended, and we were at peace."

"What will you tell Joseph, then?"

"I'll tell him *no*, absolutely not. We have an Indian war coming up, and I will need every able-bodied man on the frontier to defend our homes."

"I can see how difficult this is going to be for both of you," she sighed. "Nancy Ward wants our Joseph to marry one of her daughters to make a strong alliance with the Cherokees. Shouldn't Joseph be allowed to make up his own mind?"

"I want Joseph to marry for true love, like I did."

"Then maybe Mary Finley has a chance, like I did."

"We will see about that." John smiled and drew Bonny Kate into an embrace, and they kissed.

Chapter 34

The Return to King's Mountain

The Sevier family trip to the Watauga Valley was a pleasant respite from the burdens of entertaining that had weighed heavily upon the mistress of Plum Grove continuously since her wedding day. At Watauga Fort an armed escort was arranged to take Mrs. Grace Bowman and her daughter back to Quaker Meadows in Burke County. Young Joseph Sevier had volunteered for the mission, but Colonel Sevier steadfastly refused to assign his son that duty, because he was concerned the young man's motivations might lead him into danger. The disciplined, obedient son submitted to the older and wiser authority but never pretended to be happy about it.

Old Colonel Carter received his lieutenant colonel warmly and with great enthusiasm for the remarkable accomplishments of the Washington County volunteers. The officers needed time to discuss campaigns and court business, while Bonny Kate had only a brief visit with Mrs. Carter.

Before dark, Bonny Kate led her family the remaining two miles up to Stony Creek Farm, the home of Major Valentine and Jemima Sevier. They were greeted with joy and hospitality. Captain Valentine, Amy Sevier, and their clan were also present for the family gathering. Colonel Sevier joined his family the next day and set up a system of receiving his dispatches daily by express courier from the detachment at Watauga Fort.

A report came in that the Chickamaugas under Dragging Canoe had left their villages with the intention to attack the Cumberland settlements.

"I hope James Robertson is prepared for war," John remarked to Bonny Kate.

"He should be," she replied. "I sent him all the powder and shot we had."

"That was a decision that will no doubt prove to be the salvation of James Robertson's Cumberland district."

A letter arrived from General William Lee Davidson of the Salisbury District requesting Isaac Shelby and John Sevier to bring their men back to eastern Carolina for a new campaign to capture Fort Ninety Six. General Gates had approved the plan, and General Morgan would be assigned to the project also. Maybe there would be time to mount another campaign to the east before the Chickamaugas returned from the Cumberland and reunited with the main branch of the Cherokee Nation for a new war on the white settlers. It was a difficult decision for Colonel Sevier and he weighed his options carefully, considering also his dwindling financial resources.

One evening at Captain Valentine Sevier's home on the Watauga, John, his brother and his father watched the children playing games in the meadow from the comfort of the spacious porch. Inside the cabin was heard the animated conversation and laughter of Amy, Bonny Kate, Jemima, and the two thirteen-year-old cousins both bearing the name of Betsy Sevier.

"Heaven is here at home and hearth," John declared philosophically. "Why do we ever leave home?"

"Because there are wicked men out there who want to take all this away from us," the younger Valentine answered.

"Why can't they be satisfied with what they have and leave the rest of us to our own peaceful pursuits?"

"That's a fine dream for the Sons of Liberty," the elder Valentine observed. "But envy, hatred, jealousy, fear, and greed are the wild animals that surround, snarl, and snap at the condition of man. It was ever thus."

The laughter from inside the house rose to a peak, and the hilarity spilled out onto the porch. Bonny Kate marched out to where John sat and appealed to his judgment. She held her cooking apron bunched up in her right hand, and her other hand smoothed out the pleats of her petticoat at her waist.

"John dear, Amy says I'm showing more than she, and I have vigorously denied it. We need a man's opinion!"

"Whoa, John," Valentine the younger laughed. "Be careful with that. There'll be no easy way out of it."

"Hush, Val," Bonny Kate admonished. "We know whose side you'll take in the matter. I want to know what the colonel thinks."

Amy Sevier appeared at the window and testified. "We measured with the apron string and sure enough, Bonny Kate has greater girth than I."

"John, they fudged the measurement to my disadvantage. Is that any way for sisters to treat one another?"

"I should think not, my Bonny Kate," he answered. "In all fairness to you, I shall consider the matter. Come; sit on my knee, dear lady."

She stepped over and lightly seated herself in his lap.

"Whoa," John reacted playfully. "It seems a certainty that the case carries greater weight in favor of the plaintiff."

"What do you mean by that?"

"He means you are heavy," Amy giggled. "I told you, Bonny Kate. I think you're having twins, and I should know. I got big really quick with mine."

"Twins have to run in a family for that to happen, and there are no twins on the Sherrill side. Are there any Sevier twins in earlier generations?"

"Papa knows the answer to that," John said.

Val Sevier grinned. "I know my family all the way back to the time of good Saint Francis Xavier, and Amy's twins are the first ones I've ever heard of."

"There," Bonny Kate gloated. "You've heard it from the greatest authority on Sevier family history."

"That don't mean nothing," Jemima Sevier weighed in. "There were no twins on Amy's side of the family either; none with the Youngs, and none with the Douglass family that I recall."

"So you can't say it won't happen," Amy said.

Bonny Kate stood up and pulled John up out of the chair. "The moon is rising. Let's take a romantic walk along the river."

"Excuse us, folks." John smiled as he left with his wife.

Across the darkening landscape of the upper Watauga the lovers strolled. "John, what did you learn from Colonel Carter? Has he resigned as colonel as he promised he would?"

"Not exactly, but he did recommend me to Governor Nash as his successor; at least he told me he did. I don't mind the rank so much as the lack of resources to mount another campaign. The money we drew from John Adair covered the King's Mountain affair, and Isaac Shelby kept the rest to fund the next campaign in the East. I'll have to fund the Indian campaign myself."

"The grist mill is showing a profit even after I pay the Georgians their wages," she said. "The lead mine has large balances of receivables, if the state assembly approves payment."

"Don't count on that," John said. "The state is trying to raise the money to equip an army against Cornwallis. Settling old public debts is not as great a concern to them as the present emergency."

"What are we going to do?"

John took a deep breath. "I have a firm offer, in silver, for Plum Grove Plantation. We could live in the Mill House, now that the addition has been completed."

"Why not sell the mill and keep Plum Grove?"

"Mr. John Clark from Georgia is prepared to pay top dollar for Plum Grove. I have no buyers for the mill; besides the mill is closer to Jonesborough where my headquarters will be."

"Oh John, I wanted to have this baby at Plum Grove. I would be so disappointed to leave a home where so many happy memories were made."

"I thought you wanted a big house at Mount Pleasant for the happy memories."

"I do, but to give up Plum Grove right away is an uncertain prospect."

"Our war for independence is an uncertain prospect as well. The money from the sale would pay for the Indian campaign and allow me to finance the Mount Pleasant home. We could have that big house and new farm in less than two years."

"So in two years I'll have my dream home with wide porches for a view of the Nolichucky Valley?"

"It would solve all our problems fairly easily," John replied. "And in the short term, when business calls me to Jonesborough for court and military meetings, I could easily be home with you every night at the mill."

"Why doesn't Colonel Carter sell *his* big plantation to finance the cause?"

John laughed. "Colonel Carter doesn't have a ready buyer. For some reason this fellow John Clark has a powerful hankering to grossly overpay me for Plum Grove."

Bonny Kate remembered each time she had spoken to Mr. Clark on various matters. "I understand Mr. Clark's appraisal of the value of Plum Grove, and it was me that misrepresented certain features of the farm."

"Bonny Kate, we need that money if I am to be God's instrument to save our young country and chastise our enemies. This offer from Mr. Clark seems like the workings of Divine Providence."

"I'll do it for you, my dear."

They embraced and John breathed in deeply the essences of Bonny Kate's day: cook fire smoke, fresh baked bread, cinnamon and apple from the pies the ladies baked.

"I love you, Bonny Kate."

"I love you, John Sevier."

John noticed the little catch in her voice, and the tears on her face in the soft moonlight. "I can find another way to borrow the money if this is too hard for you."

"Nothing is too hard for me. I'll survive this move, and together we'll build a strong community and a new commonwealth."

The next morning the men went turkey hunting up Stony Creek and were still gone when a visitor arrived at the farmstead. She was a worried woman on an exhausted old plough horse, and she climbed down from her mount before she said a word. Amy Sevier greeted the stranger kindly. "Good day, ma'am, can we offer you a hot meal and a place to rest?"

The woman smiled and nodded her thanks, but got right to business. "I was told to ask for Colonel John Sevier. They said he could help me."

"I'm Bonny Kate Sevier, the colonel's wife. He's turkey hunting now with the boys."

"That's fine. Let me tell *you* what I need."

"Won't you come in out of the cold?"

"Yes, ma'am, I will." She walked into Amy's great room and saw the large gathering of cousins. "What a passel of young'uns! Are these all yours, Mrs. Sevier?"

"Actually I'm just getting started with *my* family."

"Whew, honey, somebody needs to sit down and explain a few things to you. You'll never last at this rate!"

Amy laughed. "My dear sister is a master of deception between the said and the unsaid, Mrs. ... I don't believe we learned your name."

"Moore; the name is Lizzy Moore."

"Well, Mrs. Moore, I'm Amy Sevier, and half of these children are mine by Captain Valentine Sevier, and half belong to Colonel John Sevier by his first wife. Bonny Kate is their stepmother and she is pregnant with her first baby."

Lizzy Moore washed the road dust from her arms and face at the basin, and she appeared younger and more at ease that at first. "Mrs. Sevier?"

"Please call me Bonny Kate so there's less confusion. There are too many of us around here that answer to *Mrs. Sevier.*"

"Well Bonny Kate, I came here to get my husband back..."

Bonny Kate looked at Amy before she answered. "Do we know your husband, Mrs. Moore?"

"His name is William Moore, and he marched away with Colonel Campbell to the Carolina war. His friends returned to Virginia without him, but they told me he was still alive down there at King's Mountain. I want Colonel Sevier to help me go get him."

"Why come to Colonel Sevier?"

"Colonel Campbell and Colonel Shelby have not yet returned from the campaign. Colonel Sevier is the only man in the West who can help me, and besides that, he has a good reputation for kindness to women. I will not rest until I have my man back home."

"I am deeply touched by your serious trouble, Mrs. Moore, and I am sure my husband will do his best to help you. John will be back from the hunt shortly, and we will see what can be done."

The ladies served their guest a meal and visited with her as the younger children napped. By midafternoon the men had returned from the hunt.

Bonny Kate ran out to meet her husband and explained about the visit of Mrs. Moore. "John, Mrs. William Moore needs our help, and she's the sort of woman who won't take no for an answer."

"Thanks for the warning, but I have plenty of experience with such women."

"How was the hunt?"

"Joseph and James had all the luck; they each got a bird."

John washed himself from the hunt and once refreshed, he greeted Mrs. Moore and discovered the nature of her request. As they sat on the porch of Val and Amy's farmhouse, John responded. "I know William Moore. We got him safely settled with a man by the name of John Finley, and I provided him with the means to pay for his care until he could make his way home."

"How will he make his way home on only one leg?"

John at first didn't have an answer for her. He thought a moment and remembered General Davidson's plan for a new campaign in the East. If the army of the West returned to South Carolina, a detachment could be sent to Mr. Finley's home and inquire of William Moore's fate. John held out that hope to the distressed Mrs. Moore.

Bonny Kate found Joseph Sevier back by the cookhouse preparing the fresh game for cooking. "Your father is meeting with Mrs. William Moore. Do you know who she is?"

"Moore is a fairly common name," Joseph replied.

"But William Moore went to King's Mountain and didn't come home."

"Oh, Billy Moore, the fellow we left with Uncle Robert at Mary Finley's house!" Joseph washed his hands quickly, dried them, and grabbed his waistcoat from a peg on the back porch. He hurried around to the front porch with Bonny Kate, where they listened to the rest of the interview.

Mrs. Moore seemed to be pretty worked up when they arrived. "I can't wait another month while your captains organize an eastern campaign. My husband needs to come home now!"

"Mrs. Moore, it's a long way down there and very dangerous territory for patriots. The Tories are fighting back everywhere across that countryside. I can't spare a company of men to go on a rescue mission for a man who is not even a citizen of Washington County. I could not justify the loss of any man on a mission like that."

"It's because my Billy is a cripple now, isn't it? A one-legged man isn't any good to the army, so you just don't care."

"That's not fair, Mrs. Moore. Your husband could still overcome such an injury and continue to serve his country."

"I don't give a hang about the country. How's he going to serve me?"

John stood up quickly when he saw Bonny Kate and Joseph watching.

"Mrs. Moore, excuse me, but it seems my wife and son have joined us. This is my eldest son, Joseph."

"Hello, Mrs. Moore." Joseph held out his hand, and she took it in greeting. "I'm pleased to meet you, ma'am."

"Joseph, is it?"

"Yes, ma'am; I'm sorry your husband was wounded."

"We are all sorry, Mrs. Moore," Bonny Kate added. "Are we making any progress on the rescue plan?"

"Not yet," John sighed. "I don't think we can provide a military solution."

"Please, just tell me where to find him, and I'll go get him myself," the brave lady said.

"I'll go with her," Bonny Kate volunteered.

Mrs. Moore looked at Bonny Kate and admired her courage. "Dear Mrs. Sevier, you're pregnant. This mission is too dangerous for you. The care of your unborn baby is now your first priority."

"I'll go," Joseph spoke up. "I know exactly where to find the home of John Finley."

"Oh, would you be willing?" Mrs. Moore asked. "Can we leave today?"

"I'm a good scout," Joseph said. "If we moved like scouts and kept to the untraveled ways, moving at night and avoiding the Tories, we could get the job done."

"I would not recommend this job for a solitary scout, and having a woman along will draw too much attention," John said.

"I can fix that," Bonny Kate said. "My brother John has been itching for action, and he knows North Carolina like the back of his hand. We can dress Mrs. Moore in my hunting shirt and breeches and make her look like a scout, too. All we need now is the approval of the Washington County colonel."

John shook his head. "Colonel Carter would never approve such a risky plan, but the lieutenant colonel might, provided you make me two promises."

"What promises, Father?"

"Deliver Mr. and Mrs. Moore home safely and give my regards to Miss Mary Finley."

Joseph grinned. "I'll promise anything to get back to King's Mountain and see that little lady."

"Then go with my blessing."

John Sherrill was summoned from his duty post at Watauga Fort and readily agreed to the opportunity for heroic action. Preparations were made rapidly for the scouting trip. As Mrs. Moore dressed in Bonny Kate's hunting clothes, she thanked the colonel's lady repeatedly for her help and persuasive influence.

"I'm overwhelmed that your husband would send his own son with me and that you would offer your own brother."

"It's all about family caring for one another," Bonny Kate explained. "Joseph is sweet on Miss Mary Finley; that's why he volunteered. As for my brother, he's always looking for adventure. Now Mrs. Moore, we have you looking like a Washington County scout, but you will need a better horse to complete your disguise. Take my horse; she's good for thirty miles a day."

"Oh, I couldn't do that."

"You will have to be well mounted to keep up with Joseph Sevier and my brother John. Scouts have to move very fast, especially in enemy territory."

"I don't know what to say. I'll never be able to repay your kindness."

"Don't worry about that. Just keep my boys from getting into trouble."

Mrs. Moore laughed. "Trouble has always been my constant companion."

"Mine too," Bonny Kate laughed. "And I have never been able to turn my back on an old friend!"

The three traveling companions made the trip over the mountains in nine days. John Sherrill's knowledge of the back country and the scouting business was invaluable to the success of the mission. Colonel Sevier had promoted Joseph to the rank of first sergeant, and he was gaining valuable experience as a decision maker. Mrs. Moore was a strong woman and entertaining in conversation. She always offered encouraging words to the two young men. It was dark by the time they rode up to the Finley cabin and observed no signs of life.

Across the road a man came out of a neighboring house with a lantern held high. "Who is that out there in the road?"

"Friends," Joseph answered, without revealing whether they were friends of the king or friends of liberty.

"Don't go near that cabin. It's the small pox."

"Are you sure of that?" Joseph asked.

"I'm not sure of anything these days. I know they took in a rebel who was wounded at the battle. A few days later they posted the quarantine notice of small pox when Bloody Bill Cunningham came through here hunting rebels. He threatened to burn the house down over them after the disease was done ravaging them. I still see the girl every day going out to fetch water, but I never see the old man."

"Mary?" Joseph called to the dark cabin.

"Who is out there?" replied a man's voice that Joseph recognized as John Finley's.

"It's Joseph Sevier."

There were noises of haste inside the cabin and the door flew open, "Mary, stay back!" Finley shouted.

A darkly cloaked figure cleared the threshold and paused at the edge of the narrow porch. "Joseph?"

"I'm here." Joseph strode quickly toward the cabin as the girl rushed into his arms. He pulled back the hood of the cloak, and it was indeed the girl of his waking thoughts, his hopes, and his dreams.

"You came back! You came back! Oh Joseph, you came back for me."

"Mary, what about the small pox?"

"It was all a ruse to buy us a few more days. We'd nearly given up hope, but you came back!" Her soft lips found his, and she kissed him repeatedly.

"Mary!" Mr. Finley called sternly from the porch. "Get back in the house, girl."

A lantern was lit inside the cabin, and a man on crutches appeared in the doorway. He was missing the lower half of his leg, but obviously still alive.

"Billy!" a woman's voice called out from her manly disguise. "Billy, I've come to take you home!" Mrs. Moore ran past the kissing young couple intent on doing some kissing herself.

John Sherrill watched and grinned. He turned to the neighbor with the lantern. "Don't you just love happy endings?"

"There will be no happy endings here if Bloody Bill Cunningham catches up with you." The man turned and rushed back into his cabin and barred the door.

The next morning Mary Finley climbed down from her place in the loft and dressed quietly for a trip to the spring to fetch water. Her mother was already up starting the cook fire.

"Mary, there's one small slab of bacon left in the smokehouse," Mrs. Finley said in a low voice. "Today would be as good a day as any to finish it up."

"Yes, ma'am. I'll fetch it in."

Joseph had watched her preparations from his pallet on the floor and followed the girl out. The Moores were still asleep under a bearskin, and Mr. Finley snored from the opposite side of the room as John Sherrill rose also. He pulled on his moccasins and smiled at Mrs. Finley. "I'll tend to the horses."

When John Sherrill was dressed for the day, he opened the back door of the cabin and saw the young lovers involved in another tender kiss at the doorstep. He quickly closed the door and strode across to the front door and carefully surveyed the roadway up and down before stepping out on the front porch. As he breathed in the cold December morning air, he spied the neighbor across the road mount his horse and spur the animal to a gallop in an eastern direction. "I don't like the look of that," he muttered.

Mary fixed a fine breakfast from the provisions the travelers had brought and the bacon she found in the smokehouse. It was clear the Finleys were almost out of food and just short of desperate about what to do next. Joseph was treated with much kind attention by the young lady, and it was evident to Mrs. Moore that the feelings being expressed were genuine.

John Sherrill buttered another fluffy biscuit and posed a question to Mr. Finley. "Where does the road go east of here?"

"It forks a mile farther up. The left fork goes to King's Mountain, and the right fork goes down to York."

"Is York a pretty good-sized town?"

"Naw, you wouldn't think much of it. There is a camp of Tories there now."

"I saw your neighbor light out this morning in that direction."

"Damn that busybody!"

"Who is Bloody Bill Cunningham? Your neighbor mentioned him twice last night."

"He's the worst of the Tory leaders, when it comes to house burning and hanging defenseless citizens. He rode by here a week ago suspecting we were harboring a rebel. Mary had the idea of the quarantine sign and after a few threats and curses, he figured we would suffer more with small pox than anything he could do to us. We've had to live with the terror that he's coming back."

Sherrill turned to Sevier. "The neighbor has gone to fetch the Tories, but our horses need a day of rest. What do you think we should do, Sergeant Sevier?"

"What's the soonest a man could ride to the Tory camp and make it back with a mounted detachment?"

"Two hours, I reckon."

Joseph Sevier was thinking fast. "We leave immediately, proceed slowly for the sake of the horses, and travel cross country in unexpected directions."

John Sherrill scooped up the remaining biscuits on his plate and put them in his haversack and stood to go saddle the horses. "The horses will be ready to travel in an instant, Joe. You get the people ready."

The attention turned to William Moore and his ability to travel. Mary removed the leg bandage and showed the healing progress. "I am amazed at how the skin has grown back across the bone here, and with the herbal poultice we kept it moist and pliable. The center of this area still has a way to go, but there hasn't been any infection, praise the Lord."

Mrs. Moore turned away and had to open the shutters on the nearest window. She took deep breaths, and her husband called to her. "Are you all right, Lizzy?"

Through her tears she spoke softly. "I don't see how you lived through this."

"Very few people expected me to, and I had my doubts at times. But I just kept thinking about you and our children, and I never gave up."

"He was the perfect patient," Mary said.

"And Mary was the perfect nurse."

"Can he travel?" Joseph asked.

"Slowly," Mary replied. "I don't want that one spot to reopen and bleed again."

Everybody prepared to leave knowing full well the peril of being caught by the Tories. Only Joseph Sevier had a clear idea of where they would be heading. John Sherrill arrived at the front porch leading the horses, and Joseph met him.

"Johnny, take them west, down to the first creek, and make no effort to cover your tracks. Turn into the streambed and walk them up to the north side of the road and come back to a point about a hundred yards out behind the neighbor's house. We'll meet you there, mount up, and head northeast for a little while."

"Are we going toward that hill?"

"Yep, right across the battlefield, then on to Charlotte. General Gates is supposed to be there with the army. We'll find safety there."

"King's Mountain, is it? It don't look like much of a mountain to me."

"It seemed a lot bigger the day we conquered it," Joseph said.

John Sherrill completed his misdirection maneuver and met the other five travelers in the woods to the north of the main road. The Moores were mounted together on the strongest horse, and Mrs. Moore had to hold her husband in the saddle as the horse rocked along in a walking gait. The pace was slow from the start, with everyone on foot leading their horses except the Moores. Mr. Finley had only a pair of plough horses for himself, his wife, and his daughter. Joseph was keenly aware they were not bred for running. The first hour passed with John Sherrill following, doing his best to cover their tracks where he could. He knew the Tories could easily use hunting dogs to track them and probably would.

Two hours later Mary paused at the foot of King's Mountain and looked up in awe at the slopes that had been so hotly contested just weeks before. "Wolves are all over these woods since the day of battle. Their howling makes the most mournful sound in the night."

"They didn't dig the graves deep enough to keep out the wild animals," Mr. Finley shared. "This route will not be pleasant to the nose."

"But it will keep the Tories from using hunting dogs to track us," John Sherrill pointed out. "That's the genius of the Sevier in charge of this little tour."

Joseph was well up the slope when he turned around to encourage the others. "Well, are you coming with me?"

"We are coming," Sherrill answered. He thought he might have heard some dogs far behind them.

When everyone had reached the crest of the lonely hill, they walked along the length of it. "This is the place where the hospital tent was set up," Billy Moore said solemnly. "I remember a fellow named Adam Sherrill helped me get here."

"My brother; he is the kind and thoughtful one of us," John said.

They came to the northeast slope where the land fell away again. By now the sounds of the baying hounds were quite distinct.

John Sherrill looked back and scanned the woods for signs of their pursuers.

Joseph Sevier stopped to listen for a moment. "Mr. Finley, can you get to the Charlotte Road from here?"

"Why yes, you'll strike it in less than a mile due north."

"Go now, quickly, with the fastest horses and leave your plough horses tied at the foot of the hill for Johnny and me. We will be a little delayed in joining you at Charlotte, but don't stop until you reach the American lines."

"What are you boys doing?"

"Yeah Joe, what *are* we doing?" Johnny asked.

"What we came to do, Mr. Sherrill," he replied with cool confidence. "We are getting these good people to safety in Charlotte."

"I won't leave you, Joseph," Mary cried.

"I'll be along soon," he tried to calm her.

She threw her slender body into his embrace. "Don't let them hurt you."

"Go quickly and allow me some space to do my work..." She silenced him with a long kiss.

Joseph broke away from the clinging girl. He thought she would have been tougher when the pinch came.

"Perhaps I should stay and help you," Mr. Finley offered.

"Get Mary to safety, sir, and that's an order!"

"The lad knows what he's doing. Come along, Mary."

The Moores and Finleys were soon down the slope and gone.

"I didn't know you were planning on this," Johnny said.

"I didn't think it would come to this."

"The dogs will bring them right up the ridge. We'll have some easy targets if the Tories want to play our game."

"Well Johnny, you wanted to see King's Mountain. What do you think?"

"I think I've seen enough. Let's go home."

"I thought we could use these trees for cover and just kind of back down slowly tree to tree, reloading and firing until we get to the horses."

They positioned themselves and waited. "Look at these trees, Joe; they are all torn up with bullet holes. Y'all must have thrown a ton of lead up here."

"Captain Lenoir and Major Winston came up this slope. We attacked the hill at the other end. See that pile of stones down yonder? That's where they buried Ferguson."

Shots rang out in the distance as Mr. Finley led the well-mounted refugees in the direction of the Charlotte road. There were as many as a dozen shots fired back at the mountain. Mary Finley listened with anguish to every report until the firing stopped. Still, her father pressed the horses on toward safety. The wind stung and froze her tear-streamed cheeks as Joseph Sevier's powerful horse galloped along beneath her. She had loved, truly loved, a man for the first time in her life and now agonized over the fear she might have already lost him. How could those two brave western men have survived so much shooting?

"Joseph Sevier, dear Joseph Sevier, will I ever learn the depth of your courage and sacrifice, all for the love of me?"

Mr. Finley heard her lament. "Hush, Mary. You never really knew that boy."

"I knew him, Father, just like I know my own heart." She wept bitterly all the way into Charlotte.

Chapter 35

Charlotte Town

"Can't these old farm horses go any faster?" John Sherrill complained.

"The first quarter mile was respectable, but now they have but one gait—slow," Joseph Sevier replied. "I wonder how far it is to Charlotte."

"It shouldn't be more than about five more miles. My leg is really burning now."

"We'll find a doctor first thing and get that bullet out. I'm sorry you got hit."

"That bunch was determined to show us a fight, but they sure forgot about us when their dogs tangled with that pack of wolves. That's the Sevier luck, Joseph. You have it just like your daddy has it."

"I don't think we could have escaped without a fight. Those Tories would have run us down if we hadn't turned and faced them on the mountain. I hope I can find Mary safely arrived in Charlotte."

"I hope we can get our horses back," John said.

Charlotte Town was a small village for such great continent-shaking events taking place there. The taverns were filled with noisy Continental soldiers when the two scouts from the western waters arrived about dusk. The village doctor was still in his office, and he went to work immediately on John Sherrill. He explained all the excitement that had been produced when Lord Cornwallis pulled out suddenly leaving behind a wealth of supplies still packed in the wagons.

"General Gates moved in, and his regular army soldiers are swaggering about like they won the victory. The funny part of it is, none of the soldiers now occupying Charlotte had anything to do with the battle at King's Mountain. But they brag to the ladies like they did."

"I was at King's Mountain," Joseph said. "I saw my uncle shot down, and I saw Ferguson killed. I saw the mountain covered with the wounded, bleeding, and dying. I saw the prisoners huddled together and shivering in the cold, for lack of food and blankets. I saw men driven to the ends of their endurance and saw them hang the

Tories by torchlight. What in all that experience could a soldier go bragging about to the ladies?"

"What your name, young sir?" the doctor asked as he laid down the forceps with which he had just extracted a bullet.

"Joseph Sevier."

"Of the John Sevier family?" the doctor asked.

The patient supplied the details. "He's the son of John Sevier, and my sister Bonny Kate is the colonel's wife."

The doctor was greatly impressed and offered to buy the boys a dinner at the best tavern in town. Not having eaten since breakfast, they accepted the hospitality readily.

"Now take care to stay off that leg, and keep it elevated when you sit or lay down," the doctor instructed Johnny Sherrill when he had finished. "And let me see you again in a couple of days."

At the tavern the doctor paid for their dinners and talked while they ate. "You'll have to camp outside town tonight, because you won't find a bed in the entire town."

"Why is that?" Johnny asked.

The doctor pointed to a table of continental officers eating, drinking, and laughing in fine spirits. "That's General Nathaniel Greene, Washington's favorite and most trusted man. He takes over command from General Gates in the morning, hoping to reorganize the southern army. He's got a big job ahead of him and brought a sizable staff. That's why there are no beds in Charlotte."

"I have to find a girl before I think about bed," Joseph said.

"Spoken like a true red-blooded American lad. Every soldier in here is thinking the same thing. In nine months I'll have an upsurge in the baby business like you wouldn't believe."

"Doctor, have you seen a one-legged man by the name of William Moore, traveling with his wife? There is also a man named John Finley with his wife, Anne, and a daughter named Mary. They would have arrived in town this afternoon riding well-bred horses."

"No, I'm sorry. I was so busy this afternoon in the surgery that I never looked out."

"He's sweet on Mary Finley," Johnny explained. "That's the girl he has to find."

"Why don't you inquire at all the taverns and the livery stables? If that doesn't give you results, go up Main Street and ask at the Presbyterian church. Sometimes they take in the sick and wounded, or the occasional weary traveler. But you'll have to behave like a gentleman with that girl of yours, or they'll throw you out."

Joseph grinned. "That goes without saying, Doctor."

The doctor stood up and loudly proclaimed. "Well boys, enjoy your stay in Charlotte. It was my great pleasure to meet a couple of real King's Mountain heroes instead of all these regular army pretenders."

The room hushed and looked their way as the grinning doctor put on his hat and cloak and stepped out. An officer approached them from General Greene's table and politely addressed the boys. "Are you gentlemen from the King's Mountain expedition?"

"Yes, sir," Joseph replied.

"General Greene requests the pleasure of your company for a toast to your brave officers."

Joseph Sevier and John Sherrill crossed the room to the general's table and Nathaniel Greene stood up, prompting all the men at the table to stand and face the mountaineers. The boys saluted, and the great man returned the salute. "What are your names, men?"

An officer who was seated with his back to the boys now exclaimed loudly, "For the love of God, it's Joseph Sevier!"

"Uncle Rich!" Joseph replied with even greater enthusiasm. The two men embraced in a bear hug.

"General Greene, this is my nephew, Joseph Sevier, the eldest son of John Sevier."

"What a coincidence," the general laughed. "We have been talking about your illustrious father for the better part of the evening. Who's your companion?"

"This is John Sherrill, Colonel Sevier's brother-in-law."

"Well, I'll be blessed," General Greene exclaimed. "It a pleasure to meet you both. And this one was wounded in the service of his country. Where did that happen, son?"

"King's Mountain," Sherrill replied.

"We have a couple of real King's Mountain heroes. What an honor! Bring these men some of that West India Rum. Boys, the innkeeper claims this rum was taken from the baggage wagons left behind by the great Lord Cornwallis. That gives us even greater delight in these toasts."

"Gentlemen, I give you Colonel John Sevier and his Washington County Volunteers!"

"To Colonel Sevier and Washington County!" all the men answered, and drank the toast.

General Greene invited the mountaineers to sit and talk with him, but the general was a better listener than he was a talker. He questioned Joseph at great length about the Indian situation in the West and seemed disappointed that so much work remained to be done in securing the West from the ravages of savages.

"Now, Mr. Sevier, tell me the nature of your relationship to Colonel Richard Campbell."

Joseph smiled at his Uncle Rich and replied, "He married my mother's sister, Rebecca. Aunt Becky and Uncle Rich have always been very dear to me."

"Sarah's children have always been very dear to us, as well."

"That's mighty fine, Colonel Campbell. Can't we use that family connection to persuade Colonel Sevier to join the Continental army? We could sure use an officer of his caliber."

"Yes, sir, I believe we could."

"General Greene, thank you for honoring me like this, but may I be excused?" Joseph asked. "I'm on a mission to bring home the wounded that we had to leave behind last month, and I have to see about their care."

"I completely understand the duty of a soldier."

"Then he has to find a girl," John Sherrill added with a wink and a grin.

"Now the truth comes out," the general laughed. "Ah, what joy I'd find to be young again, in the active service of the country. Yes, sir, it's been a real pleasure."

The boys saluted again and then shook hands with the general and his staff and took their leave.

Joseph walked up dark Main Street with a hurried purpose.

"Slow down, Joe. I'm still trying to learn how to work these crutches. Where are we going in such a hurry?"

"The Presbyterian church," Joseph answered.

"Aren't we going to search the stables and the taverns?"

"I just know an angel like Mary would most likely be found at the church."

"Oh man, you have a deeper wound than I have. It's one of Cupid's arrows lodged in your heart."

"Hurry up, Johnny."

The men arrived at the Presbyterian church, and Joseph Sevier settled John Sherrill on a hard bench in the sanctuary and elevated his leg with a haversack. "Get some rest and say a prayer for healing. I'll join you later."

"Hey Joe, can you get me a drink of water? Can you tuck me in? Can you read me a bedtime story?"

"Later," Joseph called over his shoulder. He was intent in his search and would have searched the whole town for that girl if the first door he knocked at hadn't been the pastor's manse.

"Yes?" the pastor's kind wife answered the door.

"My name is Joseph Sevier, and I have lost my traveling companions today. We were going to meet in Charlotte this evening, and I can't find them. The names are Finley and Moore. Mr. Finley has a daughter named Mary, and Mr. Moore lost his leg at the battle of King's Mountain. I know I'm rambling, but I'm very concerned about their safety with all this military activity in town."

"I'm glad you are here," she said soothingly. "I know where your friends are. Please, come in."

The Charlotte Presbyterian manse was grand compared to the rough log cabins of the West. A staircase went up in the candle-lit central hall to rooms on an upper floor.

The rooms were painted in bright colors, and the furnishings were beautifully crafted. Joseph had never seen such a fine home except for Colonel Carter's mansion. He was ushered into the parlor, and there he found Lizzy Moore with John and Anne Finley. They were surprised and delighted to see him. Mrs. Moore rushed to embrace him.

"You're unhurt? I can't believe it! We heard all the shooting and despaired of ever seeing you again. What became of Mr. Sherrill?"

"That joker took a bullet in the leg because he didn't take cover when I ordered him to. The doctor fixed him up, and he's asleep in the sanctuary. Mr. Finley, you have the slowest horses in America!"

"I know it, son."

"Where's Mary?"

"She took it terribly hard," Finley said shaking his head.

"She wept uncontrollably, hysterically. We couldn't console her," Lizzy said.

"She cried herself to sleep, up in our guest room," added the pastor's wife. "It was deep grieving like I've seen widows do."

"Can I see her?"

"I don't know that she could handle the shock of seeing you alive again," the pastor's lady said.

Joseph grinned. "She better get used to seeing me, because I intend to marry that girl, if she will have me and if Mr. Finley will allow me to court her."

Finley didn't respond, leaving an awkward silence that the pastor's wife was obliged to fill. "It seems Miss Finley has invested considerable emotional energy into the idea of a romantic attachment to Mr. Sevier. How long have you known each other?"

"About two months," Joseph answered.

"Two days is more like it," Finley corrected him. "You spent a day with her back in October, and we didn't see you again until last night."

"Oh my, this is a strange circumstance," the pastor's wife appreciated, "a strange circumstance indeed."

"I have nothing against the lad. His courage is unquestioned, and he seems to come from a good family..."

"A family that treats their women like queens," Mrs. Moore added.

"And I'm much obliged for today's rescue from the Tories. But my daughter is a young and inexperienced farm girl who hasn't seen much of the world. Mary doesn't understand what marriage is all about. She is the only child we have left, and we can't let her go with a fellow she's only known for two days."

"I noticed that Mary had a Bible packed among her belongings," the pastor's wife said. "Does she read it?"

"Right regular," Finley answered. "That was the inheritance from her grandmother."

"Then I will tell you with great confidence that Mary has centuries of experience packed away in that pretty little head. She understands as much about family and marriage and children as any woman could teach her. And if she believes what she reads, she has tremendous resources of faith on which to build her life."

There was again an awkward silence that Joseph felt obliged to fill. "I don't believe there's any great need to disturb her sleep at this hour. I'll check in with her in the morning. Good night, Mrs. Moore, Mr. Finley, Mrs. Finley, and Mrs. ..."

"Green, Patience Green. My husband is the Reverend Sterling Green. I'm sure you'll meet him in the morning. Breakfast is at seven if you wish to join us."

"I'd be delighted, ma'am, and could you set a place for my stepuncle, John Sherrill? He's a good Presbyterian and a good patriot, too."

"Yes, bring Mr. Sherrill. We would like to make his acquaintance."

In the sanctuary of the church Joseph found a wooden bench next to his Uncle John, who was still awake pondering the full day of strange events.

"Did you find that girl?"

"Yes, I did."

"Is she all right?"

"I don't know. They wouldn't let me see her. They said she was upset, and cried herself to sleep. Mr. Finley doesn't approve of me and won't let me court her."

"That's a heck of a note to end our day on. We liked to get ourselves killed to save that old hoot owl and his empty-headed daughter."

"She's *not* empty-headed! She has centuries of experience packed away in that pretty little head. She's a regular Bible reader; I learned that much about her tonight."

"And you'll learn a lot more before we get back home. Mr. Finley has the slowest horses in America."

Joseph smiled. "But can Mr. Finley be persuaded to go out to Washington County with us?"

"Offer him land for a farm, and a good job, and I think he'll go along. Hey Joe, he could work for Sherrill and Sons. We need wagon drivers for our transport business."

The light of a lantern shone from the front door of the parsonage, and it moved rapidly across the yard toward the door of the church. Joseph noticed it immediately and saw three cloaked figures in full skirts enter the sanctuary.

"Joseph," called the voice of a young woman. "Is it really you?"

The brave young man stood and answered. "Yes Mary, we are safely arrived." In less than a moment the girl was in his arms, overcome with relief and crying with joy. Joseph smiled broadly at her companions, Mrs. Moore and Mrs. Finley.

"She woke up crying for her knight in shining armor," Mrs. Moore said. "We had the pleasure of telling her the good news."

"Thank you," he replied. "Everything is going to be all right, Mary. The doctor said that Mr. Sherrill's wound is not life threatening."

Mary smiled at the wounded hero. "I'll see that Mr. Sherrill gets the best care in Charlotte."

"Mary, these gentlemen plan to leave Charlotte very soon," her mother said. "Mr. and Mrs. Moore have to get home before the winter snows close the mountain trails."

The young woman held her man tight and looked into his eyes. "How long do we have?"

"The horses need rest, so it won't be tomorrow."

"Good," Mrs. Finley said. "That will give me some time to work things out with your father."

"What things, Mother?"

"Mrs. Moore has offered to pay our expenses to Washington County from the funds provided to her by Mrs. Sevier. She assures me that Mrs. Sevier would receive us with great hospitality if we make the trip."

"Oh Mother, could we?"

"I can assure you that Mrs. Bonny Kate Sevier would welcome you with every comfort affordable at Plum Grove," Joseph said.

"I'm curious to meet this Bonny Kate," the mother said. "I just need a little time to reason this out with my husband. Come, Mary, we have much work to do tomorrow, and we will need a good night's sleep."

Mary smiled broadly. "Good night, Mr. Sevier. Good night, Mr. Sherrill."

"Good night," the men replied, bowing courteously as was the custom of the time. The ladies left with their light-giving lantern, and the sanctuary became dark again.

Joseph sighed with satisfaction as he found a comfortable position on the hard wooden bench. "Well, Mr. Sherrill, what's the best way to get home from here?"

"We can follow the Catawba up to Sherrill's Ford, where we can stay at Uncle William's place. Then a day of travel to the west will bring us safely to Brother Uriah's farm. After that we follow the mountain trails home to the Nolichucky."

Far to the west, that very same December night, Colonel Sevier and his lovely bride made a soft bed of bearskins and blankets on the clean scrubbed floors in the deserted great room of Plum Grove Plantation. Moving day was never easy, and many tears were shed as the last wagon rolled away bound for their new home at Sevier's Mill on Little Limestone Creek. The honeymoon couple had ridden up to the crest of Mount Pleasant to enjoy the sunset, raced their horses through the twilight shadows back down to Plum Grove, eaten a candlelight supper at the fireplace in the Great Room, and made ready for that last night to themselves. Ahead lay the Indian Campaign for John and days of unpacking and settling in at the Mill House for Bonny Kate.

"I'm not looking forward to the coming month," Bonny Kate said sadly.

"I'll be back before you know it, and we will secure a long period of peace with the

Cherokees," John said.

"I hate leaving Plum Grove. It holds so many precious memories for me and the children."

"I understand, but the Mill House is bigger, closer to Jonesborough, and better protected if the Indians attack while we are gone. You let that Cherokee scouting party get too close last month. It's not safe here anymore for you and the children."

"Did you warn Mr. Clark about that before he bought this place?"

"Yes, and he is not moving here until spring planting time. We should have the Cherokees pacified by then."

Bonny Kate rose, stirred the burning embers, and then put another log on the fire. "It's a chilly night," she said staring into the fire. "I guess our honeymoon is over."

"Every moment with you is a honeymoon for me."

She turned to him and smiled. "You're so sweet, John. You always know how to delight me whenever we are together. But the fact remains, you were gone a month to the Carolina War, you sold Plum Grove Plantation to finance an Indian Campaign, and you are about to leave me again for another month of campaigning. I should be angry about all this, but I know that none of it is your fault. What am I to do with you?"

"Why not warm yourself with some hot love?"

She laughed at his expression and joined him under the blankets. She lay back and embraced him eagerly as he leaned over to kiss her.

Author's Note: To my dear, patient, long-suffering reader: We who have journeyed far together should give our generous host and beautiful hostess some time alone. We have intruded far too often into their public and private business, but the benefits of our observations have been many. We have learned countless lessons about eighteenth century life that can be applied directly to life in our own time. We have learned our Revolutionary War history with a unique emotional dimension and far more entertainment and humor than academic disciplines are permitted to teach it. We have traveled to King's Mountain and mentally participated in the battle that turned the tide of the War for Independence. We have observed the miracle of unique and improbable circumstances that led to an overwhelming American victory on that remote little hill in northern South Carolina. We also have had the opportunity to experience the anxiety of staying on the frontier farm, guarding the well-beloved homes, sheltering the less-fortunate refugees, and worrying about the safety and success of our troops. There were many dangers, toils, and snares along the way that might have arrested our progress, but with courage and self-discipline you read on with the determination of an over-mountain settler. Dear reader, I am proud of your accomplishment. Let us return to the twenty-first century now, far richer for the experience, more appreciative of our history, and more capable in the struggles of our own times. Fare thee well!

Epilogue

Bonny Kate's Honeymoon is a strange title for a novel about the legendary hero and heroine of Tennessee's Revolutionary War days; stranger still to be labeled with the subtitle Victory at King's Mountain. When a twenty-six-year-old bride plans her honeymoon trip, it doesn't usually turn into a military campaign in which the combined militias of four states destroy a third of the British Empire's invading army, providing a major turning point in America's War for Independence. Yet, that is what we have seen in the pages of this book. Several of the early Tennessee historians reported that Bonny Kate "spent her honeymoon sewing uniforms for Colonel Sevier and his sons," but if the complete story were to be told, we would see that her participation went much deeper and broader than the historians relate.

When my first book, *Bonny Kate: Pioneer Lady* was published, readers would often ask me whether Bonny Kate was a real person and if she really said and did what is written in the book. The first answer I want to share is yes, she was a real person who helped raise ten stepchildren and then raised eight children of her own. She assisted her husband in winning the American Revolution and became the very first "First Lady" of the state of Tennessee. She ran the Sevier household and plantation as a productive, profitable, diversified farm for fifty-six years, through good times and bad. She also managed John Sevier's many other enterprises during his long absences in service to state and nation. Among the family businesses were horse breeding, grist milling, iron forging, mining, banking, and land development. They lived modestly and always provided help to needy members of the community in the spirit of commonwealth, which was their peculiar model of self-government.

The next question about which parts are true, what persists as legend, and what was invented by the novelist from an undisciplined creative imagination, is more difficult to discern. All that could be discovered about Bonny Kate from scant historical writings is included in this book. There were family events, favorite sayings, notable quotes, and family anecdotes about her activities that were naturally included in the proper time and geographical contexts. In general, greater historical accuracy is found in *Bonny Kate's Honeymoon* than in the first Bonny Kate book because more information is available from historical sources about her life during this period.

You will observe that Bonny Kate and John Sevier arose from backwater obscurity to state and national prominence through a long process of self-sacrifice and service to others within and under the authority of the established social and political structures of the day. Even though they were revolutionaries in a revolutionary era, they remained faithful to the principles of liberty, justice, and political authority vested in democratically elected national, state and county governments.

The first book, *Bonny Kate: Pioneer Lady* was a classic romance about people in preparation for predestined roles as instruments in the plans of Divine Providence. The characters were polite, noble, and unaware of the challenges and responsibilities that lay ahead. In *Bonny Kate's Honeymoon* the challenges emerge immediately, and we begin to discover the strength that was always present in their characters and watch as God's plan begins to unfold. Bonny Kate and John Sevier become historically important for their contributions in the American Revolution and later for his leadership in the state of Tennessee. There is obviously much more of this story to be told about their remarkable lives as an example of human achievement directed by a divine plan.

John Sevier was a community builder and became governor of the first state to be formed after the original thirteen states. They named the new state Franklin in honor of Dr. Benjamin Franklin, and it existed for four years until North Carolina reclaimed the territory and cut a better deal for the transfer of title to the national government shortly thereafter. John Sevier was regarded an outlaw by North Carolina until he relinquished his title and role as the new state's first and only governor. His friendships and political skills helped him recover his political fortunes, and soon he was elected to the General Assembly of North Carolina and his experimental state forgotten. North Carolina was slow to ratify the Federal Constitution, set up congressional districts, and hold elections. When they finally got their house in order, John Sevier was elected a representative to the First Congress of the United States in North Carolina's 5th District. He took his seat in June of 1790 and served out the remaining year of the session. North Carolina ceded the western over-mountain district to Congress to become part of the Territory South of the Ohio River. President Washington appointed William Blount as the governor of the territory, and Sevier served as the territorial Brigadier General.

In 1796, John Sevier became the first governor of the new state of Tennessee and served three consecutive two-year terms. The state constitution barred him from a fourth term, but two years later he became eligible for three more terms, which he served from 1803-1809. In 1811, he returned to the national level as a congressman from Tennessee, serving throughout the War of 1812, until his death in 1815. In the United States Capitol building there is a statue of John Sevier representing the state of Tennessee.

Throughout his political career he was always remembered as a military hero at the Battle of King's Mountain. He was so well-beloved in his time that crowds would turn out and line the roads when people heard he was traveling through their communities. He was nicknamed "Chucky Jack" from his days of living on the Nolichucky River. He was a leader of men, charmingly polite to women, honest as the day is long, and his impulses of generosity toward those in need prevented him from ever becoming truly wealthy.

Visitors to Knoxville, Tennessee, can view the monuments to John Sevier and his wife Catharine that stand over their graves on the lawn of the old county courthouse. There is also a monument to the memory of John's first wife, Sarah, although her hidden grave is still undisturbed on some lovely hill miles and miles away. Five miles south of Knoxville, visitors can tour the buildings and grounds of the Governor John Sevier Home called Marble Springs, where some of his worldly goods are still on display.

Whether you read this book to learn more about the people portrayed in it, or you just love a good historical novel, it is the wish of the author that every reader may be blessed by the same Divine Providence that guided and directed the life of Bonny Kate. The fact that she believed in Providence and often affirmed her faith and trust in it is absolutely true!

Index of Characters

Bonny Kate's Honeymoon is set in a large community of historical characters who played significant roles in the American Revolution in the southern states, from Virginia to Georgia. There may be times when the crowd becomes overwhelming and you might become confused about who is who. This index of characters is provided as a quick reference to clear up the confusion whenever needed. The immediate household of John Sevier comes first with only Sarah's children included. Bonny Kate's children were not yet in the world during *Bonny Kate's Honeymoon*. The remaining historical characters follow, listed alphabetically.

Catharine "Bonny Kate" Sherrill Sevier, our heroine was born August 3, 1754 at Sherrill's Ford, North Carolina. She was the third child and middle daughter of Sam and Mary Sherrill. In 1776 her family moved west for better opportunities in a country that was uncontrollably careening toward war. They arrived at Watauga Fort the day before the surprise attack of the Cherokees that involved the western settlers in the Revolutionary War. Kate was searching for a stray cow outside the fort when the attack came and she had to run for her life. The help she received getting into the fort over the wall resulted in an introduction to Lieutenant John Sevier, a man she would marry four years later. She and John had eight children, while she assisted her husband in a legendary political and military career that has fascinated historians and story-tellers for over two hundred years. She died October 7, 1836 at the age of 82 and is buried beside her husband on the lawn of the old Knoxville Courthouse.

John Sevier, the hero of this story was born September 23, 1745 and was thirty-five years old at the time of the Battle of King's Mountain. He won 35 battles in his military career and never lost, rising to the rank of Brigadier General. He was a representative in the North Carolina State Assembly, and member of the House of Representatives of the first U.S. Congress from the Western District of North Carolina. He was elected the first and only Governor of the State of Franklin, six-term Governor of the State of Tennessee, and went back to the House of Representatives for the 12th, 13th, and 14th sessions of Congress representing Tennessee, and served on many committees and commissions throughout his political career. He had just been elected to Congress again when he died in 1815, at the age of 70 while helping to define the boundary between the State of Georgia and the Creek Indian Nation. Marrying at the age of sixteen, he had 10 children with his first wife Sarah Hawkins Sevier, and eight children with Bonny Kate Sherrill Sevier.

Sarah Hawkins Sevier was John's first wife who married at the age of 15 and died in January, 1780 at the age of 33 shortly after giving birth to their tenth child. Sarah was a main character in the author's first book about Bonny Kate, and her influence on the community was far-reaching as a relationship builder and matchmaker. Her sisters and female cousins married influential and prominent men of accomplishment who founded many important families.

The children of John and Sarah Sevier:

Joseph Sevier, born March 17, 1763 was probably named for his mother's father Joseph Hawkins. Joseph was 18 years old when he fought at King's Mountain. Family records often confuse him with his uncle Joseph Sevier who was approximately the same age. Tradition holds that Mary Finley of the King's Mountain neighborhood was Joseph's first wife.

James Sevier was born October 25, 1764 so he was a month shy of his sixteenth birthday when the over-mountain men gathered for muster at Sycamore Shoals. His strong desire to go on the campaign led him to persuade his new step-mother Bonny Kate to speak up in favor of letting him go. It is a fact that he did not attend the wedding of John and Bonny Kate and had a long discussion with his father at home the morning before the wedding. He never revealed what was discussed.

John Sevier Jr. was born June 20, 1766. He was 14 when his father and two elder brothers went to King's Mountain. He was the man of the house while they were gone and no doubt was very useful to Bonny Kate.

Elizabeth Sevier was born in 1768 and was twelve years old when her mother died. She went by the name Betsy and as the oldest girl in John Sevier's household, she shouldered much responsibility for the care and nurture of her younger brothers and sisters. As we might imagine she was very much in favor of her father's remarriage and readily welcomed Bonny Kate as her new stepmother.

Sarah Hawkins Sevier was born in July of 1770 and obviously named after her mother. As a child she was nicknamed "Dolly" to prevent confusion with her mother.

Mary Ann Sevier was born in 1772 and was about eight years old when her mother died. In the first Bonny Kate book, the dramatic scene of Sarah Sevier's funeral at midnight, in a thunderstorm, on a lonely hill outside Fort Nolichucky in January, 1780, is preserved from the remembrances of Mary Ann Sevier.

Valentine Sevier was born in 1773, the last of John Sevier's children to be born in Virginia. That same year they moved into their new home at Holly Bottom, in the Cawood community on the South Fork of the Holston River, arriving on Christmas Eve. He was named for John's father.

Richard Sevier, known by the nickname Dicky, was born in 1775 the same year as the Transylvania land purchase. At the time of King's Mountain, Dicky was a cute little five-year-old.

Rebecca Sevier was born in 1778 on her father's Watauga farm across from where Stony Creek enters the Watauga River. She was two years old when her mother died.

Nancy Sevier, born 1780, was an infant at the time of her mother's death. Stepmother Bonny Kate was the only mother she could ever remember.

The remaining characters are presented alphabetically by last name for easy reference.

John Adair was the land office entry taker. He collected the land filing fees and transmitted the funds to the state treasury. He allowed a grant to be made of the funds in his possession to pay the expenses of the campaign. His speech in the story is a direct quote as he justifies the use of the money to preserve the state's liberty. Mr. Adair and his son enlisted in the King's Mountain campaign.

Abram of Chilhowie was the Cherokee chief who figured prominently in the national council and led the warriors in the three-week siege of Watauga Fort that began July 21, 1776. This was the surprise attack where Bonny Kate Sherrill first met John Sevier.

Attakullakulla, often called the **Little Carpenter** for his statecraft skills in putting together treaty agreements, was the principal chief of the Cherokees, and advocated for peace with the white settlers. His death in 1780 destabilized the Cherokee council allowing the British agents to push the younger chiefs into war against the white settlers who supported the cause of American independence.

Waightstill Avery was an attorney of the Washington County Court. He is known for surviving a duel with a hot-tempered young lawyer named Andrew Jackson.

Andrew Barry was a member of Major Chronicle's group of South Fork Boys from Lincoln County, N.C. He helped the wounded Robert Henry get home and they spread the news about the great victory of the Blue Hen's Chickens. Their version of the battle reached Cornwallis and prompted him to withdraw from North Carolina and reassess his invasion plans.

Isaac Baldwin was a convicted Tory prisoner next in line to be hanged during the early morning hours of October 14th at Bickerstaff's Plantation. His younger brother in a demonstration of much emotional grief cut him loose with a concealed knife and together they escaped as Sevier and Shelby stopped the hangings. Baldwin was killed two weeks later when McDowell's scouts discovered his hiding place near his home in Burke County.

Aaron Bickerstaff was a Tory officer killed at King's Mountain. The American army camped on his plantation the evening of October 13th and conducted a trial of the most notorious Tory captives and hanged nine of them. After the Americans left the morning of the 15th, the widow **Martha Bickerstaff** had her servants cut down the bodies and provided proper burials.

Daniel Boone was a leader in the settlement of Kentucky. When Indians attacked his family on their way out to Kentucky, killing one of his sons, they withdrew to the Watauga Settlement and spent the crop year of 1774 there, as the neighbors of the Robertsons, the Carters and the Valentine Seviers. That year John Sevier lived at Holly Bottom on the South Fork of the Holston River some 20 miles away. Many of the earliest Watauga settlers knew Boone as a hunting companion and expert woodsman.

Lieutenant Reece Bowen was a Virginia officer serving under William Campbell. He refused to take cover and bravely faced the enemy muskets giving his life for his country.

Grace Bowman, the former Miss Grizelle Greenlee, was the widow of Captain John Bowman, killed at the battle of Ramsour's Mill, June 20, 1780. She and her little girl were taken under the protection of her husband's cousin, Charles McDowell, who escaped the invasion of Ferguson's army by crossing the mountains to the valley of the Watauga. There Mrs. Bowman became the houseguest of Bonny Kate Sevier.

Colonel Thomas Brandon was a South Carolina leader serving under General James Williams.

John Broddy was the serving man of Colonel William Campbell, who bore a striking resemblance to his employer in stature and dress.

Captain Jacob Brown was John Sevier's good friend and the man who bought tens of thousands of acres from the chiefs of the Cherokees. He was an early player in the real estate game and was responsible for opening up settlement along the Nolichucky River. His wife was **Ruth Gordon Brown.**

John Brown was one of the three men from Sevier's regiment killed at King's Mountain and buried on the field.

Colonel Thomas Brown was the Tory leader in Georgia who stubbornly resisted Elijah Clarke's siege on Augusta. Colonel Brown used the depot at Augusta to supply the Chickamauga and Creek Indians with firearms and ammunition for raids on the homes of white western settlers.

Colonel Arthur Campbell was Colonel William Campbell's cousin. He brought 200 Virginians to Sycamore Shoals to double the size of the Virginia Army for the King's Mountain campaign. Arthur then returned to Virginia in command of the Virginia home guard.

Lt. Colonel Richard Campbell was the husband of Sarah Sevier's sister Rebecca Hawkins Campbell. He appears in the story with General Greene at the Charlotte Tavern where he recognizes his nephew Joseph Sevier.

Colonel William Campbell was the leader of the Virginia militia who agreed to join forces with Sevier and Shelby, and ended up as the elected commander-in-chief of the expedition. His wife Betty was the sister of Governor Patrick Henry of Virginia. Campbell's efforts as commander were truly heroic when one considers the intense rivalries and bitter conflicts of all the colonels and generals who, for various reasons, coveted the command of the assembled forces.

Major William Candler of Georgia was one of Elijah Clarke's most able officers. When he and Colonel Clarke heard about the campaign to catch Ferguson, Candler led a company of thirty men to find and assist Colonel Sevier in any way they could.

John Carter was a businessman and merchant who led the early settlement of the Watauga Valley as the Chairman of the Watauga Association, first Colonel of Washington County, and County Judge. He delegated all military matters to his talented Lieutenant Colonel John Sevier. When the King's Mountain campaign was organized the Washington County political and military structure put Lieutenant Colonel Sevier at a disadvantage in rank to the full colonels representing the other counties. On the home front Colonel Carter had the challenging task of dealing with Bonny Kate Sevier every time a community emergency came up. **Elizabeth Taylor Carter**, the judge's wife, liked and admired Bonny Kate Sevier dating back to the days of the siege of Watauga Fort.

Lt. Landon Carter was a heroic and active young man in John Sevier's command. He was the son of Judge Carter, and one of Sevier's closest friends. Landon's talent for leadership on the campaign resulted in his promotion to captain in a military career that eventually would make him a general.

Richard Caswell was the governor of North Carolina in the early months of 1780. He was the one who called up the Washington County troops for the summer campaign that culminated in the victory at Musgrove's Mill. At the time of the King's Mountain Campaign Abner Nash was governor. John Sevier met Richard Caswell as early as the 1775 Transylvania land purchase and became close friends with a common interest in developing western lands. The Caswell family stayed with the Seviers for several months as refugees in the summer of 1781.

Sam Chambers was the young man who deserted the army with James Crawford to betray the intentions of the over-mountain men to Major Patrick Ferguson. John Sevier saved his life after the battle, took him home, and secured a pardon for him.

Major William Chronicle was the leader of a Lincoln County mounted ranger unit. He had been intercepting the British courier traffic between Ferguson and Cornwallis, and was certain that Ferguson would move east when threatened by the army of over-mountain men. Chronicle and his friends had used King's Mountain as a hunting camp and knew the lay of the land very well. He became very valuable as a guide to Sevier, Shelby and Campbell in the final hours of the march. When Colonel Graham was called away to attend his sick wife, Major Chronicle was promoted over Lt. Colonel Hambright to the leadership of the Lincoln County militia, a position at the head of the column that brought him into the crosshairs of a Tory sharpshooter. The circumstances of Major Chronicle's merit and usefulness make his heroic death all the more tragic.

John Clark was the Georgia soldier who fell in love with Plum Grove Plantation and purchased it from the Seviers. In 1790 John Clark returned to Georgia and sold Plum Grove back to John and Bonny Kate.

Colonel Elijah Clarke of Wilkes County, Georgia, volunteered his services in resisting the British invasion of the southern states. He served in the Carolinas with Colonel Charles McDowell in the summer campaign, attempted to retake Augusta, Georgia in September, and when that failed, retreated north with all his men and their families. His movements drew the attention of British Major Ferguson who sent all his scouts to the southwest hoping to intercept the Clarke party. This allowed the over-mountain men to approach Ferguson from the north undetected. Elijah Clarke arrived with his seven hundred refugees at Bonny Kate's door and taxed her resources severely to provide for the sick, wounded and starving. After John Sevier returned from King's Mountain, Elijah Clarke went on a campaign to South Carolina where he was wounded. He returned to Plum Grove to recover, but Sevier was mounting a campaign against the Cherokees, and Clarke went along despite his wound. After the Indian campaign, Colonel Clarke took his men back to Georgia and stayed in service until Georgia was liberated. Eventually Elijah Clarke became the governor of Georgia. He always appreciated Bonny Kate's hospitality and became a very good and useful friend of John Sevier.

Hannah Clarke was the wife of Elijah Clarke. She became Bonny Kate's houseguest for at least six months as her husband returned to active duty.

Colonel Benjamin Cleveland was the 250-pound jolly giant who kept things lively in camp. He was fond of practical jokes, gaming, eating, and drinking, but when it came to fighting Tories he was all business. Cleveland had spent some time in the over-mountain country in the early years and had traveled to the Cherokee towns to recover some stolen horses. He knew Daniel Boone, James Robertson, the Shelbys, and John Sevier from those experiences. He settled in Wilkes County, North Carolina and called his farm Round About because the Yadkin River formed a horseshoe nearly surrounding his home place. His soldiers applied the name to their Colonel because of his great girth.

Lt. Larkin Cleveland was Benjamin Cleveland's brother who was wounded by Tory snipers on the way from Wilkes County to Quaker Meadows.

Captain William Cocke was an important figure on the frontier, but known better as a lawyer and politician than a military leader. From Sullivan County, he went with Colonel Isaac Shelby on the summer campaign, but not to King's Mountain.

Lord Charles Cornwallis was the British commander-in-chief in the southern campaign to retake the colonies of Georgia, South Carolina, North Carolina, and Virginia. King's Mountain cost him a third of his army and the talented Patrick Ferguson, then Colonel Tarleton lost a major battle to General Daniel Morgan at

Cowpens the following January. Finally, Cornwallis faced Nathaniel Greene at the Battle of Guilford Courthouse in North Carolina, March of 1781 and although he held the field at the end of the day, the cost was too great to repeat, so he retreated to Wilmington, N.C. Seven months later his army was trapped by the French navy, and the American army at Yorktown, Virginia and Cornwallis was forced to surrender.

Dr. James Cozby was the western doctor who was John Sevier's steadfast friend. He went along on almost every military campaign that Sevier led. Dr. Cozby married one of the Hawkins girls; a sister to Davy Crockett's mother and they were Sarah Sevier's cousins.

James Crawford was the man who deserted the army with Sam Chambers to betray the intentions of the over-mountain men to Major Patrick Ferguson. John Sevier saved his life after the battle, took him home, and secured a pardon for him.

John Crockett was a young man who had seen great personal tragedy when his parents and most of their children were massacred by Indians in the year 1777. Young John married Sarah Sevier's cousin, Rebecca Hawkins, and they were the parents of the famous frontiersman, Davy Crockett. John Crockett did indeed go on the King's Mountain campaign, probably serving under Isaac Shelby.

General William Lee Davidson was the commander of western North Carolina militia units, headquartered at Salisbury, N.C. When Sevier and Shelby were trying to solve the command problem they requested either General Davidson, or the Virginian Daniel Morgan to lead them. They had no respect for the Continental Army General Horatio Gates who had blundered so badly at the Battle of Camden.

Captain Abraham DePeyster was the second in command under Patrick Ferguson. He survived the battle and did his best to prevent the mistreatment of the Tory prisoners. After the war he corresponded with former enemy John Sevier and expressed his respect and friendship.

David Dickey was the South Fork soldier who reluctantly escorted Colonel William Graham home to his stricken wife. They left just minutes before the battle began. When the sounds of battle reached their ears Colonel Graham changed his mind and returned to the battle arriving in the final moments of the contest.

Reverend Samuel Doak was the minister of Salem Presbyterian Church which was, and still is, in Washington County about eight miles southwest of Jonesborough. He was a good friend of John Sevier and gave a moving sermon and prayer the morning of the march of the over-mountain men from Sycamore Shoals. His wife was **Esther Montgomery Doak**. At the time of King's Mountain they had a daughter Julia, and a son John Whitfield Doak. The burning of the Doak family cabin and Esther's escape with her infant son was a true historical event, but the novelist has no source that says it happened in October of 1780 or that Bonny Kate Sevier happened to drop by that morning.

Dragging Canoe was the Cherokee chief who broke away from the main branch of the Cherokees and started his own tribe on Chickamauga Creek near Chattanooga. The Watauga settlers had a hard time punishing the war-like Chickamaugas because they had to cross the territory of the peaceful Cherokees to get at them, whereas the Chickamaugas made regular raids on the settlers of the Watauga and Nolichucky Valleys. British agents supplied Dragging Canoe's people with munitions and supplies to encourage frontier war that they believed would hurt the American ability to continue the revolution. Paradoxically, the American frontiersmen got so good at "Indian play," that they employed it against Ferguson and won.

Jacob Dyckes was a Tory partisan living in Washington County. He cooperated with eastern Tories and the Tories working from Indian Territory to steal horses and create a state of lawless anarchy that they hoped would defeat the cause of American Independence. The goal was generous land grants that would become theirs when the King of England took back his American colonies. It is a true story that Bonny Kate's generosity to her friend **Mary Dyckes**, the wife of Jacob, resulted in the discovery of a plot to kill John Sevier. Bonny Kate's quick action to notify him of the danger saved her husband's life.

Captain William Edmondson was a Virginia officer and a close friend of Colonel William Campbell. It is true that Campbell was present with his dying friend when the battle ended in such great confusion.

Moses Embree was a Quaker industrial engineer who had the skills to build water-powered mills, forges, mines, and well-built houses.

Thomas Embree was the son of Moses Embree, and he was also very adept at building the industrial structures necessary to develop the community. The Quakers did not believe in war or slavery, and the Embrees of the next generation took up the cause to abolish slavery.

Hugh Erwin was a member of Major Chronicle's group of South Fork Boys from Lincoln County, N.C. He helped the wounded Robert Henry get home and they spread the news about the great victory of the Blue Hen's Chickens. Their version of the battle reached Cornwallis and prompted him to withdraw from North Carolina and reassess his invasion plans.

Major Patrick Ferguson was the British commander of the western wing of Cornwallis' invading army. The short, red-headed Scotsman was a professional soldier given the difficult task of recruiting, equipping, and training American Tory militias in the foothills and mountains of South Carolina and North Carolina. He was an expert marksman and invented the rapid-fire, breech-loading Ferguson rifle, which he demonstrated to the Royal military establishment in England but could not generate enough interest to authorize its adoption into the service. He served in the northern theatre of the American war at the Battle of Brandywine in 1777 where he was seriously wounded and lost the use of his right arm. He fought at Monmouth in 1778 and was stationed in New York until 1779 when Sir Henry Clinton sent him with Cornwallis on the campaign to recover the southern colonies. Savannah, Georgia was taken in 1779, Charleston was taken in June of 1780 and Cornwallis drove north through South Carolina during the summer months. The British underestimated the resolve of freedom loving men willing to fight for their liberties, and overestimated the ability of the Tories to support and assist the British invasion. Major Ferguson's threats to invade the over-mountain country, hang their leaders, and lay waste their land with fire and sword backfired with disastrous results. The leaders he threatened in the persons of Sevier, Shelby, and Campbell were men of heroic action and could not be bullied into submission. They rapidly mobilized a thousand mounted riflemen and pursued Ferguson's army to King's Mountain where they caught up with him on October 7, 1780.

Captain Benjamin Few was a Georgia Whig leader whom we find as captain of the watch at Plum Grove the morning after their arrival at Bonny Kate's. The novelist has no source that says Captain Few accompanied Elijah Clarke to the Nolichucky Valley, but Captain Few was known to the writer from another research project.

John Finley lived in a cabin close to King's Mountain with his wife **Anne Miller Finley** and seventeen-year-old daughter **Mary Finley**. Robert Sevier was taken to the Finley home after the battle for the treatment of his wound. Apparently Mary Finley and Joseph Sevier, the son of John Sevier, developed a relationship and fourteen months later they married.

General Horatio Gates was made the American commander of the southern division of the Continental Army in 1780. He was considered one of the most experienced generals available in the service. Congress appointed General Gates and in his first engagement blundered into Lord Cornwallis' army near Camden, South Carolina in the wee hours of August 16th. At daylight the two armies fought a decisive battle disastrous to the Americans. General Gates abandoned his army and escaped the field of battle on his horse so rapidly that those who observed his behavior were shocked and disgusted. Gates had ruined his reputation in the south, and in Congress. He was replaced by General Nathaniel Greene in December of the same year.

John Gilleland of Sevier's regiment was already seriously wounded when he saw Major Ferguson and two others galloping toward his position. He tried to shoot but his rifle misfired. He pointed out Ferguson to Robert Young who took the shot that helped bring the enemy leader down.

Enoch Gilmer was a very talented Lincoln County scout who worked for Major William Chronicle. He could speak and act like a Tory and express a range of emotions that could convince anyone of his sincerity. He gathered much useful information during the final push to catch Ferguson. He sang the ballad "Barney Lynn" to signal all clear at the crossing of the Broad River.

Colonel William Graham was the Colonel of Lincoln County, N.C. who received word that his wife was stricken with a possibly fatal colic, which in reality proved to be childbirth. Colonel Graham rode for home immediately, accompanied by young David Dickey. When some distance away they heard the sounds of battle, Colonel Graham changed his mind, and returned to King's Mountain. He charged up the slope in the final minutes of the contest waving his sword and shouting, "Damn the Tories!" That evening Mrs. Graham gave birth to a healthy little girl she named Sarah.

General Nathaniel Greene was a talented officer of George Washington's inner circle. He was a Quaker from Rhode Island, who had educated himself from books and built a successful business. He met Washington at Boston in 1775 and proved his value as Quartermaster of the Continental army. Greene always yearned for an operational command and finally got his chance when he was selected by Washington to take over the southern command from General Gates. General Greene was respectful of militia colonels and thought highly of Sevier, Shelby, and Campbell. In the fall of 1781, Sevier and Shelby joined General Greene in South Carolina to push the British back into Charleston.

Joseph Greer was the seven-foot-tall scout who worked for John Sevier. He was the son of Indian trader Andrew Greer. Sevier sent Joseph Greer to give a report on the Battle of King's Mountain to Congress so they could receive the unvarnished truth. He chose the impressive young Greer to display the physical prowess representative of the over-mountain soldier. George Washington was certainly impressed.

Lieutenant Colonel Fredrick Hambright was born in Germany, came to America at the age of eleven and was an early settler in Lincoln County, North Carolina. He served in General Rutherford's western campaign in 1776, in the defense of Charleston in 1779, with Colonel McDowell in the summer campaign of 1780, and under Colonel William Graham at King's Mountain. In the battle he received a thigh wound and although his boot filled with blood he stayed in the saddle and fought on bravely until the surrender. He recovered and lived until his ninetieth year.

Alexander Hamilton was a brilliant young continental soldier who rose rapidly to the rank of colonel serving on Washington's staff. We met him in the halls of Congress when Joseph Greer arrived to give his report on the Battle of King's Mountain. Hamilton later became Washington's Secretary of the Treasury, and established the New York Stock Exchange and the Bond Market.

Colonel Andrew Hampton commanded the troops of Rutherford County, North Carolina at the Battle of King's Mountain. He lost his son Noah in a cavalry charge by British Major Dunlap into the camp at North Pacolet River at dawn July 15, 1780. This event from the summer campaign embittered Andrew Hampton against Charles McDowell who had posted the pickets too close to camp. After that incident, cooperation between the two colonels was impossible.

Jonathan Hampton was a son of Colonel Andrew Hampton and served as a scout on the King's Mountain Campaign. He found out that Ferguson was sending patrols to the southwest in an attempt to catch Elijah Clarke's party of refugees from Georgia. He reported his findings to the over-mountain officers at Gilbert Town.

Noah Hampton was the son of Colonel Andrew Hampton. He was killed in a fight on the North Pacolet River about the middle of July, 1780, when British dragoons under Major Dunlap rushed the American camp at dawn.

Major Samuel Hammond was one of General James Williams' men who urged the General to join the over-mountain men to defeat Ferguson.

Lieutenant Colonel James Hawthorn was a South Carolina officer who, on the day of battle, took over for Colonel William Hill who was still recovering from a shoulder wound. Colonel Hill stayed back with the foot soldiers when the army rode out from Cowpens.

Nan Henderson was the part-Cherokee beauty who attached herself to Jacob Brown as an interpreter when he first traveled out to the west. She assisted him in arranging two extensive land purchases, and was bequeathed a farm in Mr. Brown's last will and testament. Ruth Brown and her children took the case to court to prevent Miss Henderson from keeping the farm.

Richard Henderson was a North Carolina judge and land speculator who put together the Transylvania Land Company and bought large tracts of Kentucky land from the Indians in 1775. Daniel Boone, Isaac Shelby, James Robertson, Charles Robertson, and John Sevier all had connections with Judge Henderson in the business of western lands.

Robert Henry was a member of Major Chronicle's group of South Fork Boys from Lincoln County, N.C. He received a bayonet wound through his hand and into his leg. After the battle he was taken to his mother's home about twenty miles north of King's Mountain. With his friends, Andrew Barry and Hugh Ervin, they spread the news about the great victory of the Blue Hen's Chickens. Their version of the battle reached Cornwallis and prompted him to withdraw from North Carolina and reassess his invasion plans.

Major Joseph Herndon of Colonel Cleveland's regiment was left in command of the foot-soldiers. His orders were to bring them forward as rapidly as possible to support the 910 horse soldiers who rode to King's Mountain. The army was reunited in camp on the Broad River the day after the battle.

Colonel William Hill was one of Colonel Thomas Sumter's South Carolina men who with Colonel Edward Lacey resisted the efforts of General James Williams to take over their army to attack Fort Ninety Six. Hill was suffering from a shoulder wound from an earlier battle, so he turned over his command to Lt. Colonel James Hawthorn who led the unit at King's Mountain.

Samuel Huntington was the president of Congress at the time young Joseph Greer burst into Independence Hall and gave his report about the great victory at King's Mountain.

Captain Shadrack Inman was the heroic Georgia trooper who came up with the idea to draw the British into an ambush at the Battle of Musgrove's Mill. In the rout of the enemy that followed Captain Inman was shot and killed.

Colonel Alexander Innes was the ranking Tory commander at the Battle of Musgrove's Mill. Although badly wounded he avoided being taken prisoner, and recovered to continue in the service of the king.

Francis Jones was the courier from Charles McDowell who arrived after the Battle of Musgrove's Mill with the news that General Gates had suffered a disaster at Camden, SC.

Dr. Uzal Johnson was the army doctor who served under Major Ferguson and had so much work to do after the battle.

Joseph Kerr was the crippled spy serving Colonel James Williams who brought in definite news about Ferguson's location during the officers' meeting at Cowpens the evening of October 6th.

David Knox was a prisoner at Cornwallis' headquarters in Charlotte, N.C. who crowed like a rooster at the news that a powerful American army called the Blue Hens Chickens had wiped out Ferguson's command.

Colonel Edward Lacey of Thomas Sumter's South Carolina regiment was famous for his midnight ride to find the over-mountain men. He and William Hill suspected Colonel James Williams of trying to hijack the mountaineers for an attack on Fort Ninety Six in upland South Carolina. Lacey rode all night to intercept Campbell, Shelby and Sevier at Green River and redirect their course to the east making it possible for them to catch Patrick Ferguson's army.

Captain William Lenoir was from Wilkes County. He went west in 1776 on General Rutherford's campaign and served several months on the frontier until the peace treaty was made in 1777. His wife was Anne Ballard. On the King's Mountain campaign he commanded a company of foot soldiers serving under Colonel Cleveland. He left his company at Cowpens and rode to glory in the company of Major Joseph Winston. During the all-night, rain-soaked ride to catch Ferguson he voiced a wish to God Almighty that the rain would stop and it stopped immediately. Then he witnessed the mysterious officer on the white horse, directing Winston's unit to the proper place in line to complete the encirclement of the enemy. Captain Lenoir arrived in time to witness the death of Major Chronicle and help rally the Lincoln County men to press the attack. Captain Lenoir was wounded twice, but lived to write about the miracles he witnessed, and to serve his state and his country for many years.

General Alexander Leslie was the British commander of the Virginia invasion force which landed from naval warships to meet and resupply Lord Cornwallis after the conquest of the Carolinas. Together they would capture Virginia and move north to take on the rest of the continental army. The grand scheme stalled at King's Mountain, suffered another setback at Cowpens and was abandoned after Guilford Courthouse.

Michael Mahoney was one of the three men from Sevier's regiment killed at King's Mountain and buried on the field.

Captain Casper Mansker, an early long-hunter and pioneer station builder from the Cumberland settlement makes his appearance to pick up a shipment of powder and shot that Bonny Kate has donated to save Fort Nashborough.

Major Joseph Martin was a Virginia officer who also had an officer's position in Sullivan County, North Carolina. He was married to Nancy Ward's daughter Betsy Martin and served as Virginia's State Commissioner to the Cherokee nation.

Captain John Mattocks of Lincoln County was killed in the first moments of battle near his friend and hunting buddy, William Chronicle.

Colonel Charles McDowell of Burke County was one of the greatest organizers and strategic planners of his day. He gathered resources, assembled men, invited colonels from every county to join the campaign and used his influence with the governor to sanction the efforts. The western men considered his methodical strategic approach too slow to deal with the dual threats of Indian attacks in the west and Ferguson's insolence in the east. At Shelby's insistence, Sevier arranged a smooth transition from Colonel McDowell's leadership to a more active, tactical, and unconventional approach for dealing with Major Ferguson.

Major Joseph McDowell was Colonel Charles McDowell's brother. "Fighting Joe" had all the quickness and tactical common sense that his strategic brother lacked. Joseph McDowell understood the necessity for a change of command, and led the Burke County troops to glory at King's Mountain.

Mrs. McDowell was the mother of Charles and Joseph McDowell. She bravely stayed at Quaker Meadows and suffered the occupation and use of her home as Ferguson's headquarters in September of 1780. The Tory officers bragged about the success of their invasion and threatened her with ghastly punishments to her sons as soon as they could be apprehended. Mrs. McDowell had the pleasure of hosting those same Tory officers a month later as defeated, and humbled prisoners of war.

John McCrosky, a Virginia soldier, brought news of the surrender of the Tories to Colonel Campbell where he was attending his mortally wounded friend Captain Edmondson.

John Miller was the blacksmith who settled near the Shelving Rock on the main path to North Carolina. The over-mountain men camped near his place the first night of the march. He re-shoed their horses and also volunteered to go on the campaign.

Little is known about the real John Miller, but the novelist has greatly expanded his character in both Bonny Kate books for the purposes of entertainment.

Captain Samuel Moore was at the Battle of Musgrove's Mill. He led a dozen men upstream to Head's Ford and crossed to get behind the enemy. Moore's charge into the enemy camp panicked the Tories who abandoned their equipment and ran toward the safety of Fort Ninety Six. Captain Moore destroyed the Tory camp before rejoining Colonel Shelby across the river.

William Moore was a Virginia private soldier who was badly wounded at King's Mountain and lost his leg to amputation. The story of Mrs. Moore going to fetch her husband home is true. Her first name could not be determined from the novelist's resources so he called her character **Elizabeth "Lizzy" Moore**. The novelist also blended two other traditions not supported by historical documentation; that of Joseph Sevier's desire to return to Mary Finley, and John Sherrill's claim that he went to King's Mountain and was wounded there. Mr. and Mrs. Moore survived the hard trip home and lived to build a large family of descendants.

General Daniel Morgan was a respected leader of Virginia riflemen with vast experience in the French and Indian War and in the northern phase of the American Revolution. His heroic actions at Saratoga, and Quebec are well remembered but his victory at Cowpens on January 17, 1781 was his crowning achievement. There his 900 men defeated 1200 Tories including the hard charging dragoons of Colonel Banastre Tarleton.

Patrick Murphey was one of Sevier's soldiers who was wounded at King's Mountain but survived.

Lewis Musick was the Georgia scout who went with Anthony Twitty into Ferguson's camp to get the scouting report for Shelby and Sevier. The capture of Ferguson's cook was a true incident.

Governor Abner Nash was the governor of North Carolina at the time of the Battle of King's Mountain. The state capital was at Hillsborough where General Horatio Gates and South Carolina Governor John Rutledge had taken refuge as well. Nash's predecessor was Richard Caswell, John Sevier's friend.

Oconostota was the aging war chief of the main branch of the Cherokee nation. When peace was arranged with the white settlers in 1777, Oconostota had a hard time keeping the younger chiefs from aligning with the break-away warriors of Chickamauga. When the principal Chief Attakullakulla died in the summer of 1780, Oconostota and Nancy Ward found themselves without sufficient political support to prevent war with the white Americans.

Mary Patton was the owner and operator of the gunpowder mill on Powder Creek. She had learned the trade from her father and was apparently very good at it. The widow Patton supplied the King's Mountain expedition as well as all John Sevier's

Indian campaigns.

Virginia Paul was one of two red-headed camp ladies that worked for Patrick Ferguson. She survived the King's Mountain battle, but the emotional shock of so much death and suffering overwhelmed her. She marched away with the prisoners into North Carolina, eventually was released and made her way back to British headquarters.

Harmon Perryman was one of the three men left behind at John Finley's cabin by Colonel Sevier to take care of Captain Robert Sevier. At Robert's insistence they attempted to travel home without the operation and rest prescribed by Ferguson's physician, Dr. Uzal Johnson.

Sam Phillips was a cousin of Isaac Shelby who was captured by Major Ferguson in the summer of 1780. The British paroled him to carry the threatening letter from Ferguson to the leaders of the west that motivated the over-mountain men to action.

William Rabb was one of Major William Chronicle's men who like his commander, was shot down in the beginning moments of the battle.

Lord Rawdon was the British second in command to Lord Cornwallis. He served as both a staff officer and also commanded troops in the field detached for special duty.

Major Reives is "Sevier" spelled backwards. The novelist made up the name to explain the apparent historical discrepancy found in the King's Mountain muster list in the book by Pat Alderman. The list of officers has two separate entries for Valentine Sevier; one is a major and the other is a captain. We know that John's brother Val was the captain, but who could have been the Major Valentine Sevier? Despite no family tradition of the father's participation, we believe that the seventy-seven-year-old strong and healthy "Big Val" did indeed go along at least as far as the foot soldiers went, and as a former general store owner and tavern keeper would have provided valuable services in the commissary of the over-mountain army.

Major Charles Robertson was an original member of the Watauga Association and served as the principal land trustee for the Watauga purchase. He would collect the fees and issue the deeds on all original land claims. He also served as the next in command to Colonel John Sevier. He was the uncle of James Robertson a main character during the siege of Watauga Fort. His wife was **Susannah Cunningham Robertson** and their daughter Kesiah married Robert Sevier.

James Robertson was an important leader of the Watauga Settlement and by 1780 he was establishing a settlement on the Cumberland River called Fort Nashborough. His wife was **Charlotte Reeves Robertson**. Bonny Kate is asked to help save Fort Nashborough and commits to sending all their available gun powder and lead shot.

William Robertson was one of the men John Sevier left at John Finley's cabin to care for his brother Captain Robert Sevier. This William Robertson might have been the brother of Kesiah Robertson Sevier.

Captain George Russell was just a lieutenant at the battle of King's Mountain, but his meritorious service earned him a promotion and he commanded the company that Colonel Sevier detached for a "long patrol" back to Sycamore Shoals. Russell's company would help reinforce the frontier stations and spread the news of the success at King's Mountain.

Governor John Rutledge of South Carolina continued to run his state from Hillsborough, the capital of North Carolina. He commissioned James Williams a general upon receiving the report of the Battle of Musgrove's Mill, the only good news they had all year until King's Mountain.

Virginia Sal was one of two red-headed camp ladies that worked for Patrick Ferguson. She died at King's Mountain, killed by gunfire, while rushing to assist the wounded. As tradition tells us, she was buried with Patrick Ferguson in a shared grave.

Abraham Sevier was a younger brother of John Sevier who also went on the King's Mountain campaign. Born February 14, 1760, he had a distinguished military service record as a scout and private soldier on many campaigns. He married Mary Little and had ten children.

Joseph Sevier I was a younger brother of John Sevier who was about the same age as John's son Joseph II, causing much confusion for family history researchers. Brother Joseph, intelligent and capable, was always very helpful to members of his family. He cared for his wounded brother Captain Robert on the battlefield of King's Mountain. He married Charity Elizabeth Cawood, the daughter of John Cawood of the South Fork of the Holston and had several children.

Valentine Sevier was the father of John Sevier. He brought the Sevier name to America, married a Virginia girl, Joanna Goade, and had seven children. He operated a store, a tavern, an inn and a mill in the Shenandoah Valley of Virginia. Joanna died about 1773 and "Big Val" followed his sons to the Watauga Valley. At the time of King's Mountain, he lived on the farm next to his son Valentine the Sheriff, in the area where Stony Creek runs into the Watauga. His second wife was a widow with grown children, Jemima Young Douglass Sevier. Jemima was the mother of Amy Sevier, Val the Sheriff's wife. Big Val lived to be over one hundred years old.

Valentine Sevier, the second son of Big Val Sevier was born in 1747. He was the first of the Seviers to move into the Watauga Valley and got into cattle ranching. He and his wife, Naomi "Amy" Douglass Sevier would have fourteen children, but at the time of the King's Mountain story, they only had eight: **Elizabeth** (1768), **John**, (1769), **Ann** (1771), **Valentine** (1773), **Robert** the twin (1775), **William** the twin (1775), **James** (1777), and **Jemima** (1778). Valentine was an important member of the Watauga Association, served as County Sheriff, and was captain over a company of the militia. He had an active military career and rose to the rank of colonel.

Captain Robert Sevier was the third son of Big Val Sevier and was a popular leader and a good soldier. He went with a company of Watauga men to help defend Charleston in 1776 and the patriots successfully turned back the British attack. He commanded a light horse company in patrols of Washington County to suppress Tory activity and protect against horse rustlers and Indian marauders. He married Kesiah Robertson Sevier the daughter of Charles and Susannah Cunningham Robertson and they had two sons: **Charles Sevier** (1778) and **Valentine Sevier** (1780). Captain Robert was shot in the back during the Battle of King's Mountain and disregarded the doctor's orders to get an operation to remove the bullet before traveling. He started for home on October 8, 1780 and died eight days later on the mountain trail.

Evan Shelby, Sr. was of Welsh extraction and came from western Maryland to the Holston River Valley. He was a Captain of the Virginia militia at the Battle of Point Pleasant, 1774, and advanced up to eventually become a general. His sons, Isaac, Evan Jr., and Moses all had important roles at the Battle of King's Mountain.

Major Evan Shelby, Jr. was at the top of the mountain to receive the sword of surrender from Captain DePeyster at the end of the battle. He also served at Cowpens in January, 1781 and also in central South Carolina in the fall of 1781, to confine the British to the city of Charleston.

Colonel Isaac Shelby commanded 240 men from Sullivan County which was newly created in 1779, just north of Washington County in the over-mountain country. He was one of John Sevier's best friends and was the youngest of the full colonels. He had seen service in the summer campaign under Colonel McDowell, participated in the Battle of Cedar Springs, helped in the taking of Thicketty Fort, and commanded the right wing at Musgrove's Mill. Isaac Shelby was red-headed with a temperament to match. He was impetuous, always ready for action, and had not yet learned the social arts that always pleased the ladies. In those days he had no patience for women's business. He was interested in the development of Kentucky. Eventually he would marry **Susannah Hart** the daughter of **Colonel Nathaniel Hart**, and become the first Governor of Kentucky.

Captain Moses Shelby was another son of Evan Shelby Sr. He carried messages from his brother Isaac to Colonel Campbell and others during the days of preparation for the campaign. At King's Mountain Moses was badly wounded, but he recovered in time for the Battle of Cowpens, January 17, 1781. He also helped Elijah Clarke recapture Augusta, Georgia later the same year.

Sam Sherrill was the father of Bonny Kate Sherrill Sevier. As a good friend, neighbor and father-in-law to John Sevier, Sam felt obligated to serve on the King's Mountain campaign. He also knew the lay of the land in western North Carolina up and down the Catawba River having lived at Sherrill's Ford for nearly thirty years. Sam took three of his sons, Sam Jr., Adam and George with him, and met a fourth son, Uriah who served in his uncle Capt. William Sherrill's company. **Mary Sherrill,** Sam's wife, was a supporting influence for daughter Bonny Kate who, as we have seen, had more than her fair share of responsibilities while her husband was away.

The children of **Sam and Mary Sherrill** with their birth years are as follows: **Samuel Jr.** (1748), **Susan** (1752), **Catharine "Bonny Kate"** (1754), **John** (1756), **Uriah** (1757), **Adam** (1758), **William** (1759), **Mary Jane** (1760), **George** (1762), and **Aquilla** (1778).

Adam and Elizabeth "Granny" Sherrill were Bonny Kate's grandparents who had a tremendous influence on young Kate when they all lived in Sherrill's Ford, North Carolina. They both died in the early 1770's when Kate was a teenager. After Adam Sherrill's land was willed to eldest son William, second son Samuel moved his family west to Watauga.

William Steele was one of the three men from Sevier's regiment killed at King's Mountain and buried on the field.

Colonel Thomas Sumter was the patriot military leader of South Carolina, known as the "Fighting Gamecock." He was outraged when General James Williams showed up at his camp with a general's commission from the governor, and tried to take command of his army. Sumter immediately rode to Hillsborough, N.C. where the South Carolina state officials had taken refuge. Sumter wanted to set the governor straight. Colonels William Hill and Edward Lacey were left in charge with strict orders to ignore General Williams. When Charles McDowell passed through with news of the over-mountain men hunting Ferguson, Williams, Hill and Lacey were all inspired to join the campaign. Colonel Sumter did not return from Hillsborough in time to take part in the Battle at King's Mountain, but the South Carolinians were well represented and served with great distinction.

Isaac Thomas was a merchant and trader among the Cherokees. From his travels he knew the country extremely well and had become an expert on the language, traditions and customs of his customers. He was frequently coming and going among the Cherokees and naturally collected information and carried messages back and forth.

Mathew Talbot was the grist mill operator on Gap Creek who supplied corn for the King's Mountain campaign. His son Mathew Talbot Jr. went on the campaign as a private soldier. The Talbots were early Watauga settlers who had come to the area about 1772 with James Robertson.

Colonel Banastre Tarleton was a dashing young British cavalry officer who made quite a name for himself as a fast-moving, efficient, fighter on the southern campaign under Lord Cornwallis. After Charleston was taken Colonel Abraham Buford of Virginia leading a company of foot soldiers was overtaken by Colonel Tarleton. The Virginians were in the act of surrendering to the overwhelming force when Colonel Tarleton led his saber-swinging dragoons into their ranks and massacred them without justification. The outrage over this action motivated the King's Mountain men to use

"Buford" as a watchword and "Tarleton's Quarter" as an excuse for harsh treatment of the Tory prisoners. Tarleton continued to pose a very real threat until he was defeated at Cowpens in January, 1781.

William Tatham was an Englishman who worked for Colonel John Carter in the mercantile business. He served as Clerk of the County Court when John Sevier was away campaigning. Tatham wrote about his experiences on the frontier and generally had good things to say about the people he knew. His writings, while very hard to find as published works, are great sources of early frontier history.

Isaac Taylor was the son of Andrew Taylor of Gap Creek. Isaac went on the King's Mountain Campaign and distinguished himself as a good soldier. He accompanied John Sevier on several Indian campaigns. He became a constable of Washington County in 1780. He learned the art of surveying and was made county surveyor for the newly established Greene County in 1783. He married Bonny Kate's sister, Mary Jane Sherrill in 1785 and established a farm in Greene County. His surveying business boomed, but Isaac died sometime before May of 1787.

Leroy Taylor was the husband of Bonny Kate's elder sister Susan. It's possible their marriage occurred prior to Sam Sherrill's family moving to the west. Leroy and Susan had several children and lived on a farm on the north side of the Nolichucky, close to Daisy Fields. Susan died in 1785, but Leroy distinguished himself in county government, and state government, as a great supporter of John Sevier. Leroy eventually attained the rank of Colonel in the militia.

Major Jonathan Tipton was one of John Sevier's regimental majors. He was second in command of the Washington County troops on the King's Mountain campaign.

Anthony Twitty was a South Carolina scout who went looking for Major Ferguson, found his camp, and gathered valuable information for the patriots about Ferguson's strength and his movements. He was joined by a scout from Georgia named Lewis Musick. The capture of Ferguson's cook at the Green River camp was a true incident.

Brian Ward was the South Carolina merchant who carried on a valuable trade with the Cherokees during the French and Indian War. Accused of being a spy and sentenced to death, Ward's life was spared by the intervention of Cherokee princess Nanye-hi, who held the office of "Beloved Woman" in the Cherokee nation. Ward later married her.

Nancy Ward was the Cherokee princess Nanye-hi who was the "Beloved Woman" of the Cherokee nation. She was a promoter of peace and prosperity between the white settlers and Cherokee people. She introduced weaving cloth and raising livestock to supplement gardening, hunting and fishing for the economy of the Cherokees. Her first husband was Kingfisher with whom she had two children. Kingfisher was killed in a battle against the Creek Indians. Nancy who had accompanied her husband to the battlefield took up his weapons and inspired her people to a great victory. She was made "Beloved Woman" for her valor, and the title made her the chief of the women's council. She also had a voice on the national council. Her office gave her the power to save the lives of captives, a power she used often. Her second husband was Brian Ward whose life she had saved. The Wards had two more children, both girls.

George Watkins, a patriot soldier who had served with James Williams at Musgrove's Mill was captured by Ferguson and paroled the morning of the battle. Sevier's scouts picked him up as they approached King's Mountain and he gave detailed information about the enemy's situation.

John Watts was a Cherokee chief who followed Dragging Canoe. Watts spent much of his time among the peaceful main branch of the Cherokee nation and was well known to the white leaders. Sometimes he would pretend to be a friend of the whites while sending information and warnings to the Chickamauga towns. He was as dangerous a friend, as he was an enemy.

General George Washington was the commander-in-chief of the American Continental army. He was a Virginian and greatly admired and respected by John Sevier who suggested that Washington County be named in his honor. Sevier even named his eldest son by Bonny Kate after Washington.

Daniel Williams was the young son of General James Williams who stayed at his father's side until his death from the wound he had suffered in battle.

General James Williams was a South Carolina colonel at Musgrove's Mill in chapter 2. He marched the prisoners to Hillsborough and received a promotion to general from SC Governor John Rutledge based on his exaggerated report. James Williams reappeared in chapter 24 and tried to claim the command of the over-mountain army with his general's commission, but the other officers prevented his doing so. General Williams died a hero's death on King's Mountain.

Major Joseph Winston commanded the Surry County, North Carolina troops at King's Mountain, coordinating with Colonel Benjamin Cleveland of Wilkes County. Winston had considerable experience in the west on Rutherford's 1776 expedition, and as a commissioner to the Cherokee peace talks in 1777. Winston's wife had just delivered triplets shortly before the King's Mountain campaign. Winston's assignment was to take the right wing to the far end of the mountain and complete the encirclement of the enemy, but he lost his way. With Captain William Lenoir, he experienced some sort of spiritual apparition of an unknown officer on a white horse directing them to the battle. When they did arrive at their appointed position it was exactly the right place at exactly the right time to surround and defeat the enemy. Both Winston and Lenoir always believed they had experienced a miracle.

St. Francis Xavier was born in 1506 in Navarre, a small kingdom between France and Spain. He helped to found the Order of the Jesuits and was sent to East Asia to minister to people in Japan and the East Indies. He died in 1552 while on a mission to

China and was made a saint in the Roman Catholic Church. His faith, his mission, and his charity towards others established a model for members of the Xavier family which continued after they left France for England where their name changed to Sevier.

Jean Xavier was the ancestor of the Sevier family who served as military commander for King Henry of Navarre in a war for the French throne. He wore a white plume on his hat and told his men to "follow the white plume for there will be the thickest part of the fighting and the greatest glory." This courageous behavior became an ideal for generations to follow and was certainly present in the Sevier men at King's Mountain.

Robert Young, Sr. was a neighbor with family connections to the Seviers. Robert was the brother of Jemima Young Douglass Sevier, the second wife of Valentine Sevier, John's father. Robert Young fired his rifle "Sweet Lips" and helped to bring down the enemy commander. His son **Robert Young, Jr.** also went to King's Mountain.

Bonny Kate

PUBLISHING COMPANY

Bonny Kate Publishing Company Book Order Form

More Information: Explore our website at www.bonnykate.com.

Fax orders: 1-888-822-7585. Send this order form completely filled out.

Telephone orders: Call toll-free 1-888-822-7585.

E-mail orders: Go to "Orders" page at www.bonnykate.com.

Postal orders: Bonny Kate Publishing Company
c/o Mark Strength
112 Prindle Drive
Smyrna, TN 37167 USA
Telephone: 1-888-822-7585

I wish to order the following books and materials. I understand that I may return any of them for a full refund – for any reason, no questions asked.

Bonny Kate: Pioneer Lady

Hardcover edition: Quantity: ____ x 29.95 ea.   Extended cost: _____

Paperback edition: Quantity: ____ x 19.95 ea.   Extended cost: _____

Bonny Kate's Honeymoon: Victory at King's Mountain

Hardcover edition: Quantity: ____ x 29.95 ea.   Extended cost: _____

Paperback edition: Quantity: ____ x 19.95 ea.   Extended cost: _____

Shipping: U.S. orders add $5.00 for each order.   _____

Tennessee Tax @ 9.75% (Tennessee Residents Only)   _____

Total order $_____

Name: _____

Address: _____

City: _____ State: _____ Zip: _____

Telephone: _____

E-mail Address: _____

Printed in the United States
148070LV00003B/1/P

9 780979 951435